Whisper of Death

Paige Elizabeth Turner
2016

Whisper of Death

Paige Elizabeth Turner

Copyright © 2017 Paige Elizabeth Turner

The moral right of the author has been asserted.

Apart from any fair dealing for the purposes of research or private study, or criticism or review, as permitted under the Copyright, Designs and Patents Act 1988, this publication may only be reproduced, stored or transmitted, in any form or by any means, with the prior permission in writing of the publishers, or in the case of reprographic reproduction in accordance with the terms of licences issued by the Copyright Licensing Agency. Enquiries concerning reproduction outside those terms should be sent to the publishers.

This is a work of fiction. Names, characters, businesses, places, events and incidents are either the products of the author's imagination or used in a fictitious manner. Any resemblance to actual persons, living or dead, or actual events is purely coincidental.

Matador
9 Priory Business Park,
Wistow Road, Kibworth Beauchamp,
Leicestershire. LE8 0RX
Tel: 0116 279 2299
Email: books@troubador.co.uk
Web: www.troubador.co.uk/matador
Twitter: @matadorbooks

ISBN 978 1788036 825

British Library Cataloguing in Publication Data.
A catalogue record for this book is available from the British Library.

Printed and bound by CPI Group (UK) Ltd, Croydon, CR0 4YY
Typeset in 11pt Adobe Garamond Pro by Troubador Publishing Ltd, Leicester, UK

Matador is an imprint of Troubador Publishing Ltd

MIX
Paper from
responsible sources
FSC® C013604

Acknowledgements

Many authors rely on cooperation of government and private enterprise to assist with information that might allow us to accurately detail our fictitious settings. To that end, for advice pertaining to coronial inquests, I thank Gemma Tibbatts of Regan Peggs Solicitors.

I also recognise other contributors who, for various reasons, chose anonymity. To those, and one person in particular who forgivingly tolerated my impatience, I sincerely thank you.

Again, I am indebted to draft readers, Wayne Harvey, Ian Loader, and Frederick Dickson.

Thanks must also go to Rebecca, whose encouragement drove me from pencilling soppy rhymes to writing fully fledged novels.

Also by Paige Elizabeth Turner

Beyond all Doubt

Prologue

4 April 2017

Chief Constable Davidson
Area Commander
Metropolitan Police
New Scotland Yard
London SW1H 0BG

Dear Sir
I respond to your questioning my working relationship with MET officer DCI Stafford.

Between August 2016 and March of this year, I worked under Detective Inspector Marchant investigating a series of murders in Evesham, Worcestershire. Concerns raised by me (which saw the exoneration of a convicted man) subsequently fostered an internal affairs enquiry. Force command supported my ideal that the welfare of an innocent man must survive over the doctrine of 'back your partner at all costs' – even if that ideal should jeopardise a serving officer's career. My consulting DCI Stafford resulted in the apprehension and conviction of the true offender.

Your enquiry into my current alliance with DCI

Stafford is, with the greatest respect, beyond the scope of police authority and non-conducive to maintaining a working relationship between police and private investigators. You are aware of my resignation from the constabulary in favour of my own investigations agency. As a licensed Private Investigator, I was engaged by Newquay-based lawyer, Mr Alexander Beecham, to inquire into the suspicious death of his mother, Joyce Beecham. My liaison with DCI Stafford in that matter was wholly professional and a vital conduit by which to flow information to your command.

I present herewith the circumstances of my engagement, together with comprehensive detail of the Beecham enquiry.

Yours faithfully

Olivia Elaine Watts
Watts Happening? Investigations
Worcester, Worcestershire.

PART ONE

1

Saturday 4 March

Meredith Bennington reaches for the shrieking mobile. Knocks it to the floor. Pads her fingers across the bedside rug. Probes for the recently updated iPhone.

She grabs the vibrating sliver. Checks the time. 1.14 a.m.

Answers.

Gasps.

Calls Roslyn and Alexander: 'Get to the hospital. Quick. Mum's deteriorated. Doctors reckon she hasn't got long.'

Alexander's *'How come they called you?'* query sets her on edge. The topic has the potential to widen their cracked relationship into a huge abyss. 'Not now Alex. I think mum might be more important than our squabbling over who's calling who.'

2

Friday 3 March

Twin glass doors retract. Medics struggle with the gurney as if it were a wayward shopping trolley. An intern sweeps aside a plastic curtain while a nurse jots vital statistics onto an admission form. She clips a label above the bed: Joyce Beecham. Age 70. Stroke (cause not identified). Diabetic.

With great fortune, Alexander had extended his lunch break from his job as a lawyer in a successful legal practice to sneak a surprise visit upon his mother. Overcome with delight on seeing Alex, Joyce wobbled on her feet and dropped to the floor clutching her chest.

Excitement. Has a strange effect on the elderly.

Alexander assisted her to a couch. Failing to recognise the seriousness of her guttural cough and rasped breathing, he produced a glass of water, believing life's elixir would cure all. He touched the glass to his mother's lips. Before taking a sip, Joyce slumped into the couch, motionless, eyes glaring to heaven's gate, willing it to swing open and bless her admission.

Alexander rolled her into the recovery position, punched 999 into his phone and ordered an ambulance. 'Please hurry.

My mother's dying' – the statement founded on panic rather than fact.

Joyce Beecham's habits mirror those of the aging population, most of whom pay no heed to the benefits of maintaining health and elasticity. Save for bowling a few sub-100 games at her local ten-pin bowling lanes, Joyce has not participated in exercise since playing attack in the school hockey team, some fifty-five years' earlier. She contends that rearing three children in the intervening years kept the blood pumping – although she neglects to add that once those children had left home, boredom fell upon her like waiting for the regularly delayed 16.06 Paddington to Plymouth train. She allayed that boredom by worshipping two idols: television and eating. The television satisfied her emotional needs while the food mollified physical cravings.

Having managed Type 2 diabetes for fifteen years, Joyce now turns to chocolate for instant hits. She's unfazed by the creeping monthly weight gain, and she ignores study results that alarm the public with bleak outlooks for those who carry excess weight and elevated blood pressure. As if that weren't enough, her ailing marriage finally crashed when George, her husband of 45 years, cited her ballooning figure as his reason to exit the marriage. In despair, Joyce turned to the bottle. To her credit, she *had* ceased smoking during her first pregnancy, but that was countered by her love – some would say addiction – of alcoholic liqueurs. She continues to sink a half-glass (albeit a large one) per evening, under the mistaken belief that consuming a daily litre of water will annul the alcohol's effect.

Joyce's children attend Cornwall and District General Hospital's Ward 6B. The gathering is a rare phenomenon.

Never do Joyce's children simultaneously attend family gatherings. They long ago developed intuition to stagger arrivals to avoid potential conflict with their siblings. Those attributes demonstrate the competitive edge rooted within each child, and also defines their absence of affection for each other.

The dynamics plummet as the three draw alongside their mother's bedside. Trapped beneath a taut sheet, Joyce's arms and chest germinate tubes and electronic monitors which wind their way to life-sustaining technology. The trio argues over who will accept responsibility for their mother's care – provided she pulls through – the verbal spat evolving from the perceived burden of future medical appointments and rehabilitative processes necessitating around-the-clock attention.

'We're here to help,' Meredith whispers to her insentient mother. Confident her mother cannot hear, Meredith's words are uttered only for the benefit of Roslyn and Alexander. 'There's wonderful staff to help you,' she continues through quivering lips.

Roslyn raises her eyes in annoyance. 'Bit late for *you* to be caring, isn't it?'

Meredith's strong resolution holds court: 'Mum's best prospects will be realised through professional palliative care.'

'And I suppose you'll be providing that care?'

'No more than any loving daughter would,' counters Meredith. 'There'll come a time when this will be too traumatic to deal with. Mum will never be able to resume life as it was, and even if she could, she'll never manage on her own. I suggest we prepare her home for sale and administer the proceeds under Power of Attorney.'

Despite two years separating their birth, Meredith and Roslyn were once seen as twins. They share the same star sign. They followed similar school curriculums and sports interests, and hung in the same circle of friends. The onset of puberty spawned radical change. Their interests diverged, perhaps as a protest against years of sharing the same clothes, hairstyles, and bedroom. Teen years saw Meredith prefer dogs, Roslyn horses. Meredith struggled to get out of bed, Roslyn excelled in sport. Meredith attracted boys, Roslyn was content with her own company.

Meredith's schooling at Cornwall Comprehensive energised her chequered personality. Regularly achieving high grades, she attained the coveted role of school prefect in her second year, allowing her, within the confines of toilet blocks and sports change rooms, the opportunity to wrest cigarettes and money from unsuspecting juniors and weak-willed seniors.

Today, she is a reliable and ambitious part-time employee of her local council, but not without issues. She clashes with co-workers who choose to disagree with, or ruffle the feathers of, the ebullient Meredith. She has pledged that no one will block her quest to achieve long-standing goals, and those goals fix upon one word: money. In pursuing that objective, she foists her persuasive nature into the face of others. Perhaps the trait was inherited from an obscure branch of the family tree, although no member of the paternal or fraternal line has ever demonstrated overbearing authoritarian or domineering behaviour. That is not to say that buried somewhere within the roots of family history lies an achiever who had mastered the art of obtaining results through others. He could have been a slave-master, ship's captain, Earl or Lord, or even an eighteenth century criminal entrepreneur in the vein of Fagin.

Imbued with those genes, Meredith grew into a woman of niggardly nature, shielded by a translucent screen bearing the deceptive facade of a smiling politician. She is a chameleon who can do no wrong – a trait that saw Meredith assume, from a very early age, an imperious role over the younger Roslyn and Alexander.

Meredith has carefully masked her true intentions since resolving to hasten her mother's demise. She harbours no guilt over the inhumane wish. She loves her mother, but not in the clingy mother/daughter union enjoyed by model families. Her affection is a mercenary demonstration of responsibility for which she seeks reward. She is driven not by malice or revenge; she simply harbours the desire to remove an obstacle that barricades her enjoyment of life.

Strange expression, psychoanalysts would agree, that a person in a loving kinship could so easily sweep aside an 'obstacle' in the same manner they would kick aside refuse on a footpath; swat a fly that threatens to crawl over a freshly baked cheesecake; or callously dispose of an unwanted Christmas pet.

She's researched the effects of various poisons, but discounted the mode after learning that latent trace elements could expose her complicity. The next bullet-point for consideration was a fall in the bath. *That* could easily be organised, and be easily justified as an accident. The subsequent drowning would likely see a coronial enquiry return a verdict of death by misadventure. She has also considered adjusting her mother's medication to overdose levels. The task would be effortless, because Meredith sets out her mother's tablets into a weekly dispenser of morning and evening doses. For that very reason, Meredith would inherit the label of prime suspect.

The plan remains unresolved. But not abandoned, for history has shown that Meredith's dogmatic disposition sees her accomplish all ambitions. She has greater hopes for life than spending thirty hours per week imprisoned in her mother's home, cooking, cleaning, shopping and overseeing financial affairs. It is the breadth of her mother's wealth that impels her to drain the abundant financial pool.

She was therefore, wrought with mixed feelings when her mother suffered the severe stroke only two days' shy of her seventy-first birthday.

Roslyn's DNA spiralled away from her sister's, both in personal characteristics and ambitions. *Her* school reports repeatedly commended achievements in the 'women's' skills of home economics, needlework, and other now politically incorrect challenges a young girl once encountered at school and college. Lacking the confused genetics and tainted personality determiners of her sister, Roslyn is now the virginal, church-going, god-fearing girl as different to Meredith as is Ellen DeGeneres to Oprah Winfrey.

Unlike Meredith, who married at nineteen, Roslyn has left a trail of broken hearts and relationships. She blames introversion for her inability to maintain steady friendships. Often taunted by Meredith's: 'What's wrong with you? Don't you *ever* want to get married?' Roslyn retorts: 'When I'm ready. Yours wasn't exactly a model marriage.'

Roslyn now manages a flourishing real estate agency, founded on the back of her foray into weekend markets and car-boot sales where she once marketed a range of children's and teenage casual clothing, illegally screen printed with copyrighted motifs of Disney and Warner Bros. characters.

* * *

Joyce Beecham braces herself as a doctor and his colleague approach her bedside. She digests their well-rehearsed spiel: 'We have to be down-to-earth with you, Mrs Beecham. As with all operations, a by-pass presents an element of risk. That is not to say that we do not exercise all due care and diligence – this hospital has an enviable record. Quite obviously, we cannot guarantee that all operations will fall within the one hundred percent success rate.

'We do not wish to alarm you. We merely ask patients to think about putting their affairs in order, solely to relieve pressure that may later fall on the shoulders of your loved ones.'

Joyce glares at the pair. Wonders if they might be joint proprietors of the local funeral home. Double-dipping the system – they win either way: get paid for the operation; get paid for the funeral. Straight to the point, she sums up: 'So what you're saying is that I might cark it as a consequence of the operation and you'd like me to have a will prepared?'

'I prefer to be more succinct, Mrs Beecham, but yes, that would be the ideal solution.'

'All right. You've got the details. Call my son – he's my next of kin – and ask him to come in. I'll do that just to satisfy you. But let me tell you – I'm not going anywhere.'

A nurse interrupts: 'We've tried contacting your next of kin, Mrs Beecham. She's not answering.'

Joyce crunches her brow. 'No wonder. It's not a she, it's a he. It's Alexander, my son.'

'No, Mrs Beecham. We have a Meredith Bennington listed. There was an Alexander, but it's been changed.' The nurse solemnly rearranges a magazine and glass on the bedside table and peeks at the few cards.

Joyce springs from the pillow. Winces in pain. Utters the fresh revelation: 'Just a moment. Nothing can be changed without my authorisation. No one can simply walk up to your Nurses' Station and say: 'I'd like to change Mrs Beecham's next of kin. Well can they?'

'Ordinarily not, Mrs Beecham. But there are some circumstances that would permit such an amendment to be approved.'

'Approved? By whom?'

'The administration manager.'

'Good. I should like to see him.' Joyce glares at the nurse, who mirrors the hypnotic stare, not knowing whether to seek out the administration manager or medically resolve the confrontation with a 20-ml shot of Diazepam. Joyce breaks her stare and continues: 'Perhaps he or she will enlighten me as to why my medical record was changed without my consent?'

'I'll see what I can do' – the generic response to all conundrums. The nurse spins on her heels, contemptuously lifts her head and squeaks from the ward in her synthetic-soled shoes.

Joyce weeps in amazement that the hospital, the very institution charged with protecting her interests, has randomly permitted a person, quite possibly her own daughter, to instruct a change to the hospital's records.

The nurse returns.

Joyce dabs tears from her cheeks and studies the bronze name badge: Nurse Susan Allsop. Allsop is a human replica of her badge: squarish features, rectangular eye sockets beneath which rest small black briquettes – the penalty of too many night shifts – and her complexion is an artificially-enhanced golden-bronze. 'Are we feeling better now, Mrs Beecham?'

Joyce remains mute, the patronising question not warranting response.

Allsop continues: 'The administrator's off until tomorrow.'

Joyce draws her hand to her chest, takes a deep breath and glares at the nurse. 'The hospital doesn't rely on one person only to carry on its business. Better you let me see his deputy or assistant. Even better, just let me know who's authorised the change. I'll bet you a pound to a penny that it wasn't me.' She maintains her trademark glare, intimidating the nurse into a response.

'I'm sorry, Mrs Beecham. For privacy reasons, we can't divulge that.'

'Goodness me! Privacy reasons? You're talking to the very patient whose privacy's been invaded by your allowing someone to change my records. Where was the privacy concern there?'

'Come now Mrs Beecham. We can't go getting our blood pressure up can we?'

'Give up with your "we" this and "we" that. I want to see the administrator or manager now, or I'm checking myself out, blood pressure or no blood pressure.'

'Oh, you can't do that. We haven't signed a release, have we.'

Joyce's cheeks glow like hot embers. She is a woman prepared to afford latitude to anyone, but when a person returns contemptuous mannerisms as she now faces, her fuse ignites and detonates violent tantrums.

A tirade ensues between the two; a double-edged trade-off over whether the administrator will attend to resolve the problem, or whether Joyce will cement her protest by walking out of the hospital. Nurse Allsop desperately summons assistance to quell Joyce Beecham's pertinacious constitution with a rushed dose of Diazepam.

Drifting into the haze of catalepsy, Joyce looks beyond the operation: an afternoon relaxing in her favourite easy chair; sipping a decent cup of tea and snacking on Jaffa Cakes; and preparing proper meals. She warms to the elation of going home; to its comfort, warmth, and familiarity; to its radio programs, television, and classical CDs; and to its garden of roses and azaleas. The mural is fractured by the realisation that for all the love she bears her children, they would not even stoop to remove weeds or errant leaves that might flutter in from neighbours' trees. Despite that, she focuses on grabbing a second bite at life and mentally lays the table for a huge homecoming dinner…

3

Saturday 4 March

A nurse enters and orders the squabbling trio to show more respect to their mother, *and* patients in adjoining wards. Her suggestion that only one visitor remain in the ward is met with disapproval, yet two siblings immediately retreat to the cafeteria.

Joyce remains motionless behind the flimsy nylon curtain which surrounds her bed like a mosquito net shrouding the sleeping quarters of a tropical hut. She looks grim – an understatement considering her state of health – although it could be said that the only hospital patients who do glow with pleasure are those confined to the maternity ward, and then, only post labour.

To one side a huge diagnostic machine beeps, flashes and heaves, monitoring heart-rate, oxygen uptake and blood sugar levels. Opposite, a chrome 'T' hanger suspends an intravenous drip from one side and a 500-millilitre bag of blood marked 'Blood Group A' from the other. Polyurethane tubes loop like a Los Angeles freeway interchange to shunts inserted into Joyce's arm. Hues of blue, yellow and purple resemble an oceanic oil spill across her forearm, leaving only a small atoll of sandy-white flesh.

Beset by hemianopia – a legacy of the stroke – Joyce is unable to determine who is adjusting the intravenous drip. She makes out the blurred outline of a white coat as she struggles to grasp why the IV needs attention only ten minutes since its last check. She squints. Tries to sharpen the image now injecting a syringe into the IV bag. *Why can't I recognise the figure when I can easily read the syringe's tiny label?*

Fortified by caffeine, the three siblings reunite with a pledge to not further inflame hospital staff. Meredith and Roslyn prop at the bedside, each clasping a limp hand. Alexander stands at the foot of the bed, stealing occasional glances at the patient history chart. The scrawled stats and hieroglyphics are barely decipherable, although he does identify hourly blood pressure readings in the 100/70 range. From a long-expired first-aid qualification he recalls a reference to systolic and diastolic pressure and that the reading falls in the acceptable range for his mother's age. Her present situation, though, could distort the reading thirty points either way.

He reaches down to flip the page when Joyce forces a guttural groan. Her jaw falls open and lips quiver as she desperately tries to speak. She lies moribund, casting anxious glances to each child, eyes flickering, curious why all three children are in attendance. She answers her own question: they're here because it's time.

She breaks into a violent spasm, torso arching high above the bed. She gags. Reflux pools in her throat. Her face reddens. Stretches into a huge, warped grimace. Lights flash. Monitors buzz. Nurses rush through the nylon curtain: 'Out. Out!' Alexander lunges forward and takes his mother's hand. She squeezes it with a fierce grip, summons a surge of energy, and utters, in a hoarse whisper of death, 'Help me, Alex.'

Scientists and doctors have long sought to capture dying persons' experiences. Tomes of medical journals expound incidences of super-human strength, premonitions, chronicles of purported previous lives, and blind people suddenly witnessing the Lord's brilliant white beacon of hope.

Alexander is not a scientist, but he recognises in his mother's voice an uncharacteristic plea. He looks to Meredith and Roslyn and then back to his mother. She returns his gaze – lifeless.

Alexander clutches Roslyn in a mutual embrace of consolation. The sudden shock elicits a bizarre reaction: 'What's happened to us that we hardly speak to each other? Why should it take this to get us to communicate?'

Roslyn empathises, 'We're not kids anymore. We've gone our own way. Some families remain cohesive and over-reliant on each other for love and friendship, never being able to separate or live apart. Our family, though; we've all done our own thing. You've succeeded in law, reliant on no one; I've got my estate agency – achieved through my own efforts, and Merri, despite her occasional disappearing acts, seems to have also done well for herself.'

Alexander scratches his head. 'Yes. To a certain extent, you're right. But not all families shun each other as is our habit. You know, mum looked fine yesterday; we were feeling more positive. I dropped in last night to cheer her up with some magazines and a block of chocolate.' A freeze-frame of the previous evening dazzles before him. The chrome bedside bin, Mars and chocolate éclair wrappers crumpled in the bottom – a vibrant giveaway of earlier visitors' generosity. Rather than add to the confectionary refuse, he pocketed the purple and yellow wrapper of the 200-gram Cadbury's Caramello he'd handed his mother. A swell of guilt castigates him for a loving gesture that might be the precursor to a fatal insulin imbalance.

'You know we're not supposed to do that, Alex. I took one too, and I think Merri snuck in a bag of chocolate éclairs. You know mum's supposed to limit her sugars, 'cause of the diabetes.'

'Bloody hell. Don't go off at me. Mum's always said a small block picks her up. How was I supposed to know you two would even be here, let alone bring chocolate?' On that, Alexander withholds mention of the extra treat he'd smuggled into the ward. A deft hand in the kitchen, he had followed his mother's recipe to make a large bowl of rich Chocolate Mousse. Only now does he realise how irresponsible the compassionate deed had been. The six egg yolks, half cup of sugar, 500 grams of Cadbury's Dark Chocolate, 300 ml of thickened cream, and a few drops of vanilla essence would have sent her glycaemic level off the scale.

He went to just as much effort to smuggle the treat into the ward; the airtight container lying in the bottom of the bag in which he carried magazines and flowers. He walked past the nurses' station to an audible mumble: 'He's such a nice man. Takes such good care of his mother.'

Had nurses seen the hidden treats, they'd have withheld their compliment and marched him straight into their office.

* * *

Meredith turns in her sleep like a rotisserie spindle. Her mother's final moments hang before her: the grey-white complexion, the glazed eyes, the straggly hair that sat on her shoulder like moulten cat fur, and the bruised arm punctured by a succession of IV drip insertions.

Meredith has excelled in portraying the compassionate daughter with the same veracity as she disguises her joy at being a step closer to inheriting her mother's estate.

Yesterday, she'd discussed with Roslyn the prospect of either of them shouldering the responsibility of next of kin, given they were both accessible to doctors who might one day seek consent for an emergency operation. Never had the girls objected to their brother – the 'baby' of the family – being endorsed by their mother as next of kin, but Meredith expressed awkwardness as both she and her sister had always enjoyed a much closer relationship with their mother than had Alexander. Meredith lamented her mother's decision, which she believed was made only because of Alexander's profession in the legal arena. She believed her brother would not cope with the responsibility, and questioned how he'd react to a critical situation. Could he make an immediate decision in his mother's interest, or would he, in his usual manner, procrastinate for fifteen minutes before proffering an answer?

With that perception, Meredith advanced to gain leverage over her own future. Without her mother's knowledge or consent, she attended the hospital one hour before visiting hours and confided in an admissions' nurse. On providing her mother's detailed medical background she raced to the point: 'My mother is now incapable of making her own decisions. She has previously attempted to take her life, and we, as family, believe she may do so again. That might explain why she brought a knife into the hospital with her – maybe to try to take her life for a second time.'

Joyce had done no such thing – as if in a state of cardiac arrest she had the foresight, inclination, and ability to seize a knife and place it in her bag. If she were so intent on dying, she would have hoped for the stroke to finally claim her. Joyce could not know about the knife, because Meredith had covertly placed it in her bedside drawer.

Meredith's action was malicious and calculated to discredit her mother. She knew that duty of care responsibilities would now compel the hospital to assess her mother's mental capacity. She continued: 'I have documentation to change mum's next of kin.'

'We'll need your mother's permission, of course.'

'She's already signed it. And I also have a signed authority with her bank,' said Meredith as she produced a signed letter and bank acknowledgement of her being co-signatory on her mother's account. 'Also, mum was admitted to an institution a few years ago; she said it was for observation, but of course it was much more than that. Thames Valley Health Services holds the file.'

Credibility and persuasion is a lethal and productive combination. Minutes later, Meredith Bennington's name filled computer screens as Joyce Beecham's next of kin.

4

Three hundred miles north, in the county of Shropshire, Lord Robert Bennington skulks in his study, fine-tuning yet another invention.

Born into the class of grandiloquent British, he's never had to work to maintain his eccentric lifestyle. Not one to lounge about his estate in silk smoking jackets, he focuses on realising his personal goal – as a hobby rather than career – to be a successful entrepreneur. None of his projects has yet conquered the world. Far from it. Most investors have raised eyebrows at his off-the-wall inventions.

One renowned failure, satirised in *Farmers Weekly* and other rural magazines, was promoted as a breakthrough in irrigation. Lord Robert had endeavoured to combat the effect of prolonged dry seasons leaving dams and reservoirs as jigsaws of dry, cracked earth. He prophesised that siting a huge block of ice in a strategic position on select acreage and channelling its melting water to the furrowed acres, would see crops flourish like never before.

Promotional material raved: 'For crops to rise before your eyes, you ought'a use our Lord's water.' It went on to explain: 'We harvest water from local rivers and snap-freeze in a range of mega-litre sized cubes. We deliver to your property and guarantee sustained-release water to your crops.' Lord Robert happily included the government's trendy buzzword, 'sustained', for any new product or service marketed to the community must hail integrity and boast elements of sustainability.

His cubes were formed in huge shipping containers, snap-frozen with nitrogen injection and then transported by low-loader to the farmer's property where they were off-loaded and cracked open like a jelly mould, releasing a huge, glistening, frozen monolith an ice carver would kill for. 'The 187,000-litre block of ice melts nourishment into your produce like slow-release fertilizer.'

The project received fascinating reviews and responses from rural correspondents, with a variety of Letters to the Editor offering opinions both for and against the project. The worst, came from a farmer who claimed his block had fully melted before irrigating his 320-metre seed drills.

Another widely-publicised invention detailed converting passenger aircraft cabins to rows of black cubicles. Rationalising the Black Box as the only piece of equipment to survive an aircraft catastrophe, Bennington claimed he could offer passengers the same protection as afforded the electronic circuitry and transmitting devices housed within the indestructible data unit. He saw a Nobel Peace Prize on the horizon as well as the ill-conceived prospect of a knighthood. Fitting rewards for a gentleman of his station.

The prototype was constructed with five-millimetre carbon fibre, reinforced with tempered steel. The interior featured high-density foam rubber, which, on contact with the body's median temperature of 36.8 degrees, would mould itself to a figure-hugging cocoon, thereby securing all limbs during transit. A comprehensive menu sat at eye level, encouraging passengers to obtain meals or snacks via the individual pod's speech recognition program. On requesting food or drink, a feeding tube descended from the bulkhead, allowing the passenger to place his or her mouth over the tube to ingest the selected alcoholic or soft drink, or puréed snack or meal. It was this facet of Lord Robert's invention that created the most work – and laughter – within the manufacture's premises.

Vita Foods, the successful tenderer to the Black Box challenge, experienced early difficulties with public acceptance of its product. Conducting sample tests in supermarkets throughout England and Europe, Vita Foods learnt that Business Class delicacies such as Lobster Mornay and Chicken Breast Fricassee were not appreciated as a pulped mash via a plastic tube.

Bennington adopted the premise of successful marketing campaigns: the secret of customer satisfaction lies not in the product's merit, but by the way the buying public is hoodwinked into believing that the product will deliver its promised benefits. Consequently, after retraining sample demonstrators, Lobster Mornay became the top-rated in-flight food on British aviation departures. Ex France, the blended ham and cheese croissant gained notoriety with its consistency somewhat thicker than the Lobster Mornay, but by all reports, equally palatable.

The natural consequence of having consumed the foregoing delights is, at a later stage, the need to expel them. Lord Robert pondered this for days, until, inspired by his new wife's suggestion, proposed the idea of fitting catheters prior to take-off. '*A small amount of pain in exchange for huge relief,*' became the catch cry of nurses fitting the tube and bag.

The promotional publicity and consequent criticism embarrassed both the medical profession and Lady Bennington's reputation, despite her unreserved support of her husband's ideals to slash aviation deaths. She had been taunted 'Lady Ice Block' during the irrigation flop. Within weeks of the Black Box release, she was dubbed Queen Catheter. Her embarrassment over the catheter controversy 'pissed her off' (her select words) so bad, that despite her devotion to her husband, she simply up and left the manor and the seven-month marriage.

It was Lord Robert's mother, Victoria, who, through a most peculiar set of circumstances, engineered Meredith Beecham into her family.

While sauntering around an antique and craft exhibition, Victoria buckled to the ground, capitulating to breathing difficulties. By chance, Meredith Beecham, herself a craft lover, and a trainee nurse, caught sight of Lord Robert's frantic waves and rallied to his aid. The non-life-threatening situation resulted in Lord Bennington extending to Meredith a gesture of gratitude by inviting her to lunch – an invitation Meredith gratefully accepted. During the less than elaborate spread inside a caterer's tent, Meredith enquired into the nature of Victoria's health, and gradually pieced together that she had entered the final trimester of her years – reliant on pillows, pills, and morphine. Atherosclerosis could be easily managed by a younger patient able to take on mild exercise. At 92-years-of-age, Victoria Bennington was far beyond commencing any sort of fitness regime or even extending her five-minute daily walk in the garden.

Meredith compassionately volunteered to attend twice

weekly to coax her through a mild exercise program. 'You could probably do with some company too,' she added.

Victoria protested: 'When I'm going, I'm going. There's nothing worth prolonging life for.'

Lord Robert was sympathetic to his mother's declining health. He had long regretted the close relationship he once enjoyed had evaporated in his eighteenth year when he assumed responsibility for himself – at his father's insistence. He engineered total independence, his parents morphing into figureheads like an alabaster king and queen on a chess board. Robert continued to accept invitations to family banquets, conversation parties and other celebrations only because he understood that being seen by the right people in the right places is *the* key to a successful life.

Lord Robert now extends to his mother the same cohesive love he had received as a young child. He has forecast that losing his mother could be like the trauma he once experienced upon losing his favourite sports coach. Worse still, would be to lose his mother through a disease that could be, if not remedied, eased by the introduction of a few hours' exercise. Meredith's offer was meritable. If he were rewarded with even an extra few weeks with his mother, he'd feel that he'd excelled in prolonging her quality of life.

Victoria's physician subsequently rubber-stamped Meredith's structured routine of fifty metre walks and low-impact callisthenic exercises.

After a fortnight of successful half-hour sessions, Victoria sprung a surprise on Meredith during the morning walk. 'You know, Meredith? You'd be very good for my Robert. If you're as good to him as you are to me, I think you would make an excellent addition to the family.'

'Thank you, Mrs Bennington. I do try to fit into families, but I have not thought of myself in any other way than a professional contracted by your son. I can't be seen to be too close to my patients or clients.' Meredith concealed her elation. She'd presented her best profile, relying on her closeness to reap rewards, although not necessarily by taking the arm of a much older man.

'I'm not going to be around forever, my dear. I've held onto a final wish for years now, and that is to see my Robert marry within these walls. The last wedding here was my own – nearly 70 years ago.'

'Meredith grinned off the consideration of her being a worthy wife to the much older Lord Robert. Her smile broke into a loud chuckle at the thought of the age difference being greater than her actual age of nineteen. 'Well, time will tell, Mrs Bennington.'

'Oh, do stop with that Mrs Bennington formality. It's Victoria. You should address me only as Victoria. I insist.'

'Very well, Victoria. I am happy to.'

'I shall speak to my son and have him make the arrangements. A spring wedding will look simply marvellous in the Anglia Gardens. The Magnolias will be prolific. I shall instruct my courtier to outfit you.'

'I haven't said "yes", Victoria.'

'But you will, won't you my dear?'

'Of course I will.'

Tension dominated the engagement that was founded upon an exercise program and progressed to a pledge to marry. She had viewed Lord Robert merely as a casual acquaintance from whom she could enjoy the fruits of the upper class, and in so doing elevate her own status. But with perception beyond her years, she saw that all before her could one day be her own, simply by marrying the quiet, eccentric, older gentleman. Her mind spun like a stuck CD: 'I can't go wrong. I can't go wrong.'

There was no surprise, fainting spells, or kaleidoscope of fireworks when Lord Robert asked Meredith to marry him. She ogled the diamond ring, not so much for its 4.2-carat princess-cut solitaire, but for the sparkling accompaniment of six half-carat pink diamonds – collectively worth more than the glistening centrepiece. Sparkles of wealth radiated into her future. Love did not rate even a speck of dust.

The wedding, celebrated on the tenth day of spring, commemorated no family history. It was merely the earliest occasion to satisfy Victoria's exceedingly urgent desires to see her son married.

Anglia Gardens was a regal brick paved geometric layout bordered by English Box hedge. Standard roses flourished in freshly dug garden beds while recently sown annuals and clusters of lavender waved their fragrant spell over the gathering's 160 well-wishers. Not one of the large group was family or friend of the bride. Meredith, on seeing marriage as an opportunity, chose to not reveal to anyone – including her family – that she was marrying a gentleman some twenty years her senior. Victoria, who revelled in managing the preparations, had no difficulty recruiting bridesmaids, flower girls and page boys to attend Meredith. Perhaps to the annoyance of some, she even coerced a local pastor into giving Meredith away – despite Meredith having never set foot in a church.

Behind the group, a huge, white marquee sat like an

igloo on the vast expanse of clipped lawn. Weeping willows and silver birches waltzed to the melodies of the local college's choral group whose 'auditorium' was an open-ended tarpaulin that subdued harmonies in the manner of the Royal Albert Hall's pre-1960 performances.

At Victoria's insistence, the wedding service was brief. 'Let's just get it over and done with,' she'd instructed local celebrant Carol Dickenson, who ultimately uttered the sealing words: 'Lord Robert Bennington. Do you take this woman, Meredith Louise Beecham, to be your lawfully wedded wife, from this day forward?'

Robert gazed lovingly into Meredith's eyes. 'I do.'

'Meredith Louise Beecham. Do you take this gentleman, Robert Maxwell Bennington, to be your lawfully wedded husband, from this day forward?'

Meredith was not sure. She certainly didn't love him, but had resigned herself to maintaining the happy facade solely to wed into riches. Many before her had done so, as would many after.

She looked to Robert and then to the celebrant. 'I'm so sorry. The excitement overcame me. I do.' The congregation cheered as rose petals rained over the married couple.

The petals wilted as Lord Robert spent an inordinate amount of time in his study, a room of sizeable proportion; perhaps a former library as evidenced by the five-metre wall of meticulously crafted and corbelled shelving, its centre cabinet's lead-light doors a striking focal point. Arched ceilings soared seven metres above.

Remaining examples of exquisite stone masonry transport admirers to the sixteenth century when knights in armour emblazoned with clan insignia proudly rode across vales to attend feasts where they'd drink and gorge themselves in preparation for a session of lecherous debauchery to prime their ego should they not survive the next battle. The poor stonemason had only a family and a small sack of tools as his life's score. But those same tradesmen left a legacy of treasure to be enjoyed by future generations. The true artisan aspired to create works of art; art they would bequeath to God, and to the world.

Clerestory windows sit high in Lord Robert's study, affording added security and more usable wall space. Two 60-inch plasma television screens feed sweeping images of the gardens. A motion sensor detects activity around the front entrance gates – some 200 metres beyond the residence.

Gracefully accepting her husband's encouragement, Meredith continued nursing studies to better support her new mother-in-law. Combining those studies with the increasing burden of Victoria's needs, Meredith began to feel her role more akin to a maid than a wife.

She introduced brandy shots to Victoria under the auspice of medicinal value, fully cognisant of the possible adverse effects. Meredith cleverly covered her tracks by 'mistakenly' leaving Victoria a flask to sip at her will. The following morning's sunrise would shine on the empty flask as it lay beside the soundly sleeping Victoria, or from its resting position after toppling to the floor.

Had Lord Robert been aware of his mother's drinking, he would have severely chided Meredith. To him, there was no one more important than his mother.

In the same manner Meredith had married Lord Robert

as a road to riches, Lord Robert had married Meredith Beecham to facilitate his mother's recovery.

Four months into her marriage, Meredith tapped a customary 8.30 a.m. knock on her mother-in-law's door. No answer. That was not unusual. Victoria had lost nearly eighty percent of her hearing. Meredith knocked again. Entered. Victoria lay peacefully in bed. Death presents itself in serene finality. With resourcefulness displacing compassion, Meredith approached the bed, snatched the empty stainless steel flask from her patient's grip, straightened the sheets, and then proceeded directly to her husband's room.

Despite her accomplished acting, Meredith couldn't muster even one tear. 'Mum's gone, Robert. She's gone.'

'Where to, for goodness sake? It's too early for her to be out.'

'Robert, she's at peace. She left us during the night.'

Over following weeks, Meredith devoted more time to consoling her husband than she had previously devoted to the fragile Victoria. Incompatibility and trivial arguments fell between them, forcing them apart until they withdrew to separate quarters of the home. Their infrequent meetings could be best described as 'tolerable', their individual interests forcing continued separation.

Lord Robert worked incessantly on a new invention – a baby's bottle that did not require inversion to facilitate milk flow. The Bennington Breathing Bottle project was cut short for Lord Robert's attendance at the reading of his mother's will.

At the offices of Bartholomew and Bartholomew,

the family's legal counsel since 1752, Brigham Oswald Bartholomew chaired the meeting attended by Lord Robert and Lady Meredith Bennington and Marianne Troquét, who, as Victoria's personal valet and head of house had also been called to the reading. Lord Robert's marriage had produced no known beneficiaries.

Bartholomew dispensed with introductions, tapped the circular table and waved a document before him: 'I shall read the late Mrs Victoria Anne Bennington's Last Will and Testament, executed before me, at this office on March 11 of this current year. *"To my only surviving son, Robert, I bequeath the estate of Wiltshire Manor and its environs together with all contents and chattels of the estate, both fixed and unfixed, for a period so long as he remains married to Meredith Louise Bennington – nee Beecham."*

'Should the marriage not survive the passage of time, I am instructed to transfer all hereinbefore stated property to one Miss Marianne Troquét, who joins us in the reading of this document.

'Irrespective of the aforementioned, the said Marianne Troquét shall, 30 days beyond the reading of this will, receive the sum of £250,000 in recognition of her devoted service to both the late Mrs Victoria Bennington and Wiltshire Manor in general. Further, the said Meredith Louise Bennington shall, 30 days beyond the reading of this will, and I quote, *"receive the sum of £500,000, to afford her life's luxuries that I know my son will not provide".*'

Lord Robert blushed. Faced Bartholomew and quipped: 'Maintained her humour to the end.'

'Very well, my Lord. That is your mother's instruction nonetheless. In conclusion, Mrs Victoria Bennington orders her beneficiaries to not discuss, to or with any other person, any provision, benefit, or detail of this meeting.'

Meredith returned to the manor, surprised beyond expectations to have access to half a million pounds within the month. She wondered why Victoria executed the will in such a manner, awarding the bulk of the estate to Lord Robert, but conditional upon him remaining married to her. Meredith was not subject to any similar condition. It seemed to be a penalty or imposition upon Lord Robert, binding him to Meredith for life – should he want to maintain ownership of Wiltshire Manor.

Meredith had no reason to challenge the will's provisions. Her husband though, now eternally controlled by his mother's wishes, would have to ensure the marriage's stability. Meredith believed that Victoria had provided her son a means of securing that stability – a tall order destined to fail.

As did the Bennington Breathing Bottle project, because it did, colloquially speaking, run out of breath. Like many inventions in infancy, the idea had merit in principle, but fell far short in practical applications.

The separation between Meredith and her husband widened. Lord Robert retreated to his library. Meredith continued her nursing studies. There was no emotional disharmony. Each party accepted (without letting on to the other) that they'd married for a purpose – and the purpose had nothing to do with love. They attempted a form of reconciliation, as do many quarrelling spouses, while living separate lives under the banner of holy matrimony. They endured the customary I'm-not-talking-to-you-until-you-apologise, so perfected that after one whole month neither had apologised because neither would accept responsibility to reignite conversation.

They dined in expensive restaurants, talked all evening, went home to engage in pleasures of the flesh, only to rise afterwards, each smiling in unison: 'This doesn't resolve anything. Changes not one thing. I hope you realise that.' It mattered little, because after an evening release of pent-up sexual desire, which could hardly be described as lovemaking, the supposed cure-all and restoration of marital harmony failed to strengthen their union.

After the expiration of the will's 30-day withholding period, all emotional attachment had dissolved – from Meredith's perspective at least. She had no desire to inflict further emotional injury upon Lord Robert, so left Wiltshire Manor to pursue her own dreams.

PART TWO

5

Monday 27 February

I tip the remaining clothes from my floral suitcase and stack them in groups against the bedroom wall: formal, casual, underwear, gym and running attire. In the kitchen, Tupperware, steel bowls, Argos plates and cutlery, and assorted packets of food totter on the benchtops. Six taped boxes cover the tiled floor like stock awaiting attention by Tesco's nightfill crew.

Where do I start? I'm Olivia Elaine Watts, former Detective Sergeant of Worcester CID. I've made a life-changing move by setting up a flat in Newquay, a beachside town in Cornwall. I left behind a modern upstairs apartment in Worcester; threw aside the continually deceitful and unfaithful DCI Dave Stafford, and distanced myself from the back-stabbing, two-faced former best friend Sharon Fowler. I have as much difficulty ejecting painful memories as I do in facing this new chapter of life.

I've never been much of a homemaker. I'm the practical woman who clings to basic standards. I don't care for forty-eight-inch plasma televisions – my twenty-four inch is quite okay; I don't need a souped-up Dyson vacuum cleaner – my £24.99 Argos special does the job just dandy; I don't crave fancy, expensive furniture that my few guests would be afraid to sit on; and I don't treasure the new kitchen equipment gifted to me that I never use, and never intend to use.

My prudency leaves me with very little to arrange in the new apartment. I am more interested in re-arranging myself. I think that facing a life-changing challenge and embarking on the 'I'm-starting-all-over-again' personal change for the better, compels me to sweep away the past. All of it.

Yesterday, while scoffing a habitual take-away lunch, I walked past Newquay Hair and Beauty. Checked my reflection. A line of dark regrowth marked an axe cut through straggly blonde tips. Twists of hair fell upon my face. I looked like a 24-year-old Scottish Terrier. I shoved my cheese and tomato baguette into its bag, and sashayed into the 'No Appointment Necessary' salon. Monica, who I summed up as an apprentice, convinced me that my structure would 'pull off' a transformation so wild that not even my mother would recognise me. I didn't dare reply that she wouldn't recognise me under any circumstances. Of course, Monica couldn't do anything about my five-foot-four petite, or once petite, frame. Nor could she change (and never would I allow anyone to change) my belligerent, self-centred and pedantic disposition.

Two and a half hours later, I bounded out of the salon with auburn hair trimmed into a short bob; a little too short for my liking, but not so short as to look butch.

Since my late teens, I've brushed on generous applications of azure eye shadow to contrast the blonde highlights. Monica applied her take by brushing on a dark mauve – adding depth and sparkle to my deep blue eyes – and finished off with a gloss mauve lipstick leaving me with a pair of kissable Polynesian lips. The downside of that is that I have no one to kiss them.

I retrieved my baguette and flounced along the High Street like an aspiring model taking to a shopping centre catwalk. I smiled. I whistled. I felt renewed and reinvigorated. Passers-by looked at me as if I were on a drug-induced high. They frowned as I acknowledged them with a smiling: 'Nice day isn't it.' And then shot me an indignant glare on walking by.

Ten days ago, after a night of juggling thoughts and ambitions, I walked into my Worcester landlord's office, gave 30 days' notice, and slammed a cheque for the following month's rent on his desk. He gave me the 'you're-a-great-tenant' line and followed up with: 'Is there anything wrong? Anything I can do for you? We don't want to see you go.'

I returned my 'girl's-gotta-do-what-a-girl's-gotta-do' sermon, smiled, and then rushed home to pack.

Newquay was far from heading my list of top twenty towns in which to hide and start over. Maybe 'hide' is too strong a word. 'Laying low' might be more apt. To those who question my unexpected uprooting, I offer woman's favoured standby: 'I'm leaving a few bad memories behind.' How much farther behind could I leave them than the vast rural tapestry stitched between Worcestershire in the West Midlands and Cornwall in England's south?

I am fortunate to have had a brief introduction to the town after accepting a posting whilst still a serving police member. To cut a long story short, my tenure with the police became unbearable after I failed to weather flak from the outfall of the Evesham Murders case.

My present situation came about after Alexander Beecham, an adversary I'd encountered in a minor legal battle some months earlier, had phoned me to requisition some statements and exhibits of a concluded matter. As a reliable and professional operator, I would ordinarily have returned case material on the hearing's conclusion. I explained to Alexander that problems threatening my career and personal life had hampered my professional capacity.

I should add that we developed a very close rapport over a short time. Surprised us both, I think. The nature of our legal acquaintance, a regulation traffic matter that had escalated to a contested hearing, had necessitated frequent personal contact. There was no avoiding regular 'plea-bargaining conferences'. As the informant, my attendance was mandatory. Over those few meetings, an inexplicable attraction drew me to him. After the hearing, which I won – because police rarely lose traffic contests – I succumbed to Alexander's coffee invitation. Casual outings followed: shopping, cinemas, sightseeing at Land's End, and more shopping. Alexander considered them dates. I didn't. I resisted the faintest hint of commitment, remaining aloof and reserved, still wounded and scarred from Dave Stafford's callous betrayal. At the height of our friendship, I would have instantly married Dave – had he proposed. That dream was shattered upon finding, in the most embarrassing way possible, that he did not subscribe to the ethos of monogamy.

The experience left me guarded about entering or even thinking about a new relationship, especially within only weeks of ending my previous. It's fair to say, though, that stars definitely shone brighter each time I met Alexander. During one of my heart-emptying confessions, I blurted out how I wanted to throw everything away and start again. Watts Happening? Investigations, which I'd started in Worcester, was in its infancy and yet to gather regular clientele, despite the business's promise. It would not suffer by relocation.

Alexander professed the advantages of moving south: 'We've got plenty of accommodation and office space, and it's not as if we're a crime-free area.'

I returned the age-old excuse: 'I'll think about it,' recognising it as the same lame excuse people use when they're put on-the-spot. The cliché is one of my favourites. Recently, when in the throes of purchasing my new car, the salesman crunched me with his closing question: 'Would you like to drive it away today, or early next week?'

I'd not yet decided if I wanted that particular vehicle! 'I'll have to think about it.' Did I? Heck no! I just hightailed it out of the yard and kept dealer-hopping until I found the perfect combination of the right car and an easygoing salesman.

Considering Alexander's suggestion, I toyed with the idea of relocating to Newquay. Sure, it was near the end of the earth, or more correctly, near the appropriately named 'Land's End' — a collection point for all of England's rich, poor, escapees, backpackers, surfers, authors struggling with work-in-progress, artists duelling with mid-life crises, and those contemplating their future, funded, not surprisingly, by the government purse.

'Come down for the weekend and see for yourself,' he crooned. I did, politely refusing an offer of his spare room, preferring instead to book a budget Bed and Breakfast to preserve my professionalism and to dispel the male thought process that I might actually be spending a weekend *with* him. I pursued the trip as an exploratory mission: a bit of soul-searching; evaluating a business opportunity; and checking-out a haven where I might re-ignite the fire of life. I live by Jeff Probst's *Survivor* catch-cry: *In this game, fire represents life and when your fire's gone, so are you.*

On driving into Newquay, it felt like home; like a magnet drawing me to a place I should have discovered long ago. The first sights were somewhat off-putting: wetsuits hung like liquorice straps from windows, balconies, trees, and anything that would allow surfers' attire to air and dry in readiness for the next excursion to the surf beach, which is a short walk from the High Street.

The town promised a similar bustle to that I had enjoyed at Worcester. The shopping precinct was equally exciting, and a row of fine eateries boasted a variety of cuisines that would satisfy my cravings on 'eat out' nights. Not quite so easy to determine during the day, the entertainment district forecast a vibrant diversion from trekking the streets as I sought to promote my business. The experience paralleled my feelings upon returning to Worcester after short absences: the appreciation of home transmits a shiver through the body, confirming one's belonging – this *is* home. I considered making Newquay home.

I checked vacant office space and found a superb location with a two-bedroom apartment directly above. The clincher was that its monthly rental was less than I had paid for office space alone in Worcester. Ever cautious, I left a conditional holding deposit, telling the agent, 'I'll think about it over the weekend.'

As I drove home, my thoughts synchronised with the

motorway's drone. *I wonder if this would work? Might there even be a future with Alexander? What have I got to lose?*

Romance is one facet of my life I had never been inclined to rush, but my feelings for Alexander had intensified over those few days – and I hadn't even slept with him. At forty-seven, he exceeded the maximum age I would normally date, but I justified my rationale with the fact that he was only two years older than Dave Stafford. Attached to the debit side was his effeminacy, both in appearance and manner, which prompted me to wonder if he might be gay. 'Not that there's anything wrong with that,' Jerry Seinfeld once parroted.

He shaved so close that layers of skin must have peeled off with each passing of the razor. His hair emulated the rolling waves of Newquay's International Surf Beach. Not a tsunami like the coiffured, 50's look, but as blonde-tipped ripples spreading across his crown in the effect of a wake from a speedboat. His body evidenced a musculature once envied at college, but ensuing decades had mashed the taut sheen into a spongy white pelt. Green eyes darted from deep sockets, his broad flat nose bore traits of West Indian or Jamaican heritage, and his mouth, often twisted in confusion, spoke with eloquence and understanding.

His right ear was pierced twice in its lobe where two small diamond, or, heaven forbid, cubic zirconia, studs glistened and refracted prisms of light. Perhaps that's what he is. A rainbow. An inverted colourful smile.

I left it until the following weekend before I returned. Forty-eight hours in Newquay had convinced me to take a further look before committing myself either way. Alexander caught me off-guard when he hinted that I'd not be long in finding work. It wasn't so much my suspicion of his trying to capitalise on his personal interest in me, it was the ego boost I experienced upon accepting, *Yes, I can do this.*

'I might even be able to slip a few summonses or enquiries your way,' he continued.

'Alexander, I'm not sure the lure of a few quid dropping papers is enough for me to upheave my life to move more than two hundred miles from my home.'

'Call me Alex, Liv. I'm only saying that I can help you with immediate cashflow should you decide to come down. Of course, the final decision is yours.'

'Okay. I'll bite the bait – but I'm only chewing it. I'm not going to jump into anything. One thing though, I will jump if you call me "Liv". I'm sorry, but I hate it, not for anything really bad, mind you. My dad, well, stepdad since I'm opening my heart here, used to call me "Livi" – still does sometimes – I guess it's just a name I want to keep locked away with all my treasures.'

'Sorry. Won't do it again.'

He spent the next ten minutes repeating how Newquay would guarantee an enviable lifestyle and business. I'd heard it all over the previous weekend, but his continued glowing report was more than enough to whet my appetite. I asked him to accompany me to the High Street where I showed him the vacant office and upstairs flat.

'Alex. If I confirm this and move in, it'll not be because of anything you're offering. I'll be glad to help you with any professional enquiry, but I don't want to be obligated to anyone. That's what I want to leave behind.'

'Fine by me,' he replied, raising his hands in retreat. 'Just trying to help.'

But the irresistible challenge lay before me.

Thirty minutes' later I'd paid three months' rent, and from a nearby Kwik Print outlet, ordered a pack of 200 business cards.

6

Sunday 5 March

What the hell. Bloody 2.30 in the middle of the night. I snatch my squawking mobile. I'm not expecting a call. Even telemarketers show respect for normal sleeping hours, although that's now subject to change as organisations increasingly outsource marketing activities to India and the Philippines. It won't be long before we're inundated with 1.00 a.m. calls, surveying us about banking customs, electricity usage and telecommunications providers. We'll berate them with a mouthful of profanities, and then fume at the pacifying: 'Oh I am sorry. I forgot to account for the time difference.' *Yeah, sure you did.*

I sit up. Pull the duvet to my neck. 'Hello. This better be important.'

'Is this Olivia?'

Duh. Why do people ask the most ridiculous questions? 'Who else would it be at this time?'

'I'm sorry. It's Alex. Something terrible has happened. My mother's just died. I'm at the hospital.'

'Alex. Sorry. I don't know what to say. Is there anything I can do?' I immediately regret my groggy who-the-frig's-this attitude I level to anyone who dares disturb my sleep full of romance and fanciful experiences. 'I'm sorry, Alex. I didn't mean to sound insensitive, I just woke up.' I hoped he'd get the subtlety that he's wrecked my night's sleep. 'I'll come on over.'

I don't mind supporting people in times of need – and this surely is one of those times – but why call on me to console a guy I don't *really* know. Well, I can't just ignore him.

I pull on a pair of crumpled jeans, grab my bag, rush into the hallway, and stumble downstairs to the front door. Scold myself: *I must get used to this place.*

My Ford Focus sits at the kerb. On expiration of daytime parking restrictions, I move it from the rear car park to the main road. I know that doesn't necessarily guarantee its safety and security because if someone is desperate enough to steal a car, they'll take it from anywhere.

A few months earlier, I wouldn't have given a damn about where I parked my car. A 1973 Reliant Robin painted in sickly blue would hardly raise the testosterone levels of a hardened car rustler. Yes, I ashamedly admit to having owned one of those three-wheeled relics, but that was all my budget would allow in my first year with the constabulary. As I progressed in the job, I considered upgrading, but living close to the police station convinced me to save my money and wait. Until when, I had not decided.

On leaving the police seven years' later, I preserved most of my final salary to cover living expenses while establishing Watts Happening? Investigations. Knowing that image is everything when promoting a business, I supplemented my remaining £1,000 with a small top-up loan and treated myself to a five-year-old Ford Focus.

For my purposes, it's functionally equipped with a six-speaker sound system, iPod connectivity, air conditioning and comfortable velour seats. Sometimes the most insignificant extras stand out as winners. The cup holder, for instance – within arm's reach – because I'm always buying coffee at take-aways or service centres; the little make up mirror glued to the sun visor – because a woman can't do without a mirror; and the glove box and door pockets deep enough to store my assorted paraphernalia and notebooks and maps – although I have discarded most fold-out maps after having installed an integrated GPS system. Yep. Suits me down to the ground.

The exterior, however, is disappointing; not from a manufacturer's point of view, but from my own. I tend to switch from introvert to extrovert as the wind changes. My extrovert persona insists that I drive around in a yellow, vibrant orange or iridescent turquoise car. However, my introversion recognises the nature of my work as requiring me to lay low, be unobtrusive and assimilate with society. That limits me to white or silver. Silver is the more appealing, but plain old white is less conspicuous and blends easily with Britain's twenty-one percent of white cars.

* * *

Cornwall and District General Hospital is accessed via a half-mile-long road divided by double yellow lines and flanked by bluish-white halogen lights. I could have been driving along Heathrow's Runway 3 East.

I rip a ticket from the automated financial controller of car parks and roll under its rising yellow arm. Anyone who's had the misfortune to drive into a full car park will agree that one spends more time searching for an elusive parking spot than they do attending their loved one. At 3.00 am there is no such drama. I leave Fiona in the closest bay and rush to Accident and Emergency, signposted only as A & E.

Fiona? Um, yes. I have a penchant for naming my cars. Fiona Focus. It's a juvenilistic trait inherited from my over-alliterative father who animatedly named his vehicles. I clearly recall Victor Volkswagen, Adrian Audi, and Verity Vauxhall. There was also an old Renault, late 50s maybe. I think he was restoring it. The model name, designated by the factory was 'Frigate'. Dad prefixed it with a crude name – and it wasn't Freddy. I merely uphold the tradition.

The glass-fronted entry glows orange from towering floodlights that stand like enormous Chupa-Chups. Hoping to avoid an out-of-hours inquisition, I walk with authority up the wheelchair ramp, showing my distaste – and laziness – for the twenty-odd steps. My resolve fades upon seeing a dishevelled Alexander pacing the foyer.

Alerted by the automatic doors, he greets me with a welcoming hug. Catches me off guard. Holds me with greater intensity than is respectable in the circumstances. It's not one of those European kiss-each-other's-cheek-and-break-off kind of hugs; it is something deeper – I'd describe it as latent desire – reminding me of the 'first date' hug, where the guy holds you, waiting to see if you clench your arms around him as an indication of whether you're going to let him kiss you, but with each breath he draws you into his body as if trying to cast an abstract mould of your breasts pressed into his chest.

Before I crave more of this little interlude, I return to earth with the realisation that it is probably innocent. *Perhaps I've been left to pasture in fallow fields for too long, spelled to my own paddock to wander in expectation of what the mating season – if ever there is to be one – will deliver.* And then my investigative bent weighs in: *Is this an expression of guilt? Is Alexander looking to me as his saviour?* I tilt my neck just enough to see not one tear in his eye. I extricate myself from his tentacle-like grip.

'Sorry Olivia. It shouldn't have happened. She was fine yesterday. No sign of any need for concern. All vitals were within acceptable limits, or so I've been told.'

'These things happen, Alex. Perhaps it was meant to be.'

'Don't give me that sympathetic crap! I've heard enough already from the hospital with their buck-passing and non-acceptance of responsibility. That may wash with some, but it certainly won't with me. I've witnessed far too many bureaucratic cover-ups at work without having them pandered to me in a situation like this. That's why I called you, Olivia. This is a clear case of negligence. Start your timecard or whatever from 2.30 a.m. You're on the job.'

I reel at the aspect of Alexander's nature I had not yet witnessed and certainly do not deserve. I'm not here touting for work – I'd much preferred to have stayed in bed – and I don't see this as a time to be discussing business. I soften my approach: 'Alex. I know this is a sensitive time. I've come here as a friend, not as a business proposition. Let's work this through, ask a few questions, *and then*, if there's a reason to explore behind the scenes, I'll take it on. For the moment let's find the charge nurse. And by the way, I'm just a friend, okay? I'm not here in an official capacity; we don't want anyone to have to think twice about what they're saying. Okay?'

We pass the ward where a vacant bed evidences Joyce Beecham's departure. Barely forty minutes after my receiving Alexander's call, the hospital has erased all signs of its recent patient. I shouldn't criticise that, but I do resent the hospital's insensitivity in preparing to admit the next fortunate, or unfortunate, patient. The curtains hang open, ready to welcome the morning sun and chirping birds who will sing joy into the freshly bleached, scrubbed and disinfected three metre square of hope. So much for the future. At this minute, only death's darkness fills the ward.

Commanding the Nurses' Station is a diminutive, weary-looking charge nurse, the antithesis of what I expected. 'Nurse Kosinski' shines on an enamelled name badge pinned to the bodice of her uniform. I introduce myself as Alexander's friend, fully intending to soft-pedal around the issue before I hit her with a double-edged leading question. 'Nurse, I wonder if you could tell—'

Alexander rushes in: 'When am I able to find out what caused my mother's death?'

Good one Alex. That's certainly set the scene for refusal.

Kosinski offers: 'You'll have to speak to Dr Patel about case details.'

'This is not a "case detail", it is a question about a patient who was vibrantly alive only hours ago, but now lays dead somewhere in the bowels of this building.'

I thread my hand through Alexander's arm, not wanting him to eject another blast at the nurse. I also don't want him doing, or saying, something he'll later regret. 'Come on Alex, just a moment.' Then to nurse Kosinski I say: 'Can we please see Dr Patel, or perhaps a copy of the death certificate?'

'Dr Patel is unavailable, and we can't produce the certificate to anyone other than registered next of kin.'

'I am the next of kin,' retorts Alexander.

'Just let me check that.' Kosinski clicks through a computer. 'No, we have a Meredith Bennington recorded as NOK.'

Alexander leans over the counter's pedestal and glares at the nurse. 'That can't be – she's my sister. I helped my mother with the form in your own administration office downstairs.'

'You may have completed a medical authorisation form or similar, Mr Beecham, but Mrs Bennington *is* your mother's next of kin. All we can say is that Mrs Joyce Beecham was taken by natural causes.'

For the third time, I take Alexander's arm, and this time drag him from the verge of passionate confrontation. 'Let's go now. We can't achieve anything tonight.'

He replies, wilfully enough for Kosinski to hear: 'First thing in the morning I'm seeing the hospital registrar. They're not getting away with this. I'll formally challenge it.'

At 3.45 a.m. I accede to Alexander's request to leave him alone in the car park. Some people handle grief better on their own. I drive home, detouring via an all-night garage to top up fuel for Fiona and caffeine for me. Two taxi drivers stand alongside their cabs, chatting and slurping coffee as they impatiently inhale huge gulps of nicotine should the next fare be only a radio call away. They're probably recuperating after spending half an hour sanitising the cabin, cleaning out pizza crusts, potato chip bags and all manner of refuse deposited by late-night partygoers. A quick spray and wipe, and they're ready to re-join the excitement and dangers of their occupation – all for little reward.

I complete the ten-minute journey, wondering how best to help Alexander ascertain the cause of his mother's death. Facing me is an investigation that could morph into a malpractice suit or, at worst, a murder enquiry. *That* challenge inspires me to burrow into the Beecham family background from where I might unearth a starting point. Would someone actually murder a seventy-one-year-old grandmother? Logic determines my answer: *Not bloody likely*. Despite Alex's belief that his mother was quite all right yesterday, there is nothing to suggest Joyce Beecham is a victim of foul play.

I accept Alexander's invitation to a hastily arranged memorial lunch. Being of conservatively strict morals (discounting my changed persona in the face of libidinal urges) I consider it unethical and inappropriate for an outsider to attend such an intimate function. To console a grieving family on the arm of the guy who is essentially my de facto employer is exceedingly hypocritical. It's not that I can't slip into the role of the new girlfriend – I've graduated with honours in the subject of deceit.

Morals give way to practicality when I realise that attending Joyce Beecham's memorial will enable me to siphon information from other family members and anyone else innocently dropping reckless gossip. From there I can consider the merit of Alexander's murder theory.

I don my black suit and wait.

7

Sunday 5 March

My nerves shudder as Alexander raps the front door. I greet him and blurt my misgivings about infiltrating his family's private mourning. The encounter ripens into a doorstep disagreement until Alexander escorts me to his waiting Jaguar.

'Far cry from my Focus,' I compliment.

'Can't beat the Brits.'

As far as I am aware, from my limited interest in all things mechanical, Jaguar is no longer British. I remember the hoo-hah in 1989 when the Ford Motor Company trumpeted taking over our Coventry-founded slice of history. And then in 2008, it fell to Tata Motors – India's largest motor vehicle manufacturer. I play my submissive self and hold my tongue.

'How are we going to handle this?' I continue.

'By finding a way to uncover the truth.'

Cryptic reply. Reeks of sarcasm.

'My mother had been in hospital for a few days. Friday, she went in. Had a bit of a turn at home. Nothing life threatening. You heard the interchange yesterday about my being removed as mum's next of kin. For some reason,

Meredith, my estranged sister, is now recorded in my place. On the surface, it's no big deal – she can have it. It's how this has happened that concerns me. I could subpoena the hospital's records and administrators, but that would be costly. The hospital would, of course, with its limitless resources, defend its position all the way. If you were to sniff around, I think we'd get a better and quicker result and perhaps find a motive not only for the administrative change, but also for mum's sudden death.'

'You realise we won't be popular? The starting point must be your sister.'

'My sentiments exactly. I was hoping you'd see it that way. You'll need to be discrete. I can't afford to have this look like a family vendetta.'

'Well, is it?'

Alexander glares with fierce intensity. His eyes laser through me as if I'm a sheet of half-inch steel. 'There's more, Olivia. During mum's hospitalisation, some bastard cleaned out her house. The bloody low-life took nearly everything. I haven't been able to narrow it down to exactly when – I only realised when I dropped by this morning to do a bit of a tidy up.'

'I'm figuring you're going to suggest that's no coincidence?'

'I don't know, but it's safe to say I'm thinking along those lines. Seems the louse had a key. There was no visible sign of forced entry.'

Alexander scuffs the kerb as he enters the parking bay. 'Get ready, we're here.'

We stroll along a lavender-bordered path. Alex takes my hand. I soak up the warm feeling. Treat it as an appetiser of things to come. The front door stands ajar, just enough to release waves of conversation and laughter. I've never attended a wake, so I'm surprised at the joviality of what I presumed would be a sombre event. We step into the reception room. Other than two people standing in a corner, the room is bare, save for a worthless, paisley fabric couch. A corner cabinet, of the type that might have hosted photos and mementos, now stands empty. Tell-tale geometric, dustless impressions evidence where pewter frames, international relics, and acrylic stands framing family snaps had proudly stood.

Alexander gazes in desperation. He has experienced loss like everyone else: a lost or stolen wallet; a power tool lent to a trusted friend but never seen again (both the tool and the friend) and the worst loss of all, the premature passing of a family member. I discern that he's never felt such complete emptiness and irate anxiety. I see it in his watery eyes as he struggles to compose himself. I squeeze his hand. 'You want to go outside for a moment?'

'I'll be right.'

I hope he will be. I nod to a woman of similar age. Gesture with open palm and mouth, 'We're fine. Give us a moment.'

'This was mum's favourite room,' Alex confides.

It reminds me of my parents' room – far from opulent but meeting their every need and comfort. I take in the bare walls and the carpet's dotted impressions. I reconstruct the missing chair, television stand, coffee table, and a two-seater couch.

Alexander mumbles: 'Who the hell would do this? Why mum? It's a personal violation. The place looks like the remnant of a cyclone whose eye sucked a path through her home, taking with it every irreplaceable road map and street sign of her life.'

We walk into the next room. The kitchen. More chaos. Alexander's not ready to make eye contact with anyone, he merely gazes at the clear benchtop which once held an array of appliances. He drops to his knees. Looks in the cupboards and picks up a scratched aluminium frying pan and a warped saucepan. On the lower shelf, he discovers one of his mother's secrets – an emergency stash. Inside a box of Corn Flakes a folded fifty-pound note is concealed beneath the inner wrapper. The money is crisp and fresh – the cereal's use-by date long expired.

Many will relate to the elderly's hidden reserves. Tins under beds, in freezers, and buried in the rear garden. They all have them. Why? Because they don't trust banks. They fear that on the day they sign a withdrawal form for £2,000 for a holiday to Blackpool, the bank will not have the funds. The elderly are sceptical: the bank might succumb to another Global Financial Crisis or corporate takeover that will dupe investors of their retirement fund and savings. They fear taxation and ever-increasing fees: account keeping, service charge and miscellaneous debits – all eroding their life-sustaining deposits; and they fear the spiralling effects of inflation further diminishing the substantial amount once entrusted to the most honourable of British institutions. Many, like Joyce Beecham, after hearing of friends' life savings being whittled away to tiny sums representative of their grandchild's school savings account, took radical steps to conserve their cash. And the result of those radical steps often saw the elderly forget exactly where they had stashed their biscuit tin of life savings. Years later, a DIY renovator, while repairing a loose floorboard, chances upon a dusty metal receptacle chock-full of crisp, twenty-pound notes.

I help him from the floor. 'This place was a shrine,' he says. 'Typified homes of the aged. Last week, photos clung to walls, the mantelpiece struggled to support a dozen knick-knacks, and faded photos and mementos stood like Academy Awards on huge granite pedestals. Our childhood craft and paintings dotted walls and crowded tables. There was a pipe cleaner figurine; a wooden bowl I'd turned at school in the era when 'technical' schools represented the academic choice for trades' entry; there was my sister's first doll – minus hair, one eye and a leg, and a collection of certificates, ribbons and trophies from school sports and other curricular activities in which we Beechams excelled.'

He leads me to his mother's bedroom. A mahogany dresser, which Alexander explains had been a ruby wedding anniversary gift from forty years earlier, has evaded the pilferage. It parades wedding photos, a Wedgwood statuette celebrating the Queen's Coronation in 1953, a framed cutting from a regional newspaper dated July 30, 1969, announcing George and Joyce Beecham's acceptance into the local Lions' Club, and the host of tourist spoons and postcards confirming the numerous British resorts they'd visited during their forty-plus year marriage. He peers into the cheval mirror sitting askew on the dresser. Four lace doilies yearn for the missing jewellery boxes containing irreplaceable wedding and engagement rings, gold pendants, rare opals, and a treasured ruby bracelet, all of which commemorated significant milestones of Joyce Beecham's marriage.

Beneath the bed, stuffed boxes of paraphernalia hoard memories that most would have off-loaded to charity many years earlier. 'Look, Olivia. Mum's got her whole life here. Seems like she's got rid of nothing.'

It is often said that one's home reveals volumes about its owner. This home has much more to reveal.

A woman pokes her head through the door; haughty deportment objecting to our presence in the bedroom. Her eyes scan me like an airport security wand. 'Oh hello, and who do we have here?' She addresses Alexander rather than me. I study her warped grin and suppress the urge to respond with an articulate Westminster oratory: *Thank you my dear loyal subject. Allow me to introduce myself to this esteemed congregation. I beg your indulgence to formally accept the company of Olivia Elaine Watts.'* The sarcastic thought spreads across my face until I simply reply: 'Hello, I'm Olivia—'

'Hello Meredith. This is Olivia, a close friend of mine. Olivia, meet my sister, Meredith.'

I offer my condolences.

Meredith levels an icy glare, perhaps over her brother having snared a girlfriend. I shift uneasily – I am not anyone's girlfriend; I am merely a subversive digging dirt on selected guests. I melt the frozen atmosphere by changing tack. 'Alex mentioned his ill mother. We've only been seeing each other for a short while. It was actually me who insisted on supporting him today.' I pull Alexander close. 'If my presence offends anyone, I sincerely apologise.'

Meredith raises her glass. 'No dear. I did not mean to

be overbearing. Your presence took me by surprise. You see, young Alex has not had a girlfriend for quite some time… have you Alex?'

Alexander shoots a furious scowl. 'Meredith. You would not know who I see or when. It's none of your business, nor a topic for discussion. Also not to be discussed is the conniving you've been up to at the hospital. In mum's memory though, I must raise it: How come you're registered as next of kin? You know I was. Have been for years.'

I feel the swirling undercurrent gain momentum like a powerful rip whose surge claims the weak and unsuspecting. Meredith's voice is the rolling waves, crashing down with a town crier's announcement: 'Always have to prove your superiority, especially in front of others, don't you? I did it for mum. It was me who was always at her home, me who cared for her, and me who was on the spot for her every need. All you do is see next of kin as a token title like a company director who sits as an honorary figurehead.'

'And that's exactly why mother recognised me as the most appropriate person. I was, and am, level-headed. In comparison, any decision you make is in your own interest—'

Guests gather in the hallway. Good on them. Nor would I want to miss this.

Meredith stands toe to toe with Alexander, relishing her audience's attention: 'What are you on about? This day's for mum's memory. I'm not here to cop your abuse. If you want to argue, we'll do it later, but not here.'

Alexander stands proud. He leans into his sister's ear: 'I couldn't be stuffed looking at you later, let alone talking to you.'

Meredith bears the aggressive carriage of a lioness protecting her pride. 'Very well Alexander. Come along—'

Meredith looks to me. 'What's your name again? Come and meet my sister, Roslyn.'

'*Our* sister,' Alexander snaps.

I cannot comprehend how two sisters can be so different. I relish the benefits of being an only child. Meredith, who appears to have a core as harsh as her facade, is short and frumpy with bold features, bloated face, flared nose, and a thick neck that belongs in a rugby scrum. I'd say that she's average, which on my scale is one rung above ugly, whereas Roslyn's lithe figure will capture even the most uninterested company's attention.

Course golden hair falls upon her shoulders like an evening sunset while her facial features radiate constant attentiveness. Crystal-blue eyes, finely plucked eyebrows that dance with inquisition, a slender nose able to detect the scent of money from miles afar, and thin lips quick to respond to all manner of conversations, accusations, innuendos, slanders, and criticisms are Roslyn's finest attributes – or so I discern. She will command the top tier of the winner's podium – no matter what.

She is accompanied by her latest beau. He looks out of place both as a partner and family member. Roslyn's penchant for accumulating lovers and discarding them with the frequency of full moons is well known, but not favoured by her siblings. Meredith, notably, frowns upon her sister's election to remain unmarried – yet far from celibate – with money being her sole idol. Roslyn's disposition is not inherited from the oldest branches of the family tree. An aggressor and purveyor of initiative, she is one of few who believe that happiness can be achieved only through money. She devised her own mathematic formula: wealth = possessions = happiness.

Roslyn views sales as a conduit to riches. In her late teens, she commenced training at a renowned Vauxhall dealership, believing she could create a niche market of female clientele. The vision was prophetic and generated huge commissions, rewarding her with the top salesperson award – nationally – for two consecutive years. When asked how she achieved the accolade, Roslyn was coy, claiming: 'It's my customer service.' From experience, she'd learnt that women shun high-pressure salesmen who rate selling their product equally with making a move on the female client.

Upgrading to a real estate office changed her life's course. Starting as a receptionist, she enunciated her wish to progress to the sales team where commissions are a tangible result of the effort generated by each person. During her first month of answering phones and opening mail, she'd estimated salesmen's commission and resentfully found that they had paid more in tax than she had earned for her 40-hour week. That explained the tailored suits, Italian shoes, Rolex watches and gold chains that could easily mistake the professional salesmen for West End pimps. Their huge salary also explained the manors, farms, and expansive properties that some staff, unbeknownst to the seller, procured (through their wife or other family member) far below market price from 'insider knowledge'. So impressed was Roslyn with their lifestyle, she adopted it as an intermediate goal.

A transfer to the rentals department painted a broader oversight of the market. Showing further initiative,

Roslyn completed a series of Real Estate Agent courses through Bristol University and soon after approached her office manager – who she had twice dated – pleading for an opportunity to join the sales team, emphasising her intention to achieve wealth and recognition in the once male-dominated industry. She sat out three months until a staff resignation opened the promotional door. Once instilled in the role she quickly adopted the salesperson's creed: *Anything can be achieved if you really want it.* Two weeks later' she sold her first property, a small bungalow, and was so hyped that she pledged to her manager that she would sell at least one property per week. And she did. For fifty-six consecutive weeks.

With her first commission, Roslyn purchased mining stocks and shares, and continued to increase her portfolio with interests in gold trading and futures markets. This diversion from real estate was at the behest of one of her casual boyfriends, calculatedly 'recruited' from a pool of investment advisors. Needless to add, Roslyn ensured there was only one-sided emotional attraction. And it was not hers.

She siphoned information from Peter, (whose surname she's forgotten) who laid the framework of profitability by reinforcing the investors' cliché: 'Don't store all your eggs in one basket.' Roslyn knew the consultations weren't free; they were bartered with physical investment which she would 'trade' only until she had gleaned sufficient knowledge. And Peter was only one of Roslyn's 'boyfriends' who specialised in financial arenas.

She once considered leaving real estate to concentrate fully on her share and investment portfolios, but rationalised that as a foolish career move. And so would it have been, for Roslyn ventured into property investment and later boasted to her family and social circle a pretentious, sprawling mansion. 'The Gables' was not a home in which one would comfortably live; it was a show home, where shoes were placed in a box at the doorstep; where children were banished to a 'playroom' – monitored by the home's internal video system; and a home where one fingerprint on a wall or light switch would set Roslyn on a course of furious rage.

Today, Roslyn mourns. She whisks me away from Alexander and enthusiastically welcomes me to the family fold with a trip through a family photo album where I pack away nearly half a century of Beecham history. Roslyn is softly spoken, demure and reserved – in total contrast, I imagine, to her business persona. Her rolling commentary adds life and depth to the brief outline earlier provided by Alexander. 'Here's Merri on her first school day. Little Goody Two-shoes pompously walking off on her own as if she's starting two grades above her level.'

'That's not unusual, is it?' I query, having no knowledge of how children react to their first day of school – other than my own memory of crying at the school gate.'

'I'm not sure. Look, here I am, clutching my mother's skirt and looking straight into the camera. I was pleading with dad to save me. The lens captured it most dramatically, don't you think?'

I don't let on that I care nothing for the photos or Roslyn's interpretation. It is the family dynamics that interest me; just absorbing the interaction between the three siblings is more than enough to keep me occupied. What does interest me though, is the effort Roslyn employs to promote herself – even as a young child – to an elevated station within the family. The competition between the girls is a parade of personal supremacy.

Roslyn turns the pages like months of a calendar, which I view as a flickering narrated newsreel of the young Beechams maturing into their teen years.

'Your father the photo buff?' I ask.

'Yes. It wasn't a hobby-like thing; he just got so annoyed at looking at photos of beheaded children or family members who'd suffered indiscriminate amputations of arms and legs. I remember him snatching the camera from mum, never to relinquish it again.'

I chuckle at the analogy, remembering that I'd captured similar portraits with my first Kodak Instamatic. Now, stashed in my shoulder bag, I have the mandatory mobile phone with its eight-megapixel capacity to shoot photos and videos of equal clarity. I envisage using both facilities during the afternoon. 'Where's your dad now?'

'Another story. Next question.'

The rebuff hits me with the power of a backhanded slap. *Now that's something to pursue with Alex.* I don't stop there: 'What about Alex. He seems to be left out.'

'Oh, you would have noticed that, wouldn't you? I mean, you'd be so interested in seeing him as a young boy. Yes, dad did favour us girls somewhat, but the photo bug chrysalised and flew off as we grew older. Look, here's one of Alex when he was thirteen, taken at our mother's fiftieth birthday do.'

Alexander looks splendid; neat dress pants, white shirt, and Disney tie. He could easily have been mistaken for a roving Seventh Day Adventist spreading the gospel on a Sunday morning.

'So where did you two meet? How come we haven't seen you before?' Roslyn's face lights up in expectation of a dose of good gossip.

I won't disappoint.

Anticipating that very question, Alexander and I had spent the previous evening concocting the plot of our romantic meeting. The result is worthy of publication in *That's Life* or *People's Friend*. It could be a plotline for a Barbara Cartland or Danielle Steele tell-all, and believable enough to satisfy all as to why, dear, single, Alexander was suddenly making a family appearance with a much younger woman on his arm.

God knows I have hung off very few arms. All my romances – if I could describe them so – were of the quick to prepare, quick to dispense with, two-minute noodles variety: unwrap, heat, devour and clean up. Never have I dined with a purveyor of entrée, main course, and dessert.

I wink at Roslyn: 'I'd been selling flowers at a local car-boot sale when I noticed Alex walk past, peevishly glance at me and continue on, only to see him glance back from an adjacent row. Initially, I was concerned, because no one knows what sort of cranks wander around markets, shops or anywhere else for that matter.

'Ten minutes later he approached my stall, set two coffees on the table and asked for my largest bunch of long-stemmed roses. I said, "They only come in bunches of six."

'He replied, "Make it twelve."

'I nearly made a fool of myself by gathering twelve

bunches, but corrected at the last moment. "Would you like them gift wrapped?" I asked.

'Alex said, "Yes thanks. And have you any cards?"

'I joined the two bunches and wrapped them in silver cellophane – the most romantic complement to red – and handed him a card. He proceeded to write a short message. Summoning my investigatory skills, I craned my head to decipher the inverted hieroglyphics: *You are a most beautiful woman. I would be honoured to be part of your life. Coffee? Alexander Beecham 0777 600 3633.*

'What a wonderful guy, I thought. The recipient would be swept off her feet. He handed back the pen, secured to the card behind the flowers' ribbon and passed the bunch to me.

'I was flummoxed. He seized the moment: "Please don't think me too upfront, but I'd like to give you these from my heart."

'I could have been married for all he knew. I thought of quickly unwrapping them and making a double profit – no, just joking!

'He handed me a business card – which eased my mind – and my eyes settled upon his occupation. Acting with artificial grace, I was at first reticent, giving only an inkling that I might be interested. But as soon as I arrived home from the market I phoned him and arranged our first date.'

In detective training school, one of the most important things I learnt when having to identify points of interest in photos or film, was to ignore the subject matter and scan the periphery. *That* is where the picture tells its story.

Forensic photographers, when called to arson scenes,

strive to arrive while the fire still rages. They'll film the entire perimeter, zooming in on spectators' and rubber necks' faces and profiles, knowing that amongst their number probably stands the arsonist orgasming over his (or her) handiwork.

And it remains true, for in the innocent family snap I now admire is eighteen-year-old Meredith shooting a piercing stare at Alexander, presumably because it was she who wanted the attention. I recognise the look of anger, of jealousy, of a young woman so selfish that she cannot accept her brother's position in centre stage obscuring her buxom pose.

'I'm so sorry, Roslyn. Here I am questioning your family photos, yet I haven't even extended my condolences. I *am* sorry for your loss.'

'That's fine. Goes without saying – that's why you're here.'

I feel her genuine emotion and respect. I'd succeeded on my part – another Academy Award nomination on the way. I also feel a touch of guilt by having empathy for Roslyn, who, I now believe, was not complicit in anything unlawful. I take a huge gamble: 'Well not really. With no disrespect, I'm a private investigator and I'm here with Alex at his request to learn something of your family background. Alex believes that your mother did not die of natural causes.'

'That's a terrible thing to say. Alex put you up to this? What's the implication – that one of us killed our own mother? Where is that fucking Alexander?'

Woops. Guess the gamble's backfired. 'Roslyn. Please. Allow me ten minutes. For how long was your mum ill? Alex has told me how you and Meredith cared for her daily needs.'

'She hadn't been *ill*. There'd been complications after a stroke a few days ago, but I'm sure that's got nothing to do with this. Our only concern was her diabetes and high blood-pressure, but she'd coped well with that. She was scheduled for a by-pass. You know that, don't you?'

'Yes. Alex told me. I didn't feel it proper to go to the hospital because I hadn't yet met your mother. This must have been unexpected? You had no idea that your mother's health was so bad?'

'Right. Mum, or Meredith, if I'm honest, called us to a bedside meeting on Saturday. I was frantic because Merri relayed the hospital's concern about mum. I never thought of it as a be-prepared-if-something-goes-wrong meeting because Merri does tend to dramatise things for attention – if you haven't noticed.'

So that's where you get it from, I conclude, weighing both Roslyn's and Meredith's natures. 'When did you last see her? Your mum I mean.'

'Just the evening before. Merri and I went in together. Alexander was there too – I saw his car – but I don't know whether he went in before us or after. He wouldn't dare join us. Rarely does. Well, he's more withdrawn from Meredith than me. The conflict started years ago. Don't know what over. Something stupid probably. I'm sort of swept into it because I'm close to Merri. So Alex hardly sees me either. Anyway, mum was fine then. She was busting to go home.'

Roslyn edges aside, scanning faces for recognition, beckoning their attention. She's obviously had enough of me.

I ruthlessly continue: 'And Meredith didn't mind looking after her?'

'Look, we both didn't mind; she's our mother after all. But to Meredith, everything's a chore, right down to brushing her own teeth. Fancy tea and cake?'

I accept the offer as a means of extending the conversation and directing the discussion to my own course. I accompany Roslyn to the kitchen where another photo album, whose pages of sepia moments beg to be relived, lays open on the table. This room too, is festooned with family memorabilia. A "Goodbye Mum" iced cake commands focal point on a table of tea, coffee, and biscuits. Guests congregate, recounting memories of bygone years.

I feel an affinity with Joyce's home although little sign remains of anyone having lived here. Not knowing whether the house had been *legitimately* burgled, I surmised the vultures had begun their pickings, or had been over zealous in packing away their mother's possessions. Nails and picture hooks jut from the walls like abseiling cleats hammered into a rock face; a cheap calendar suffering leaf-curl hangs askew; the pantry is stripped, leaving only a few generic products sitting on a bed of dusted sugar, coconut, salt, and coffee. It is very different from the standard of living I had been led to believe the Beecham girls were accustomed.

As for Alexander's home, I anticipate viewing that under more relaxed and intimate circumstances.

After stomaching Roslyn's CV of triumph in the financial and property markets, I steer the conversation back to Meredith.

Meredith had no matching status. She'd trained as a nurse and later specialised in consultancy and palliative care. She demonstrated a small slice of her sister's business acumen by recognising the great financial rewards in caring for the aged, for there are none more eager to spend money on preservation of life than those who unreservedly accept that death's door has finally been unlatched. Meredith's decision to enter a nursing career, according to Roslyn, was founded as a young teen who cared for her fellow beings and felt strongly about alleviating pain and loss from sufferers and their families.

To me, that was at odds with her reported stand-over tactics in the schoolyard. And I have the advantage of knowing how well history can be adapted to suit a given cause.

As she progressed through training, the power of the weekly pay packet began to reward her with more joy than the accomplishments of care, compassion, and repatriation that she had bestowed during the working week.

Some would define her resolve to worship the pound with greater fortitude than the needs of the patient as hypocritical. Meredith, however, would profess that by not respecting the patient, she would not receive the pound. There is merit in her analogy.

I conclude that Meredith is as equally aggressive in the financial arena as Roslyn – they just chose different vocations from which to reap their rewards.

Later that afternoon, after the tears had dried and the Beecham rivalry had settled (for the time being) I return to the disorder of my new home.

Eager to unfold Alexander's theories, I phone one of my former associates.

8

Sunday 5 March

Hamilton Holt was born into the burgeoning computer phenomenon of the late 80s, growing up with microchips and motherboards over rattles and alphabet blocks. That upbringing saw him develop and mature in line with computer and internet technology. On the eve of his twelfth birthday, Hamilton queued with his parents outside PC World, awaiting the midnight release of Windows 98.

Never have I confirmed whether his version of childhood history is true. I just can't accept that rational parents would introduce such meaningless and dangerous items to a child. Now, with hindsight, I think the Holts might have possessed an uncanny perception of the future.

I met Hamilton Holt when he worked in the constabulary's IT department as a network installer and technician monitoring the MET's Help Desk. We later reunited after I had need to call upon FALCON, the Metropolitan Police Cyber Crime Unit.

I am one of few privy to Hamilton's unofficial experience, more aptly described as a clandestine hobby of breaking into, or hacking – as is the official term – any type or number of secure web sites. Hamilton relishes the challenge; the more secure the site, the greater his determination to breach its security wall. He's cracked them all: banks, Department of Work and Pensions, Conservative Party's private emails, and lower level shopping sites. His one regret is not being headhunted to assist in identifying the perpetrators of the *News of the World* phone hacking scandal which caused the 168-year-old newspaper to cease publication in July 2011.

He is the classic archetype nerd: ginger hair, thick rectangular glasses, four pens in the top pocket, and a pair of stainless steel stretch bracelets securing shirt sleeves to elbows. His short stature ensures abysmal failures in the dating scene. As a result, he pays scant attention to his appearance and hygiene. It would not matter if he did, because the after-effects of his regular Bratwurst and horseradish sandwiches repels all within a ten-metre radius. Courts have granted Apprehended Violence Orders for lesser affronts to the community.

On the plus side, he has a repertoire of manners and eloquence that would be appreciated by all feminine women, and best of all, he is an altruist always prepared to rally to my assistance.

Today, he's gone out of his way to appease me. I explained the investigation and my urgent requirement to obtain background information on the three Beecham women: Joyce, Meredith, and Roslyn. Nothing would be out-of-bounds, I want everything: bank statements, mortgage accounts, welfare claims and payments... My initial brief is to report on the changed next of kin authorisation that resulted in Meredith Bennington having control of her mother's decisions. I'm cautious about discussing the topic with either Meredith or Roslyn until I clutch pages of evidential documentation – whatever that might turn out to be.

Within hours, Hamilton dispatched to my office an envelope swelling with 122 pages of 'restricted access' files. The comprehensive clutch of documents includes Joyce's marriage Certificate of 40 years' earlier, children's Birth Certificates and immunisation notices, school placements and records of child endowment payments, and rolling accumulations of Census declarations and Inland Revenue returns.

I am enlightened to find that Meredith's savings account is credited fortnightly with £152 from Care Services Ltd. Hamilton highlighted the payment – care rendered to Mrs Joyce Beecham – and attached a Certificate of Incorporation disclosing Meredith Bennington as company director of Care Services Limited. I baulk at the thought of a person tendering an invoice for looking after their own mother – but my constitution and ethics are above those of the general community. I would never charge for looking after one or both of my parents because family care should be provided for compassion, not reward.

I appreciate the sensitivity of broaching this topic in the preliminary stage of my investigation, and for that reason set aside the need to identify a motive behind Meredith's submitting an invoice for weekly two-hour attendances upon her mother at the rate of £38.00 per visit. On the plus side, I might be able to eliminate Meredith from involvement in her mother's demise on the basis that no one would do anything to end that sort of windfall.

On the very next statement a monthly credit of £1866.70 jumps from the page; an amount that I am unable to cross-reference within the documents. Further checks reveal the sum has been credited over a long period. My initial thought, without foundation, is that the amount relates to a share portfolio, assurance fund, pension plan or monthly rent from an investment property. Hamilton has noted in the margin that he'd been unable to glean any detail, other than a succession of shelf companies, from the payer's account number. Also, he has not yet established the origin of four regular credits varying between £55.00 and £336.00 per month. Incomplete detail annoys me.

I leap to the phone.

Hamilton is stunned to hear that I am calling about the smaller rather than larger discrepancies, but he convinces me that there's no offence in having money credited to an account, provided that the money originates from a legitimate source. Of that I have no argument. He mentions a fortnightly credit of £40.00 made over the previous eight months by a N. Geddes, and details his efforts in trying to ascertain the transaction's details.

I counter, 'You can't go querying every person who transfers money between accounts because you think there's something wrong.'

'I can when the recipient is a suspect in a suspicious death. It's not as if she's running a party-plan company for over 70s, selling nylon ankle-length negligees on a monthly plan. You tell me, Olivia, how a woman who works solely in aged care can amass such a pile of wealth and regular flow of credits from undetermined sources? You asked me to gather information – well, you've got it!'

'Have you got Inland Revenue details on her?'

'No, but that's no problem if you want it.'

'Good. You do that, before we probe further.'

'But wait,' enthuses Hamilton, ebulliently trumpeting a conquest like a child winning their first Little Athletics event. 'We have history.'

'And what might that be, Hamilton. Come on, spill it.'

'I'd rather draw it out a little. How about we get together over dinner?'

'Hamilton. Why do you keep trying it on? I'll give you the same answer I gave on the last fifteen invitations: thanks, but no thanks.'

'You disappoint me so, Olivia.'

'Come on, Hamo. I've got a lot riding on this. You know I need success down here.'

'Olivia, you're not going to believe this. There are credits going into Meredith Beecham's – her maiden name, remember – accounts, plural, dating back years. We're talking quite a few thousand pounds overall – it could even top £100,000. I have scant info at the moment, but it seems a police enquiry into two untimely deaths, both of which occurred at the Northampton BUPA Hospital might be a common thread.'

'You saying she's *involved* in the deaths?'

'Not saying it. For the moment, I'm just thinking aloud. So did a few others, but post-mortem found nothing untoward; certainly nothing that would indicate suspicious circumstances.'

'If there was nothing suspicious, the MET would not have been involved. I have a few contacts, but I half burnt them before leaving Worcester. If I were to start behind-the-scenes digging, I'd have to offer something bloody good in exchange.'

Hamilton whispers: 'I have a secondary channel of info piping through later on.'

The phone call confirms that rewards will flow from the mysterious finances of Meredith Bennington slash Beecham. That doesn't suture the loose ends. I desperately need something concrete.

'So,' I continue, 'Where's the husband?'

'Some estate way out in Shropshire. Bit of an eccentric recluse. Harmless though. Do you think we should go see him?'

'We? Why should you think you'd be tagging along with me?'

'Because you've refused me dinner sixteen times now, I thought you'd be about to crack. Also, you never know when you may need a second person for safety, so as a person with many talents, who better than I to assist? And you never know; you might need some urgent on site info.'

'And you think I couldn't phone you? Come on H. You know how I work – quick and methodical with no shenanigans. I'm on an investigation here, and it could very well be murder. I can't afford to make errors.'

'Exactly! That's why you need me. When do we leave?'

I huff impatience into the phone. 'First of all, Hamilton, what're the goods on this Bennington guy?'

'No criminal history. Well-to-do Lord of the manor, although probably through legacy of an inherited title. Has family money and plenty of it. Turns out he married Meredith when she was 19, but they haven't lived together now for something like thirty years – yet they remain married.'

'Something odd about that!'

'Why, Olivia? Makes sense to me, because if we were married, you'd never want to forgo me – no matter what.'

'Get real, Hamilton. I've got as much chance of marrying you as I have of becoming the next Duchess of Cornwall. Actually, that could be an each-way long-shot, couldn't it? Look, some people drift off and do their own thing. Nothing wrong with that, though you'd reckon that by now one or the other would have remarried. I'll contact the good Lord Bennington and see if he'll have a casual chat with me. You got anything on the hospital cover-up? I mean, have you hacked into any incriminating emails whizzing between doctor's offices, matron's desks and insurance companies?'

Hamilton despondently mumbles: 'No. Nothing.'

'Think I'll have a word with Alex about the death certification. The hospital won't volunteer information about Joyce's final hours. I suppose they're sworn to silence on any comment that might be interpreted as a medical conclusion. Their mouths are secured tighter than a clamped wheel in a Tow Away Zone. We must have sufficient evidence to force a post-mortem. If we haven't got it, we'll get it. Just before I go, how's Roslyn looking?'

'Clean as the Queen's corgis. No overdue debt. The usual credit cards, bank, Argos and Amex, and a business loan with a bal' under five grand. Has a couple of investment properties, both purchased over the past five years and both tenanted; rates up to date etcetera; has reasonable liquid assets 'round ten grand. Don't see a financial motive there.'

Doesn't mean a thing. Even the rich strive to be richer.

I end the conversation, flip open my laptop and click to BT's search page. Enter Bennington, Robert, Shropshire. Three results flash onto the screen. I click on the obvious:

Bennington, Lord Robert Maxwell. Press the number into my phone. Jab 'call'.

'Good afternoon. Wiltshire Manor, Marianne speaking.'

'Er, hello. My name's Olivia Watts, calling from Cornwall. Could I speak with Lord Bennington, husband of Meredith Bennington?'

'Oh no. Nothing's wrong is there? What's happened?'

Good sign. I've got the right number. 'No real problem, but we do need to clarify a few details.'

'I'll see if he's in—'

The phone echoes a wooden thud as it clunks onto a table. *Here we go with the filter-the-phone-call routine.* The guy is plainly in, otherwise she would have said at the outset that he wasn't. Just like an office secretary – nosy but efficient. Every call they're unsure of is greeted with: 'Oh, he's in a meeting. Can I leave a message?' Or, 'Can I tell him what it's about?' Cheeky bitches. I always feel like saying: 'Just put me through so I can tell him myself – that's what I rang for, isn't it?'

They call them 'gatekeepers' now – the sweet young blonde decorating the front desk. Keeper of messages, information, and secrets. And keeping the company's clients away from the very person to whom they wish to speak. Argue with a gatekeeper at your peril. She has the power to connect you with your intended – or terminate the call. Beside her sits a Golden Syrup cocktail on a coaster, in readiness to enhance the silky, seductive voice: 'Mr Smith will speak to you now. Just putting you through. Bye'ee.'

'Hello. Robert Bennington speaking.'

I jump to the present. 'Hi. I'm Olivia Watts, a private investigator working on a case in Cornwall where the name

Meredith Bennington, who I understand to be your wife, is a subject of our enquiries. My purpose for calling is to make an appointment to see you.'

'There's nothing wrong is there?'

'No, sir. But there are some personal matters we'd prefer to not discuss over the phone.'

'Very well. I understand. You name a time. I'll fit in.'

'Tomorrow morning, say 10 o'clock?'

'I must say, that's prompt.'

'I can make it later. You tell me.'

'No, no, ten's fine.'

I confirm the address details and punch them into my phone's GPS to double-check the referenced location. I bid him good afternoon, certain that he's about to pace the parquetry, wondering what the heck is going on with his estranged wife.

I call Hamilton to ask if he has the means to monitor Lord Bennington's phone lines.

'I can do anything,' chirps Hamilton, 'but such activities are illegal. There's a massive risk factor. I'd prefer not.'

Sometimes I expect far too much.

My day's business completed, I plan an early night before embarking on the monotonous journey to Shropshire. I stroll along the High Street, intending to drop into Subway to order supper – a footlong Meatball with everything, including jalapeños.

Having been an 'upgrade' girl since the term was coined to extract the maximum amount of money from every customer, I purchase the 'meal' which includes a refillable Coke plus a cookie of my choice. Cookie? Bloody Americanisms. I hate them, which, I admit, conflicts with my partaking of Subway. I have a propensity for challenging anything non-British: 'Why can't you call them biscuits? This *is* England.'

The sandwich artist replies: 'Because cookies are different to biscuits. They're a different mix.'

'Well, I don't understand how we've had chocolate chip biscuits for generations, made with a variety of mixes, and many taste the same or even better than your famed cookies. Have a nice day,' I smile as I terminate the conversation with another annoying Americanism.

I phone Alexander to let him know that I'll be off to Shropshire the following morning. He seems surprised, or disappointed, to hear that I'm acting so quick. His attitude disappoints me, especially after I've pulled out all stops in my quest to obtain a result. Alexander is one of those guys who has to keep a stranglehold of control over everything he's involved in. (Excuse my personal view, but I reckon *all* guys are like that). I expect some feedback or at least an expression of gratitude. Perhaps he is annoyed that I haven't yet produced anything tangible to assist his cause. I rally on regardless: 'Alex. In working behind the scenes to establish a cause of death, there are various processes, many circuitous, that we must follow. As a lawyer, you are well-equipped to recognise that. For the present, our best shot is through Meredith, and it therefore follows that her recent history might provide a connection to the present. I'm asking you to support me on this, otherwise it's hardly worthwhile my getting further involved.'

'Don't know if I can. Meredith knows something's going on. You know I've already barrelled her about dropping me as next of kin.'

'Of course she knows something's going on. She's shit-scared, Alex. And she doesn't know half of what we've got. So let me open some doors here. Okay?'

'Yep. All right. I'm sorry. The whole thing stinks. To *think* that my own sister might be involved is hard to take. Continue on. I'm all right with what you're doing.'

Sleep descends slowly on private investigators. Tactics and procedures, interviews and enquiries, and pursuits and observations act out pantomime scenes as a curtain raiser to the night's dreams. Flashes of the future punctuate my dreams. 'What ifs', we call them in the trade. *What if I arrive at Wiltshire Manor and find that Lord Robert is a lecherous predator? What if Meredith left with a promise to not expose him? What if it's not a manor but just a tiny council house featuring a grandiose brass nameplate? What if I arrive, only to be greeted by Meredith herself who would be perplexed at my appearance there?*

I wake at an ungodly hour. Crane my neck to the bedside clock. It flashes erratically. Victim of another blackout – a regular Newquay inconvenience. Or is it my building's switchboard? I check the time on my ever-reliable mobile phone and wish I'd not woken. 6.22 a.m. I won't get back to sleep. Not one to waste time, I spring out of bed, jump into a track suit and with banana in one hand and a two pound coin in the other, commence the short walk to the news agency. The morning stroll serves as a good brainstorming session to help me prepare the coming day's tasks. The aroma of fresh pastry – apple pies or jam tarts, I guess – entice me towards its origin. I explore the surrounds of my new environs, criss-crossing back streets and lanes until finally chancing upon High Street in a location far from where I expected to appear.

While looking at watches in the local jeweller's shop I jerk to reality on noticing that it is nearly 7.00 a.m. Needing a minimum of two and a half hours' transit time to Shropshire, I overlook the morning paper, turn around and jog home.

9

Monday 6 March

I made good time, feeling no guilt for hoofing it along the motorway. Knowledge of police officers favoured hiding places for detecting speeding motorists is one of my prized assets. In the unlikely event of Fiona creeping over the speed limit, another of my assets is a sweet and seductive disposition able to melt the pen of any police member who chooses to rest his infringement book on my bonnet.

I park in front of huge electric gates protecting Wiltshire Manor. From what or who, I am yet to discover. A discretely mounted camera, camouflaged by the fanned foliage of a huge cypress pine, swivels from a brick pier towering above the gates' spiked top. I open the car door and the gates open – activated, I assume, by a motion detector or a person monitoring a bank of security screens. I fall back into my car and proceed along the white-stoned driveway which snaps, crackles and pops like a bowl of Rice Krispies. Closely-planted poplars border the edge, allowing the early morning sun to etch yellow stripes across the drive, transforming it to a 200-metre Zebra Crossing.

As the manor emerges, I discard my earlier impression of it being a glorified council house. The manor replicates a huge hotel that has been extricated from the French Riviera and plonked square in the centre of Lord Bennington's expansive estate.

Two huge marble and granite columns support a giant portico designed to protect guests and their attendants from inclement weather. The entrance door resembles the underside of an old drawbridge, because it is, by far, the most immense door I have ever seen. It spans the width of a fire station's huge glass doors and its height soars above twenty feet.

I park beneath the portico, expecting James, Jeeves or a rigid, upright male dressed in starched shirt and black vest to assist me. Surprisingly left to my own devices, I resort to the age-old tradition of knocking on the door. I ponder the conundrum of why a person would install an electric camera on a gate 200 metres away, only to neglect having a bell or pull cord on the front door.

The door creaks open. 'Hello, Miss Watts? Lord Bennington is expecting you.'

'Thank you. You're Marianne?'

'Yes. You recognise my voice?'

'No. Not at all. Just presumptuous.' I have an answer for everything.

Marianne directs me through the ballroom-sized entry foyer that might once have admitted two hundred of Jane Austen's fictional guests. A parquetry floor with marble inlay glistens beneath hundreds of faux-candle globes balancing on a chandelier.

'You're here about Meredith?'

'Yes. I'll speak to her husband first. No need to be alarmed; we only need some information to assist an enquiry. I may chat to you after.'

Marianne knocks on the study door and admits me into a room where Lord Bennington sits behind a huge desk, gingerly constructing a deck of cards into a contorted building.

'Come on in Miss Watts. Sit down, please.'

'Thank you, sir. What a huge room.' I feel like an idiot as soon as the words leave my mouth; sort of like an aspiring actress fluffing her first lines. *What the heck did I say that for? I probably sound like a young schoolgirl who for the first time had met a pop star she's idolised for years and upon seeing him goes weak at the knees and incoherently dippy.* I nervously continue: 'I have been engaged by a client to investigate a hospital's role in his mother's death. Meredith is not an *official* suspect, so I pledge to you confidentiality of our communication.' I stress the word 'official', hoping to dilute the strength of my accusation.

'I'm not sure there'll be communication until and unless you give me sufficient cause to speak about my wife – and in her absence, mind you. Not really up-front, is it? And you're not police, are you? So, this isn't sanctioned by law?'

First score to the good lord. 'Sir…' I stall to consider how to establish ground rules and preserve my credibility. I must set him at ease. 'No. I am not the police, although I did recently serve as a detective sergeant for Worcester CID. I've since established my own investigations practice in Worcester, but transferred to Cornwall at the behest of a local lawyer. Mrs Joyce Beecham died in hospital while recovering from an unrelated illness. My client is the deceased's son.'

'Beecham, you say? So where does my wife fit into this fanciful story?'

'Your wife, as you must surely know, is the daughter of

Joyce Beecham and the sister of my client, Mr Alexander Beecham. Our investigation focuses on malpractice or the unthinkable prospect that Mrs Beecham was actually murdered.'

'Should you not wait until it's established whether or not the lady was murdered before you conduct such a penetrative investigation?'

'Fair enough point, sir. However, the present difficulty is that the hospital claims natural causes by 'frailty of old age' as they so nicely put it. The doctor signed the death certificate to that effect, thereby bypassing the need for an autopsy.'

'I see. So you're going to hedge around a few questions rather than ask me directly if I think Meredith's the type of person who would kill her own mother?'

'That's not how I would put it. I'm merely seeking background information that might assist my client.'

'I've never heard of such a preposterous scenario. Meredith devoted many hours to caring for *my* mother – even before we were married. I have no doubt that her compassion was founded on exemplary Christian ideals. My mother died of natural causes at 92 years-of-age. There's no way on God's earth that Meredith could have, or would be, complicit in anyone's death.

'Perhaps if she'd devoted equal energies to our marriage she'd be by my side and sharing this conversation – but that's not the issue. There's nothing here for you Miss Watts, so if you'll excuse me, I have some pending matters.'

'Certainly sir. I'm sorry for having caused you grief. These enquiries are never easy.'

'I'm sure they're not, but you might have armed yourself

with fact rather than speculation before embarking on your crusade which I consider is a reverse investigation. You have what you believe to be a crime, and now you're trying to find, or fabricate, facts to support your theory.'

'That's not correct. I prefer to leave on a good note, so I'll bid you good morning sir.'

Marianne suddenly appears in the doorway, discretely summoned by a buzzer concealed beneath Bennington's desk. 'You're ready, Miss Watts? Let me show you out.'

I'm certainly not ready, but decorum dictates the favourable time to depart.

Marianne directs me to the door. She's perfected the walk learnt in etiquette and deportment classes: head held high, taking quiet, tiny steps while looking straight ahead and uttering not one word.

I detect that as out of character. Upon my arrival, Marianne was overly pleasant and inquisitive. Now, she presents as if she'd experienced a personality disposition during the previous ten minutes. I conclude that she has either been silenced by her employer, or that she heard our entire conversation from beyond the door and now chooses to not become involved. The latter is the more plausible because butlers and maids strive to ensure they're abreast of the events of their masters, just as a secretary strives to know more about her employer's business than does his wife and shareholders.

I clamber into Fiona and scurry along the driveway, scattering stones into orbit, while others chip and tap against my abused car's tinny wheel arches. The gates allow me through and then slam closed as if to angrily bar me from future visits. I stop a few metres farther along the road and enter details of the conversation into my notebook. I make no mention of Bennington's attitude, applying the rationale that any responsible person would defend their loved ones. The fact that Lord Bennington struck me as over-defensive must be a consequence of his compassion for his estranged wife. I speculate that Bennington would, right this minute, be on the phone, quizzing his mother's former doctor.

Before driving off, I phone Alexander: 'Just left his lordship's. Bloody hell, you wanna see this place; it must have once been home to royalty. Anyway, I learnt nothing, but did get a few negative vibes after mentioning his estranged wife. I reckon he'll be rifling drawers of old files later on, just to satisfy his curiosity. Hopefully, I've planted enough seeds of inquisition. Perhaps he'll feel more at ease when I speak to him again, later in the piece. For the moment, have you got anything from the good doctor Patel or the hospital?'

'No. Nothing further. They're sticking by mum's death as old age. They have to, don't they? Can't go back on what they've certified! In their view, there's nothing suspicious. That's their official stance.'

'Alex. That's old news. We need a reason to demonstrate that a post-mortem will contradict their conclusion.'

'I thought that's what you were getting from your Little Lord Fauntleroy or whoever he is.'

'Very funny. I tried, but he employed the same tack – "bring more evidence and we'll talk". This really is one of those Catch-22 situations. Perhaps we could put pressure on the hospital? There must be a legal means of initiating an autopsy. That's your bag, Alex. The legal stuff. Can you look into it?'

'Yep, okay. Leave it with me. What's your next plan?'

'Can't tell you. Don't get the wrong idea, but sometimes we have to do things that are best left unsaid.'

10

Monday 6 March

I rehash my scene to be played in the Cornwall and District General Hospital with a ruse I'd I perfected in a small regional hospital. Research for the project required a preparatory visit where I took particular notice of the cleaning staff's uniform. I then sourced a replica online. Duplicating the identity tag was more difficult. I'd propped in a waiting room that lay in the path of the cleaners' progress through a general admission ward. I dropped a few breadcrumbs from an out-of-date sandwich won from a nearby vending machine. I say 'won', because the machine jangled out more change than the two one pound coins I'd inserted. Anyway, the cleaner interrupted my pretend phone conversation, motioning – not asking – me to move aside. I pinged my phone's camera, stood up, and discretely snapped shots of her ID tag.

I could have adopted my pickpocket con where I bump into a cleaner and unclip her tag during a small fracas. I decided against that because a missing tag would have put the hospital on alert, resulting in all cleaners being scrutinised at the commencement and end of their shifts. I prefer to operate under-the-radar. So I left the hospital, sped home and downloaded the photos into my computer. After a few minutes' clicking, colouring, and resizing in Photoshop, I became a bona-fide part-time cleaner.

During my years with the constabulary I was, by necessity, required to employ borderline illegal practices in pursuit of penetrating criminal activities. It's the backbone of investigatory procedure. People rarely surrender or volunteer information at will; it has to be coerced from them like a dentist extracting teeth from an unanaesthetised patient. That is why, in most cases, the suspect's determination to protect himself and his loved ones from incrimination or blame will see him yield to his interrogator.

Never will I shirk a challenge. I explore all channels in my quest to unearth the smallest clues. I am the proverbial dog seeking a bone and once upon the scent I will not heel until the delicacy is retrieved.

I ponder the challenge facing me and consider suspending the investigation until I hold tangible evidence that positively establishes unlawful interference in the deaths of either or both Joyce Beecham and Victoria Bennington. Only flimsy information, innuendo and hearsay has led me to Meredith. I can't act on those falsities. I am bound by law – appearances and hunches are best left to those of lesser ability, like my old foe, DI Michael Marchant.

Before phoning Alexander to discuss my predicament, I head to the hospital. I calm down during the drive, exorcising the panic and reservations of failure that course within me. Professionally, (and to a lesser extent, financially) I can't afford to flop on my first case – I'd never live it down, and I'd quite possibly never again get work in the industry. When I apply logic to Alexander's dilemma, I have no option other than to label the hospital a crime scene. That becomes my starting point and the reason I should covertly check its layout to determine the most practical future approach.

It's time to stop second-guessing myself and start making positive inroads.

Cornwall and District General Hospital has been recently modernised. Built in 1924, it was extended in 2012 to include a fast-track admission wing together with an Accident and Emergency section to accommodate six ambulances at any one time, courtesy of prolific drug users booking out the holiday seasons.

The admission area itself boasts a huge laminate counter of mailbox red – perhaps not the most pragmatic decor for a hospital. Nurses and clerks mill behind, taking enquiries, answering phones, checking computers, and liaising with doctors and medical staff. Cleaning staff flit about, unnoticed by their professional colleagues. Care staff rush by, wheeling patients to operating theatres and respite wards.

Two contractors drag a trolley of canned soft drink between vending machines. I envy those who would later traverse the hospital filling chocolate and sweet machines. I could easily assume *that* role; it would be like having a *Survivor* immunity idol to protect me. The downside, unfortunately, would be the lack of opportunity to access restricted areas. Nonetheless, I snap off a photo of one of the contractor's identity cards for future use.

Hanging above the admission counter, a huge signboard directs visitors to wards and clinics, clearly specified by different colour designations for each ward. *Follow the red line to casualty, blue line to maternity, black to x-rays and so on.* That's how it works now, just follow the lines. No

'Fifty metres to accounts' or 'Personnel, second door on left'. Today, we just follow the lines. One day, the whole of Britain's road network will be awash with colour-coded directions: Birmingham, take the green road; Manchester, the red motorway; 10 Downing Street? Skip along The Yellow Brick Road.

Pointers to 'Accounts', 'Administration', and 'Chapel' capture my interest. A series of coloured arrows direct me to the accounts section where I flop onto a seat and adopt the jittery demeanour of a waiting patient – attentive and anxious – whilst trying to gauge the level of activity in the administration area.

It is larger than I expected, which isn't necessarily a problem. The presence of hideous fabric-covered orange partitions is. I'll need to be alert to the prospect of a staff member popping out from behind one of the screens. If Joyce Beecham's medical record is suspended in one of the filing cabinets lining the rear wall, I'm going to need quick and uncompromising access.

Alternatively, the file could still be with Dr Patel, or concealed in a drawer at the nurses' station or even enroute to an unknown destination, wheeling through corridors and offices, up and down lifts, across desks of clerks and administrators to be checked, rechecked and 'signed off' by team leaders and supervisors, and then recorded on the hospital's 'File Tracking System' to generate a completed file that will later, when required for audit or investigation, be declared 'misplaced' within the bureaucratic motherboard.

Of the eight staff seemingly dedicated to clerical duties, only three appear to be actively engaged. The remaining five exchange chatter about husbands, boyfriends, weekend parties and how hard they'd worked over the past few months, dodging workmen, sheets of plasterboard and trekking through an orienteering course just to attend the toilets.

I remove my wallet, and inside the clear vinyl sleeve insert a recently manufactured Lloyds Insurance Accredited Agent identity card. I approach the enquiry counter. A young girl chewing a half kilogram of gum stretches me an elastic smile and whinnies: 'Can I help you?'

'Hello. I'm Olivia from Lloyds.' I return my own smile as I wave the false ID in front of Miss Gum Chewer's eyes. 'I represent the family of the late Mrs Joyce Beecham who passed away on Saturday. I'm with the Field Investigations Unit assigned to authenticate claims. There's nothing particularly out of order with the file, save for the next of kin having submitted a life policy claim with little regard for a period of mourning.' Having perplexed the young clerk with my verbosity, I continue: 'I wonder if we might check the death certificate date and number so we can confirm that all's above board?'

The clerk points a thanks-for-interrupting-me glare and proceeds to the bank of cabinets I'd spotted on my way in. From a top drawer, labelled A – C, she removes a file and flings it on the counter. 'Here. Check what you need, it's all there.' She walks away, leaving me with the confidential file of a deceased patient. I gaze at documents. I desperately want copies. At that precise moment I sense being watched. I look to the ceiling to see a big, black, bug-eyed security camera capturing the unsuspecting public. I am no longer unsuspecting.

I toy with the possibility of creating a diversion by

yelling 'fire' so that I can shuffle some of the documents into my bag, but decide against rash action, choosing instead to hand back the file to Miss Gum Chewer. I memorise its return placement, having already planned a clandestine return to photocopy the documents.

My route home takes me straight past Alexander's office. I feel obliged to give him a sit-rep (situation report in police jargon). I also want to see his office – an omission (of no bearing) I'd made while considering my move to Newquay. Now, I'll bill him for the pleasure.

I expect to walk into a cavern of bookshelves, portraits of his father and esteemed members of the legal profession within a plush reception area where leather Chesterfields, crystal ashtrays and a huge marble counter will impress the most discerning client.

I am grossly disappointed. The office is a grey cube in a new development; one of those buildings erected by bolting together four huge concrete slabs and then whacking on a silver-paper-insulated iron roof. Inside, the walls are painted Elephant Grey. African or Asian? – I wouldn't have a clue. The whole complex is insufficiently drained, because the second thing to hit me is the moist, musty smell of damp concrete. Timber architraves and doorframes shine a darker grey – in vogue twenty years' ago – and two, four-foot fluorescent lights hang from shiny brass chains.

The fit-out is equally bland and would rival a dentist's waiting room. A black laminate desk squats in the centre of the reception area. An equally black gentleman, an articled clerk I later learn, taps and clicks on a computer like a descent of Woodpeckers. A budget settee hugs one wall, an odd-shaped table supports an acrylic stand of Legal Aid brochures, and a water cooler hums in a corner. One wall is assailed by degrees, practice certificates, Law Society membership and a huge Plexiglas-fronted graduation photo that distorts the graduates' identity.

The efficient Mr Singh shows me to Alexander's office, which is one of two accessed via a small hallway beyond reception. That's when I see the bookshelves. Heavy duty storage. Sections of steel shelving support statutes, files, and reference manuals. Scattered files occupy another shelf and pending briefs folded in half and tied with pink ribbon await court process. Pink? Differentiates between defence and prosecution briefs.

Alexander welcomes me from behind a desk piled with legal texts, exercise books and files. I offer a précis of my progress. He shows me a copy of an application (he called it a 'submission', but that's a bit over-the-top for me) to the Cornwall Coroner to appeal against the MCCD (Medical Certificate of Cause of Death, he explained) issued by Dr Patel. The thrust of the submission challenges the doctor's conclusion of 'frailty of old age' on the basis of the patient's natural functions having been monitored *and* documented within acceptable limits. The lengthy document annexes a two-page history of Alex's mother's previous good health, and states: 'An autopsy will confirm the aforementioned and provide ample evidence that Cornwall and General District Hospital's duty of care to Mrs Joyce Beecham was grossly mismanaged.'

Alex stops short of levying specific allegations, but from what I read, well, he doesn't really need to. I am ecstatic to learn of the application's grounds, and hope that the coroner will discover the true reason behind Joyce Beecham's death. The findings will become a matter of public record, a vital outcome if I am to convince the sceptics – and they are growing by the moment.

On the debit side, I am now under extreme pressure to obtain Mrs Beecham's hospital charts and records to bolster the forthcoming enquiry. The hospital and certifying doctor will learn of the application, and that concerns me because the hospital, in supporting its staff and systems, will have many opportunities to 'doctor the records'.

'Probably already have,' says Alexander. 'I spoke to the Registrar first thing this morning. Clammed up like a politician after being sprung for abusing his expenses. So I offered the courtesy of letting him know that I was referring my concerns to the coroner. As expected, he didn't say a word.'

My familiarity with administrative process dovetails with Alexander's account. 'Yeah. They'll bury their heads until the last minute and then request an adjournment or extension of time, depending on what is required of them. You'll probably have the autopsy before they decide to act.'

Alexander smiles. 'So much the better, although I know a couple of girls who won't be particularly pleased. Nor myself, for that matter, because it means delaying mum's funeral. But at least we're on the way.'

'Yep.' I shudder at Alexander's reference to 'we', knowing that I will soon engross myself in risk and impropriety.

I reveal nothing of my intentions.

11

Monday 6 March

One facet of working as an investigator is combatting the job's invasion into our private life.

I've been paternally programmed for this work. As the stepdaughter of a proud senior police officer, (now retired) I groomed myself in his mould. As a child, I learnt to query anything that didn't make sense or wasn't entirely clear. On one occasion, I overheard dad quiz my mother, 'Honey. Where's my wallet?'

'Probably where you left it,' mum replied.

'If I knew where I'd left it I wouldn't be bloody asking!'

I was eight-years-old and so eager to help my dad. I embarked on my own scientifically-based search procedure, based on snippets and smatterings of investigative procedures I'd heard from dad's boasting. I trundled up to my room and pinned my Junior Police Constable badge to my tunic and collected my official police notebook which was unofficially imprinted with Birmingham CIDs mail stamp. I remembered that dad arrived home at eight o'clock, fell through the front door and threw his coat on the hall stand.

With a beaming smile, I approached my father: 'Dad. I think you should check the pockets of your coat.'

'No Livi dear. I wouldn't leave it there. You run along back to your game.'

Dad continued protesting: 'I left it on the fridge. I always leave it on the bloody fridge!'

Mum would always egg him on: 'Come on now. You didn't leave it there. You probably left it in the pub 'cause you were too sodding pissed to pick it up off the bar that you'd obviously collapsed on.'

Dad often recounted brawls and arguments he'd witnessed in the pub. It made sense that he would conceal and protect his wallet which secured his treasured police identification and warrant card.

I drew in the backchat from the lounge room, so upset about mum being berated by dad. It forced me to help dad. At that age, I hadn't a clue what 'sodding pissed' meant, but I did know that dad frequently attended the pub. He'd even taken me a few times. I was sworn to secrecy. But we were sprung on returning from one of those sessions, and that was when I heard mum call dad a 'sodding idiot'.

I crept upstairs and into my parents' room. On their huge bed, dad's briefcase lay in a shallow indentation. I snapped open the locks. The lid sprung open as if releasing a Jack-in-the-Box, and revealed files, papers, a row if pens, handcuffs and two small notebooks. Attached to the lid was a sleeve from which two manila folders peeped. I reached into the sleeve and felt dad's wallet. I pulled it out, just to make sure, and then replaced it.

Overjoyed, I withheld my excitement because I knew I'd be in big trouble if dad knew I'd been in his room without asking. Even more so for opening his briefcase. I was glad

I'd been able to squash it closed after struggling to align the brass latches.

I went back to my room and entered in my notebook: *To find a solution, first look at the most obvious. If that fails, double check. If the problem remains, look to the second most obvious conclusion and you shall be rewarded.* To this day, I've retained that little book and never fail to copy the childhood scrawl into every new notebook.

Crime, in general, is never committed with great foresight. The late Ronald Biggs might argue otherwise, nevertheless, many of the clues leading to the arrest of the Great Train Robbers resulted from exploring obvious conclusions.

During the challenging Evesham Murders case, the most obvious clue was that Barry Simmons had murdered Juanita Morales. But it was too obvious. I looked beyond that, to the second most obvious clue, which was that another person had committed the crime. As an open-minded investigator, I solved the case on the back of that decision.

I took my notebook in to the lounge room and faced my father: 'Dad. You found your wallet yet?'

'No Livi. Don't you worry. I'll find it later, I'm sure.'

'But dad, I can help. I followed the logical progression procedure, however you call it, that you talk about. Look at my inbestigation. You took off your coat and hung it on the hallstand. You said the wallet's not there. You went upstairs and put your briefcase in your room—'

'Have you been in my room, darling?'

'No, dad. But that's what you always do; you call it MO – that Latin name.'

'Modus Operandi, Livi.'

'Yeah, that opera. Anyway, you've still got the same clothes on, so the wallet's not in your pocket, it must be in the briefcase or mum's right that you left it in the sodding pub.'

'Olivia! You can't say that. "Sodding's" not a nice word for a little girl.'

'But dad—'

'Enough!'

I stood stunned, wondering why I couldn't say words I'd learnt from mum. I didn't see dad head upstairs, but I saw him walking down, scratching his head and holding his wallet. I forgot all about my chastisement and nearly peed myself with pride.

This might be an appropriate time to let you know something I rarely talk about. Although adopted at the age of four-years-old, I refer to my stepmum and stepdad as my parents. My biological mother and father remain unknown to me, save for a half-day meeting with my biological mother, Elaine, shortly after I'd turned eighteen. This dark side of my life haunts me and makes it exceedingly difficult to open my heart to repair the unhealed wounds that remain sutured within me. One day, circumstances might allow me to pluck the supernatural courage needed to detail the tragic series of events that precipitated my being abandoned. Now's not the time.

What started as a productive day is wiped out by phone calls from Alexander. And Hamilton Holt. Topping that, Meredith left messages on my voice mail as if she were trying to unsettle me.

There are times when an investigation's progress will be

gauged not by those to whom we speak, but by those to whom we do not. For instance, Roslyn had been over-helpful and over-friendly at her mother's memorial afternoon, but since that day she has not contacted Alexander or me to learn of the enquiry's progress. Quite obviously, there is no necessity for her to do so, but given the field of conflict laying between her and Meredith, I would have bet a pub meal that by now, she would have dropped subtle snippets to implicate her sister. Their opposing points of view about removing Alexander as next of kin now makes me wonder if Roslyn is wearing a darker mask of subterfuge than I am prepared to accept.

Another unresolved matter, of a very personal nature, is my status as single. One of the three men within the sphere of my work is seventy-four-year-old Lord Bennington. Never would he be my eligible bachelor – no matter his wealth.

Hamilton Holt, despite inviting me out more times than I've had dates, has failed to shoulder my sixteen rejections. His offer stands ad infinitum, and will remain so, because Hamilton's aesthetic handicap causes me great embarrassment – a fact I shamefully admit.

Then there is Alexander, out of bounds because of my strict work ethic against fraternising with clients. The code is moral, rather than cast in stone. Nevertheless, I am surprised to receive Alexander's phone call, suggesting an 8.00 p.m. meeting over dinner, ostensibly to discuss my progress. I offer my professional let-down: 'I'm having an early night. I've got another case to prepare.' I think I uttered it half-heartedly, knowing that I really want, and deserve, (by my own justification) a night out. Urgent pangs of desire brew within me. I need to renew my bond of womanhood.

We agree to meet at the Butcher's Den, a restaurant specialising in, not surprisingly, meat dishes. It is equally renowned for its 'butcher's bar' where hits against the underworld have been arranged by gang identities so noted for 'butchering' their adversaries. The promise of tacky clientele reminds me of what I'd left behind in the constabulary, for 'The Den' is reputedly a meeting place for local Mafia and euro gangs – with great food.

I arrive first and take a table, upon which doilies resembling soiled bandages sop up evening spills. Cowhides decorate the walls; other nondescript pelts and coats of lambswool complement racks and hooks, and a huge open-view cold store displays varieties of beasts, their fleshy white and pink carcasses highlighted by fluorescent orange branding symbols. This meat connoisseurs' haven offers an entrepreneurial variation on the theme of selecting a live lobster from a salt-water tank. A waiter dressed in Blues Brothers' discards plonks a Gin and Tonic on my table. Since absenting myself from Worcester's bar and club scene, I find it easy to fall into a quiet, evening wind-down. Minutes later, Alexander sidles beside me. 'What's happening?'

'Don't think you're the first to use that line – and you won't be the last! Nothing much. Just sampling their G and Ts. Very nice.

'I'll top you up then. Just a tick.'

Alexander returns with another tumbler of Gin and Tonic and a pint of what appears to be flat stout. 'What are you drinking?

'Coke. I'm driving.'

'Don't be a stick-in-the-mud. You can have a couple, and if you do get into trouble you can just bail yourself out!'

'My point exactly. There's no way I'd risk my professional credibility, let alone my licence, for the sake of a few drinks. You go right ahead, but count me out.'

'I should have met you at your place so you'd be more relaxed.'

'I'm fine, Olivia. Just fine.'

We paddle around the shore of small talk as we each down a garlic prawn entrée. I'm conscious of the gin and tonics loosening my mind (and secretly hope they'll loosen my morals) but still I need to probe Alexander about his family background. 'Alex. I don't want to speak out of turn, but something doesn't ring true about Meredith adopting herself as next of kin. She didn't discuss it with you, so we can presume your mother knew nothing of it. We're blind to Roslyn's role in the decision other than what she's told you. Can you come up with a reason why Meredith would see being next of kin as so important?'

'Apart from being a control freak? Nothing.'

'She's left me a couple of messages. Makes me wonder whether she's onto me. Theoretically she should know me only as your 'close friend' as I was introduced at your mother's memorial.'

Alex shifts in his chair: 'I haven't said anything about you to anyone. I want this to be low-key as possible.'

Truthfully, it doesn't matter to me whether Meredith knows who I am. What I am more concerned about is *why* she felt the need to call me. 'Alex. This could be a dicey situation. Other than you, I'd confided only in Roslyn about my true role, and I've spoken to Meredith's estranged husband, who, I might add, isn't too impressed with me. Very defensive of Meredith though – for someone who's supposed to have been living apart for yonks. I can only imagine that either Roslyn or the good lord, and I don't mean God, has blabbed that I'm investigating Meredith. Strange thing is though, that my interest in Meredith only surfaced from your original concern of her being recorded as next of kin in lieu of yourself. But there is something else to her shadow – a succession of unusual deposits into her bank accounts.'

'I don't know anything about that,' Alexander mutters, 'but it wouldn't surprise me if Roslyn did speak to her sister and spill the beans on you. They can be close when it suits them.'

'Are you aware of the possibility that Meredith was being paid to care for your mother?'

Alexander twists in his seat: 'You're fucking joking! Sorry. What do you mean? How do you know that?'

'I have reliable information.'

I choose to not reveal anything other than the most basic of my enquiries lest I proffer information that could later be used against me or, perish the thought, be used to clear the very person it implicated. 'For the moment, Alex, just accept it. Meredith has been billing the NHS for her part in caring for your mother. Sure, it seems crass, but in her defence, she is a registered carer and entitled to account for her services.'

'Fucking services! Bloody hell, Olivia. She's our mother. Shall I slip back up to the office and whip up a back-dated claim? While I'm there you could phone Roslyn, and ask that she do the same. Or is she already?'

'I've got no idea about Roslyn. I'm planning to contact her later, but don't you go tipping her off.'

'Stuff the both of them. That's what I reckon.'

'Settle down, Alex. Settle down.' I take Alexander's hand and feel tension and anger pump furiously to his fingertips. Main course has just been dropped, literally, on the table before us. My honey-glazed chicken breast is dwarfed by Alexander's rump steak with its steaming pepper sauce inching like a mudslide toward the plate's edge. 'Forget about this stuff for a while. Enjoy your steak. After, we can take a walk to the beachfront.'

Alexander winks a glint of acceptance. He orders another Coke for himself and a Gin and Tonic for me. I don't want another one. I am already numbed by the first two and very nearly entering the zone of incoherent happiness where anything can happen – and usually does.

Alexander's home is spacious and modern, but missing the distinctive 'bachelor pad' fingerprint. I remember nothing of leaving the Butcher's Den or walking to the beachfront. I have no memory of salty air or sand squishing between my toes, and no memory of arriving in this lawyer's sanctuary. All I do recall is pitching from side to side as his car swerved around corners and careered through roundabouts.

Wailing from a hi-fi system is Leona Lewis' cover of Roberta Flack's 'First Time Ever I Saw Your Face'. *People still play Leona?* His lounge room reminds me of a Curry's technology section. A 60-inch plasma television squats between banks of matte black speakers. Alexander had once bragged about this prized home theatre as a hook to invite me to a movie night. As is a girl's intuition, I'd sensed an ulterior motive. Not wishing to waste an evening in front of a television, I declined the invitation.

The remaining furniture appears to be hand-me-downs

or charity shop bargains. I cannot accept that a lawyer on good money would succumb to what looks like pickings from a hard-rubbish collection.

'Who's your designer?' My belated return of sarcasm. *Okay, not the best way to ingratiate myself.*

'It's a bit dated, yes. Just some of my parents' things I saved from being thrown out.'

'I guess your parents were the winners.'

Alexander shoots me a puzzled look, either not comprehending my one-liner, or he does understand and chooses to repay it with a non-approving glare. And then he shocks me by leaping forward, wrapping his arms around my waist and standing still – just holding me. I rest my head on his shoulder and smell the diluted blend of aftershave, cigarette smoke and the stale, yeasty, odour of an unventilated pub.

'Olivia,' he whispers, 'You still drunk?'

'I never was drunk. Just merry.'

He cradles my cheeks in his hands, presses his lips to mine, tastes the residual peppermint lining my mouth, and then chases my animated tongue around the cavern of sensuality.

I'm one of those girls who kisses with closed eyes, but sometimes I can't resist sneaking a peek at the guy so I can get the heads-up on his enjoyment or disappointment. Alexander is the proverbial blank canvas. He expresses vacancy like a taxi patrolling The Strand at three o'clock on a Monday morning. I imagine him reviewing the *'Dummies Guide of How to be a Successful Lover'* (which I could have written) or the once widely criticised *The Joy of Sex* now eagerly sought and treasured by octogenarians.

The lingering kiss borders on eligibility for entry into the *Guinness Book of Records* for the joint record of longest and most boring. A kiss is a kiss all the same. My lost libido finds itself. Warm flushes course through my body, preparing me for a night of lust that last week was not even on the horizon. Tonight? Hmm, anything goes.

Then it hits me. *Bloody hell, am I slow. I should have seen it days ago.* He is a mummy's boy. It all makes sense; the sibling rivalry; the doting son appointed next of kin, and his status as a single, never married, forty-seven-year-old.

'No. You're not drunk,' he belatedly replies. 'I would never take advantage of a drunk woman.'

I reconcile that he'll never take advantage of any woman, crapulent or otherwise. Despite my earlier craving for his company, I change my mind, as is a woman's prerogative, and decide that he would not take anything of me – advantage or no advantage. The one-night-stand fades from the menu.

He releases my face. 'So. Shall we sit down and talk about us and how compatible we are as working partners?'

'We could, but I've got more work I should be doing back home. I'm heading off now. Sorry to cut the night short. Have a good night.'

'But Olivia.'

'Alex. You're about to doze off.'

'Without you?'

'Yeah. Sorry. Can't spoil a good thing.' With that, I say goodbye and leave Alexander perplexed in the doorway. He looks like a child who, for the first time, has not got what he wants. I imagine him once throwing toys around the room and nagging his mother until his tantrum was rewarded. I've witnessed a side to him that is extremely changeable; he can switch from hot to cold, and vice-versa, without notice. I recall his venomous interaction with Meredith and wonder if he could have been the same with his mother. For all I know, he might have argued with his mother over *her* decision to appoint Meredith as next of kin. Perhaps he's fed me a line about his being rebuffed, and just maybe, what if Alexander can't accept reality and resorts to blaming others as a means of freeing himself from scrutiny?

I clear my head beneath a row of orange streetlights and hail a taxi to return me to the comfort of solitude.

I slump into my recliner and thank God and every other deity for saving me from surrendering to Alexander. In the middle of the night I twitch to the haunting scene of Joyce Beecham's final words: 'Help me.' I see pain and desperation fill her face, the exclamation punctuated by fear. Juanita Morales' exophthalmic eyes gazed that same stoned look – fixed in a merciful plea – after her body was dragged from the River Avon.

There is a universal fear attached to dying. I've thought about it when previewing dangerous operations, and I continue to question why our inevitable demise seems to accelerate after we pass the Fabulous Forty milestone. While I'm sixteen fabulous years from that celebration, I still worry. Joyce though, by all accounts, had no need to fear death. So why the plea: 'Help me, Alex'? She must have *known* something was wrong.

Talking to myself. Not a good sign. Why the fuck am I dilly-dallying with this? Joyce had feared something and she'd expended her final breath not on 'I love you' to her children, but on a plea directed to Alex. Why? Was she trying to tell him something? Did she know *he'd* done something? Or was it delivered through a premonition of death, a final gasp to the assembly?

12

Tuesday 7 March

A crippling calf cramp wakes me, but I cannot understand why. I don't suffer sodium or potassium deficiencies, both of which are abundant in my predominantly 'take away' diet. And when I prepare the rare home-cooked meal, I upend the whole salt-shaker into a saucepan of vegetables. As for potassium, bananas are my favourite fruit because I can't be bothered with cores, seeds, and rind. Bananas are nature's fast fruit – rip off the skin and the job's done.

I leap out of my chair and stretch my leg. I grip my toes, thankful this is happening on my own rather than during a romantic spell where I would feel like a freak and probably look the part too. As my lower leg regains mobility, I glance at the clock to see that it is only 2.37 in the morning. Tiredness had departed my body after only three hours.

I've always thought the leather recliner a domain of the aged, where grandpa elevates his slippered feet, lights a pipe selected from various smoking paraphernalia scattered on an adjacent table, and then spends the morning reading every column inch of *The Daily Telegraph* and *Daily Mirror*. Each twist and turn of his arthritic body causes the chair to groan like creaking floorboards or trumpet flatulence guaranteed to elicit stifled sniggers from grandchildren.

I found mine (leather recliner, not grandpa) back in Worcester in one of those shops that claim to sell antiques, family heirlooms and deceased estate. The only genuine antique in the store was the old biddy – God bless her – behind the cash desk. The dark, gloomy shop displayed reproduction bureaus, dressers, study desks, chiffoniers and portmanteaus, tables, chairs and bedsteads, and a neat array of recently handcrafted pottery, jugs, and bowls for placement upon one's own antique nightstand. Resting on each item sat a folded, gaudy-yellow fluorescent 'sale' tag, which made a walk through the showroom feel like a journey on a ghost train through a tunnel in which scores of haunting yellow eyes peer from cobwebbed walls.

The recliner looked out of place. My meticulous sense of order picked it straight away, because its purpose was reduced to displaying embroidered pillowcases and handkerchiefs instead of selling itself for £199. I loved the deep cherry colour, having long shied away from traditional dark brown and bronzed leathers then in vogue. The elegance of cerise stands above all, and, I'm embarrassed to say, appeals to my pretentious aspirations.

After convincing the proprietor that the colour was not in fashion and that she could be stuck with it for a long time, I came right out with a contemptuous offer: £100. She scoffed and barked that she'd rather take it to the tip than sell it for a pittance.

Bet you wouldn't.

And she didn't, because ten minutes later, after less

haggling than I'd conduct over a £10.00 top at the market, I handed over £120 and arranged free delivery.

I shuffle into my tiny kitchen and click on the electric jug. I'm a pot of tea at home, tea bag at work, person – reinforcing that same laziness that draws me to bananas. For a long time, I've believed that if one is listless enough to rely on instant tea bags and microwave meals, they might as well extend their laziness to sleeping in their clothes, leaving the television on one channel (for even operating the remote contradicts their lifestyle choice) and, if you'll excuse the parallel, wearing incontinence pants because going to the toilet is too much of an imposition on one's day.

I accost the television for company, bypass American CNN news, a couple of religious sermons where arms sway to the chorus of Hallelujahs bellowing from Mississippi mamas, and I check a ninety-seventh rerun of *Bewitched* where blinking eyes are not necessarily symptomatic of a facial tic. I settle on Sky news.

This too, is run of the mill: Prime Minister Theresa May announces a new tax initiative (only half negating tough measures earlier inflicted on taxpayers); further tension mounts within the Royal family over a former duchess's debts; a former Cadbury's board member regrets selling to American interests (too late I yell at the screen); and local identity, Nora Geddes dies in a Cornwall nursing home: *'Nora Geddes, whose family links to the first Welsh settlers, died in her sleep, aged 74. Mrs Geddes, nee Griffith, was a lineal descendant of Prince Llewelyn ap Gruffyd who was renowned for challenging English sovereignty. Mrs Geddes leaves a son and two daughters.'*

I hear that the weather will be fine in most parts of the country and that our day will be so much brighter because the bulletin is sponsored by Lux washing powder. I care little for the weather after my ears resonate the word 'Geddes'.

I'd heard it recently, the name among many in the usual plethora of matters associated with enquiries, new neighbours and townsfolk, and the continually lengthening list of names annexed to Alexander's family dramas. The pieces fall into place: 'Geddes' had featured on Meredith Bennington's bank statement. The fortnightly credits. *Thank you, Hamilton.*

Nora Geddes dies in a care home. Meredith Bennington is carer. Too much of a coincidence? Again?

I cannot wait until first light to satisfy my curiosity. I phone Sky news to obtain the name or location of the home in which Mrs Geddes resided and I receive the stock response: 'We don't have any information other than that broadcast.' After bluffing that I'd missed part of the bulletin and that I wasn't after any detail other than that released, the tune changed. 'Oh, is that all?' the receptionist drones after resuscitating herself. 'It's the Happy Valley Care home. I'm sure you'll find it in the phone book.'

I'll do better than that. I'll drive there right now. 'Thank you. Have a good morning,' I enthuse, allowing her to return to her crossword, nail painting or television show on the opposition's channel.

Overdue for a freshen up, I have a quick shower and transform myself with minimalistic make-up of mascara, eye liner and a smear of lipstick. I search my mobile for the care home's postcode. I jump into Fiona, finger the postcode into her GPS and head for Happy Valley.

A half-moon rests on the horizon, scaring darkness from the road. Doesn't worry me. I'd drive blindfolded to get to my destination. Twenty minutes' later a huge yellow smiley face welcomes me to Happy Valley. And the home looks happy. Lime-washed masonry sets off large windows across which hang happy yellow curtains. Inside, I imagine two-dozen bingo players snoring happy Zzzs from their smiling, toothless gums.

I have no idea where to start. How does one justify an investigation at four o'clock in the morning? I first have to discover whether Meredith Bennington had been Nora Geddes' carer. A delicate, mischievous approach is necessary, because staff will be barred from divulging information of their high-profile patient. If I object, they'll push privacy laws in my face: 'I'm sorry. The *Data Protection Act* prevents us from releasing personal information.' That is truly a catch-all that allows any office or department to freeze all requested documents and prevent them being thawed into the public domain.

The spontaneous tack has previously reaped results. Often found to be the most productive, I am relieved by the prospect of having a double-chance to hoodwink the morning shift also, due to commence at 7.00 a.m. In the meantime, I leap from my car and bound to the main entrance. The electronic doors ignore my approach. Suitably snubbed, I walk to the side of the building where a hand-drawn arrow directs me to a night bell. I press the button. A red-eyed staff member approaches, fumbles a dangling chain of keys and opens the door. 'Can I help you?'

'I hope so. I know I'm early. I'm on my way to work. My sister, Meredith, left a bag for me. Said I could collect it any time, but it looks like I've inconvenienced you. Sorry.'

'Meredith? And who might she be?'

'The nurse who looks after Mrs Geddes.'

'Oh, Merri. Apt name. Always so happy. You obviously haven't heard. Mrs Geddes passed on only hours ago. Merri left in such a state. She certainly didn't leave anything because I'd have noticed. I've been behind the desk most of the shift.'

'Sorry. I guess she must have had more on her mind. Could you check when she's next on duty? I'll come back at a more reasonable hour.'

'She's not on roster because she's agency. Perhaps you could phone or call in after 9.00 a.m. Reception might have a list of her patients and scheduled visiting times.'

I restrain myself from jumping with joy at the confirmation. Now I can start building a solid case against her, although I might be hard-pressed to acquire witnesses keen to support my theory. Three are now dead.

I correct myself. I am not 'building' cases anymore; I am merely completing a file for my client, Alexander Beecham. This has swollen into much more now that his sister, Meredith, is linked to the death of her mother-in-law, plus the added coincidental connection to Mrs Geddes. This has blown far beyond reporting my findings to Alexander.

There is one contact with whom I can exchange total faith and trust and that is DCI Dave Stafford of London's MET police.

13

Friday 10 March

Mrs Nora Geddes' funeral service is held at St Austell cemetery on a bleak Friday afternoon. [I'm fortunate that it's not Friday the thirteenth, for my superstitions would prevent me from reporting this detail in Chapter Thirteen.]

Grey mist clings to jagged memorials of family long departed. The cold, sombre service attracts a cavalry of friends and family, including the rare appearance of those seen only at Christmas and birthday functions. Because my investigation into Meredith Bennington's activities has fragmented into three separate enquiries, I had scoured daily papers to ascertain the service venue, my intention being to view the congregation to glean a deeper understanding of family dynamics. Other than a professional hunch, I had little else to fuel my belief that Nora too, was a victim of ill will.

From a nearby plot bearing the gold-inscribed name, 'Alan W. Aitkinson 1927 – 2005', I survey the squabbles of the unfolding service. All right, I am ashamed and embarrassed by my conduct. I totally agree that it is abhorrent to use someone's dearly departed shrine as cover for an investigation. But, and this should be noted, if my actions identify a perpetrator of the very act that I believe put Joyce Beecham, Nora Geddes and possibly Victoria Bennington into their graves, my indiscretion must be forgiven, or at least viewed through a blind eye.

My position affords a great vantage point. The congregation stands like veins of coal whose ridges of obligatory black identify the respective clans and generations. Glaring like a flashlight in the mine, Meredith Bennington's persona evidences her overabundance of nerve and audacity. She has ingratiated herself to Nora's kinfolk, her carriage almost Thatcheresque – single-focused and commanding respect from all, but at the same time oblivious to slanderous innuendo.

Why is she *here?* Had she have been involved in anything sinister, she would surely evade the sensitivities of a funeral service. Her attendance puzzles me. I conclude that nothing Meredith Bennington does is low profile. She has not disguised ex-gratia payments into bank accounts held with regular banks – Lloyds, Nationwide and HSBC – when she could easily have transmitted it to offshore trusts or Swiss accounts routed through unregistered shelf companies and third party nominees.

Nora's direct family obviously know Meredith, her invitation presumably made in appreciation for services rendered. With immediate effect, my assumption proves wrong. I see a man, who I later learn to be Nora's son, Gerald, stride up and challenge her attendance. The couple share no pleasantries or formalities. To the contrary, anger and dissention fume from both. I turn my good ear to their direction and pick up Gerald: 'And who invited you to our family's mourning?'

'No one invited me. I'm paying my respects and celebrating the life of a patient who was very dear to me. I give you my condolences for your loss.'

'Yes. Thank you. This is *my* dear mother. I'll not make a scene, but I'm asking you to leave gracefully; perhaps make your way over there as if you're returning to your car for something.'

'I shall do nothing of the sort. It seems you have little knowledge of your mother's friends or wishes. You should know that your mother and I formed a close friendship over the past six months, a friendship that is deserved of respect, and a friendship that should allow us both to continue the process of grieving without any sort of altercation at the door of God's resting place.'

'Very well, miss. On that you are most correct. You continue your grieving – from some distance I suggest – and I'll continue this discussion later. Don't think you're going to mingle with our family.'

Meredith flares at Gerald's aggression and quickly sinks the verbal knife: 'Oh, but I am, Mr Geddes. Your mother transferred Power of Attorney to me not ten days ago. I am very much a part of this.'

'What!' Gerald fulminates as he weaves between mourners to his family. An over-animated discussion erupts, unsettling nearby grievers.

My interest too, is unsettled. I have the ringside seat to the best exhibition of family dynamics I could ever wish for. And Meredith is on the ropes. What happens next though, *really* questions Meredith's psychological state.

Raging with fury, she rips off her black suit, leaving her covered only by a black camisole and black tights. She throws the clothes at Gerald's feet, turns and walks off, ignoring curious stares and whispers from the congregation. All she could possibly gain from that would be Gerald's suffering the indignation of having to explain the strange commotion.

I've pegged Meredith to a tee. Whilst she has no deep emotional bond to Nora, she is tinctured with the burden of death. She accepts the loss with more grace than a lawyer losing a client, and with greater regret than a retailer losing a valued customer. She cannot simply flick a switch to dissolve the friendship developed between a patient and herself. More so, she won't forget the financial advantage. But she is incensed by Gerald Geddes' acrimonious attitude and his nerve to question her presence. She might expect him to turn the Geddes' family against her, a challenge that would be made so much easier if Gerald learnt of Meredith's monthly financial consideration.

And he will – because I am going to tell him.

The service proceeds without incident. I wait in my car, expecting (or maybe hoping for) another altercation. From my phone's camera, I capture the departing guests and family, accomplished by feigning a text message while leaning against the car door. My other hand takes charge of a thick, crusty cheese and pickle sandwich. I focus on Meredith's departure and snap off stills that I hope DCI Stafford will run through the METs Facial Recognition Program – just in case Meredith had previously fallen under police notice.

I have no idea when, or if, I'll phone Stafford. I have not yet recovered from being dumped because of his deceptive philandering. Serves me right though, I should never have been so possessive. I had truly believed my future lay with Dave (in more ways than one) so I was decimated to find my dream had ended so fatefully. Still, he is the only police member I know who will acknowledge my professionalism and assist me. He holds such power over me – sweeps my mind clear of everything but him and me. Even now, despite our having not spoken for nearly six months, he has the ability to pop into my head, or I have the disability to not reject him.

I chomp into the last piece of sandwich. Most of the congregation has departed, leaving only the priest and his associate ambling towards their black Rover. I pack away my camera and resolve to phone Stafford the minute I arrive home. His number had orbited my mind until self-ejecting into cyberspace, along with other useless cerebral matter including logarithms and cosines from seventh grade, the archaeological history of Stonehenge, which I studied on a whim, and the *Pitman* guide to shorthand which my mother insisted I learn 'to get a nice office job.' Who needs shorthand when I'm proficient in text messaging, emoticons, and reading my own code of contractions and hieroglyphics?

I cast a final look at Nora Geddes' resting place. Gerald hovers over the fresh earth, weeping last respects. Even though I've gleaned pages of info from this location, I plan to extract every last morsel. I do the right thing and wait until he walks from the plot before I approach him and introduce myself. I apologise for the insensitivity and take a few minutes to gloss over the events that compelled me to disrespectfully intrude on his mother's funeral. Finally, I confirm that I am deep into an investigation that I hope will prove that his mother had died under suspicious circumstances.

Gerald rejects me with the customary: 'You're not a cop, what can you do?' which I counter with: 'I don't need to be a cop to value life. You've already had words with the Bennington woman – I overheard it all – so I know that you firmly believe there are questions to be answered. And let me tell you this: The reason I'm here is because I'm already investigating a suspicious death for my client who is a local lawyer. The link is that Bennington had ties to both deceased.' That enhances my credibility and paves the way to open communication.

We prop on a nearby seat where Gerald dictates a comprehensive background of his mother's illness. I learn that Nora had received her family's love and care for eight years after the onset of Alzheimer's disease necessitated her leaving the matriarchal home. The traumatic loss of her husband, four years' earlier, was blamed for intensifying her memory lapses to a point where she often failed to recognise her own family. Nora would not impose on her children, despite their ready insistence to participate in a regular care roster. Gerald and his two sisters eventually worked a rota to cook, wash and maintain the modest home. He ashamedly concedes that Ann and Maxine wore the brunt of the load with his mother's demanding and demeaning personal care and hygiene needs.

Gerald veers off track to offer his view of how women's roles change through life's advancement: 'Children born fifty years ago are now called upon to reciprocate love and care to their mother. A young mother has no qualms about bathing and changing nappies of her newborns, yet when those babies, decades later, are called upon to bathe and change incontinence pads of the very mother who cared for them, the protest is loud and clear: "I can't do that. We'll get someone in".

'My sisters jointly decided to employ a visiting carer. I simply went along with it. Meredith Bennington was ultimately hired as the most suited and enthusiastic applicant. We put together a contract for three hours per day over a six-day week. The girls agreed to alternate Sundays. Big of them, I thought, because that was the day of routine family visits. It was hardly an imposition.

'The roster succeeded without flaw for six months until Meredith learnt that mum was neglecting morning and evening meals and surviving only on a lunchtime snack. She discussed her concerns with the family, adding that mum's propensity for losing balance and falling could result in an unnecessary injury requiring hospitalisation. Meredith recommended the local Happy Valley as one of the better facilities. She floated the idea to mum, but was sternly rebuked. I was in the room when mum protested: "I'm not living anywhere other than my home of fifty years. My entire life is within these walls". Mum's one to stand her ground.'

Gerald speaks with a great deal of compassion and sincerity. Nothing seems out of the ordinary. I think any responsible carer would want to see the best for their patient. When a loved one faces injury, just through normal, daily activities, full-time care must be considered.

He continues: 'Meredith persisted. Kind of worried me in a way. My experience with nurses is that they have a take it or leave it attitude. Somehow or other, this Meredith managed to win mum over. She stuck her nose in everything – way beyond the bounds of personal care, I might add – assisting with shopping, running errands and posting mail, much to the annoyance of my sisters who believed *they* were best qualified to help mum shop. Despite their originally agreeing to contract Meredith, the two girls sharpened their claws. Didn't faze Meredith though, because she continued on her way until she coaxed Mum into a sunny corner room in Happy Valley.

'Now this is where it gets interesting,' says Gerald. He glares at me to satisfy himself of my attention. 'Meredith confided in mum that she knew someone in real estate who would obtain the best price for her property. Mum told me that she was considering a deal by which the proceeds of her home would cover the Happy Valley fees twelve months in advance while she'd still make a tidy interest on the balance. Meredith would monitor that account to distribute payments to different accounts under the pretence of maximising interest, saving tax and preserving mum's pension. It all sounded so believable.'

I jump in. 'Money has been flowing out of your mum's account. I've seen Meredith's statements that show monthly credits of £80 from N. Geddes. The problem we'll have is authenticating whether the authority was legally executed.'

'Leave the execution to me,' Gerald gruffs.

On returning home, I retrieve my old police directory, locate Stafford's office number, and jab it into my phone. I also enter his mobile number – just in case. This wasn't as simple because I had to rummage through old bills, packed in haste to leave Worcester, and try to recognise the number from crumpled service provider registers. I press 'send'. And then it happens. Again. I chicken out. I am not ready for his how's-you-been-going-Olivia and the we-must-get-together-for-a-drink spiel. Shamefully, I would probably encourage the thought, because as soon as we'd get together for a drink it would be only a matter of hours before we'd end up at my place writhing over each other's bodies, savouring salty flesh, erogenous zones and combining to attain convulsions and explosions not seen or felt since the last eruption of Krakatoa in 1883. And that would be before we even got into bed. No. I am now a responsible self-employed investigator. I have a reputation to establish. No more one-night stands.

I erase the sparkle of sex from my mind and think of Dave only as DCI Stafford. What can I do to support my enquiry? A moment of serious questioning provides the answer. I need to raid – or burgle – Meredith's home. I am sure that I will find something I can use to either nail her or clear her of complicity in her mother's demise. I pluck her address from Hamilton's pile of information and recognise it as one of Cornwall's affluent areas.

That prompts another question: How does a nurse afford to live on a two-acre property amongst well-to-do doctors, dentists, lawyers, and politicians?

14

Friday 10 March

I speed to the address with the intention of conducting an intensive search. On arrival, I prop under a tree in Pin Oak Avenue and wait.

Across the road, a decorative wrought iron gate provides no security to the target property. It stands open, attracting leaves and garden debris, fish and chip wrappings, flavoured milk cartons and crushed Coca Cola cans into a levee beneath the gate.

A glimmer of yellow light huddles in the corner of a front window. It is surely too early, at 8.30 in the evening, for anyone to be in bed, so I assume that an occupant is either reading or watching television. I quickly discount the television because there are no strobing lights darting about the windows. I am acutely aware of the householder's ploy of leaving an inside light burning to fool prospective burglars like myself into believing that someone is really home. As a member of Worcester's Neighbourhood Watch team, I'd educated residents to adopt that very ritual. Here, it has the opposite effect. I am drawn to that solitary light like a lost ship to a beacon. One solitary light in a house of at least ten rooms paves the way for me to peek through the front window.

I progress towards the house, concealed by the shadow of four-metre-high Leylandiis which soar above a brick fence. All good things come to an end. An automatic security light, activated by my clumsy entry into its sensor's perimeter, scares the crap out of me. I dart to my right. The light was a bad investment. It does little to promote security other than send squirrels scurrying up trees and dispatch me to the cover of a privet hedge. It highlights the gardens, both for my benefit and for any prospective night photographer seeking snaps for council's Beautiful Gardens award.

Needless to say, I have a back-up plan to counter these sort of hiccups. I am disadvantaged by being known to Meredith so I can't just knock on the door and ask for Mr Smith. Meredith might have already been suspicious of me and found that I am *not* her brother's girlfriend. As I haven't yet returned her phone calls – not through want of trying – I could simply say that I couldn't get through and thought that I'd just drop by in case she wanted me for something urgent. Not too original or credible, but it could save me from an awkward situation.

Once again, I'm thinking too far ahead. A crumpled fold in the front window's curtain allows me to peer into a vacant reception room. With confidence regained, I creep around the side of the house, through another unlocked gate and into the rear garden. I duck beneath overhanging shrubbery and spider webs before slipping on a strip of mossy concrete. I fall to the ground with a heavy thump; an impromptu reminder of my first ice skating adventure. No light flashes through the side windows – which is another good sign – so I continue around the perimeter of the house until I reach a glass-enclosed sunroom.

On discovering the rear door is secured by a new multi-lock system which set pins into five locales around the door frame, I decline into panic. Over the past few years, I've become proficient at gaining access by springing open latches with old credit cards or employing hair pins on older locks. Today, new technology continues to defeat me. My best hope is to pluck a nocturnal burglary practitioner to train me in the finer aspects of defeating security doors.

I'm not being critical when I say that the most security-conscious are often the most forgetful, or the most lazy. My view is proven when I chance upon an unsecured sash window. I pull my knife from its ankle strap (which I illegally carry for self-protection) slide it between the two sashes of window, and flip the latch into its open position. I lift the window, clamber over the waist-height sill and drop cautiously to the floor.

I've entered the far end of a sunroom which is faintly illuminated by the half-moon. Thank goodness, because I hadn't brought my penlight. Bamboo tables and chairs sit perfectly aligned in a rectangular setting. A stack of magazines rest square on the table, so neat that guests might be reluctant to even look at them. I take a closer look at the table and chairs. It matches exactly Alexander's description of his mother's missing setting. I'll deal with that later.

The sunroom is a late add-on to the early 1900s Tudor construction. The brickwork and plumbing of the original home remain exposed, and painted white, on the inner wall – as does the original rear door, which presents me with a further challenge. I expect it to be locked, but Meredith, or whoever else who lives here (information of which I am blind) practises the it'll-be-all-right-I'll-only-be-gone-for-a-short-while security measure of closing the door without locking it. I walk straight into a kitchen of grandiose proportion: granite benches, island hob, huge AGA, a host of electrical appliances (two of which match items on Alex's stolen goods list) cluttered at one end of a work bench, a double fridge-freezer, cappuccino machine – which I feel like cranking up at this very minute – and a tumble dryer whose cycle lights flicker green and orange in a vain effort to alert someone to rebalance the load.

That momentarily sets me back, because it suggests that Meredith might have left for only a short time. As my eyes adjust to the darkened room, I rifle several kitchen drawers, but find nothing other than stainless steel and plastic utensils, recipes, and a few crumpled shopping reminders.

I step into a general-purpose room where a bureau sits against a wall upon which hangs a huge portrait of Lord Robert Bennington. *No mistaking I've got the right house.* I wonder why his picture is here. A memory of love, or a means of torture? Lord Robert himself confirmed they are separated. I don't know to what extent, because to me being separated is like being pregnant – you either are or you aren't. There are no gradations. I scoff at those who report an 'amicable' separation. If so 'amicable', why separate?

Regardless of whether they are divorced or just living apart, it does strike me as strange that one would have a life-size portrait of their ex watching over their every move. Perhaps that is its purpose. Like the *Picture of Dorian Gray.* Staring from the wall to taunt all before it, Lord Bennington's features growing angrier by the moment and his face changing daily, tormenting Meredith for using his lordship as a route to riches. I make a mental note to ask Hamilton to dig further.

From inside the top left-hand drawer of a lacquered cherrywood bureau, I remove a plastic folder crammed with assorted papers. Two slips near the top bear Happy Valley's logo and Nora's weekly meal selections. I can think of no reason for their being stored in Meredith's home, unless she had substituted, or removed entirely, her patient's orders.

I also find a building society savings book in the name of Joyce Beecham, showing a substantial balance, and notably, a withdrawal made only two days' earlier. My scant probate knowledge tells me the account should be held in trust to await division under Joyce Beecham's will. Also by my reckoning, there is no way on earth that Joyce would have passed the account exclusively to Meredith, for to do so, Joyce would have had to exercise a conscious decision to exclude both Roslyn and Alexander. More to the point though, it reinforces Alexander's assertion that he was removed as next of kin because, and this is crucial, if Joyce were to have passed an account to anyone, it would have been to Alexander.

There are letters from the Department of Work and Pensions addressed to Joyce Beecham, care of Meredith's address. I do not recall Alexander mentioning anything about his mother having lived with either daughter. Not in recent times anyway, because Alex told me about the stroke at his mother's home, and it was from there that she was conveyed to hospital. Given those circumstances, I can't reconcile why Joyce's mail would be addressed to her daughter's home. The conundrum solves itself as I delve further into the pile. Another letter addressed to Joyce Beecham from the

Department of Work and Pensions announces: *'Thank you for advising your change of address and updated bank details. Our records now show your residential address as 54 Pin Oak Avenue. Revised direct payment details will be confirmed by separate letter. If you have any queries, please contact one of our friendly Customer Service Consultants.'*

I crave for enough light to snap a few shots of the documents. Eerily, as soon as the word 'light' enters my mind, the front of the house floods with light. *Bloody sensor's gone off.* I race to the front door. A dark sedan coasts into the driveway. The automatic garage door hums its electronic whir. I hum electronic panic. My first instinct is to race out of the front door while the car's occupant, presumably Meredith, alights from the vehicle. I quickly reason that the element of risk is far too high.

Female heels clunk along the footpath like a drunk cobbler fixing a shoe. I have time only to scamper to the bureau, drop the folder back into the top drawer, and retreat through the kitchen to the sunroom. The front door squeaks on its hinges. Light tumbles along the hallway and shoots into the kitchen. I have no time to bolt through the window, so I pull down the sash and conceal myself behind a convenient floor to ceiling curtain.

Footsteps scuff into the kitchen. 'How are you, Gerry?'

I recognise Meredith's voice, but have no idea who Gerry is. I'd discerned only one set of footsteps.

'Oh, aren't you beautiful this evening, showing yourself so proud and shiny?'

"Proud and shiny?" Has she got a bloody dog in there? If so, he'll sniff me out in no time. Why haven't I heard him padding about?

'Let's give you a good slurp of water and freshen you up. Look at this dust on your leaves. I've neglected you these past few weeks. I'm so sorry. I've had too many things happening. Here, have these slow-release granules, they're good for your roots.'

Now I'm the first one to be happy about good roots and everything organic, but this woman's off her head – she's talking to a bloody plant? Gerry indeed. Must be a bloody geranium. Woops. For a grown woman who calls her car "Fiona", I guess I'm in no position to criticise – although I don't talk to my car.

I edge the curtain back just a smidge. See nothing beyond the sunroom. As I release the fabric, Meredith walks straight into the sunroom, staring in my direction. I freeze. There's no other way to react. I consider grabbing the element of surprise and rushing her, pushing her over and pacing out of the back door – if I could open it. She certainly wouldn't expect me, or anyone else.

I maintain my observation through a four-millimetre strip between the curtain's edge and the wall. She wears a blue evening gown, and not very well. It is a basic off-the-rack after five – available in sizes 14 to 24 – that women buy, hoping to replicate the image of a Hollywood starlet walking the red carpet. Meredith wouldn't even make Bollywood. I surmise she'd attended an important function, probably charity, where she'd mixed it with socialites, drinking champagne and boasting donations to this cause and that. I discount the prospect of her having been accompanied by a hot date. She's arrived home alone – something I rarely do on my dates. She might have left some poor guy hanging. From my perspective, I reckon most guys would have begged for the noose.

Her footsteps advance. I prepare for the curtain to swish aside. I brace myself, roll my fingers into fists and wait. I don't even breathe. And then I smile.

She stops, bends down, picks up a newspaper from the table and returns to the kitchen. A moment later she places Gerry on the newspaper, carries him to the back door, unlocks the door with the key that had been sitting in the lock for the whole time, and then sits Gerry on the step. I presume exposure to moonbeams will initiate a massive growth spurt. Who knows how this weird woman thinks?

I chastise myself for not earlier checking the door. I could have easily prodded the key to the floor and pulled it outside, rather than go through the charade with the side window. What I am now thinking is that with the back door open I might have an easy opportunity to escape while Meredith is outside pampering her stupid plant.

The female psych differs little amongst our number, so I know that there's very few of us who arrive home from an event, whether it be a family function, a hot date, or even a shopping trip, without performing at least two rituals. The first is to throw off our shoes. Tick 'one'; she's done that. The second is to rush to the toilet. She must be overdue – surely?

And she is, for when she steps back inside she walks purposely to the hallway. Although I have no idea where the bathroom and toilet is, I hear a door open and then close with that hollow clunk that only a toilet door echoes. I walk to the open back door, drop down two steps, and knock over friggin' Gerry. He makes a soft clunk, nothing Meredith would hear while she's tinkling away, so I bend down, stand him upright, tip the spilt soil from the newspaper back into the top of the pot and set him back on the path. Aside from the clay pot's broken rim, no one will ever know.

I creep around the side of the house where the unmistakeable toilet window lights my way. I negotiate the mossy pavers, this time without losing my footing, and rush through the side gate. The front yard lies in darkness and shrubs challenge me to stealth around the perimeter lest I again activate the sensor light. I exit the front gate and into the blush of Pin Oak Avenue's orange street lights. By unknown means I trip the sensor. The front yard lights up like Wimbledon's Centre Court. I look straight ahead and run across the street, evading a fatality with the Number 27 bus to Bodmin Moor. Once in my car, I glance across the road and see only wavering Leylandii in Meredith's front garden.

I have safely executed my mission without detection.

What I need now is a spell of relaxation in the sanctity of the nearest McDonald's. No matter where I drive, whether it be through large cities or small counties, I can rely on homing in to a 'drive thru' where I'll order my customary Quarter Pounder with Cheese, small fries, and vanilla shake. When I'm truly stressed I'll add an Apple Pie. If I'm lucky, they'll be promoting the special offer of two for 99p, which I down with ease.

I deploy my GPS, in which, I'm embarrassed to confess, is the location of every McDonald's in England and Wales – the result of inputting ten hours work with Google Search and Google Maps. I drive to the nearest site and stroll in to the throes of evening clean up. The staff, resplendent in uniforms that would incite jealousy in Harrods' advisors, scurry about mopping floors and polishing stainless steel.

In the dining area, a girl wipes a cartoon-decaled table, leaving a white arc of diluted thick shake smeared across its surface. Another girl mops the floor so diligently that I wonder if it might have been more hygienic for the girls to swap chores.

'Get some more fries down,' another girl shrieks. I could not discern whether she was encouraging a colleague to drop a basket into the deep fryer, or pleading with him to scoff the remainder of his super snack.

I glare at the illuminated menu and wish for the day when I unwrap my Quarter with Cheese and find it as thick and succulent as the appetising meal depicted on the larger-than-life illuminated sign box. Needless to say, I am not deterred from ordering the delicacy.

'Sorry. Shakes are finished now.'

'Finished? You don't close for an hour.'

'Yes. But we clean up early so we can leave on time.'

I feel proud that I don't let my clients down because I have to clean my venetian blinds or scrub clients' ashtrays in preparation for the next day. 'Any Apple Pies?'

'Sure. Three left.'

'Since you're closing, will you do three for the price of two?'

'Sorry. We can't do that. The registers aren't programmed for it.'

I think back to my after-school part-time job in Sainsbury's where a customer could request whatever they want and I could process it through the register without bar codes, alarm bells and a digital readout of change that I had to tender to my customer.

So, I have one Apple Pie with my meal, convinced the

other two will be thrown out at the end of their holding period. And they are.

I glance through the tattered customer newspaper with its 'features' pages missing, together with crosswords, television guides and cinema screenings, in effect leaving me with the front page proffering how an Australian soap star has made it 'big in Britain' – as so many have – and the rear page lamenting Manchester United's third consecutive loss.

If anything can clear my mind, it's sitting down to an enjoyable meal while leisurely flicking through a *complete* daily newspaper. I hoped that the day's newsworthy events would topple those I'd just experienced at Meredith's home.

Stuff this. I grab my phone and press 'Dave Mobile'.

'Hello.'

'David? Are you home?'

Stafford answers with a question: 'Olivia?'

'Yes. Long time, isn't it?'

I can't recall exactly how long, but six months would be my best guess. I've not forgotten him. He'll still look like a cop. Typecast. At five-foot-ten he stands three inches taller than me, his black hair is cropped shorter than an army recruit's, and his deep brown eyes are piercing, yet inquisitive. What particularly draws me to those eyes is the left eyebrow that jumps dramatically at surprise or agitation. I remember in court, his brow rising with counsel's objections and witness's lies, and falling with favourable judge's rulings and carefully elicited witness answers.

He plays his ace: 'Sure is. We must get together for a drink.'

Gee. How well do I know the guy? I knew that would happen; knew that would be his reaction, no matter the reason for my call or whatever else is happening in his life – we'd have to have a drink. Now, I should summon all my strength and resist the temptation.

'That would be great, but hold on a minute. The reason I'm calling, I'm working on a case. Involved and multifaceted. There's some matters that might interest you, and, well, I could use a little help.'

'This an official call, Olivia?'

'I can make it official, but that's a bit premature. You see, I've got some info I shouldn't have, but it helps support other official information I do have.'

Having not spoken to Stafford since I'd started Watts Happening? Investigations, I hoped he would recognise that I remained as conscientious with my work, or more so, despite my having left the constabulary. I give him the complete rundown from my initial briefing to the history I'd obtained through Hamilton Holt, and up to the deaths of Victoria Bennington and Nora Geddes.

'My client's sister,' I explain, 'Meredith Bennington, nee Beecham, is implicated in the whole shebang. I've seen documentation on Meredith's premises from DWP agreeing to divert her mother's pension payments to her own account.'

Stafford is quick off the mark: 'You know there's nothing legally wrong with that. It could have been done by agreement.'

From what I've learnt of Joyce's independence, I am sure she wouldn't have consented to that. 'Quite true. It could. But what about the withdrawal of money from a dead woman's account? The very woman to whom she was providing care.'

'If you can prove it.' Stafford stalls. I can see the eyebrow jumping. He's thinking of the past and wondering whether to take a gamble on me. 'Okay. What do you want? I'll keep this under my hat for the time being. You want a full history check I suppose?'

'Yep. Meredith Louise Bennington, formerly Beecham, 21/6/60. I'll send a photo in a few secs.'

'Still in that dingy office?'

'Nah. Got a new one in Newquay. You should come down one weekend.' *Shit! Why the hell did I say that?* 'I'm tied up on this case for a while. Perhaps we should wait at least until I've sewn it up.'

'Okay. I'll be in touch.'

15

Saturday 11 March

Stafford opens with a whinge about the extra hours he'd worked just to help me. Despite arousing me from sleep, I thank him for calling, but withhold guilt, and the offer to 'make it up' which I assume he's expecting. He is tactful enough to not mention Sharon. He will never forget (I hope) his embarrassment after I stumbled upon Sharon at his front door. I'd completed the 200-mile Worcester to London haul to finally confess my love, and open the door to our future as a married couple. The door was opened all right, by Sharon, who had been my close friend throughout the police academy (and later, a *very* close friend). She filled the doorway and taunted me with, 'Hi Olivia. You've come to congratulate David and I on our engagement, have you?'

I had no inkling that Dave had been interested in anyone else, nor that Sharon was selfish enough to do what no woman should *ever* do to another woman.

Nevertheless, to the point of today's mission, I have no reservations about Stafford's work ethic. He is beyond reproach. I am confident of his doing all he can to assist me, whether official or surreptitious, and that he will handle matters with utmost discretion and transparency. Stafford envies my enthusiasm and knows I pursue enquiries with vigour, especially where I firmly believe that a suspect is treading beyond law's boundaries.

He dispenses with the small talk and recites:

"Meredith Louise Beecham. DOB 21 June 1960:
16 April 1976
Shoplifting
Chief Constable's warning.

4 September 1976
Shoplifting
Children's Court – fined £10. Restitution £10.

17 June 1978
Theft
Magistrates' Court – convicted and fined £50.

30 November 1978
Obtain financial advantage
Magistrates' Court – convicted and sentenced to three months' imprisonment, suspended for twelve months.

July 1979
Person of interest in death of Bennington, Victoria Anne (mother in-law). Exonerated."

'She's had an active childhood, but hasn't come under our notice for thirty years. Doesn't mean she's clean though.'

I study the history. 'Maybe she is on the level, or she's

graduated to a career criminal proficient in covering her tracks. Dead men, or women, tell no tales.'

Stafford claims to have no grounds upon which to proceed, if in fact, a crime has been committed. 'My assessment of Meredith's involvement,' he continues, 'is, at best, speculative. You have no witnesses, no evidence. Nothing more than circumstances that in all probability could also be tailored to implicate other family members.'

I protest that there is more than coincidence hovering over the head of one who has been so closely related to three deaths. I wonder whether he is taking me seriously or just sitting behind his desk in hope of renewing our casual relationship.

I have been so dedicated to Alexander's ever-expanding problem over the past week that I've done nothing to personalise my new flat or venture to weekend markets to purchase interesting knick-knacks discarded by those who'd recently undertaken their own redecorating plan. I love the tables of goods offered by those wanting to recoup money from precious items that could just as easily have been left on their footpath for the hard rubbish collection, and I love the items sourced through local classifieds, shop window ads, garage sales and eBay, all laid out on blue plastic tarpaulins and priced at a mark-up rivalling the retail standard.

The phone interrupts my breakfast of poached eggs.

'Olivia. We must meet to discuss this case of yours.'

Stafford astounds me. I am sure he would not have called had he not made a substantial breakthrough. I'm also certain he will be extremely cautious about what, and how much, he's prepared to discuss.

'Hello to you too. You've checked her out already?'

'Let's say I've familiarised myself with her background. We can make this an official enquiry and open or re-open, whatever the case may be, an investigation into Victoria Bennington's death.'

'I don't want to disagree, but I think we would have a better shot, so to speak, by looking at Joyce Beecham, who is the closest family victim and whose son engaged me to investigate. That gives you a reason and credibility for your involvement.'

'I don't need credibility. We'll discuss this in my office. Two this afternoon?'

'Fine. You in the same place?'

'Yep. Be here until my retirement kicks in – the sooner the better.'

I terminate the call, pleased to have convinced Stafford of the merit of my investigation. It is a change from the many hours I'd once dedicated to passing information to senior officers.

It's not unusual for police to pursue some incidents with vengeance – fully focused on prosecution to improve their conviction rate. The lunchroom banter captures all: 'Yeah, I did him for six years', or, 'Stitched him up well. Magistrate had to accept my version, didn't he!' The laughter increases, 'He only coughed to one, but the beak accepted my evidence, and why wouldn't he? The scroat had done another four burgs earlier in the year.' For those loose cannons, upholding justice and protecting the community is merely a secondary consideration.

Juries too are swept away by evidence put before them, evidence that is often selective or restrictive because counsel and prosecutor have already exchanged case detail before a trial begins. Those discussions often result in the famed 'Plea Bargain' – a deal put to a client 'in his interest.' Whilst the foundation of law provides that an accused is innocent until proven guilty, he is offered concessions, sometimes very generous, to plead guilty to save the cost and time of a trial, and in some cases to save trauma to alleged victims who must recollect and recount the most graphic testimony – or fabrication.

The jury will hear only the evidence placed before it. That evidence can be heavily edited, so the jury will not hear, for instance, an accused's complete Record of Interview which is a series of questions and answers taken by police shortly after arrest. There have been cases where a defendant's denials on the Record of Interview have been withheld from the jury, yet the jury is expected to decide guilt or innocence from such a contrived deposition. The jury is therefore deprived threads of evidence that both the defence and prosecution have agreed to omit from a defendant's testimony. The jury might not even hear the accused give evidence because defence counsel, following the long-standing creed: 'do not put your client on the stand', does not want his client 'exposed' to cross-examination.

Strolling down Newquay's High Street while enjoying a bout of therapeutic shopping, I spot Meredith standing outside her brother's office. I prop beside an adjacent store and assume the role of window shopper – drooling over things I could only wish for but never own. I wonder why she would choose to wait outside, rather than enter. I answer my own thought: the two are presumably not on speaking terms. It therefore makes sense that Meredith is there without Alexander's knowledge and without good reason. So intrigued am I by her non-objective presence that I maintain a vigil of the frontage for forty minutes. I deduce that she is either waiting for her brother to meet her in neutral territory, or she is involved in a stalking campaign I am yet to understand.

The nature of her odd behaviour prompts me to enquire further. I rip out my phone: 'Roslyn, hi. It's Olivia Watts, we met the other day at your mother's. I want to have a brief chat with you. Could you allow me fifteen minutes or so, as soon as possible?'

'I've got no appointments this afternoon. What about two o'clock?'

'Can't do that. Seeing someone else dead on two and I can't change it. Can I drop by now?' I shouldn't have used the expression 'dead on two' to a woman who'd just lost her mother. I let it slide rather than highlight the faux pas with an apology.

'Bit early, but that's fine. Just hop into my office and we'll hit a good café down the road.'

'I'll be there. By the way, how are Alex and Meredith getting along?'

'That's a strange one out of the blue. They'll never get on. She'd kill him if she could – figuratively speaking of course – especially with the drama he's creating over her changing mum's next of kin.'

'Uh, okay. Just wondered. See you soon.'

16

Saturday 11 March

Roslyn's extravagant office is testament to a thriving real estate business. I enter the palatial enterprise and approach a commanding granite-topped reception pedestal. Roslyn materialises from an adjacent door, firmly befitting her role as branch manager and partner of the franchised agency.

I am relieved for having not invited her to my four-square-metre office, where its reclaimed desk and dented four-drawer filing cabinet successfully bid from a government auction contrast my two plastic Argos outdoor chairs covered with a drop of linen curtain. My sporadically used high-backed leather recliner is a king amongst serfs.

'Good morning, Olivia. Nice to see you again.'

Really? You've seen me only once, under the most solemn of circumstances – what makes you so gregarious now? I respond with my own false conviviality: 'Thank you. Nice to see you too. Love your office, and the location. Must be a gold mine.'

'Serves its purpose. We're the leading agent in the Plymouth area. Turned over more than 45 mill' last financial year.'

Shit! I'll be lucky to turn over 45 hundred.

I calculate from the agents' commission scale that the agency receives two to three percent of the property sale price with the salesperson receiving two percent of that. My most conservative estimate means that the agency earnt more than £2.2 million in commissions. I note three staff offices, one of which has been reduced to a chaotic hold-all, and deduce that after staff salaries Roslyn would pocket in the region of £200,000 per year. Plus perks. Unless she is extremely greedy, psychopathic, or disturbed, there is no logical reason for her to resort to hastening her mother's demise for the sake of pocketing a few thousand pounds.

'I thought we'd have lunch at the Wander Inn. Sounds a bit ordinary, but the food's good and the coffee's exquisite.'

'Fine by me.' I've had my share of instant, aromatic, decaffeinated, caffè latte and cappuccino. I can't wait to see what she has in mind.

Roslyn carries herself with confidence as we listen to each other's silence during the short walk. Whether we are exercising mutual caution, or just waiting for the other to speak, I can't be sure.

Roslyn performs the chivalrous deed: 'Right then. What'll you have dear?'

Dear? Don't start that Rotherham speak. Dear? As if I'm some old biddy like the dearly departed Ena Sharples of early Coronation Street *episodes, or a customer awaiting service from the counter of a Salvation Army (bless them) soup kitchen. I must gain control without demeaning Roslyn.* 'Can we dispense with the "dear"? My mum calls me that and I just loathe it. Sorry. On a happier note,' I continue, glancing at Roslyn, 'I'll have what you're having,' to steal the double entendre from the movie, *When Harry met Sally*.

We command an outside table beneath a coffee-house sponsored umbrella. Roslyn lights a cigarette. She slides over the pack, then recoils as I gesture 'no' with my arm, far too vigorously, as if I'd intended to force the pack into the next county. I thought we'd chosen the outdoor setting to capitalise on the spring sunshine and gain a little more privacy, but it seems that Roslyn's nicotine habit drew her to the promenade. She searches my eyes, hypnotising me into opening the conversation, thereby proving that she is well practised in the salesman's lore after closing a deal: *he who speaks first, loses.*

I'm certainly not going to lose. I haven't lost sight of my goal, and that is to unearth information to help Alexander determine whether or not his mother had died from another's hand. 'Roslyn. This is a very sensitive situation. I must ask for your complete confidence and discretion.'

Smoke hangs over the table like London's 1950s smog epidemic. Roslyn glares at me as if I'd told her that her agency is about to be audited by Inland Revenue. She grinds her cigarette into the ground. 'What's going on here?'

Nearby patrons twist their heads to Roslyn's accusative tone.

'You know I'm retained by your brother to inquire in to the circumstances of your mother's death.' I hand her another business card bearing my accreditation from the Security Industry Authority.

Roslyn sits open-mouthed, wondering if Inland Revenue auditors really are standing before her. I continue: 'I was formerly a detective sergeant with Mercia Police and had been a police officer for seven years.' I add the tag to endorse credibility, knowledge, and experience, for there are many private investigators who, to put it bluntly, do not have the benefit of my past. I must tread carefully with Roslyn, given that I'd already riled her at her mother's memorial. She didn't accept my intrusion then, nor will she, I am sure, welcome it now.

'As you know, Roslyn, your mother was recovering well. You must accept that, based on your observations.'

'Well, yes. But anyone's health can deteriorate under one of many circumstances.'

'Quite so, Roslyn. And it's those circumstances that aroused Alex's concern. There's two trains of thought he's asked me to pursue. I'll get to those in a moment, but before I do, there seems to be some discrepancy over who's next of kin.'

'I thought it was set. Alex has been next of kin for as long as I can remember. It's natural, isn't it – the male takes on the role? Also academic. Just a name on a form. It's not as if we expected mum to die.'

'Of course not. No one expects it. Not in normal circumstances, anyway.' My barb clearly pierces her carapace of honour.

'What are you getting at? You're hiding something, aren't you?'

'I did say this is sensitive. Remember I told you about Alexander's theory, and I stress the word "theory" that someone possibly did something to hasten your mother's death, although not necessarily with malice.'

'Fuck me. You still trying to blame someone? What the fuck are you saying? You bitch! What's in this for you? A fat cheque and a spot in Alex's bed?'

Roslyn's reaction floors me, although I suppose it is not

so unnatural. I would probably respond with the same anger if someone accused my sister (if I had one) of murdering my mother. Worse though, is the implication that I am sleeping with her brother just to further my career. I congratulate myself for having not succumbed to his earlier invitation, for had I have done so I would now be blushing the colour of that huge central-Australian rock.

'Roslyn. I'm not in this for any reason other than to satisfy some queries. You can probably solve this right away and then we can put it to bed. Why was Meredith so anxious to be next of kin? I believe she discussed it with you.'

'"Practicalities" is what she told me. She was more available than Alex. She was out and about and always in touch with hospitals because of work.'

I conceal my theory that Meredith was *expecting* something to happen and for that reason she effected the change. 'And Alex was *not* available?'

'I'm not positive, but he's often in court and unavailable – he may as well have been in Antarctica…'

I let her ramble for a while – I do not wish to disarm her by cutting her short. 'So. Why wasn't Alex included in the discussion to remove him as next of kin? Surely he had a right to be involved rather than you both sealing the deal behind his back?'

Roslyn stalls, collects her thoughts. 'I don't know. I didn't think that much of it at the time. Meredith made sense, but as I said, it was just so academic. I really didn't see the point in fostering more family flack.'

'So there's little harmony between you three?'

'Just the way it is, and has been for years. We each stick to our own space.'

'The outcome of this, Roslyn, as I've mentioned, is that Alex is considering a malpractice claim against the hospital on the grounds of neglect with respect to monitoring medication and misdiagnosing examinations.'

'Bloody hell. What's he doing? Can't he just be satisfied that mum had reached her time? Is he looking for a payout or something?'

'I have no such instructions, and I sincerely believe that's not his angle. He honestly believes, as do I, from information I can't yet divulge, that your mother died prematurely and not of natural causes. Whether the cause be malice or misadventure is what I'm determined to uncover.'

Roslyn calms and looks genuinely concerned at the possibility of her mother still being alive if it were not for the scenarios I'd suggested.

'That brings me to why I rang you today. I'd noticed Meredith standing at the front of Alexander's office. Seemed to have no purpose because she occupied the same spot for forty minutes. Any idea why she'd be taunting her brother?'

She raises her eyebrows. They speak for her: *I don't give a damn*. 'You're supposed to be the sleuth, why don't you ask her?'

'I probably will. I just thought—'

'All right already. Merri's got something happening, but I'm not sure what. She phoned me maybe yesterday or the day before and said that she was acting for a client and seeking a business appointment. Very la-de-da, if you ask me.

'I said something like: "What kind of client have *you* got?" and Meredith went on to explain her relationship to a woman who'd recently handed her Power of Attorney over her affairs. Her "duty" as she called it, was to settle the estate, and that included selling her home – hence her approach to me.

'I asked Merri why she had been appointed to act under Power of Attorney. It struck me as weird that she was named on two within a fortnight, but strange things have a habit of following my sister. I asked if the woman had family, to which Merri replied, "Well, yes. But she confided in me. They're all right with it."'

I knew straight away that Meredith had spun her sister a line, because there was no way known that Gerald Geddes, at least, would have vetoed Meredith Bennington holding Power of Attorney over his mother. 'So, have you accepted the listing?'

'Yes. It's one of those deals the client wants sealed as soon as possible, almost with the same haste as a mortgagee sale. It's listed on open sale for 30 days. Failing a positive result, the property will proceed to auction. There is an added condition though. Merri stipulated that twenty percent of the sale's proceeds be directed to the Happy Valley Care Home.'

That seals it for me. Even though Roslyn hasn't mentioned the name of Meredith's 'client', the mention of Happy Valley confirms the connection to Nora Geddes. I deduce that an 80% profit out of the deal is more than a win.

'All right. that leads to something else, Roslyn. I'm either going to lose you on this or cause you the most dramatic grief. For that I apologise in advance. Have you heard or seen news reports of the death of a lady named Nora Geddes?'

'No. Why would that concern me?'

'Your sister was her carer. At the Happy Valley home.'

'Where do you get off, Miss what's it? Occupational hazard, don't you see? Anyone who works with the frail and elderly will always be the last ones to be with them. Christ, no one else wants them, do they? The seniors of our society left to rot in a care home like compost in a backyard bin. Some of those old dears, and excuse my use of the word "dears" which you plainly detest, have dementia and Alzheimer's. Even when their family visit they don't even know them; they just sit around watching TV. Maybe someone will strike up a few chords on an out-of-tune piano while others crotchet a few more squares of their lap-rug. They're just left for dead. And now you're saying that when they die, someone is *responsible*? You tell Alex he's got a nerve getting some broken-down copper to come sniffing 'round here causing more upset and distress to our family.'

'Okay. I understand you're upset. Just before I go, were you aware that Meredith was also caring for her late mother-in-law, and she, too, died in her care?'

'Fuck you. I'm finished. I'll fix the bill; you sit here and enjoy your afternoon.'

Roslyn flounces out with more grace than a Chelsea socialite.

It takes another cappuccino to settle me down. Perhaps I'd pushed too hard and gone too far. *Nup. all in the interest of extracting info.* Still, I do hope that in the sanctity of her office, she will mull over pertinent points of our discussion.

There are few bonds closer than sisterly relationships. Sisters grow up sharing rooms, toys, and clothes; confide in each other about wagging school, share gossip and tales of boyfriends, and compete for, rather than share, their mother's love. Years later, they attend each other at their respective weddings, share the joys and demands of pregnancy, and support each other through the latter months of pains, immobility, and contractions. Within days of the child's birth, they've offered more help than had their brothers-in-law during the whole term of convalescence.

For those reasons, I tend to believe that on entering her office, Roslyn will phone Meredith and blather away the very confidential matters I had discussed. Taking that to its conclusion, I anticipate Meredith will prepare rebuttals to my suspicions as a means of insulating herself from a prospective enquiry.

Stafford. Shit! His London office is three-plus hours away. I rush to my car, which I'd left standing in the patchwork of autos comprising the railway station's Pay and Display. I retrieve a file that I'd concealed beneath the spare tyre in the boot (one can't be too cautious) and scamper aboard a London-bound train that will deposit me at Paddington Station at 1.52 p.m. – all being well. Using a service plagued with timetable revisions, signal failures, maintenance outages and staff shortages can never guarantee a scheduled arrival time.

I settle into a seat, intending to review case notes during the three-hour-twenty-minute journey to London. Big ambition, no result. The burden of impatience grabs me. Eagerness to solve my first case of substance is too much. I juggle the Beecham family's traits and idiosyncrasies: Caring. Jealousy. Greed. Motivation. Vengeance. Competition…

… the carriage's pitch and sway rocks me to sleep. I

backtrack to Roslyn. Might she be trying to pull information from Meredith, rather than give it to her? Is her defence of Meredith a sham, conceived to divert attention from herself?

Long ago, as a four-year-old only child, I was the topic of an interaction I'll never forget. It was crèche day, but mum didn't take me to crèche; she took me to a huge office building. I was too young to read, but later learnt it was the Department of Social Services. I found out that my mother left me there because, in her words, she 'couldn't afford to keep me.' Understandably, I hold passionate views about mothers who discard their babies, but I won't unleash that anger here.

For twelve months, Elaine Waterson had been engaged to marry Peter Watts. Elaine had been thrice let down after Peter hedged and changed the wedding date. The weasel had cold feet, but Elaine could not see it.

When Elaine was eight months pregnant she pressed the marriage issue. 'Peter, I don't want our child to be born out of wedlock. Please. We must confirm a date, and soon. I don't care about a fancy ceremony or hundreds of guests. The Registry Office is fine. I just want to be married before we have the baby.'

'I'm sorry love. Things have to be just right. You know I won't let you down. I just want to save a bit more money. We've still got four weeks; we'll be married – don't you worry.'

And Elaine didn't worry – until two weeks' later when early labour forced her to take a taxi to Manchester Royal Infirmary. Peter received a phone call at work. Slid Elaine's panicked message into his pocket.

I was born at 5.00 p.m. I'm told that my father strolled in some time after finishing work. 'You didn't even care enough to come straight away,' my mother wept.

'The money, honey. I would have lost two hours' pay.' The story is that my dad stayed with mum for only thirty minutes, before complaining that he'd had a long day and had to go home and shower. He kissed mum and me on the forehead. That was the last we ever saw of Peter Watts.

When mum brought me home four days' later, Peter's personal belongings were gone, as were a few of mum's CDs. Mum struggled to support me with welfare as her only means. Her monetary mismanagement escalated to a point where she was spending more money on Vodka and Orange than on formula and baby needs.

She battled for four years before giving up and surrendering me to the authorities. I learnt all this on my eighteenth birthday when my foster parents sat me down for a heart-to-heart. I thought it was going to be the big lecture about sex; the Birds and the Bees and all that stuff, backed up with subtle advice to go on The Pill – 'for your own protection, Livi'.

I could have given them a lesson about the friggin' birds and the bees: *'Fly high for a few moments and suffer the sting for the rest of your life!'*

Anyway, I listened to the story of how they'd adopted me within weeks of mum abandoning me. I'd often wondered why my surname was different to that of my foster parents. It fell into place after the big revelation.

Like many in similar situations, I set about finding my birth mum, the Salvation Army doing more than I ever could have expected. Within three months they'd located her and made arrangements for what they termed a 'soft reunion' – more of that namby-pamby political correctness crap. I was keen, rather than excited, and looked forward to the day with mild apprehension.

In a tiny office, a Salvo's counsellor introduced us. I noticed straight away that I'd inherited my mother's looks, but I hoped my years of health and fitness activities would immunise me from her weather-worn appearance. I'm embarrassed to confess that I was disappointed to learn that mum was now Elaine Mc Roberts, and had been for fifteen years. Her husband knew nothing of me. That elicited mixed feelings. Deep within, I celebrated her happiness, but mourned not meeting my birth dad. I think all of us adoptees are a little selfish in that situation. It is all about us, isn't it? *Why did you abandon me? How could you do that? Didn't you ever think of making contact?*

'I've put alcohol and my past life behind me,' my mother explained.

'Put me behind you too,' I countered. 'Didn't you think of me after you'd come good?'

'I've got other children, Olivia. You went to a good home. We all moved on.'

Ah, the old 'moved on' cliché. Two words that supposedly excuse past aberrant behaviour: *I used to be a thief, but I've moved on – I'm on the straight and narrow; I used to be a philanderer, but I've moved on; I used to be a bitch, but I've moved on – I'm now a model wife.*

'Olivia. I agreed to come here for your sake, to fill in the missing pieces of your life. I don't really know how to put this, but I'm asking you to respect *my* wishes and not contact me again.'

Whilst the request was emotionally difficult, I had no problem foregoing a relationship with a woman who could *never* be my mother. We spoke for another thirty minutes, during which time Elaine (I can't call her "mum") gave me the history that I had for so long craved. She had registered my name as Olivia Elaine Watts in anticipation of marrying Peter. The explanation of my surname resolved the dilemma I'd harboured for twenty-six years.

Now I struggle to carry my middle name – 'Elaine' – knowing I share the name of a woman who forsook me for bottles of Vodka and Orange.

A rickety set of points jolts me awake. I pledge to give my stepmother and father a huge hug next time I visit. They are my *real* parents and have given me everything – and everything I am today I owe to them.

17

Saturday 11 March

The carriage shakes, rattles and rolls over junctions and crossovers as it weaves through a landscape of steel stanchions and parallel lines radiating like a shattered window. Metal-strapped packs of sleepers await nightshift crews, and a nearby chain-mesh compound rears piles of ballast rising conically from the earth. On the adjacent line a train pulls a rush of air, the blurred image revealing the familiar blaze of red paint and tinted windows. Another Virgin. I smile as its growling engines reverberate through my seat.

As the train hums into Paddington Station, I pick up the unread folder and habitually feel under the seat to ensure I do not become the next 'lost umbrella' statistic. I leap into a City Circle tube to St. James's Park were I drop on to platform two and stretch my legs to the MET office, a task made difficult by lunch hour tail-enders scurrying back to workplaces secreted in the sacred legal district. I shirk the encumbrance of trying to dodge people devoid of spatial awareness, their attention directed to smart phones, iPods, pedometers, and other damn-fangled pieces of technology.

Having relinquished membership to the exclusive police brethren, I announce my appearance to the dual-roled receptionist-come-security officer and await an escort to DCI Stafford's office. A leggy, olive-skinned lass masquerading as a part-time dancer from the West End, presents a Colgate smile: 'Miss Watts? I'll show you to Mr Stafford's office.'

Huh? I remember office protocol dictating that all commissioned officers be addressed by rank. Admittedly, Detective Chief Inspector Stafford is a mouthful (in more ways than one) but public service staff have been reprimanded for lesser indiscretions.

I trail her sashaying torso through a double door: 'Miss Watts, sir.'

Aah, she redeems herself by addressing him 'sir'. Then it clicks. Her absence of protocol is fostered by a degree of familiarity that I had once enjoyed. *Is Sharon still on the scene, or has Dave paved the way for this Bollywood wannabe?* It doesn't matter to me. I don't care. I'm over him – until I see him. My George Clooney clone.

'Hello,' I offer, conscious that I reflect his expression of desire.

'Hello Olivia. You're looking well.'

We press on with the common preliminaries of weather and football. I explain the circumstances of my move to Newquay, although I neglect to mention his infidelity hastened my decision. I blurt out a précis of the pressing situation, confirming Alexander Beecham's concern over the altered next of kin, which has now faded to the background. I voice the recent coincidence of Meredith being Nora Geddes carer at the time of her death, and I recount Victoria Bennington's history.

Stafford listens half-heartedly while he twists and cranks a Rubik's Cube into non-conformity. I'd spoken for nearly ten minutes, which is nine minutes and fifty-five seconds longer than the world-record time for re-assembling the cube to its six correct faces. (Fourteen-year-old Lucas Etter had done so in 4.90 seconds. Stafford poses no threat.)

He pushes the cube aside, its jumbled mess resembling the present state of my life. 'How long you been on this case?'

'Week, maybe. Seems like forever. I just get going in a certain direction and then something else happens, like when I was watching TV the other Tuesday night. A news bulletin announced the death of Nora Geddes. Meant nothing to me at the time, until I remembered her name had turned up on a bank statement crediting money to Meredith – Alexander's sister.'

'And I suppose I shouldn't ask how you got to see this woman's personal statement?'

'You know me. I walk a straight line.'

'Yes. So long as it leads to where you want, Olivia. The reason I suggested we meet is because this may be beyond the scope of a newly-registered private investigator.'

I fix him a look that intimates nothing is beyond me. 'I understand that. That's exactly why I contacted you and provided sufficient information to ring bells. Are you suggesting my concerns are justified?'

Stafford leans back in his chair. 'I'm not suggesting anything, but we do have information that puts a cloud over your Meredith Beecham slash Bennington.' He picks up the cube and clicks and twists while he floats me diluted information.

The creaking and twitching infuriates me. I know he is holding back, probably because I am now an outsider and not one of the boys, and one who could be seen as a risk if given classified information. I despise the thought of being considered perfidious. My taking the Evesham Murders case behind DI Marchant's back to implore help from the man playing with a child's toy sitting before me will forever stain my character, despite a police internal enquiry finding that I'd acted with total professionalism. I have since been tainted with labels of backstabber, turncoat, deceitful bitch, and a host of other less than complimentary terms. My sincerest wish is that Stafford will trust me. Given my turning up out of the blue, as it were, there is little, or nothing, I can do to promote that. All right. I do admit there is one way, but I am not going to resort to offering him an hour with my body in exchange for information I could more than likely obtain under less debaucherous terms. Nevertheless, I commence bargaining: 'That cloud must be pretty much light-on, otherwise you'd already be investigating her.'

'Very good, Miss Watts.'

Sarcastic bastard.

'But we don't always run like a bull at a gate, do we? Remember, those who wait, take the cake.'

'Yes. But if we wait too long there might not be any cake. More to the point, there could be another death. Look Dave. Alexander Beecham has an application before the coroner to order an autopsy on his mother's body. He expects the application to receive prompt attention. Therefore, we might have barely forty-eight hours to get the goods on her. If the autopsy favours Alexander's suspicions, you can arrest her and I'll give you all my case history notes.'

'Sounds like you're trying to do me a favour. You know I only have to subpoena them?'

'Of course you can. But I've been forgetful since leaving the constabulary. You've got no idea how many things I lose.'

'Tell you what, Olivia. Turns out your Meredith has some juvenile form; shoplifting and deception.'

'That's not new. You told me that on the phone. Shows we're on the right track.'

'Proves nothin', Olivia. Thirty years ago. Clean ever since.'

'That we know of, Inspector. That we know of! She married at nineteen. We don't know if someone has covered her cellulite-ridden butt for further crimes or paid someone off, but we do know that her mother-in-law died only four months after Meredith became one of the family. What I've learnt from Lord Robert is that Meredith, as Victoria's carer, grew extremely close to her. That arouses suspicion, given continent-wide history of new wives competing against mothers-in-law. You need to read the incredibly bizarre Last Will and Testament that favours Meredith to the tune of £500,000 – conditional upon her remaining married to the old geezer. Doesn't it then strike you as peculiar that they've spent the past twenty years totally separate?'

'Tell you what we'll do. You bring me something a bit more substantial than coincidence and a will, and I'll assign a detective to the file. You give me your client's details and I'll have a chat with him also.'

I hand over one of Alexander's cards. 'This guy's a lawyer, Dave. He's not just out for sour grapes or a hunk of estate. He suspected something was wrong before his mother died.'

'Perhaps he should have called us instead of you.'

Ouch! That was a low blow of the type I wouldn't ordinarily expect from Stafford. 'Come on Dave. If you're negative about this now, what hope would he have had back then? Anyway, I'm going before I say the wrong thing. Bye.'

Stafford swivels in his chair, arms behind his head: 'What? Not staying for a drink?'

'It's not even three o'clock. Got things to do, places to go, and a file to prepare so you can receive more accolades on the back of my investigatory skills!'

'Very good, Olivia. Perhaps you should rename your company "Watts-a-joke"?'

I leave his office returning the Colgate smile to his walking coffee bean and head to the station.

Within hours, I'm reclined in my own leather chair, musing what ifs. A missing link nags me; something not yet surfaced in the investigation, a vital clue that could cement all the pieces together. I remember the father I never had, and think of the father who is missing from Alexander's, Meredith's, and Roslyn's life. Sure, he'd divorced Joyce, but why did he not bother to attend her funeral or wake, even if only for his children's sake?

When I wake early on Sunday morning I care nothing for Meredith's father, or for that matter, any Beecham. For the past seven days, I've given my all, trying to satisfy Alexander's curiosity and suspicion.

I step into my crumpled tracksuit, which complements my crumpled face and electrified hair, and shuffle into my kitchen. Coffee. I open the pantry to find that I'd delayed shopping for so long that I have neither coffee nor tea. I blame Alexander.

I slam the door, grab my purse, and walk to the High Street in hope of finding an open cafe. Typical of British towns and villages; nothing awakens before ten o'clock on a Sunday morning, save for the shrinking farmers' markets and the odd convenience store. I can't rationalise why large shops receive carte-blanche trading approval for Good Friday (the second most sacred day on the Christian calendar) yet on any given Sunday they are restrained until 10.00 a.m.

I abandon my quest for an English Breakfast, cappuccino and muffin and amble to One Stop to purchase a jar of Nescafé, a litre of full-cream milk and a 200-gram block of Cadbury Fruit and Nut. I hurry home, slide my percolator into its spot beneath the sink and prepare to suffer instant coffee.

I down the block of chocolate, helping it along with a very ordinary flat white. I am a disciple of research attesting to the stimulatory effects of caffeine and chocolate and one who singlehandedly supports the heart-thumping effects.

In the absence of pressing matters, I decide to stay home and revise my notes should Alexander make a last-minute request for me to give evidence to support his application – not that I could contribute much. I stop at Nora Geddes' history (I don't know why, because it has nothing to do with the court hearing) and reflect on Meredith's bizarre undressing routine at Nora's funeral.

I read a passage I collated from my conversation with Gerald Geddes:

Prior to the Happy Valley move, Meredith took the opportunity of familiarising herself with Nora's home. Under the pretence of offering extra help, she toiled for two days, scrubbing, tidying, and setting aside items she would later retain for herself. As a mark of respect, and to satisfy any enquiry as to her motives, she'd filled a box of memorabilia she deemed most important to the Geddes' family history. After the funeral ruckus, she left it to charity.

Her next task was to place the house for sale with a reputable agent – and she had just the person in mind. For the time being though, she is burdened with enough problems trying to access her mother's estate.

Meredith went about her daily business unperturbed by peripheral events and with no compassion for her departed mother. She continued to work, and continued to accept new clients. She is a woman of no empathy. Or conscience. She is a woman who will not put a foot wrong, or if she does, she'll pull out all stops to cover her tracks.

Contractually, the Geddes matter has nothing to do with me, but it does intertwine with Meredith's recent activities. I've done the right thing by handing pertinent information to Stafford, who, in turn, will hopefully transfer it to the appropriate team – if one has been assembled. Because of my closeness to three deaths, I easily recognise glaring similarities: each woman died under the care of Meredith Bennington, AND (at this stage) each death was signed off as natural causes. For a reason I'm yet to fathom, I had failed to convince Stafford that Victoria Bennington could also be a victim. His response of: "You bring me something a bit more substantial than coincidence and a will, and I'll assign a detective to the file" showed what I consider to be an abusive lack of vision.

I have concerns for other patients under Meredith's care, but accept I have no legitimate means of accessing or viewing her client/patient list because Meredith is self-employed through her own company. I can't imagine her being involved in another death within a few days, but then again, Nora's death was only five days after Joyce Beecham's.

I phone Meredith's number, courtesy of Hamilton's bundle of documents.

'Hello. Bennington.'

'Hi. My name's Julie. I got your number from our local medical centre; I'm looking for some help for my mother.'

'Oh right. Where is she?'

'In her home, here in Newquay. Things are getting on top of her. I'm here most mornings, but I need someone for three days a week to help with dressings for some burns mum got off the cooker.'

I hear the crackle of turning pages.

'Some spots have just become available. Monday, Wednesday and Saturday – would that suit?'

'That'd be brilliant. I don't mean to be rude, but reliability is important to me. I've been let down before. How many patients do you work with?'

'Just three at the moment. No need to worry. I've plenty of references.'

All self-made, I bet.

There isn't much more I can achieve over the phone: 'Okay, thank you. Perhaps I'll call again soon and make a time for you to meet my mother.'

'Yes. That's the best thing. Just have her doctor's name and DWP details handy, just for processing purposes.'

Done. Now I've got to find someone to stand in as my mother. I jot down a few more notes and in large letters write 'JULIE'. I don't want to blow this by calling back with the wrong name. While in a phone mood, I call Alexander to find out if he knows that his sister has been lurking about his office.

18

Monday 13 March

I've never attended a court so well preserved as Truro Magistrates' Court – a petrified slice of the 1800s. Rich mahogany timbers panel the walls, judge's bench, and witness box; banks of contoured oak seats relax anxious family, friends and press, and counsels' bar table reflects convictions and acquittals from deeply lustred Maple. From the high ceiling, scalloped opaque light fittings hang like inverted baker's mixing bowls – their tell-tale entry into the twenty-first century evidenced by power-saving fluorescent globes.

The courtroom, today sitting as the Coroner's Court, reeks of beeswax. I hope Alexander's submission will be similarly polished.

Courts don't intimidate me as they do first-timers. I am accustomed to police uniforms and eloquently robed and bewigged barristers wearing crisp white shirts looped with burgundy bow ties. Alexander fits the bill in his coal-black suit and navy blue tie, confirming that clothes do maketh the man.

I don't know why I am so nervous. I don't have a part to play other than to observe the hearing in which the coroner will take evidence from a short list of witnesses, including Alexander and his sisters. I presume Dr Patel and the hospital will justify their stance as one of correctness and professionalism to save implicating themselves in a possible medical 'oversight'. Their answers will be short and sharp to insulate them from being misquoted by circling freelance media scouts.

Alexander had subpoenaed general practitioner, Dr Johnston, who will testify of Joyce's good health over the preceding twelve years. The doctor will agree that his patient suffered a 'manageable' heart condition and that her diabetes was equally manageable. He will conclude that in 'normal circumstances' neither of those conditions would hasten Mrs Beecham's death.

With the hearing well underway, Dr Patel's mixed recollections of circumstances under which he signed the death certificate swing the pendulum to Alexander's favour. He claims that working long hours in combination with a heavy patient load 'might have given rise to an uncharacteristic lapse'. Under cross-examination, Doctor Patel concedes 'an unfortunate omission' by relying on previous observations and chart statistics to record the reason behind his patient's passing.

The coroner finds that both the family's and the public interest will be served by his ordering an autopsy and inquest.

On later attending Cornwall and District General Hospital, Alexander and I are surprised to learn that the autopsy has been set for 3.00 p.m., chiefly to take advantage of a coroner-appointed pathologist already in attendance.

We adjourn to the hospital cafeteria where we are scrutinised by doctors and nurses, perhaps trying to decide whether we're foreign colleagues or the pair 'stirring up trouble' as has been the not so silent whispers. I sip coffee while Alexander relays his victory to Roslyn. Despite the phone being jammed firmly against his ear, I manage to hear Roslyn's profane objections. Alexander's, 'Calm down, calm down. It'll be all right,' has no effect.

I know it won't be all right, for if my mother or father (step parent or not) were to be dissected like a frog in a school science laboratory, I would also be doing all in my power to prevent the peccadillo of our dearly departed. However, regardless of my view, I am anxious for the hours to spin to three o'clock.

I don't need to ask why he doesn't phone Meredith. He made that clear at Joyce's memorial function. But I do pose a nagging dilemma: 'Alex. This mightn't be any of my business, but why wasn't your father at your mum's memorial?'

'Wasn't invited. Wouldn't have been welcome. What would you do with a bloke who'd been married to your mother for nearly fifty years, then, just because she adds a few kilos to her hips – due to illness mind you – uses that as a reason to claim incompatibility. Bloody hypocrite – had a beer gut the size of Gibraltar. "I'm sorry", dad confided in me. "We'd been on the rocks for ages, this was the last straw".'

'Shit Alex. Sorry, but don't you overlook those things or put them aside at a time like this?'

'Some might, but I have my sisters' support. Probably the only thing we've ever agreed on. Still, old George never even sent a card; maybe he doesn't know.'

I don a serious look: 'For what it's worth, I think you're all wrong. They *were* married for most of their life – that's hell of a long time.'

'His face warps into a smile. 'Hell of a lot longer if you're not in love.'

In a subterranean sterile theatre, the pathologist, her assistant and two gowned associates prep for the autopsy. Alexander and I are refused entry, despite Alexander pleading with the forensic pathologist, Soon Yui, that my taking notes and observations will assist his legal research. 'You look from window,' Dr Yui orders.

A two-metre by three-metre glazed sheet frames us like an aquatic centre exhibit. I note a sign: 'Video or photography of medical procedures through this window strictly prohibited,' and sarcastically visualise students' glee of witnessing the autopsy of a 160-kilogram grandmother on their 40-inch high definition plasma televisions, only to recall my own experience of watching similar clips while studying bullet trajectory and deflection through human tissue.

The theatre itself comprises two mirrored halves, each with its own stainless steel table, stainless steel instrument trolleys, stainless steel wash troughs, concrete floor painted in white acrylic and overhead lighting sufficient to light a 'B' grade movie or reprise of *Quincy ME*. I have not seen such an expanse of stainless steel since watching Gordon fucking Ramsay's *Hell's Kitchen*.

Dr Soon Yui, resplendent in blue coverall, white disposable shoe covers and latex gloves, leads her team to the table upon which the late Joyce Beecham's rest will be violated. Dr Yui's flower patterned head cover astounds me. 'More suitable for a children's hospital,' I whisper to Alexander, 'but hardly appropriate in the serious environment of searching for a cause of death.'

'Perhaps it's a lucky charm, like a footballer's favourite jocks,' Alexander chuckles.

'Strange analogy. I suppose nothing's available in Fortune Cookie print.'

An audio system pipes the theatre's activities into the viewing room. 'We start now.' Dr Yui nods to her assistant. The assistant, also Asian, is a young male of about 25, but could be 45. Who can guess the real age of an Asian's wrinkle-free and unblemished complexion? He towers over the diminutive Dr Yui and accentuates his height with ridiculous peroxided wild hair that looks as if he's travelled ten stations through The Tube with his head poking out of the carriage window.

'Peroxide' hands Dr Yui a scalpel. She slices a dramatic 'Y' across the subject's chest and sternum. Seeing the knife glide through the bleached and mottled flesh sends me cowering to the floor. 'I won't last long, Alex,' I groan. I stand up, only to see Dr Yui grasp a tiny electric disc saw and slice through the deceased's ribcage like a home handyman running his nine-inch De Walt through the centre of a palisade fence. Her open chest weeps residual fluids. I silently thank Dr Yui for barring my participation as a hands-on spectator, thereby saving me the trauma of inhaling odours that would surely send me scurrying to the ladies' room.

I'm compromised in my ability to relay further because I close my eyes to the most gruesome procedures. I glimpse

Dr Yui pulling back white flesh as if she is skinning chicken breasts. I wonder if Alexander and I were not present, might she ruthlessly rip skin and tissue aside with disrespect? (I'll never know because I am not returning to an autopsy theatre unless directed by a High Court judge.) Huge globules of yellow coagulated fat hang from the flesh like stalagmites suspended in a coastal cave. I cringe as the doctor prises open the rib cage and sinks her hand into Joyce's core. Into separate stainless steel receptacles, she places heart, lungs, kidneys, liver and stomach, and, what appears to be two metres of digestive tract.

Dr Yui attaches a new disc to the saw and runs it around the circumference of Joyce's head quicker than I could open a can of baked beans. I cover my eyes as she removes the deceased's brain.

'You take,' Dr Yui motions to her assistant. 'Check very careful the brain. Look swelled and discolour.'

Peroxide wheels the trolley of organs to a station where they will be analysed and recorded by scales, microscope, computer, and radiological equipment. The faint audio feed convinces me that all is acceptable – until Peroxide performs calculus on the brain.

With a concerned frown, he signals his leader to check the calculi. Dr Yui's lapel microphone captures her conversation: 'Brain weight, 1.2 kilogram. That in normal range. There evidence of ischaemic stroke caused by atherosclerosis. Arterial deposit minor, I think was transient, only minor blockage. Not cause death. Both temporal lobe and occipital lobe evidence swelling. I check tissue, and find sedative. Maybe Pethidine or Diazepam. Maybe too much for sedation. Also find insulin. Too much for diabetic. Something wrong here.'

Peroxide places the brain tissue in airtight containers for further analysis.

'We look stomach. I open, you note.'

I am amazed how digested food remains in a gelatinous form of its original structure after many hours of mastication and digestion. Dr Yui continues, 'We have mash potato, 33 gram; pea, 12 gram, fluid of orange, 66 mil' – you check sugar of fluid then we know for sure if juice or concentrate – and there plenty chocolate, maybe cream chocolate sweet or dessert; there is egg – they serve egg with mash potato? – no, this egg soft, only yolk. There also sugar, gelatine and, er, this no right, there too much chocolate. They have five-clock dinner; allow digest two hours. We find when she eat chocolate. Who allow this? You please see if Dr Patel on duty. He see patient before. He treating doctor.'

While I don't comprehend all of Yui's distorted English, I do understand her concerns. Without expanding her findings, Dr Yui continues the examination. I don't need further detail to convince me that abnormal amounts of sedative and insulin have been detected in Joyce Beecham's brain tissue.

Alexander and I approach Dr Yui after she leaves Peroxide to clean up. 'I heard the audio,' Alexander says, 'and you seem disturbed by something. You're satisfied my mother's death was not natural?'

'Possible. I say no more until examine tissue. Tissue tell story then we see treating doctor. I know she diabetic, but she have so much chocolate and so much insulin. Something not right.'

Alexander withdraws and shrinks into his suit. Justifiable, I think, upon hearing the prospect of the hospital having failed to properly monitor his mother's condition, or, that the likelihood of someone having murdered his mother has just become a very real proposition.

I butt in: 'Dr Yui. When can we get the results? I suppose they'll identify the cause of death?'

'We don't guess.' To Alexander, Yui says: 'You phone tomorrow after two o'clock.'

At this stage I am no further advanced in finding out whether an insulin dose was incorrectly administered by a nurse, or whether Joyce herself had doubled up an injection. I doubt the latter because Joyce had been insulin dependent for twenty years. As a result, she would not be likely to err with pre-packaged injections. Further, in the hospital environment, I am fairly sure that nursing staff would take over patients' medication needs. That's something for me to check.

Again, Joyce Beecham's final words sting: 'Help me, Alex.'

* * *

Other than the day I sprung her hanging around Alexander's office, I haven't seen Meredith since her mother's memorial. I am certain that by now she has leeched from Roslyn everything we'd discussed at the Wander Inn. She must surely know that her mother's funeral is delayed because of Alexander's insistence on challenging the hospital's death certificate.

Fuelled by occupational foresight, I sense that Meredith might have an inkling that the autopsy will return the true cause of death, and from that, an intense investigation will follow. *If she doesn't like me, she'll definitely hate Stafford.*

Crimes are solved with the barest slivers of evidence. Body language and antecedents give suspects away with all the hoo-haa of a father giving away his daughter at the altar.

My recollection of Meredith's conduct was that it was not that of a grieving daughter – she was panic stricken. Her transfixion with Alexander's office was vivid proof. Was she stalking him? Planning a vendetta? I consider this along with Roslyn's proclamation: 'She'd kill him if she could.' Most would discount that as a throw-away line, but in context with recent events, I cannot afford to ignore the prophecy. I glare at Meredith's name on my suspect list.

And then I look at Alexander's.

Even though I have been engaged to perform an investigation for him, I must remain objective and hold foremost in my mind that *no one* is exempt from an enquiry – and that includes Alexander Beecham. With a mind to exclude him, I run through circumstances that might compel a person to employ an investigator to uncover a misdemeanour if there were a likelihood that that person could be implicated. I examine two scenarios. First, a person so confident in their complicity not being detected would feel assured that they would easily evade suspicion. The second point is that same person would be certain that the investigator *he'd* contracted would not suspect him. Reverse psychology comes to mind: *Why engage me if he runs the risk of being exposed?*

I carry on regardless, scribbling ridiculous points, expounding reasons for Alexander wanting to dispose of his mother. I stop at three: Greed. Jealousy. Revenge. Greed isn't a viable motive. He doesn't live beyond his means – he owns a flourishing legal practice with a firm grip on conveyancing and wills and probate. His home is a shade above comfortable, but from what I'd fathomed, he bears no aspirations for higher plateaus. My views aren't exactly philosophical, but I consider greed to be more than just a manifestation of accumulating wealth. For instance, Alexander could have a hidden gambling problem. He could be snorting lines of cocaine. Many of us have a side so deeply buried, even the combined efforts of the CIA and MI5 wouldn't find it.

Jealousy is a not a trait I've seen in Alexander. There is a remote possibility that he is jealous of Roslyn's success, but when all said and done, both are equally successful in their own fields. Importantly, there is no sign of his having been jealous of his mother.

The third point, revenge, stays with me. Why would a male exact revenge on his mother? I reconcile my earlier perception of him as a 'mummy's boy' and wonder if there are unresolved childhood issues. I can't see it. He is a genuine, warm, and soft man who I believe incapable of even swearing at his mother, let alone killing her. Then again, some might have once said the same of our King Henry VIII.

I am ashamed to conceive such thoughts – but work's work. I return to the fact that Alexander *is* a successful legal practitioner, and a person of such profession would *never* engage in any type of criminal conduct, despite a shrewd operator's ability to conceal behind-the-scenes activities. For the most part, never do they expect to be uncovered or prosecuted.

I imagine the revenge scenario in a different light, and see before me the bright luminescence of a woman. All I have to do is figure out who.

19

Monday 13 March

Succinctly happy that Alexander and I now have proof that Joyce Beecham did not succumb to natural causes, I type a six-page report for DCI Stafford. I am sure the pathologist's report alone will support Alexander's assertion of criminal and neglectful death. I edit my notes to reflect impartiality and direct conclusions to a family member as the prime suspect. It will be Stafford's challenge to establish who. I have fulfilled my obligation to Alexander Beecham and have, in fact, ventured beyond the scope of my charter. I write another six-page report, with annexed invoice, to hand Alexander at our next meeting.

I am one whose thoughts often race far ahead of reality. Perhaps it's a trait I should have left with my childhood. I didn't though, I dragged it into my teen years; daydreaming in the classroom and on the lacrosse field. Once, on the bus returning home from school I'd glanced at *my* bus stop as the bus departed. *I should have got off there; what an idiot.*

I picture myself pocketing Alexander's £1,000 cheque and accepting a dinner invitation. I don't care so much for dinner – been there, done that, as they say – but I do care to race to the bank, deposit the cheque, and pay a surcharge for an urgent clearance – which will cost me dearly both in fees and a later backlash from Alexander, who will protest: 'Don't you trust me to have enough money to cover my cheque?' I wouldn't tell him that I'd forgone trust long ago – especially when it comes to money. Quick cash could fulfil my dream of a brief holiday on the Spanish coast. Put in perspective, the dream is farcical, given the sparse furniture and accessories in my office and apartment.

The problem with animated dreaming is that there is always a depressing return to reality, and it's usually a dramatic point that precipitates the fall. My dramatic point is concern that one of Cornwall and District General Hospital's staff could change or 'lose' Joyce Beecham's chart and records now that the hospital is aware of the autopsy results.

I'm justifiably paranoid about authorities and instrumentalities 'covering up' their staff's and subordinate agency's mistakes. My vigilance is not without foundation. Many an enquiry has been opened by the Ombudsman's Office or similar investigating authority, only for them to later receive responses glossing over an allegation or excusing it as misinterpretation, oversight, or that the matter of concern clearly did not happen. I have personally fallen victim to bureaucratic maladministration and as a consequence, once received a £50.00 cheque as compensation for an authority's breach of its Customer Service Charter. I mention this only to underscore my concern that an affected party within Cornwall and District General Hospital (and I'll stop short of naming a particular doctor or nurse) might easily be motivated to compromise Joyce Beecham's record.

When I realise my daydreaming has eroded a great chunk of the afternoon, I spring into action, change into my hospital cleaner's uniform – graced by my bespoke identity tag – and clear the excess photos from my mobile phone. I need all the memory I can grab to capture the numerous pages of documents I'm going to photograph.

It doesn't matter to me whether I trump the hospital during the day or the evening, because cleaning staff forever roam corridors and wards. Never does a cleaner look out of place. Evening suits me – that's when I do my best work. And the administration section will either be closed or staffed only by skeleton support.

When I enter the foyer, a huge digital clock confronts me with the slogan: "We watch your health 24 hours a day". I hope they'll serve me better than they did Joyce Beecham. The foyer itself could masquerade as an art gallery. The public truly deserve to appreciate this example of artistic and architectural merit. I stand in a vault-like space beneath soaring glazed walls whose glass roof peaks at least three storey's high. Orange streaks splash across the sky, beneath which domed halogen lights float like planets in the astral panorama. The angled glass walls reflect patrons walking upside down through the foyer, their inverted moon-walk tapping and scuffing echoes off the walls. The inspired Michael Jackson might have named his album, *Off the Wall*, from this very image.

Best get moving, I tell myself, lest I be admonished by a cleaning supervisor for slacking. I head for the accounts section, gently pushing through a congregation of visitors milling about the reception desk. I am thankful for my earlier exploratory mission, which also armed me with knowledge of the cleaners' routine. Some work from portable trolleys crammed with disinfectants, detergents, cloths, and scrubbers for every type of surface within the hospital. A few carry a sponge and bucket, while others, perhaps in the final year of their hard-scrubbing career, merely flit about with duster and disinfectant wipes. That becomes my mission.

I saunter into the accounts office, surprised that it isn't locked. An employee works diligently at a centrally sited desk that commands a view over the entire floor. I assume she is a supervisor; pending retirement after 40 years' service. Her grey hair, piled in a chignon, is 40 years out of fashion, as is her bright red lipstick and black jacket – the lapels and pocket flaps paying homage to a forgotten era – the long flowing pleated skirt, and black, soft-leather espadrilles, all of which were promoted by fashionistas in a 1968 *People* magazine.

'May I help you,' she asks.

'Hi. I'll just flit 'round with my cleaning if I'm not in the way.'

'No problem. I'll be here for another hour, but might fly over to the caf' for a cuppa. In fact, I think I'll fly off now. If anyone comes in, although I doubt they will, just ask them to wait. I won't be longer than five minutes.'

I watch her "fly off", not believing my luck. How portentous. I thought I'd be winging it, having to force doors or hide in cupboards, or even have to return in the dead of night. The prospect of having to explain to night staff that I'd left my phone in the accounts office and then trying to convince them to admit me to the area would be fruitless because I'd obviously have no chance of retrieving the file with staff watching over my shoulder.

With the supervisor departed, I approach the filing cabinet where the boorish Miss Gum Chewer, only days earlier, had replaced the file. I grab the handle of the A to C drawer and it holds fast. *Bloody locked.*

Had I been thinking clearly and been more prepared when I first checked the office, I should have equipped myself with a stick of plasticine to take an impression of the filing cabinet key. Opportunity lost.

Thirty seconds gone.

I don't have to dig deep to know that Miss Supervisor's desk drawer will hold keys to the six towering filing cabinets. An embossed silver plaque sitting on the front of the desk announces: 'Muriel Hetherington – Accounts Control'. A crossword sits half-completed on the desk. I surmise she is claiming overtime to 'bring accounts up to date' when she is, in fact, struggling to complete *The Daily Telegraph* cryptic. Now she is out drinking tea and probably explaining to colleagues about the exhausting evening she is having. I've seen similar rorts in sergeant's offices where they claim overtime on the pretence of 'catching up on paperwork'.

I am bang on target – a small bunch of keys lies in a stationery tray in the top drawer. I dust the desk, remove the keys, and dust my way back to the cabinets. Four keys later, the drawer springs open. I walk my fingers to the Beecham file, but before removing it, I photograph my location within the office, making sure that I feature the bank of filing cabinets and a copy of Joyce's file resting on the steel guides within the drawer. I flip open the file to reveal some fifty pages divided by colour-coded tabs. There is not near enough time to copy the complete file.

One minute-ten, gone.

I begin with admission records, which note vital statistics, ailments, and the ward nurse's admission report. The 'Personal Details' tab leads me to a page noting next of kin and the name Meredith Bennington inked scratchily over a poorly whited-out strip – devoid of explanatory detail. That strikes me as odd, because in this computer age, when someone amends a document, they would ordinarily print out a revised copy. I wonder if Cornwall and District is over-conscientious about reducing its carbon footprint. I leaf to a header sheet which notes dietary requirements for Type 2 Diabetes. The reason for admission is relegated to the lower portion of the page in a clumsy scrawl: 'suspected heart attack reported by male relative (son)'. I read and snap shots of the pages and flick through daily charts and observation stats.

Two minutes-thirty.

Another page contains a detailed a summary of treatment and a doctor's recommendation for rest and further tests. I consider this to be 'insurance' in the event of Mrs Beecham coming to grief. The next page contains a cardiologist's report and tentative details about scheduling a by-pass operation. Another page notes Dr Patel's observation and conclusion: *Saturday, 4 March. Two-fourteen am. Patient deceased. death a consequence of frailty of old age, compounded by recent stroke and advanced diabetes.*

That was it. Not even twenty words to describe a patient's final moments. To be fair, I've never seen a death notice, so the document well be of legitimate content.

I flick to the next page and read a sheet of dietary requirements. Everything seems normal for a woman who was diabetic, but what confounds me is the location of the page. I believe it should have been placed before the death notice, perhaps along with the admission documents. That means – using an educated assumption – that pages have been removed from the file and replaced incorrectly, or, perish the thought, the doctor had neglected to make file notes at the time of death and later inserted the diagnosis ad-hoc into the file.

Three-forty.

I flick and click, click and flick, ignoring pages of routine vitals, but paying meticulous attention to copying every page near the end of the file. I reckon I've done fifteen minutes' work in about five. I am thankful that Miss Muriel Hetherington might have found gossip company in the cafeteria: 'Yes, the office is fine. I left a cleaning lady there. She'll have flitted 'round with her duster until I was well gone, and now she'll be sitting down until she hears my returning footsteps, then spring up and make as if she's been working all the time.'

Yeah, right, Muriel. If only you knew. Five minutes twenty. She's on government timekeeping.

With a smile, I drop the file onto its tracks, slide the drawer to, turn the lock until it clicks and then wipe the drawer for good measure. I turn to return the keys. Miss Hetherington is standing at her desk watching me. I panic. *Shit.* What has she seen? My nerves bristle as the cabinet key burns into my hand as if the devil himself is branding me for my sins. Sins indeed. What I've done, but not yet completed, I have done in the name of justice, although my pursuit of justice has not exactly been executed in a legally acceptable manner.

'You nearly finished? I have to lock up shortly.'

'About five more minutes. Just got a couple of desk tops to do.' Quite truthfully, I have nothing to do other than replace her keys, a task I will not achieve with her beady eyes scanning my every move. I continue to wave the duster over the desks like a fairy brandishing a magic wand. I wish that I could cast a spell over Hetherington for just a few seconds while I tip the keys into her drawer. In lieu, I'd have to pull one of my diversionary tactics before being told to leave the office.

I dust the edge of battle-axe's desk. She admonishes me: 'No dear. No need to do mine.'

'Okay, fine. I'll just finish the top,' at which time I transfer all the strength of my left arm to the duster and sweep books and files from her desk to the floor. 'Oh, I'm so sorry. Let me pick them up.'

'You stupid oaf!' she yells, 'Just leave it. Go now.' She rises from her seat and walks around to the front of her desk, examining the scattered files and papers. I step aside, and in another Academy Award winning performance, re-enact the no-contact trip perfected by professional football players: I fake a stumble. While appearing to lose my balance, I reach for the side of the desk, lower one hand to the appropriate drawer handle, and pull the drawer from its tracks. The drawer crashes to the floor with me following. I release the bunch of keys so they, too, fall to the floor as I inwardly smile and outwardly grimace.

'I think you should leave. What's your name?'

'*My* name? You're asking *my* name after calling me a stupid oaf? I made a mistake, clumsy, I admit, but I apologised and offered to help and still you yell at me and insult me. I should be asking your name! But there's no need, Miss Hetherington – I see it on your desk. *My* name? I should be reporting you to the Director. Harassment, that's what they call it. But I reckon neither of us need take this any further, so perhaps I'll just bid you goodnight and leave.'

'Goodnight indeed. You'll not set foot in my office again. Get out before I change my mind and report you.'

I accept battle-axe's tirade and opprobrious attitude. I can't afford to push too far, lest security or management become involved. I've copied Joyce's file and am now anxious to print out the pages and sift through all the goodies. All Hetherington has to do is pick up a few files and return them to her desk. If the only thing on her mind is reporting me for clumsiness, I can be satisfied that she had not witnessed me replace the file and lock the drawer.

I collect my duster and bucket, walk to the toilets, slip off the uniform and fold it into a tight square, which I conceal under my floaty T-shirt. I depart via the main entrance, watching my upside-down reflection accompany me alongside the glass wall.

The evening dusk has settled. I reunite with Fiona in the now desolate car park and head home, congratulating myself on a productive hour's work.

I have conducted many raids and searches under authority of a Search Warrant and in company with other detectives and police members. In those situations, we had an edge and an advantage – often of surprise – when seeking evidence to support a case. Persons upon whom the warrants were executed, generally suspects, were passive and obedient to our commands. Locating the object of our search was frequently straightforward and without challenge – a total contrast to what I have just achieved. I reflect on the law that as a police member I'd once sworn to uphold. Tonight, I flouted those decrees as I skirted perilously close to prosecution.

20

Monday 13 March

Such is my euphoric state when I arrive home that I brush aside small stabs of guilt and replace them with a wish to vaunt my conquest to Alexander.

Women will agree that a hot bath filled with sweet scent and relaxing salts is our favoured means of celebration. Whether we've found new love or a job promotion, soaking ourselves in soft lather, laying back and inhaling perfumed mist as we float into another world, is apt reward.

Never will the male species understand. Rather than share our enjoyment, or even sample it, they choose to head straight for the pub and down a few pints. Such is the principal difference between us: we choose to release and accept emotion through our heart; men choose the anaesthetising effects of alcohol – or sex. I'm sure you've heard, or probably even experienced the phenomena: 'Hi honey. Got promoted today. How about a quickie to celebrate?' Or, 'Chelsea won by two goals. Let's have an early night!'

Of course we all know – well, us women do – that we're obliged to accede to their request, all in the interest of maintaining harmonic levels of tranquillity within the home. So we endure (well, that's how it is for me) the quickie or early night. They perform a couple of finger-flexing exercises – maybe an adagio of Beethoven's Fifth, in C Minor – progress to an allegro, and ultimately reach the crescendo within an eight-note bar, before collapsing into the orchestral pit. What are we left to applaud? Bloody nothing!

I've already bragged of my predilection to freely accept sex, but it must be on *my* terms. Of late, *my* terms have restricted me to er, my own means. Even now, reclined in the bath, I feel pangs of sexuality and yearnings scream at me to help release endorphins that have for so long been restrained. Yes, I am in a relaxed mood, and yes, I could easily transport myself to the dizzying heights of ecstasy. But no, not tonight. For the time being I am totally obsessed with Alexander's file; I've worked far more hours than I've billed him, yet I am still apprehensive about handing over the invoice. It's not as if I don't need the money – one thousand pounds will help me along quite nicely, thank you very much.

I momentarily drift beyond Alexander, his mother and sisters, Lord Bennington, Nora Geddes, and Dave Stafford. I fear the lack of enquiries into my agency might see me struggling in the next weeks. I have no *confirmed* work on the horizon. Such is the life of freelance agents; we live from week to week. I know my business model has potential, a potential that will be fully realised after this case generates national headlines, because from nothing I will have tied together three deaths which DCI Stafford will charge as three murders.

The time devoted to Alexander's file has allowed me very

few hours in which to canvass local business interest in debt recovery. In that limited time, I've placed advertisements in the *Newquay Voice* and introduced myself to solicitors who might require investigations into suspected spousal betrayal where affairs are as common as first dates – and some affairs *are* first dates – especially in coastal, holiday and recreational areas. I need an influx of enquiry that will enable me to invoice thirty hours' work per week.

The front door bell buzzes, or more precisely, rattles. I step from the bath and drape a beach towel around myself (because I haven't yet done the laundry) and jump into clean underwear and a sloppy tracksuit. In my haste, I stupidly pull on my knickers back to front giving me that awful splitting experience of an undersized G-string – not that I've ever worn such apparel, I'm just wild with imagination.

I scurry down the stairs as I prepare a speech to refuse cleaning products, donations, or the gospel of the good Lord, but instead am horrified to open the door to Meredith. Before I can offer a surprised 'Hello' she breaks into a rant which continues as a breathless oratory. She leaves no space for punctuation, nor for me to butt in to invite her inside. She is content to glue herself to the doorstep, armed to the teeth with a vocal arsenal: 'You bitch. You've got some fuckin' hide poking your nose around everywhere it's not wanted. What's your go, telling Roslyn that I knocked my mother-in-law and Mrs Geddes and my own mother? Is there anyone else I may have murdered? The Queen mother? Whitney Houston? Maybe you're sizing me up for the death of your own parents for they'd be better off dead than having to put up with the likes of you. And what do you know of my marriage twenty years ago, before you were even thought of? I was only nineteen when my husband's mother died – she was 92 goddamit. And you're saying that if I wasn't there she would still be living now, and poor Mrs Geddes, what would I possibly achieve by ridding the world of her, she was useless anyway, couldn't even dress herself, but I was there for her; that's my job, but you drop little hints to my sister like firecrackers that explode with the power of one kilogram sticks of gelignite because you conjoin my being Mrs Geddes' carer with culpability for my being criminally responsible for her death just like you think I should be for my mother's death—'

'Mere —'

'— she died peacefully, and not at my hands. You know she'd been ill for years? Had a stroke, and a fairly major one too, two years ago, but no, you wouldn't know about that, would you? So, what's your go? Get everyone in the family offside so you can plant the seed of inquisition in their mind until it germinates into a full-blown crime tree where every branch represents a person I've killed. And here's something that'll surprise you. I know you were sniffing around Nora's funeral – goodness knows what for. I saw you sussing out everyone and trying to eavesdrop and then trying to foolishly become inconspicuous by shielding beside a grave of someone I bet you didn't even know. How sacrilegious, or whatever. Tell me, what's your agenda?'

At this point Meredith has plainly exhausted herself; her breath depleted and her body's eight pints of blood pooling in her reddened cheeks.

'Meredith,' I console. 'Come inside and have a drink. I'll explain everything.'

Meredith takes my invitation by surprise, perhaps against expectations of opposition or violence.

We enter my office. Shame again sweeps over me because of my charity shop office. I nearly offer her my own chair as recompense, but stop short, fully intending to maintain authority and control.

'Not many clients of late?' she sneers.

'Just moved in, and I've been snowed under. Nothing for you to worry about. Look, you have to understand that I can't discuss certain matters with you – but I will be up front as far as I can.

'I know your brother from my work in the legal arena some months ago. I guess you're now aware that your brother engaged me to investigate your mother's death. Have you any idea why he'd do that?'

'No. But I'm sure you do.'

'All right. There's no way to say this nicely, but you know Alex won't accept that your mother died naturally. There might be other information that supports his view.' I'm playing this very low key.

'Yes, I know about the autopsy. All done behind our back, mind you.'

I try a different tack: 'Wouldn't you be interested to find out if someone had purposely done something to ensure your mother wouldn't survive?'

'It wouldn't have happened. She just wasn't strong enough to get over the stroke. I should know. I've been looking after her for ages. As to the medical conclusions, I leave that to the doctors.'

'And you haven't thought of confirming their conclusions?'

'Not interested. I did all I could for mum. If it's her time, it's her time. Anyway, isn't my dear brother doing all the fishing? He's certainly caused enough havoc within the family.'

I side-step Alexander's involvement in the coronial enquiry. 'All I can say at this time, Meredith, is that it has been determined that your mother did not die of natural causes. Whatever happened in the past with your mother-in-law, I am not privy to. However, in the face of current events you have attracted suspicion because of the nature of your relationship to the deceased. Likewise, with Mrs Geddes. My attendance at the funeral was not to spy or monitor your movements for I did not attend with any other motive than to monitor the Geddes' family dynamics. Hell, how could I even know *you'd* be there?'

Meredith looks with acknowledgement as if to accept that I couldn't have known.

I continue: 'Certain details of my investigation have been handed to the MET. If they choose to launch an official investigation, as I believe they will, then they'll be asking you far more penetrative questions than have I. In the meantime, I've actually completed my role and I will shortly be handing my invoice and final report to your brother.'

Meredith looks relieved, perhaps as glad to be rid of me as she would be wheeling out the week's rubbish. 'Well, good for you. Get your money and get out of our business and we'll all be happy.'

'If that's your view, I guess we've got nothing further to discuss. I'll show you out.'

Her visit confirms why she'd left messages. Hour by hour she'd been building rage. In the end, it was all too much. She couldn't wait for my return call. In retrospect, I would have preferred dealing with her over the phone, but all's done now. I close the door, relieved that my association with the Beechams is over, save for banking a cheque. I suffer an uneasy feeling because I can't see a tangible result like an arrest or a conviction. I feel as if I've left a relationship, or have been dropped with the clichéd excuse: 'Sorry honey, it's not working out. I suppose we're just not meant to be.' *Yeah, sure. That's a cop out.*

So I wonder whether there is more I can do for Alexander, maybe push his barrow stronger to DCI Stafford. But my confusion continues, because Stafford and being dumped are synonymous with each other. Like many girls, I've been dumped, forgotten, neglected, and deceived. For those who haven't experienced such an event – and there can't be many – well, you're yet to suffer the humiliation of arriving at your boyfriend's home, full of joy, lust, and expectation, only to find a competitor – a close friend maybe – has stolen your beau's attention and emotion.

I will have no problems forgetting Meredith. I rearrange the two plastic chairs. Beneath one, over which Meredith had draped her coat, I pick up a small locket. I admire its fine gold chain threaded through an embossed heart-shaped pendant. I open it to find a photo of Meredith, clearly some twenty-odd years ago, holding a baby of about five- or six-weeks-old.

I have no idea who the baby is, for none of the information provided by Hamilton has alluded to Meredith having borne a child. Being over inquisitive – one of the most exciting and rewarding facets of my being – I gently prise the photo from the locket and read a dedication on its reverse:

For Rachel. Love Mum.

Does Meredith have a daughter I don't know of? Was she at the family function but I hadn't known?

I reconstruct my conversations with Roslyn and Alexander. No mention had ever been made of a 'Rachel' or any siblings of Meredith or Roslyn. I flash back to Lord Bennington. He never mentioned a child. If I remember correctly, Meredith left the marriage after seven months and very soon after Victoria Bennington's death.

On that basis, I reconcile, Lord Bennington might not even have known his wife was with child. I jolt at the prospect of Rachel being illegitimate. It is feasible. Meredith might have enjoyed a celebratory fling after escaping the clutches of her master. I shouldn't involve myself with this. I've finished Alexander's file. This revelation, I believe, will contribute nothing further. But I am driven by the conundrum of why Meredith has possession of the locket when it should be with Rachel. I draw upon my favourite resource and phone Hamilton.

He agrees to check the Register of Births.

The downside of dealing with Hamilton is subjecting myself to his continued demands for an evening's entertainment. I appreciate the art of being wooed or of being wined and dined, often under the pretence of an aphrodisiac to a romantic interlude, or, put quite bluntly – a session between the sheets; on the couch; in the car on the way home – whatever and wherever.

That's *my* downside. Once my oestrogen levels and hormones party, I have no limits. Maybe that's why I turn people down, so as to not make a fool of myself. Now, as a professional self-employed, I simply can't risk my Worcester reputation migrating to Newquay.

Nonetheless, I *am* overdue for a night out. I begin to crave Hamilton's call. *Desperately.* This time I might not resist his advances. Reward for services rendered? Maybe – provided he fronts up with the goods on Rachel.

I phone Alexander to arrange another meeting, at the same time advising him that I've completed my charter. I don't mention the invoice. I'm not giving him time to conjure an excuse to delay payment. As if reading my mind, he nominates McDonald's as a neutral venue. I am puzzled that neither of our offices are appropriate – perhaps he's due for a shift of scenery. Suits me fine. I have nothing against convening at my favourite eatery.

I hurry down the street to one of the many former petrol station sites McDonald's has transformed into red and yellow restaurants. A compatible coupling in my mind: we still get the driveway service; we still get the oil. Alexander slides a tray in front of me, crammed with two of everything. So much for making up his own mind – yet another case of 'I'll have what she's having.' I chomp into a Quarter Pounder and tuck an A4 envelope under the tray. Unable to withhold his curiosity, he opens the unsealed envelope and studies my six-page report. The lines on his face dance, twist, warp and crinkle in surprise, dismay, wonder and uncertainty.

I am extremely verbose in my reports. I believe that if I'm going to invoice a client a couple of thousand pounds, I'd best be prepared to document every single thing I've done and embellish it in such a manner that the client believes they're receiving a bargain and that I'm cutting myself short.

How I love manipulating others' perceptions. Premium rates are my best friend; a client will always have more confidence in a person who *expects* to be well remunerated. Besides, I do not wish to be aligned with the many budget operators attracted to my industry.

As he flips the final page, his frown deepens: 'I think I'll give up law and become an investigator.'

I know what he's leading to. Anyone who challenges an invoice contests it with sarcasm or aggression. I can mix it with the best: 'Really? I'm thinking of putting on someone soon. Perhaps you could email me your CV?'

'Come on Olivia. This is a heavy serve for not even a couple of weeks' work.'

'Only a couple of hours for you though, if you don't mind me saying. I've dedicated more hours to this than I've charged. Some things can't be put on paper. There's also information that I've passed on to DCI Stafford which I've withheld because I obtained it by, um, questionable means. Alex, you know I've been active on this and brought the right conclusion – your mother's death *was* suspicious and it is now a police matter.

'Can you give me a bit of a lead as to what you've given the police?'

'Best that I don't. If the police communicate with you, it's best that any questions come as a surprise. Remember that you've got the pathologist's report. I've extracted sufficient detail from that for the police to further their own enquiries.'

'Not exactly. I don't have the full report. I'll be phoning Yui in an hour. Fair enough then. I'll have my secretary drop you a cheque within the next few days.'

'Thanks Alex. I hope everything works out for you. If I hear of anything interesting through the police, I'll pass on what I can.' I leave his office without my anticipated cheque.

I've been home for only three hours when Alexander phones. 'We've got it. We've got it. Someone dosed up mum on insulin. Yui says there's synthetic insulin in the brain tissue and concerning levels in other organs. So now we know.'

I do not share his enthusiasm. 'That's good to know, but we've got nothing until we know why the levels are so high. Could your mum have made a mistake with her dose? Could a nurse have administered too much? Or might there a case of pre-meditated tampering by someone? There's a million explanations and not all of them are criminal.'

'Come on, Olivia. We've got a starting point. You've seen the hospital charts. They show whether or not there was a dosage error. All we have to do is dig deeper. Remember mum's words, "Help me"? There's something in that, and I think that mum knew what had happened – she just couldn't, or wouldn't spit it out, perhaps out of fear of her assailant being in the ward.

'Yui said it's synthetic insulin, not bodily manufactured. She explained that a diabetic injects subcutaneously, which means it's discharged beneath the skin. To account for the levels found in the sample tissues, it had to have been injected into the circulatory system. No doctor or nurse would make that sort of error. Surely?'

I stall. 'This is beyond me. You need a proper scientific analysis. Perhaps Dr Yui can refer you.'

She's already told me, but I don't understand the tech' speak; something about the molecular structure differing between natural and synthetic insulin; there's two types: fast acting and slow acting; different rates of absorption; she spoke of assimilation and metabolisation. Buggered if I know. But what I do not know is that someone put the stuff in her – and I'll find out who.'

'I'm sure you will, Alex. Do you mind if I pass this on to DCI Stafford? It'll hasten an investigation.'

'Yes, go ahead. And we got the release for mum's funeral. The service will be at two o'clock on Thursday.'

'Good Alex. Might be good for your sisters too; settle things down a bit.'

'Don't know about that. I'm worried there could be a scene at the cemetery. That's the last thing I want for mum.'

I agree. I don't know what to say, especially considering Meredith's animosity against Alexander. 'Would it help if I came with you? I don't mean as peacemaker; just to help quell any ungracious exhibitionism that I know one person is particularly capable of.' I think of Meredith's earlier ceremonial antics and her remonstration on my doorstep, and in so doing conclude that I will be far from welcome.

'Sure Olivia, good idea. There's one other thing. I think my father should attend. You were right about us putting things behind us under certain circumstances. He probably wouldn't have a clue what's happened. Might not even care, but we should at least let him know. Thing is, I don't know where he is. I've no way of contacting him.'

'Say no more. I've got connections who can find Santa Claus and the Easter Bunny.'

With my communication bent in full swing, I phone Stafford and advise him that I've prepared documents essential for his enquiry. He fobs me off. I must have caught him at a bad time. I can't determine whether he is in one of his moods, or whether he has no interest in the proposition I put to him. Had I been alerted to his indifference, I would have waited until I'd heard from Hamilton, who I hope will provide further information I can annexe to the hospital records.

I react to Stafford's abruptness by bundling together the documents and dispatching them by courier to his attention at the MET's London headquarters. By off-loading the case material, I reinforce my position as an ex-member of the constabulary.

21

Monday 13 March

For the second consecutive night, I open my door to an unexpected knock. 'Hi Olivia. Just passing. Had a feeling you would not be able to resist *this!*'

Among the things that annoy me about Hamilton Holt is his propensity of phoning or dropping in at the most inappropriate time. 'It better be good, Hamilton. You could have phoned first. And don't give me that "just passing by crap". You live 90 minutes' away.'

His face stretches to a cheeky grin: 'Yes, but I was taking the long way.'

'All right. What's so important?' I sound disinterested. Probably look it too. He could have been the CEO of Lotto delivering good news that I'd won three million pounds, but I'd still be the same nonchalant, inert specimen of womankind. All I want to do is wind down.

Hamilton looks at me, surprised to witness a glum resonance seeping from my usual effervescent dial. I study his geeky presence, overly evident by his failed attempt at dressing to impress. With a magician's precision, he conjures a file from his jacket sleeve. 'I-n-t-r-o-d-u-c-i-n-g, da-dah — Rachel Jae Bennington. Born October 2, 1980, to… guess who? Meredith Bennington. No father's name recorded, so I'd say the good Lord Robert wanted no part of the child.'

'Hang on a moment. Not so quick. That's the problem with you guys – you jump to conclusions without surveying the wider picture. This is women's stuff you know, things you'll never understand.'

'I can read you like a book, Olivia, and I'd love to open your jacket later on; perhaps you'd let me read your inside sleeve or run my fingers along the curve of your spine?'

'You'll never be so lucky. You'd reach 'The End' before you even started. Listen. Be serious for a moment. We know Meredith married Lord Robert on March 10, 1979, and we know she left the manor within weeks of Victoria Bennington dying—'

Hamilton interjects: 'Okay, okay. Cut the drama. I gave you that info. Remember?'

'Yeah, of course I do. It's a shame you haven't done enough with it. What I am getting to is that if Rachel was – and I suppose that's gospel – born on October 2, then that is ten months *after* Meredith left the manor. On that basis, we can't be satisfied that Rachel is the daughter of Lord Robert. Heck, we don't know if he even knows about her. He certainly never mentioned her to me.'

'But Olivia. There's more.'

Here we go. Hamilton and his salesman's pitch. Here comes the bribe. True to form, he continues:

'What say we go get a bite to eat at a little restaurant, and I'll reveal all. It'll be worth your while!'

'Worth my while? Why can't you just tell me what you've got without all the charades and innuendo? I can just as easily find another source. You're not the only person I know who can infiltrate secure systems and purge information.'

'Maybe so, sweet Olivia. But I'm the only one who delivers.'

Smug. Full of himself. I'm growing tired of his games, but he possesses an irresistible air of mystique and tease – an air that spurs me into submission. 'All right, Hamilton. I give up. We'll go and eat – I'm hungry enough (everyone knows that you're hungry within an hour of eating McDonald's) – and then you can reveal all. And it better be good! But that's where it stops. No dessert. No coming back for coffee. And just to deflate your overdeveloped ego, you'd never be up to handling me.'

'You say the nicest things, Olivia. It'd be fun trying though.'

We leave my apartment, me surly, Hamilton concealing a sly look of expectation, and head for the High Street where we find an Indian restaurant, ingeniously named 'The Curry House'.

Inside the door stand two six-foot carved elephants whose shiny tusks support a cane basket of menus. Very tacky. In a corner of the lounge an elderly couple crunch pappadams. A turban-headed waiter escorts us past vacant tables. During my short time in Newquay, I have not dined in this restaurant so I do not know whether the food is questionable, or whether we have chanced upon a night of sparse bookings. Then again, there are another four local restaurants specialising in Indian cuisine; three Chinese takeaways share a good income, and the mandatory fish and chip shops pick up the few pounds that would never find their way to a 'non-British' food vendor.

Hamilton pulls out a chair, its screech complementing the whining sitar drifting across the room. 'My treat,' says Hamilton as he selects Curried Lamb from the menu. 'And two Gin and Tonics, no ice.'

'How'd you know?'

'What?'

'Gin and Tonic?'

'Research, dear Olivia.'

'Better watch myself then.'

'Okay, Olivia. Here's a teaser before we eat.'

Hamilton removes a photo of a woman who looks to be about 30 years of age. Her dark brown hair is pulled back into a ponytail and secured by a sparkling diamante clip, huge brown eyes reflect shimmering light, and a fine nose contrasts rich, full lips which smile enticingly from the photo.

'Your girlfriend?'

'No. Better. Rachel Jae Bennington.'

'How the heck, Hamilton?'

'That's why you won't discard me Olivia. I deliver.'

'And that's just a taste, you say?'

'Yes. Let's eat.'

I probe the bleached lamb, which rises from a crater of rice. A creamy, yellow curry circles the chunk like a moat around a castle. On my own I would not have experienced this. I wouldn't grace an Indian restaurant; I'm more of a Thai girl – hot and spicy. I scoff my meal to rush Hamilton into divulging his revelations. He's unwrapped the present but delayed opening the box. I feel like a child deprived of a birthday gift. 'Come on, Hamilton. What else?'

'Let's trade, Olivia. Coffee at your place?'

My serene mood shifts to rage. *Why must he be so importunate?* 'Hamilton! What sort of a trade is that? Nothing you could offer would even get me boilin' the friggin' kettle.'

'Oh Olivia. You have no idea of the power and resources of the big 'double H'. But you do know I'm a gentleman at heart and that I'd never hold you to anything. I truly enjoy our working relationship and would never do *anything* to jeopardise it…'

His words evaporate into the piquant air and drift away with the resonance of the twanging sitar. I recognise his exploiting the male sympathy-seeking strategy. It softens me a little, because I know, deep down, that Hamilton is a professional, although, despite his capriciousness, he still tries it on when opportunities emerge. In the 'sympathy-seeking' stakes he doesn't cut it. And never will, because we women have perfected the mind-leveraging tool.

'… so, Olivia, here is the piece-de-resistance. I know where Rachel is – and I've spoken with her.'

'You? You took that photo?'

'Nah. That's too easy for me. I lifted it from DVLA's licence database. That's all you need to know, except that it's a recent photo – less than 12 months since renewal. So what's your angle? You told me you've finished with that Alexander guy; is this a new file you've generated in the quiet haven of Newquay?'

'I wish you'd generate your serviette; there's curry dribbling down your chin. Yes. I had finished with him, but after his sister paid me a surprise visit – that's the Meredith Bennington/Beecham connection – a new slant surfaced. She bloody exploded over *my* conduct and the fact that I'd cast a cloud over her. After she left, I picked up a locket she'd dropped on the floor. Inside was a tiny photo of a girl, together with the inscription: *For Rachel. Love mum.*

'Now, I'm obviously thinking that Meredith has a daughter, which you've now proved correct – and isn't Rachel a spitting image of her mum – and I'm left wondering why Meredith has the locket and not her daughter.'

My train of thought suggests Rachel might have handed it back in disgust, sort of like John Lennon returning his MBE. Alternatively, she might have mistakenly left it at her mother's. If that were the case, though, why have we not heard of Rachel?

Hamilton weighs in: 'If you think it'll help, despite the coincidence, I doubt her presence is related to her grandmother's death, for what motive could she have? I'll dig some more. Speaking of digging, remember those two Northampton deaths I mentioned? Turns out all was legit. Nothing to do with Meredith. Coincidence all the same; the cause was Legionnaires' – some crap in the air-con' plant infected two wards. Just a shame it got the elderly patients whose lower threshold of resistance gave them no chance at all.'

'Okay. Thanks for that. What we need now is if you can get something on Rach's schooling. That will give us a bit of an indication as to where she spent her childhood, and maybe your Inland Revenue contact or whoever can help with information that will shed light on her places of employment. Tax returns are a great source of info.' I look at Hamilton and take the plunge. 'I guess I will invite you back. I've got some photos you can look over. And yes, I'll make coffee.'

'Thanks Olivia. I knew there'd come the day you couldn't resist wanting me. You just won't admit that I grow on you.'

'Like a wart,' I snap.

Hamilton, true to his word, pays the bill, unlike a previous occasion where he'd 'conveniently' forgotten the jacket in which he kept his wallet. That time, I realised it was better for me to pay than ask him to pick up his jacket. Its gaudy turquoise velour with burgundy satin trim would have made me regurgitate every morsel of food I'd eaten.

We wobble back to my flat, stopping at a convenience store so Hamilton can buy mints to tame the curry clinging to his throat. I know the form. The celebrated grammatical equation: mints equals fresh breath equals kissing equals sex. I glance at women's magazines while he circumnavigates the store collecting enough snacks to last the whole weekend. On the counter sit Malteesers, Cheezels, a six-pack of low-fat yoghurt and a two-litre carton of full-cream milk. I don't query his shopping criteria, but still, there'll be no excuse for me to cancel coffee now.

Surprisingly, I find that I don't really want to. After living in the desert wilderness where no male company wanders – other than clients and work colleagues – I yearn for the approaching spring of my body, urging it to blossom and cohabit with nature's freshly dropped seedlings and new-born life that manifests joyous rewards of procreation. Perhaps my body-clock aligns with the emerging lunar phase because something within me churns. I haven't consumed alcohol, so I struggle to accept the miracle: I find Hamilton Holt attractive.

I open my laptop and click on the yellow folder of Meredith's charts and reports I'd copied from the hospital.

'Here. Look at these while I make coffee.' I point to my chair and say, almost instructively, 'Sit there.'

His eyes goggle: 'How the hell d'you come by this stuff?'

'Can't say. But you're not on your own for resorting to questionable practices.'

Hamilton voices bewilderment. 'You realise this is powerful stuff?'

'Of course,' I yell from the kitchen. 'I've couriered copies to Stafford.' I return with two coffees, sit them on the small table, lift my computer from Hamilton's lap and replace it with myself. 'Thanks,' I say, draping my arms around his neck and pecking him lightly on his cheek.

'For what do I owe this?' he asks.

'No questions. No answers.' I snuggle in to him, resting my head on his shoulder. He winds my hair around his fingers. I've not enjoyed the sensation for many months. Every follicle conducts electricity through my scalp until I believe my whole head is illuminated with white heat. He clasps my face and traces my lips with a finger; just soft enough to send a shudder through my body and energise the field of receptors wavering in rapture and anticipation.

By the time he kisses my lips I am delirious. And no wonder. It has been months since my interlude with Stafford and a week since my ill-fated let down by Alexander when I realised I would have more fun with a fibreglass simile of Ronald McDonald.

He leans over and traces his tongue across my lips, leaving an aroma of pepperminted curry, which, I must say, spoils the semi-romantic moment. But it doesn't stop me parting my lips to receive him. And then, like a snake striking its prey, he darts his tongue into my mouth. I pull back in surprise as he grips me with such force that I feel as if I'm being restrained by a nightclub bouncer. My excitement elevates. *So I'm a masochist?*

I have the enviable pleasure of having been wooed by soft, gentle romance, all the way through to world record quickies. Never have I experienced such animalistic urgency. No one has forecast the world ending today. I hug him with equal intensity before thrusting my hands under his shirt and caressing his chest. I could have just as easily grabbed a couple of racks of lamb. *They* would have been blessed with more flesh, for Hamilton is no more than an animated version of a clothed skeleton. But he is a man.

He recognises the deal is on, which perhaps proves that males are perceptive only when motivated by sex. He unbuttons my shirt and watches it drop from my shoulders, trapping my arms securely between himself and the chair. He leaves my mouth and commences an excursion to my neck, depositing slow, moist kisses. He slides lower and lower until he rests in the valley of my breasts. I ache for him to remove my bra and tantalise me to the lofty heights of ecstasy. He fixes on my breast, kissing and caressing.

I cannot deal with indecision or slow sex; perhaps more to the point I can't accept the anticipation of the moment. I have no patience, sort of when I'm hot, I'm hot – let's go. It then strikes me that as Hamilton's such a geek, he's maybe one of those who's fancy with words but useless in practice. With my hands still wedged by side, I manage to flex enough to undo my bra. I'm not even wearing a good one. Sort of spoils the moment. The plain, ordinary, three-for-two-pounds falls from my breasts like a pillow slip falling from a clothes line. I drop my eyes to contrasting white flesh and anxious nipples.

That is invitation enough to Hamilton. He does not disappoint as he gently kisses a route across my breasts, tongue darting over my excited buds like bursting clouds breaking over anthills. My heart races, pumping endorphins through my body, directly to my core which by now is a moist marsh waiting to trap anyone or anything into its deepness and lose them forever.

I care nothing for Hamilton's ectomorphic frame. With or without clothes he has no appeal, and there is naught within his persona that incites any manner of desire from me, or quite possibly, from any woman. I'm embarrassed to say I imagine being with my old flame Dave Stafford, not so much as a fantasy, but just enough to dull the numbness of being seduced by the most asexual being on earth.

Rejection is not in my make-up; I let Hamilton have his way, fondling and fumbling every inch of my eager flesh. So impatient have I become with his ineptitude as a lover I take the initiative.

'Now, Hamilton. Now.'

I flip open the buttons of his brown herringbone trousers and suppress a laugh when I see the same baggy white underpants I'd seen years ago in my father's dressing table drawer. I had no idea that the giant bloomers with thick waist band are still manufactured. 'Y' fronts, they call them, and that is fortunate because I do not want to waste time by removing them.

I ease out of my track-suit pants, simultaneously slipping off my knickers, reach over and guide him into me. *Goodness*, I gasp. For someone with such a sinewy, bony body, his equipment is disproportionately enhanced. Hamilton joins me, our heaving lungs matching each breath. I huff, 'Slower, slower,' to which he appears to not know the meaning because he maintains a rhythmic pace with precision of a Middle East oil derrick. I wonder if he is in pain when a grimace knits his eyebrows together and his mouth stretches into his cheeks before he expels every ounce of air from his lungs. Then he collapses on top of me. *Not now Hamilton. Please, not now.* My wish is denied. He is spent. I continue to drift in soft clouds, oblivious to all save for a 62-kilogram geek laying astride me, satisfaction etched upon his face, while disappointment and frustration falls over mine.

'That shouldn't have happened, Olivia.'

I glare at him. 'It didn't Hamilton. It didn't.'

I'm not new to succumbing to libidinal yearnings that override my rational and sensible self. I suppose that I am one of many who do things we wouldn't ordinarily consider, only to later writhe in guilt.

And so it is for Hamilton and me. As we dress in silence, Hamilton pulls a slip of paper from his pocket. 'Nearly forgot. George Beecham.'

'Thanks. I note the details and offer more coffee.

He declines.

I squeeze out a little fist-pump.

'Think I'll take these photos and see if I can make anything of them. I'll do those other checks on Rachel, too, and give you a call as soon as I have something.'

There is little else to say. I've done it again; made a fool of myself at the expense of a near colleague. 'Thanks Hamilton. I'll hear from you soon.'

I see Hamilton out, walk into my room, flop onto my bed, and think about a pleasurable way of extricating myself from the cloud of desire upon which I linger.

22

Tuesday 14 March

The sun shoots its first rays into my room, inspiring me to bring a positive outlook to the new day. Over my brief period of self-employment, I have used Tuesdays to promote my agency to local businesses and council-backed agencies. As my feet touch the floor, the name Rachel Bennington rushes to my head. I've previously mentioned my distaste for loose ends because they leave me tense and edgy until resolved. Today, I suspend my marketing plan in favour of trekking back to Wiltshire Manor and confronting, or more correctly, asking, Lord Bennington about his daughter – assuming he has knowledge of her existence.

Perhaps I am acting a tad premature because I really know nothing of Rachel apart from her age, appearance, and address. In less urgent circumstances, I would tail her for a few days, noting contacts and eavesdropping on conversations, thereby arming me with sufficient knowledge of her lifestyle.

I arrive at the Shropshire gates at 9.40 a.m. Maids are probably tidying breakfast settings, floating sheets onto beds, slicing lunchtime vegetables and ensuring their master's study or reading room is sufficiently comfortable to detain him for the morning. They'll be far too busy to expect attendance from a pertinacious investigator.

Maybe not, because again someone activates the gates upon my presence. I ease along the rustling gravel with the nerves of an Avon lady about to tender her maiden presentation. I shiver with the thought of questioning Lord Bennington about his marital wonts of thirty-plus years ago.

Marianne Troquét graces the huge door. 'Good morning Miss Watts. This is an unexpected surprise.'

I agree, and offer my profuse apologies. 'I need to see Lord Bennington. I assure you I would not attend unannounced at such an hour if it were not a matter of great importance. Might you be kind enough to announce my appearance?'

My ability to embrace an entirely different persona astounds me. I keep a spare plum in my handbag for occasions such as this, and frequently review Emily Post's 1922 *Etiquette in Society, in Business, in Politics, and at Home.*

Marianne click-clacks across the floor, leading me to Lord Bennington's study where he sits behind a collection of early edition newspapers.

'Miss Watts. I'm delighted to see you again. And surprised. To what do I owe the pleasure?'

Unsure whether he is sarcastically trying to disarm me, I adopt a solemn look: 'Might not be too much pleasure about it my Lord.' I turn my head to satisfy myself that Marianne has left the room. 'I wish to speak to you about your marriage, if I may.'

'My marriage, Miss Watts?' He studies me with reserved countenance. 'Such is a farce. It is living history. I had a marriage over the course of a few months to a young girl who did not know her heart from her mouth. It was my dear mother, God bless her departed soul, who contrived the whole performance. And that's all it was. A command performance in the gardens in which she sought to recreate the glory and pageantry of her own wedding.

'Meredith was merely a glorified maid. To be honest, she came into our home after manipulating a role as a live-in carer. She had no real qualifications, as I recall, although she may have completed, or near completed, an introductory nursing course. Certainly, she had ideals of pursuing that as a career.

'I discounted her straight away. One can't have a young, inexperienced teenager attending to the daily needs of a ninety-something-year-old, as mum was at the time. Girls then, and probably now, are more interested in going to parties, clubs or discos; they'll get a boyfriend and be off – or rob the place blind – and generally, from my observations around town, be slovenly and lazy.'

The good lord is certainly au fait with today's youth. However, I take his description of Meredith with a grain of salt. He is the jilted husband. Of course he'll not have a good word to say about her.

He continues: 'I had no say in the matter. Never did with my mother, God bless her departed soul. My mother was like a crossed cheque: not negotiable. It was she who decided who we should employ, not only as carer, but maids, gardeners and even my driver.

'Fair enough I thought; the successful applicant would be spending numerous hours with mum. She'd rejected about fourteen ideal, qualified young women – not girls – I mean women aged 25 to 40. Also had a couple of male nurses. Well, we couldn't have that type in here, could we? Male nurses indeed—'

Bennington draws a breath; his silk smoking jacket inflating like a huge black balloon. I assume he isn't forward thinking because I know the contribution male nurses make to our ailing health system. His gasp for air allows me to interject: 'So a relationship started as a result of Meredith working for your mother?'

Lord Bennington laughs jovially. 'Relationship? There was no relationship. One might be more accurate by describing it as an association. Look, I don't know what you're here for, although I'm sure we'll touch on that directly – but the marriage was one big charade for mother. It was what *she* wanted. Sure, Meredith and I tried to make it work, but never was it destined to be. Different ages, different interests, different eras.

'Mother knew that, and that's why she framed her will to penalise me should I divorce Meredith. In mum's time people rarely separated, so I suppose she devised a contingency to protect Meredith in the event of the marriage not surviving.

'However, I supported, or rather didn't object to Meredith's leaving, and provided for her, and still do mind you, with a substantial monthly allowance credited to her account. Gosh, how remiss of me. Tea Miss Watts?'

I accept. Lord Bennington has no problem divulging anything once he is warmed up. I want to keep him on the boil.

Marianne appears with tea and scones. She must be possessed of extra-sensory perception because I'm sure Bennington did not summon her or buzz the hidden button which so determinedly ended my previous visit.

I continue: 'Lord Bennington. Were there any children of your marriage to Meredith?'

'Oh goodness no. There was hardly the opportunity if you understand my meaning. After mum went, Meredith and I maintained separate quarters, separate rooms if you prefer. Meredith was a sybarite. I don't mean to sound crass; there were some, shall we say, amorous occasions, but I suspect Meredith was more interested in trying to appease herself rather than to foster any romantic cohesion with me. Tell me. Why do you ask?'

'Meredith has a daughter, Rachel, born on the second of October, nineteen-eighty, which, by my calculations, is touch and go as to whether she conceived before leaving you.'

Bennington appears genuinely shocked: 'Well, that's news to me. How do you know of this?'

'It turned up during a document search.' I choose to not reveal further because I foresee Bennington clamming up as he did during my earlier visit. Now that he is implicated as a possible father, I feel he is both surprised and interested, despite his dumbfounded persona. 'I must add that there is no father listed on the Birth Certificate. Whether that was Meredith's wish to conceal paternity, I do not know. Another possibility to consider would be that she might not have known who the father was, if, how do I put this? – if she became rather liberal after leaving the marriage.'

'I must say that is the most preposterous scenario one could contrive. I can't see Meredith being promiscuous, but having said that, I couldn't have foreseen that she'd leave the marriage – love or no love. Everything she could ever want was, and is, here for her pickings.'

The thought speared through my mind of having maids attend to every need: preparing meals, doing laundry and ironing, running to shops and markets, and caring for children when nannies were otherwise indisposed. *What value is a life of no responsibilities, save for token appearances at charity concerts and social events?*

'But she's got everything at her fingertips now, hasn't she? You've told me about her allowance; I can't imagine that being frugal.' I supposed that was the mysterious £1866.70 Hamilton had identified on one of Meredith's statements.

'Ah yes. Maybe so. But I am sure if Meredith was pregnant with my child she would not have concealed it. For what purpose? If she had ever been avaricious or a "gold digger" as you young people call it, what better way of securing a prosperous future than to announce that you are carrying a child who would inherit an earldom? No Miss Watts, it could not be my child.'

I accept the meritful point without verbal admission.

I depart the manor wondering how my life would have evolved had I been 'well born' instead of ignoble. I think about infancy and how a child identifies with its mother when a nanny attends to every whim and demand. School years arrive and the best part of seven years are spent in boarding schools, returning home only for vacations where parents endow us with gifts: horses, bicycles, computers, Play Stations, iPods, the most glamorous dolls, all manner of board games – but only those that would complement our education: Scrabble, Pictionary, Monopoly (to arouse the entrepreneur within us) and a platinum chess set so we can impress the social circle. Equally impressive would be our musical ability after the mandatory piano or violin lessons, because one must learn classical discipline. Later, if we are fortunate, we might be permitted to play guitar or banjo for our own enjoyment rather than for others'.

There would have been the spring balls and fetes in huge marquees, attendances at the theatre and opera – we'd hate it, but one must be seen at all cultural events – and perhaps a stroll around literary festivals admiring the works of authors we had not even read or heard of.

Rachel Jae Bennington might have been entitled to all that. And still might be.

So ablaze is my interest in this obscure child – despite her being none of my business – I ache to find out more. I'd burnt my bridges with her mother. Now I must rely on my own devices and those of Hamilton Holt. He will always produce something I can use as an appetiser. The main course will be up to me. I just hope *he* will never be investigated for *his* activities.

Due to the after-effects of our recent encounter, he's elected to not phone or drop in. Instead, I receive a card, bearing his name as sender, requesting my attendance at the local post office to collect a parcel of documents.

I scurry to pick up the prize and then squat in a bus stop where I rip open the package. Inside are Southampton Primary School records of Rachel's attendance as a five-year-old; registration papers of a local netball club when she was twelve, and Southampton College enrolment forms together with three years' exam results. Flipping through the pages, I learn Rachel had joined the Southern College of the Arts, she now works as a freelance graphic designer with a women's magazine, and supplements her income with weekend stints at Covent Gardens sketching charcoal portraits. How he found out the latter, I have no idea, and, of course, I know not to ask.

The bonus for me is an Adoption Certificate which states the date of Rachel's adoption – November 16, 1980 – only six weeks after her birth. Rachel, like me, would never know her real mother and father, unless she too had received a teenage birthday revelation. And what if she had? I cannot then, discount the possibility that she knows her birth mother, Meredith Bennington. The natural progression leads me to a bit of straw-clutching. Does she also know her grandmother, Joyce Beecham?

Coincidence floods my mind. I have to release the build-up of flotsam, jetsam and every incidental detail floating within me. Although I've earlier professed that if something is obvious, it must be true, I can't fathom why I have an eerie suspicion that something is not right – and Rachel Bennington stands slap bang in the middle of it. Now, less than 48 hours after handing Alexander my final report, I have more confusing tangles than I'd acquired throughout the whole investigation. There are the doctor's charts I sent to Stafford, which on their own probably mean little, but when matching their detail with the autopsy results, questions must be asked. I still await definitive answers for moneys deposited into Meredith's accounts, although that is not necessarily within my sphere of enquiry, and now there is the sudden appearance of Rachel, who could be the hinge-pin of the whole enquiry, or just another child lost to the wilderness of fragmented families.

23

Wednesday 15 March

Armed with Hamilton's research notes, I set off to the Southampton address recorded on Rachel's Drivers' Licence. I park outside a ramshackle 1950s council-owned high-rise and consider hiring a bodyguard before entering. In the car park rests a colony of MOT failures, two of which sit on bricks, blocks of wood and spare wheels. Black garbage bags decorate the crumbled asphalt's perimeter, and a concrete wall, delightfully daubed with graffiti, transforms the gloomy estate to an arts academy canvas.

The door to Flat 574, once gloss burgundy, is now cracked and blistered like the dome of the Sistine Chapel prior to restoration. The view would bring envy to owners of adjacent £1.5 million penthouses. The distant sea sparkles like de Beers diamonds, while harbour activity bustles with life I can only imagine during a Sunday afternoon on the Thames.

I rap the door. A silhouette slides by the twelve-inch square pane of smoked glass.

'Who is it?'

I introduce myself and skim a business card under the door. 'I'm looking for Rachel Bennington. Is that you?'

'Might be. What do you want?'

One of the early criminal traits I learnt is that where a person admits something 'might' be, that something or someone generally is. I once attended a drug raid with my first boss, Inspector Stafford (as he then was) when he located, in the toilet cistern of all places, two small bags of white powder. The cistern was to become one of the most popular places to stash contraband, although occupants thought themselves wise enough to always be one step ahead of the law. 'What's this?' Stafford asked when pointing out his find to the property owner.

'Dunno. Never seen it before in my life,' – the standard answer given to every police officer questioning the ownership of stolen or unlawfully possessed property.

'Come on,' Stafford continued. 'You're not preserving talcum powder in the bog. Let's have it. Cocaine? Heroin? It is drugs, isn't it?'

'It *might* be.'

Of course it might be, I thought at the time. That's the owner's way of trying to dilute responsibility. It's not a categorical admission, it's a helpful answer, so that if the seized property returns a positive certification, they will expect a deal from the prosecution because they didn't fully deny the haul's existence.

So when the voice behind the burgundy door replied, 'It might be', I knew I was speaking to Rachel.

'I'm a private detective doing a family trace and I'm hoping you'll spare a few minutes to help me.'

This is one facet of private investigating I *really* do enjoy. The ability to improvise and think on the spot. I couldn't just blurt: 'I just want to check if you're the daughter of a woman I suspect of murdering three people.'

I hope she knows she is adopted. She will then be receptive to my enquiry and perhaps help satisfy some of her own questions. To justify my actions, I instantly appoint myself advisor to Lord Bennington because he would certainly want to know if Rachel was *his* daughter.

The door unlocks, security chains rattle clear and I glimpse the world of Rachel Bennington. She urges me into the kitchen. The last time I'd witnessed such a site was the kitchen of a long-past boyfriend who'd put on a pie night in his flat. Rachel's home exemplifies the same aversion to cleaning and neatness. The table and bench tops are haphazard; breakfast dishes remain from at least three breakfasts, a cereal packet lies on its side, and an ashtray, dotted with cork-tipped and menthol filters, overflows. A pile of unopened window envelopes (presumably bills) balance on a stack of local newspapers, and shopping catalogues – colloquially known a 'junk mail' – rise from the remaining dining space. At the far end of the kitchen table an artists' palette, blotched with a Pantone chart of colours, rests atop a bundle of fresh canvas.

The once white ceiling is bronzed by plumes of cigarette smoke, and a fluorescent strip light welcomes insects to its molasses-trimmed plastic cover. The floor is a dated chequerboard black and cream vinyl tile, straight out of the 1970s. I spot a few tiles arching from their corners like a court jester's pointed boots.

I sweep my stunned gaze around the room, catching a grimy kitchen window. The ten-second appraisal stalls my announcement: 'Thank you Rachel. I'm pleased to meet you.'

'I'm sorry I haven't tidied yet. I wasn't expecting anyone.'

You can say that again. 'I apologise for intruding. I believe this is important to us both.'

Rachel looks like her home: solid structure, ravaged through the passing of time, and superficially messy. Her complexion is a mottled tan, perhaps the result of rushed make-up or a failed attempt to mask permanent signs of teenage acne. Her long hair falls in thick, brown tresses. It needs brushing and cutting. Her nails are bitten to the quick, either through nervous habit or rebelliousness against feminine beauty. (I always check a woman's nails. If a meeting or interview turns sour, fingernails become a woman's instant weapon.)

She presents somewhat 'tomboyish', but I pay little regard to first impressions. Her faded and slashed blue denims are two sizes too big – I try to weigh whether she's borrowed them or lost a lot of weight – contrast the glittering rainbow top which clings to her shapeless frame.

Her voice is mellifluous; notes, clefs and key signatures quaver from her lips: 'Come into the lounge room. It's far more comfortable.'

I do not hesitate – until confronted by a carbon copy of the kitchen. As far as I can tell, two weeks' laundry hunkers on a couch dressed with a striped double bed sheet. Rachel clears a space for us both.

Two easels, framed with canvasses of modern art in geometric prints, splashes and sponging prop beside the television. 'I like your work,' I lie.

'Thank you. I'm putting together an exhibition soon. You'll have to come.'

I see myself walking through a local village hall, catalogue in one hand, glass of wine in the other, trying to feign appreciation of art. Never could I understand what people see in a white circle painted in a black triangle, but what the heck? – to each their own. Draw or paint it? No thanks. I'm a word person; I can describe anything in words. I was once scolded by my admin' sergeant for stringing out crime reports. 'We don't need to know about this Stratocumulus or Cumulonimbus shit,' he chastised.

'But sir, the report requests: "Note the weather conditions".'

'Clouds, Watts. Just write fucking clouds.'

In my true manner of retribution, I rewrote my report. In the space requiring weather conditions, I inserted 'Fucking Clouds'. For that, I earned two weeks' penance on the front desk.

After bombarding Rachel with preliminaries of 'How long have you been painting?; Do you have work placed in shops or galleries?'; and 'Are the rewards worthwhile?', Rachel displays a confidence I did not expect in a person of questionable domestic habits.

'Artists do not expect great financial reward. Acceptance and appreciation of our craft is, like, reward enough.'

Very profound. It mirrors the sixties cop-out when hippies and flower children professed to 'live on love' although most had no reservations about claiming their fortnightly welfare cheque in lieu of 80 hours' work.

'Rachel.' I hesitate for a moment, wondering how to pursue this without lying. 'I've recently spoken with a Lord Robert Bennington of Wiltshire Manor in Shropshire. Does the name ring a bell?'

'No. Why should it?'

'I'm engaged in a paternity enquiry. How well do you know your family history?'

'I know a little. I know I was abandoned by my parents when I was like, little; don't know if it was only mum, or both, but my mum, well, the woman I know as mum, had one of those mother/daughter talks with me when I reached thirteen – it may have been my birthday, when mum said to me: "Rachel, now you're approaching adulthood, we should have an adult talk". An "adult talk"? I questioned. Like I was barely through playing with Barbies; I was trying to deal with the first pangs of monthly stomach cramps and then mum wants to put the big one on me.

'But there was no mention of that stuff. Mum had always been kind and gentle. I remember her soothing voice: "Sit down, Rachel. This is going to have a major impact on your life." I sat and listened for nearly two hours as mum cried her way through history.

'I'd been put up for adoption by my birth mother, so I was told, because she was unable to care for me. There was no other reason or information available to my mum, my stepmum I mean, because authorities closed their books and their mouths to such helpful information; like something to do with privacy laws. My step-parents are Tomasini in Southampton. They're of Italian extraction and 'chose' me because of my similar dark colouring. Christ knows what I am, pardon me; I've never been able to find out. For all I know I could be a throw-back from a gypsy clan. It meant very little to me as a thirteen-year-old, but over the years, possibly after my own maternal instincts kicked in, I thought a lot about my heritage.

'When I turned eighteen, I embarked upon a fully fledged effort to find my birth parents. As an investigator, I suppose you'd know how easy it is to gain info through the Births and Deaths register. That was my first point, and naturally I was ecstatic to receive a copy certificate in the mail.'

Glad to be able to get a word in I asked: 'Do you still have that?'

'Yes. I keep it in my 'dead family' box. Don't ask why I call it that; it's just 'cause they're not alive to me 'cause I've like never known any of my natural family. There's stuff-all in it; mum has the same surname; her Christian name's Meredith, although she's definitely no Christian for abandoning a six-week-old baby.'

'But Rachel, she may well have had a very good reason. It does happen, you know.'

'I haven't finished yet. I'll explain to you about reasons in a moment. Anyway, there's no father listed on the certificate so the obvious starting point was my birth mother. One Saturday afternoon I started phoning Benningtons from a collection of phone books. I kept track of each call and each response just in case I may have needed to back-track. I'd made like 147 calls before I struck gold. But it turned out to be fool's gold.

'I spoke with a Meredith Bennington somewhere down Cornwall. Naturally, she was like, surprised to hear from me. On second thoughts, perhaps more staggered than surprised, because I staged a question as if I were making an official call: "Records show that you gave birth to a girl at Mercy Private Hospital in Shropshire on October 2, 1980. The girl's name was Rachel. Is that correct?"

'She stalled, emitted a gasp as if trying to expel the event of nearly 30 years ago: "Oh my God. Oh my God. Yes, I had a daughter".

'I'm Rachel, your daughter. Hello mum.'

Rachel drops her head. Sorrow and embarrassment fill her eyes. 'You know what she did? Hung up the phone. The bloody bitch who abandoned me abandoned me again and hung up the bloody phone. I kept dialling for the next two hours only to receive a continuous busy tone. The following morning I phoned at 7.00 a.m. so I'd be sure of speaking to her. Speak I did, and all she – and I know it's rude to refer to my mother as "she" but I assure you it's apt – all she could say was, "This can't be real. You have family. You don't need me. Past is past and we both have our own lives to lead without complications".

'I said, "So I'm a complication even though you've had nothing to do with me since pulling me from your breast and dropping me into the 'unwanted' bin at the hospital?"

'"I don't mean it like that", my mother wept, "I suppose you've rung because you want to see me and have me in your life. No Rachel, that's not for me and I'll thank you to not call me again". And again she hung up the phone, this time with so much force the bang set me back with a fright. That's it for my mother. What brings you here?'

She surely is a Bennington judging by the way she strings words into sentences, then into paragraphs like fast-forwarding an audio book on compact disc. I'd listened to exactly the same narration from her mother. I collect my thoughts and continue: 'Lord Bennington is unsure of paternity, and I am merely asking you if you've discovered details of your father and if you've ever considered DNA profiling to establish paternity?'

'No, I hadn't considered that because my bloody birth mother wouldn't have a bar of me. The only way paternity could be established, if you haven't worked it out, is if my mother dropped the name or names of whoever she slept with nine months before I was born. I gather she was married to this Lord you speak of?'

'Yes. She was. Still is, I believe.'

'Well, I must be illegitimate. If I was his child there'd be no reason to conceal the birth, would there? I imagine there'd be no money dramas being married to a Lord. No. Whoever the father was, is nearly as bad as my mother, but maybe she never even told the guy. I've heard about those society women; she probably did it with the gardener while the good Lord was like having an afternoon of drinking port and smoking a bloody cigar. Perhaps he was Spanish or European and that's why I'm not an alabaster white pom.'

I know that in British law, a child born to a married woman is deemed to be a 'child of the marriage'. It matters not whether the birth is a consequence of a casual fling or long-term affair – the child will always be a child of the marriage. Lord Bennington had pleaded ignorance to any knowledge of a child. I believe him.

Rachel, on the other hand, has employed numerous resources to find her birth parents. I draw no conclusions from that glimpse into the past, although she has clearly made no attempt to claim Lord Bennington's parentage. To have done so would have guaranteed her a much brighter standard of living than she now tolerates.

However, she does know her mother. I cannot discount that Rachel's grudge is of such intensity that she would do anything to discredit her mother.

'Okay, Rachel. I'm sorry to bother you. I suppose I'd best just leave it there. I'm sorry to bring this up; I can see how distressing it's been for you. Good luck with your exhibitions.'

'You're not going to, like, see my mother, are you?'

'I shall ask my client, Lord Bennington. If he wants to take this any further, I'll act on his instructions. Would you mind if I gave him your contact details?'

'Quite all right. But I don't want anything to do with that Meredith. She deserves much more trouble for what she's done to me.'

I depart Rachel's home and compare our life's paths. We have both been adopted, and presumably (definitely in my case) have been reared with love, attention, and want for nothing in our foster parents' home. I didn't open up to how my life paralleled hers, but I do empathise with her gloom of being abandoned.

No. It is not gloom. Rachel harbours outright aggression that I have never replicated. I'd shed my birth-mother and let bygones be bygones. Rachel, however, carries demons within her soul, so much so that I begin to wonder what she might be capable of, or had been capable of doing.

24

Wednesday 15 March

Pieces fall into place as new information gels. I rush home, Fiona sweetly humming along the motorway, tyres whining in sync to the Black Eyed Peas 'I Gotta Feeling'. I answer my shrieking phone, too uncoordinated to hold the phone, turn down the stereo's volume and control the car. It reinforces why so many motor vehicle 'accidents' result from distractions of technology. I drift into the emergency lane and stop.

DCI Stafford yells: 'Olivia. Can you hear me?'

I had not expected to hear from him so soon. I thought the Bennington file would be buried beneath other priorities, so I am ecstatic to hear him announce: 'We're going to interview your Meredith.'

This is one of those times I wish I had not left the constabulary. To be involved in any manner with Meredith's interview would please me immensely.

'So, you got some mileage from the hospital charts?'

'Enlightening, to say the least. But you know I can't use any of it in an official capacity. However, we have dropped a subpoena on the hospital for all records and documentation pertaining to the old lady's admission and treatment.'

I cringe at the disrespect, but let it pass. 'Can I pop up and listen on audio? You never know if there might be something I can weigh in to help nail her. Besides, I got a bit more info about her and a daughter you don't know about. Peas in a pod, you might say, about glossing over their past.'

I brief him with *some* of what I'd learnt from Hamilton, and the findings of my Southampton visit. Stafford agrees to my eavesdropping on the interview, scheduled for 10.00 a.m. tomorrow. With that set, I end the call and merge into traffic with the precision of an Edinburgh Military Tattoo performance.

I approach my front door. *Shit!* It stands ajar. I'll remind you that I live on the High Street. My office fronts the footpath, and my apartment sits directly above. The flat has a separate entry, presumably in cases of the lease being split between a business and a residential tenant. I mention this just to elucidate the location of my apartment door. It appears as a doorway to nowhere, a blue door sitting in a wall between two huge office windows.

As one so security conscious, I remembered locking it when I left in the morning. Also, a trait I have practised since my father (I shall always call my stepfather 'father') tipped me off about police officers being ransacked and disturbed by fellow members from MI5, is to secrete a tiny square of newspaper between the door and the door-jamb upon closing. I'm talking about a half inch square; too small for anyone to notice, should the door be opened, but large enough for me to recognise its absence. It is also too small to blow away, for I see it sitting in a crease of the worn concrete step.

I push open the door and peer inside. My mail has been delivered, but it sits in a pile next to the skirting board behind the door, thereby indicating it had been pushed aside by the opening door. Listening for the slightest noise or sound, I creep inside and check the internal office door. Secure. I assume that if someone is still on the premises, they will be upstairs. And they are – footsteps scuffle directly above me.

I ascend the stairs, trying my hardest to stifle an advance warning from the creaking treads. The flight is original – at least one hundred and forty-years-old – as evidenced by a marble '1875' set into the building's high-pitched front gable. The carpet is somewhat newer, although its sound absorption qualities are zilch, as those who have witnessed the resonance of threadbare hessian-backed jute will attest.

With the finesse of a ballet dancer on pointe, I hug the wall, step by step up the staircase. My lounge room is accessed from the head of the stairs. Other rooms branch off: kitchen, bedroom, and bathroom. I tiptoe onto the top landing, glance into the lounge room and see that it is clear. That doesn't help, because I know that someone is nearby. It is eerie, like when I was cheating in a school exam and feeling confident I'd gotten away with it, and then I look behind and realise the teacher had been watching my every move. Such is the paranoia of expecting the unknown. Perhaps not so much a case of paranoia but more of respect for self-preservation.

Nothing appears out of place, so I pad my way along the wall, well out of view of the flanking doorways. I flip a coin, figuratively speaking of course, to decide which room to target – my bedroom or the kitchen. I reason that if someone is looking for something, despite my not having anything worth thieving, they would go from the lounge room to the bedroom expecting to find a glory box of treasures: jewellery, watches, a jar of one and two pound coins and perhaps a camera or iPod.

Given that the intruder has a head start, he might well have completed the bedroom and now be in the kitchen. That presents a problem, because if I am to surprise a person in the kitchen, he (and I say 'he' because most burglars are male) could quickly arm himself with one of many knives or my favourite Teflon frying pan.

I think of the craziest things at the craziest times. I imagine being hit over my head with the frying pan. It surely would hurt, but thanks to the inventors of Teflon, no bloodied, matted hair would stick to the pan. On the other hand, have you ever tried to 'unstick' the manufactures care label or other useless information from a non-stick saucepan or frying pan? Damn near impossible!

With waning smile, I hear rustling cutlery and a soft thump and realise the kitchen drawer of utensils has been pulled open and slammed shut. I retreat a couple of paces from my bedroom doorway. I can't risk making a sound by phoning 999, nor am I able to advance to the kitchen with the element of surprise. I have a knife in my ankle strap, but that will be useless against the might of an adrenalin-fuelled 100-kilogram desperado.

I am unable to do anything but watch the intruder walk from the kitchen to the bathroom. I know he won't spend much time in there. I have no drugs, and the solitary drawer holds only soap, flannels, and make-up. My first thought is to contain him in the bathroom, but because the door is inwards opening, I'll not have the strength to hold it closed until police arrive.

My best ploy then, is to high-tail it downstairs and summon help from the street. But I have six metres to creep across the top landing before I can hustle downstairs. I've completed four when the bathroom door opens. A figure stands in the doorway; dressed not as I expected a burglar to dress, save for a balaclava that covered most of his face. I log the attire in my memory bank: blue jeans, navy blue windcheater under a black zip-up jacket bearing a huge Puma logo on the rear. He holds a Tesco Green bag in one hand, pleasing me that my stolen possessions are walking out of my door in an environmentally friendly manner. His other hand clutches a mobile phone. Whether he was taking photos or waiting for a warning call from an accomplice, I could not know. I reason that *had* there been an accomplice, he'd certainly failed in his watchdog and reporting role.

We lock eyes. Stunned. Standoff. Who moves first?

I re-evaluate my initial assessment. He is not the 100 kilos I first imagined, but still sufficiently threatening to send me hurtling down the stairs. Our senses simultaneously kick into action. He says nothing as he turns towards the stairs intent on making a quick and trouble-free exit. I do likewise, formulating a plan to cut him off and delay his egress enough for me to restrain him with plastic ties I carry in my knife strap. I'm too slow. I reach the stairs and leap for his hips. I miss, but manage to latch onto his ankles. He trips and tumbles. Four somersaults later, he lies coiled at the foot of the stairs.

I think I'll be calling an ambulance instead of the police. I collect myself and start slowly down the treads, increasing my pace like a cat calling upon one of its nine lives after being hit at 70 mph on the motorway.

He suddenly rises and bolts out of the door. I increase my pace, bounding down three steps at a time. I yank my phone from my pocket, punch in 999 and huff a description of the absconder. I lose ground in the busy street, regretting that, as usual, members of the public ignore pleas of assistance, despite my yelling, 'Stop him. Stop him.'

He's removed the balaclava by this time to reveal long, shiny brown hair. The way he runs along the High Street makes me replay his tumbling down the stairs. There is more shape and hip in the jeans than I'd ever seen on a man. Now, I identify the run as not a male's long, stretching stride – it is the splayed motion of a woman. I suffer the humiliation of having been ransacked and defeated by a woman. *You bloody idiot. I should have put her down when I had the chance.*

I skulk back. People stare at me, trying to fathom who I am and what I'm involved in. I glide into my office. Find nothing disturbed. I recall the work I'd been doing upstairs and wonder if I'd left case notes lying about. I question myself again: *Why would the break-in be case related? Perhaps Hamilton has a girlfriend who's learnt that he spent an evening with me? Is she seeking revenge? Is Rachel investigating me? And what about Meredith?*

My concern escalates on realising that both Meredith and Rachel Bennington have brown hair of approximately the same length and colour as I'd seen flowing behind my decamping intruder. As for Hamilton, well, he couldn't attract a woman unless he'd plucked one from a 'friends with benefits' website.

A knock on my office window draws my attention. I

open the door to two uniformed constables. One scribbles a few notes from my voluminous oratory, and then suggests they escort me upstairs to ensure all is safe. I nearly blurt out that it is, but instead, allow them the grace of their duty.

We establish that nothing is missing from the loungeroom. Likewise, my bedroom is intact, my few pieces of jewellery remain in place, my camera has been inspected but it's memory card remains in place, and my Horlicks jar full of coins – future holiday funds – remains on the wardrobe floor.

'You're lucky that's still there.'

'No. You're lucky,' I reply. 'You don't have to do a theft report.'

'Let's just wait 'til we've finished before you decide what we do or don't have to report.'

I'm used to police sharing jocularity as a break to their more mundane duties. This officer is super-straight. If ever I were in trouble (and I don't count this as *real* trouble) I'd want this guy on my side for I'd be sure he'd act with one hundred percent professionalism to get to the core of my complaint.

We check the kitchen. Everything is above-board. I rustle through a mental inventory, trying to think what would be of value to an intruder who wasn't seeking money or resalable items. I have only the current Newquay investigation. Records of my previous police activities in Worcester would not be sought out, although there was a time when I feared my former colleague, Marchant, might wish to inflict damage. Thankfully, those days are long gone. I'm now safe because he is still under observation and surveillance. Last I heard, he'd been seconded to administration.

I flick through the kitchen cupboards and drawers, paying attention to my junk drawer, which is slowly filling with junk mail and sundry petrol dockets and expense receipts I store before relocating them to their rightful place in my downstairs office.

I am more accustomed to searching suspects' premises for illicit substances or illegal items than I am in searching my own home for something possibly missing. There is a certain advantage in the former because in that situation I am searching for something out of place and something that should obviously not be within the search perimeter. In my current predicament, I am looking for something that isn't here – a totally foreign and exceedingly difficult concept. Try as I may, I can't remember every little article, memento, knick-knack, and piece of paper I've chucked into my junk drawer. It is like trying to complete an insurance claim form – one just can't remember every missing object.

I reflect on the previous night's activity of entering Hamilton's information into my computer. On completion, I'd performed my usual file back-up on a USB memory stick, and then flung it into my junk drawer. That complies with the accepted practice of maintaining back-ups separate from the computer.

Certainly, it is separate. It is also missing.

Given the sensitive nature of some of the files, especially those that implicate me trespassing upon the hospital precinct and mishandling their records (well, I hadn't stolen them because they remained in the cabinet) I hesitate before admitting its absence to the police. 'There was a computer memory stick in here. It's gone.'

'Well, you can kiss goodbye to that. I can't imagine we'll be passing a file to CID to search for a £5 memory stick.'

'I can't imagine you would. But wouldn't uniform handle it?'

'Look lady. It wouldn't matter if you had national security on there. There's not a chance in hell of us recovering that.'

I have two suspects in mind, but I don't know whether, at this stage, to reveal my thoughts. Also, I do not wish to play the 'I used to be in the job' card, for fear of them treating me indifferently and telling me to conduct my own investigation. But I do need to hold my own. 'Wouldn't you check CCTV images of the person running up the street? You may be able to get an ID.'

'This isn't an episode of *The Bill*, lady. We ain't got people sitting in a cushy incident room viewing CDs and videos for hours on end looking for a person who may, and I stress, may, have stolen your memory stick. I'll submit the report to my sergeant and if it goes further, it does. You can ring the station in a couple of days.'

And that's it. They leave me standing aghast.

I had no need to ask if they had examined the point of entry, meaning the front door, because I knew they hadn't. I'd already worked out that the intruder had sprung the catch with a credit card; a common means of entry to latch doors that have not been deadlocked. My door has such a lock – an open invitation to a talented burglar.

Ordinarily, I'd phone a locksmith to arrange for a new lock. Being a new tenant I think better of that. I walk the short distance to the agent's office and advise them of my predicament, carefully assuring the agent there'd been no damage to the landlord's property, and that I don't expect any future incidents of a similar nature. I request permission to install an elaborate deadlock to both the residential and office doors. Permission is granted, thereby gifting the owner £60 of new locks.

As no pressing matters require my attention for the remainder of the day, I consider doing an hour's food shopping and trawling a couple of furniture showrooms to finally fit out my apartment to a reasonable standard. A cheap foam couch for my office will also lift my image. There's been little enquiry through the door, but the phone and answering machine have proved their worth with requests for costs and hours required to locate a missing teen, and another from a woman who suspects her husband's infidelity because of 'too much overtime, but his pay's still the same as his 38-hour rate.'

Yes. A woman always knows. Men can be so thoughtless, even stupid, when it comes to recognising their spouse's ability to spot deceit.

Unless I'm extremely lucky to see Alexander's cheque plonk through my letter flap, today will be restricted to budget items only. In the event of a *real* bargain jumping out, I could stretch myself, but one tip I've always lived by is the old proverb: 'Don't count your chickens before they hatch,' for even the most credible and professional person like Alexander Beecham will find ways of mislaying an invoice or prolonging a query on a certain item.

Before calling it quits for the day, I review the recently entered files that I'd copied to the now stolen USB stick – the very same files that someone else might be examining this very minute.

25

Thursday 16 March

I arrive at the St Austell Police Station at 9.45 a.m., in time to update DCI Stafford with the previous evening's events. Seated in reception is Meredith, resplendently dressed and coiffured, and oozing the air of confidence she'd carried at Nora Geddes' funeral. I predict that I'll see her later in the day at her own mother's funeral.

If my intruder *had* been Meredith Bennington – coincidental, I know, but entirely plausible – the content of my USB storage files will have forewarned her about the nature of questions that will soon be put to her.

DCI Stafford, accompanied by a detective constable who looks too young to be in the job, escorts Meredith to the interview room. I'm able to view proceedings through a mirrored window behind which behavioural analysts often study their subject's every twitch, labelling each as nerves, tension, surprise, evasiveness, or guilt. I hope this to be a far more rewarding experience than the earlier autopsy.

Stafford commences to interview Meredith, who has waived her right to legal representation, and is now 'assisting police with their enquiries'.

'Meredith Bennington. I'm going to ask you some

questions in relation to the death of Mrs Joyce Beecham. You do not have to say anything, but it may harm your defence if you do not mention, when questioned, something you may later rely on in court. Do you understand?'

Meredith agrees. Her face contracts into a scowl.

'First off, is it Miss Bennington or misses?'

'Misses will be fine. If you must know, my husband lives elsewhere.'

'Joyce Beecham was your mother, correct?'

'*Is* my mother. She will always be my mother.'

Stafford lets the quip pass. 'What was your relationship with your mother?'

'Her daughter, obviously.'

'I'll rephrase that. How was your interaction, your personal relationship with your mother? Frequent, spasmodic, friendly, protracted?' He throws a condescending smile across the desk.

'For the past couple of years, I've seen mum a couple of times a week. In her final few weeks my sister and I shared domestic and care duties. Earlier, we were probably like most families and visited every fortnight or so.'

'Your sister... that would be Roslyn?'

'Yes.'

'I don't mean to be insensitive here, but when was your mother's stroke?'

'The first was just over two years ago. Mum phoned me about chest pain. Knowing the prospective danger, I called an ambulance. Mum ended up in hospital.'

'She recovered from that?'

Meredith frowns a rush of impatience. 'Of course she recovered! But she had another, just two weeks ago. What's this about? I agreed to help with your enquiries, but for what? The hospital certified my mother's death as old age on the morning of her passing. Later I hear that an autopsy returned a different verdict, but I've been told nothing other than her passing was *not* natural causes. I don't know whether you're fishing, or whether this has something to do with my brother and that floozy sidekick of his, but my mother was ailing; she bloody well died from her ailments.'

I shudder at being labelled a 'floozy sidekick' and want to claw through the window to ask Meredith to repeat the insult to my face. She probably would, for she has the temerity to hold Stafford at bay, has power over her sister, and has the sweet dominance to convince or dupe the vulnerable into pledging their life's savings to the cause of Meredith Bennington. I also consider her swift response to Stafford. He merely asked about her mother's health. Sure, he'd placed the question as a land mine, hoping she'd trip over it and react. React she did. But what strikes me is her over-defensiveness because the interview could just as easily be a follow-up to the burglary of her mother's home. She's plainly dropped herself in it.

'Miss Bennington. We are not levelling accusations at you. We merely seek to understand the condition of your mother's health and who she was in contact with during her last days in hospital. As for the autopsy, yes, there are indifferent conclusions drawn from Dr Yui and Dr Patel.

'I believe our questions, whether to you, or others, will resolve that complication. I do understand this is difficult for you and I encourage you to call a halt at any time, even now, if you wish.'

Bloody Stafford. He could make mince-meat out of any

interviewer. He is the best. He's totally deflected Meredith's concern that she is implicated; he's made the enquiry generic – 'we need to understand', 'indifferent conclusions' – he's enlisting her help, yet giving her the opportunity to walk if she wants. She won't walk; she'll now think Stafford's a great guy, full of concern, understanding and compassion. Poor Meredith. She's about to be aced.

Stafford continues: 'Where was I? Yes. You were at the hospital when your mother passed on?'

'Yes, I was.'

'And you were solely responsible for your mother's welfare?'

'No. Mum was responsible for herself.'

'But you've told me that you and your sister – let me look back – yes, "In her final few weeks my sister and I had been sharing duties." Did you tell me that?'

'Yes. The duties were shared. I was not responsible.'

'But you wanted to be. Isn't that so?'

'No. I never wanted that. It was just circumstances as they arose.'

He's got her. The knife's going in for the kill. He just weasels and ferrets around an issue, gets half-a-dozen negative responses, then chucks in the biggie and hooks her. I never could do that. I can't think far enough ahead.

Stafford leafs through a file. Without looking up he says: 'I have information that your brother was recorded as next of kin in relation to your mother's affairs. What do you say to that?'

'I don't know what my brother had. All I know is that I requested to be noted as next of kin at the hospital and they changed, I mean completed, the forms.'

'And your mother consented to this?'

'She'd signed a form after I discussed it with my sister. We agreed that my consistent availability made it the right decision.'

'And your sister will support that?'

'Of course she will.'

For each question Stafford throws across the table, Meredith returns a credible response. She maintains a calm demeanour. That disturbs the officer who is more comfortable with ruffling feathers and penetrating deep into his suspect's psych.

'How long has your mother been a diabetic?'

'You've got me there. I don't know. It seems like most of her life, but I suppose it might be ten years or so.'

'She does her own blood sugar monitoring?'

'Every diabetic learns to do that within days of being diagnosed. Failure to maintain BSLs can result in blackouts, comas and even death.'

'And you're aware your mother was insulin dependent?'

'Of course I am. I'm a registered nurse as well as a daughter.'

Stafford creases a wry grin. 'Oh yes, Miss Bennington. I know all about your medical training.' He shoots a piercing glare into Meredith's eyes: 'You would be more aware than most of the effects of insulin to a diabetic. Just a couple more questions now. What is your present state of finances?'

'My financial means has nothing to do with this. I've come here of my own will to assist whatever convoluted theory you're pursuing that the hospital's somehow mishandled my mother's treatment. Whether I'm rich or poor surely has no bearing on your enquiry.'

'But I assure you it does, Miss Bennington. Do you wish to answer?'

'I pay my way; I have a small annuity from my husband, who you've obviously forgotten about because of your persistence in addressing me "miss"; I have a couple of investments and I have been fortunate to be nominated as beneficiary to the estate of some of my former patients.'

'And one of those patients was your mother?'

'Detective. You must excuse me for I won't be subjected to this line of questioning. Yes, I was caring for my mother, but I shall not be maligned in such a manner that suggests my mother was a patient for the purpose of financial gain. If you wish to speak to me further, I insist it be in the presence of my solicitor. Until that time I wish you a good day.'

Meredith rises from the table, determined that no counter-response from Stafford will change her mind. He does not even try.

'Thank you, *Mrs* Bennington. I'm sure we'll be in touch.'

I don't know what to think. Meredith had been grilled with finesse for nearly forty minutes. She'd maintained composure and control. She gave away little with her mannerisms other than anxious fidgets. I've seen them all: subtle twitches of the brow, clasping hands under the table and the quivering knees – all signs of the body under stress when one is fabricating a story or scripting a tome of work they hope will be received as the gospel truth. We investigators usually see through such smokescreens, for the truth is all-powerful and will always sprout through a field of lies.

Stafford conceals a smirk, and looks to me. He replays the interview tape, searching for Meredith's telltale rising pitch that might cast doubt over a response. He presses 'stop': *'I shall not be maligned in such a manner that suggests my mother was a patient for the purpose of financial gain.'*

He clenches his fists and thumps them against his forehead, furious that he missed putting to her the monthly invoices raised on account of caring for her mother. But he has made progress enough to ensure that there will, at a later stage, be a further interview. He ambles from the interview room, instructs his young colleague to make coffee – a task I would have once inherited – and scratches his head. 'She's a strange one. I reckon she could lie her tits off and no one would know. She even believes her own bullshit! D'ya see how she stretches her answers to add credence to her point?'

'She certainly lives beyond her means. You should see her home.'

'Done that Olivia. Did a drive-by yesterday. Couldn't even live there on my salary. Think I'll pay that sister of hers a visit. Now tell me, Olivia, how did you get your hands on that hospital info?'

I fix my eyes to the bare wall, while trying to hold back guilt. Stafford knows what I've been up to. And I know that he would face sanctions if he has first-hand knowledge of my clandestine operations. 'Can't say anything other than it came into my possession. We've been over this.'

'Yes. So we have. Just thought you may like to brag about your new-found investigatory skills.'

I can't stop smirking: 'Not "new-found" Chief Inspector; learnt them from you years ago. Anyway, you've already told me you've subpoenaed their records.'

I expect him to phone Roslyn to diffuse collusion between the sisters. I am thinking along the same lines as

I bolt from the office, pre-empting that Meredith would be straight onto the phone to her sister. I am too late, because she's sitting on the fence in front of St Austell CID shouting into her phone. I lean against a tree as if I'm waiting for a lift home, not exactly out of the way, but close enough to hear. Fortunately, she is either hard of hearing or traffic noise necessitates her conducting the conversation on speaker phone: 'That bloody Alex. He's just had me interviewed by the cops – from bloody London. I tell you Ros, he's gone too far. They asked me all sorts of stuff about mum's illness, the family relationship, diabetes. I tell you, they're not holding back on the theory that mum's death was not natural. They spoken to you yet?'

I strain to hear Roslyn: 'No. But I had that snivelling Watts woman throwing her weight around here with accusations and innuendo.'

Meredith responds: 'I'm getting a lawyer and it won't be some tin-pot conveyancing clerk like Alexander.'

Meredith's angst means little to Roslyn who seems to be growing tired of refereeing her brother and sister's spats. Long had she played the mediating role, but now her life follows her own selfish path; business and money take precedence over everything. While she is working, she is earning money; while she is earning money, she is happy; while she is happy, she does not have to think about family rivalries simmering in the background.

As Meredith blusters off, Stafford wanders over and invites me back inside for coffee. We discuss the inroads he's made into dismantling Meredith's story. He summarises that he was only 'warming up' and that Meredith will sink herself sooner rather than later. I enjoy the chat without feeling obliged to engage in the afterhours activities we once enjoyed. Perhaps he is happy with Shannon or whoever now shares his life.

I feel totally liberated.

26

Thursday 16 March

I loll at the front of St Austell CID and take stock of my situation. I've just left a police interview in a case I now have no involvement, no financial recompense, and still no clear pointer to the perpetrator of three heinous crimes. It's no longer my business. I'd be better off heading home and launching myself straight into a waiting enquiry. My problem is that I can't help embracing the bold assumption that the three events *are* related, and that had aroused sufficient curiosity in one person to raid my home. I balance that with the discomfort Meredith exhibited during her interview.

The phone rumbles in my bag. Alexander. In panic: 'What the fuck have you done? I've just had that copper mate of yours calling me to an interview.'

'I know nothing about that.'

The interview was inevitable, but I am disappointed Stafford didn't have the courtesy to let me know.

Alexander rages: 'You can't tell me you've not been exchanging info with this guy who's supposed to be helping you; you'd have to know he's planning on interviewing others. He would've told you.'

I am infuriated that Alexander thinks I'm holding out on him, but reconcile he has good reason to, after I wouldn't reveal how I came about the hospital documents. I'm more incensed that Stafford has ventured behind my back to arrange an interview of my own client without a word to me. Sure, he'd told me about the prospective interview with Roslyn, but that was all. I resolve to exercise extreme caution with anything else I might need to disclose.

I detest the way some investigations fall apart like petals of a dying flower, wilting and withering to a patch of spent stems rather than prolonging strong blooms that should later bear the fruit of its seeds. The hazy task of trying to prove Meredith Bennington complicit in her mother's murder has expanded to such a dimension that I must now include Rachel, who, separated from the family for her whole life, harbours such an intense grudge against her natural mother. I cannot omit *her* from my suspicions.

I could easily give the game away. There's easier money to be made from prancing around retail stores snaffling the occasional shoplifter, handing them over to the police who do all the paperwork, my only further role being to attend court and give evidence of the theft and apprehension of the accused. Better still, I could be driving around the countryside trying to locate a runaway teenager desperately missed by his or her parents. Invariably, those parents have never offered their children the deep love they deserve and need. One morning, their fourteen-year-old daughter drops a note on the kitchen table: 'Dear mum and dad. I'm leaving. Please don't worry about me. You never have anyway. I'll be fine and I'll contact you one day. Love, your neglected daughter.' Only then do her parents begin to ooze love and emotion.

When I receive calls from such distressed parents, I'm amazed how they're more interested in defending their role as responsible parents than they are about providing information supporting the reasons for their daughter's departure, and more importantly, a list of possible contacts or whereabouts of their distressed child. Only at that juncture do the imperious parents themselves concede that they have very little awareness of their daughter's being. They exclaim: 'Where did we go wrong?' without accepting that they'd treated their child as a possession or an article of clothing or a piece of furniture or as an inert item they send to school or trot off to his or her room. Never had they sat down to discuss anything other than school failures, dress standards, the 'unacceptable' friends, the 'bad' music and the 'outrageous' makeup.

Those same parents chip in pound after pound searching for their absconded child – in their mind justifying and quantifying the love for their child – yet that same exercise will be thrown in the child's face upon their return to the family domain. 'Oh honey, we were so worried about you. Your father's spent nearly two thousand pounds trying to find you just so we can tell you how much we love you.'

Sure, the child thinks. *You've done little to show your love while I'm at home, so why put on a show in front of the police and media?*

Thankfully, I never ran away from home, a fact that supports the love and care my foster-parents bestowed upon me.

There's no nice way of saying this, but this afternoon will be a great one for a funeral. I freshen up at the police station, but stop short of using their toilets as a change room. I've had plenty of practice changing identities in the back of my car, so it will be no inconvenience to employ my contortionist skills to squeeze into my black pants and dress jacket. Quite honestly, I am having second and third thoughts about attending, especially after Alexander's castigating me over his belief that I'd shopped him to Stafford.

As I enter Newquay cemetery's huge gates, I stop to admire two white angels floating astride alabaster pedestals. If wishes could come true, I would wish that they'd bless Meredith and Roslyn for the day – but I know that's one ambitious call. I park on a grass verge near the administration building and proceed to check the service details.

Of the few functions I attend, it is accepted protocol to arrive late. Funerals must be the only gathering where people *always* arrive early. I walk along Serenity Drive to the main chapel where the Beecham clan stand apart, except for Alexander, who hugs, presumably, his father. *Thank goodness for Hamilton.* Beecham senior appears to have changed little from the photos I'd viewed at his late wife's home. Alexander throws aside his earlier tantrum to greet me and introduce his father.

George Beecham presents far different than I'd imagined. I admire the eighty-plus, wispy-haired, laconic drawler, a stark contrast to my early perception of his being a selfish, ungrateful old bastard for abandoning his wife in a time of crisis.

As Alexander and I had surmised, he knows nothing of his wife's last days. After being ostracised by his children, he'd confined himself to a remote Welsh village with only cartons of Felinfoel Red Dragon beer and a Welsh Corgi for company. Everything Welsh is most fitting for a man who had welshed on his children.

I find it difficult to decipher the mourner's attitudes. One expects to see glum faces and downcast heads, but here, Meredith and Roslyn share smiles and joviality with all comers but Alexander and their father. As if that is not normal, the scene is soon topped by the appearance of an elegantly dressed woman in full black dress, hat, and flowing veil. She stands, head bowed, behind the assembly.

From a distance, I strain to penetrate the veil, embarrassed at deflecting my attention from the service. On making out the silhouetted features, I am flabbergasted to find that I am staring at Rachel. I wipe my eyes before double-checking, because her dress and manner separates her from her typecast image of a Southampton council flat tenant. It is like looking at the transformation after makeover on the ridiculous television show, *Snog, Marry, Avoid?* Only yesterday Rachel told me that she'd never known her natural family. She's either a brilliant liar, or has more gall than seven-time Tour de France winner, Lance Armstrong, who hoodwinked the public into believing that he was 'drug-free'.

She departs with similar grace – speaking to no one, but consoled by the fact that she'd paid her last respects.

Glad to be home, I open my door and glare at the bare floor. No cheque. I bang my fist onto the flashing answering machine: 'Good afternoon. Could you please return my call? My name is Richard Rosenberg. I represent Mrs Meredith Bennington.'

With minutes to spare before the end of the business

day, I call the number. Rosenberg warns me off further contact with Meredith, to which I advise that I have no need nor desire to speak with her. As professional protocol, and a subtle means of one-upmanship, I advise that I've passed information to police and that I believe that they might soon be in touch with his client. I decline to fill in the blanks. Quite possibly, Rosenberg might not know that Meredith has already been interviewed by Stafford, and that Stafford has information sufficient to further *his* investigation.

My disadvantage is that I do not know what Meredith has discussed with her whiz-bang lawyer. Very little, I suspect, for Rosenberg begins a fishing expedition, quizzing me about my knowledge of her marriage. I respond that my research has armed me with information freely available to the public, and that I would have to check with *my own* solicitor for advice before continuing the discussion. That quells Rosenberg's enthusiasm. His final words repeat the veiled threat against my contacting his client.

True to her word Meredith, in capitulating to Stafford's soft interview, has instructed a lawyer. Rosenberg will now insulate her from further questioning, especially from me, which is surprising because my last contact with Meredith was at her initiative – she'd lobbed, uninvited, at my door!

I don't need this. I don't need a suspect's lawyer barrelling me over my activities. I've finished my paid work for Alexander, but now, with a lawyer of a supposed innocent person begging me for information, I sense there is far more at stake in this enquiry. I have no one on side. Alexander is out of the frame with me, but in the frame with Stafford, who has dropped me by neglecting to inform me of his intention to question Alexander. I resent his negligence, but understand his motive: he does not want me to compromise my allegiance to Alexander to warn him about the prospective interview.

As I no longer have a contractual obligation with Alexander, I decide to pursue one final matter for my own interest, before handing everything over to Stafford.

Having done behind-the-scenes unearthing at Meredith's home, I decide to do similar with Alexander and Roslyn. I walk down to the local off-licence and score a six-pack of Gin and Tonic to accelerate my decision-making process.

Four cans later my lounge room sways and twists into a spinning eddy like the dizziness suffered when strapped to an out of control carousel. I dismiss thoughts of the investigation; I think only of stepping off the merry-go-round that prevents me from settling in any one place. Through the blurred haze, I see an obdurate Alexander pleading with Stafford: *How could you think I'd have anything to do with my mother's death? It was I who called the bloody ambulance a couple of weeks ago. Don't you think that if I had a motive, that would have been an opportunity – I could have delayed the call until it was too late.* He had a point there. The very point I'd floated when considering his involvement.

The haze thickens. I see Roslyn pleading with Meredith: *What the fuck you been up to Merri? You surely haven't killed three people? That's what they're saying. Is that how you've got your family house and lifestyle? You just keep them long enough to get what you want, then it's off with them. Who's next? Let me give them a sporting chance.*

And I see Rachel contemplating her future, sitting on the lonely foreshore of a pebbled beach, wondering who she really is. I sent her there. I've rekindled her memories of the past and intensified her confusion with the inclusion of Lord Bennington. I see her visiting Wiltshire Manor – maybe I took her.

With those visions so vivid, I cannot see myself recovering from my four-can intoxication – so I skull the remaining two. I feel cheap and nasty and crave personal fulfilment. I think of phoning Hamilton and inviting him for coffee. My next conscious moment is 6.00 a.m. the following day.

27

Friday 17 March

I use Friday mornings to start winding down the working week. Today, I'll just take things as they come; read papers, watch television, and listen to CDs. The demons of my Gin and Tonic hangover urge me back to sleep. Such is my inflated level of self-motivation I resist the duvet and jump into a cold shower. Ten minutes rinse drowsiness from my barely functioning body. A bizarre need to revisit Rachel springs before me. Something doesn't add up.

As often happens on mornings where enthusiasm thwarts rational feelings, I towel off and convince myself that I deserve just another five minutes in bed listening to the news. I justify it as work. Catching news bulletins is work to me, for I never know what names I might need to remember or of what criminal activities I should be wary. Had I not been abreast of the news I would never have linked Nora Geddes to Meredith Bennington.

I spring to the phone. *Bloody Stafford.* 'Why so early?'

'Early? Nine-thirty too early for you?'

Shit! I explain how I'd been ready to face the day. 'I was listening to the radio, I heard a time check of 6.22, then next thing you're in my ear.'

'Not the only place I'd like to be, Olivia.'

'You've blown all chances of that. Seriously, what brings you to my phone on a Friday morning, after you effectively excommunicated me yesterday?'

'Saw your friend Roslyn Beecham late yesterday. She's got as much chance of disposing of her mother as she's got of disposing of her own rubbish. She wouldn't do anything for herself – unless it was money-related.'

'But isn't the mum, Joyce I mean, wasn't she worth a bit? She had a home and a reasonable bank account.'

'Petty cash, Olivia. Wouldn't be her motive. Roslyn thrives on perceptions. Has to be the best. Best estate agency in the county – so she claims – and has local awards to back it up; best equestrian as a teenager, and, so I gather, wanted to be the best daughter. Could she have felt threatened by her sister's devotion to her mother?'

'Nah. You're way off track. I would bet my job she's not involved.'

'You're not staking much then, are you?'

'Very funny. You want something? If so, don't think you're getting one iota of info from me after not telling me about your wanting to interview Alex.'

'Jesus. How'd you know that?'

'Listen, Chief Inspector. I came to you with info I thought you'd be able to use to solve what might be outstanding crimes. Granted, there might be nothing in it, but the least I deserve, if you don't mind, is the courtesy of being advised of your intent to interview the very person who paid me to gather the info that I gifted you!'

'Olivia. You've been there. Sometimes we have to

proceed along the bumpy road that leads to an impartial enquiry.'

I know he is right. Morally, I would never have gone behind my inspector Marchant's back, but I was so convinced he was wrongly pursuing an innocent man – and had done so until a conviction was secured. I had to stand up for myself and justice, and seek assistance beyond Marchant's control, hence my call to Stafford. For that, I pay an infinite penalty.

Life is an eternal fight between morals and ethics, and practicalities and perceptions, for we are expected to do the right thing even if we believe otherwise. A classic example is a staff security check, in, say, a supermarket or department store. The security department is charged with the responsibility of protecting the company's assets. Staff members are checked exiting the store. Bags and handbags must be inspected. Ethically, the compassionate guard is bound to proficiency, yet he is embarrassed to fully check his colleague's personal bag. He will therefore offer only a cursory glance. The bag might be false-bottomed or have a lipstick or small item concealed within, but he has followed his corporate obligation by checking the bag, and followed his moral heart by not invading, too closely, the space of his fellow colleague.

Such emotional struggles are fought daily, just as I now struggle to believe that Stafford acted in my best interest by not telling me about the proposed interview with Alexander. 'You couldn't possibly have anything on Alex, but I agree to having an open mind. Mine's still open on this. Here's one snippet for you. Meredith's got Rosenberg. You know, Richard, the learned QC who doesn't take on a case unless he can get himself on television or in the papers?'

'Good luck to her. I reckon she'll need him. What're you doing today, Olivia?'

'Haven't decided yet. You want me to come up and listen to you barrage Alexander?'

'Just a thought.'

'No thanks. I might find something more productive. And if it wasn't within your ethics to tell me about it, I guess it's not within mine to be there.'

I hate burning my bridges, but sometimes I must make a stand to enunciate my point. I shrink and try to soften the blow: 'No hard feelings. Tell you what. I'll phone this evening, and if either of us has anything good, we'll share it. Deal?'

Stafford accepts my proposal, but I am left bemused as to the reason for his call. Surely, he has a hidden agenda; something other than revealing he'd interviewed Roslyn. That was hardly news – it was expected. How would that affect me? Doesn't mean a thing. I realise that in a roundabout way he'd siphoned my knowledge about the interview with Alexander, thereby confirming my 'closeness' to the investigation. I subsequently volunteered Meredith's legal representation and I'd broadcast that I was still involved by predicting that I'd have more info later in the day. *Stafford won.*

I regret not telling him that someone has copies of the hospital charts as well as most of my notes and files.

I map the day's activities, furious that I've wasted two hours succumbing to undisciplined sleep. I intended to return to Southampton to see Rachel, risking, I know, that if I push too far I could damage the whole case. I have a theory, but theory to a powerless private investigator is next to useless. Nevertheless, three words have plagued me for the past few days: 'much more trouble'. *'She deserves much more trouble for what she's done to me'.*

That's disturbing, because Rachel told me that the only time she'd spoken to her mother was within days of her eighteenth birthday. After having the phone hung up on her, she called the following day. That, according to Rachel, was the only contact they'd had.

Here lies the challenge of my role as a private investigator. I can make a case out of some things that flash beyond better people than me. For Rachel to use the term 'much more trouble' implies that she knows her mother's been, or is, in trouble, and she deserves more. Rachel could not possibly know anything of Meredith's troubles unless she was, or has been, in recent contact with her – or the family. So my question follows: *How does she know the family?*

I'll get to the bottom of it.

I pack a bag and phone Stafford. 'What time you interviewing Alexander?'

'You've revised your ethics, Olivia? Three o'clock. The guy's wise. Reckons he's prepared to talk down there, but he's not coming up to London. Doesn't worry me; I'm seeing him at St Austell CID.'

'Okay. I'll be there about 2.30, after hiding my car in the back streets.'

My morning is shot after spending half an hour on the phone. I have no time for breakfast. I can't drop in to Macca's because they'll be on the 10.30 a.m. menu-change as I arrive. I don't fancy a Quarter with Cheese this early and I'll be too late for Bacon and Egg McMuffins.

I ensure my windows are locked, and double-check my new deadlatch before leaving for St Austell. I plan to stroll the shopping precinct for a couple of hours before rolling in – mouth full of mints – to the CID office.

Thirty-two shops and three cappuccinos later, I enter the police station. I'm welcomed as an unwelcome guest. That's the thing with reputations – they're undeniably portable. They travel ahead of both good news and bad; they're easily embellished, tarnished, rubbished and punished. They can be so unrealistically distorted that the poor sullied person has no defence and no means of resurrecting their once fine reputation. I should expect no better from the few narrow-minded police members who don't even know me.

I sit on a moulded bench seat in the foyer, shielding my face, hoping Stafford's prompt arrival will save me from a potentially embarrassing encounter with Alexander, should he, too, decide to attend early. My wish is granted when Stafford walks in, dressed over-casual for a DCI, but then I recall his ploy when dealing with professionals.

'Dress down' he once instructed. 'They think they're above you, so let them feel it. Gives them a false sense of security. Clothes may maketh the man, but intelligence maketh the interrogator. They'll squirm in their suit while we tangle them in knots from the comfort of our cheap factory worker's attire.'

I hate derogatory slants against factory workers. I know some very professional tradespeople who work in factories, and I know production workers whose earnings far exceed the remuneration of many white-collar executives.

He extends his hand. I'm rarely greeted by handshake, but I accept the formality which I suppose is principally for show. We adjourn to a small interview room where he explains that he's been assigned a secondary room that does not have the same modern fit-out as the room in which he'd interviewed Meredith. There is no facility for live audio. Nor is there means for me to view the interview in progress. I feel as if I've wasted a trip until Stafford asks me to wait in the tea room. 'I'll run the DVD for you afterwards,' he says.

'Thanks.'

'Not so quick. I've been doing some thinking.'

I've seen Stafford in thinking mode. He's old school, preferring to work cases with the hard graft of the pre-technological era. Foregoing computer cross-referencing and photo-laden whiteboards, Stafford relies on crisp manila folders of hardcopy information. He places his hand on top of three files. The Beecham siblings: Meredith, Roslyn, and Alexander. A fourth, with Rachel Bennington pencilled on its cover, is empty. 'This is what I've come up with.' He pushes the files over.

This is like a sneak preview of a Christmas present. I start unwrapping.

> Meredith Bennington: Doting daughter who thinks of herself before anyone else. Care for her mother may be genuine, but could also be disguised as priming her for big chunk of will. Relationship with Roslyn has faltered because of sham marriage. No real relationship with brother.
>
> Roslyn Beecham: Compassionate, but not doting in the way of her sister. Has nothing to prove to anyone. Has successful business. Eager to buy into new franchise. Carries high debt levels (motive?) but is financially stable.

> Alexander Beecham: Black sheep. Calculated mind, considers all angles before speaking. Aided by Watts to reinforce his belief that Meredith Bennington complicit.

'Thanks for the mention,' I say. 'He's not "aided" by me. I've simply gathered facts that support his hypothesis. Nothing you've got here takes this any further from what I've already given you.'

'All right,' he continues. 'I took a run down to that Happy Valley place.'

'Oh yes?' Surprise raises my brows. He'd not previously mentioned interest in the Geddes death.

'And after that, I dropped into Cornwall and General. Very interesting. Spoke to a young woman with cheeks full of gum who told me about an insurance investigator wanting the same file. Don't s'pose that was you? No need to answer.'

Stafford excuses himself to attend Alexander who has just arrived.

There is no way I'm going to hang around a police station tea room, so I tender my apologies, intent on returning to the shops. I tell him to phone me when he's ready.

I waste two hours walking around shops I'd already visited. I return to the police station hoping that my presence and my dropping a few business cards in the meal room might enhance both my future relationship with station personnel and my emerging business enterprise. The office's cold atmosphere repels me. I walk by the interview room and peek through a wire-reinforced window. Stafford's jacket hangs over the back of his chair. I feel like asking for it, but do not want to give away my eavesdropping on the interview. Also, I do not want his scent clinging to my body for the remainder of the afternoon.

Stafford keeps his promise and plays the DVD. I watch him pull cards from his sleeve, as he always does when probing a suspect merely helping with enquiries. Alexander offers 'no comment' to a series of questions – the tactic infuriating the interviewer. He then follows with: 'I was not prepared for the intensity of the interview and accordingly did not arrange legal representation. Should you continue to pursue an accusatory line of questioning I should beg your leave to permit me a phone call.'

Stafford explains the momentary set back. But he is not one to be indefinitely set back– he will always force out the last word.

And he does: 'Certainly Mr Beecham. I shall conclude this at your request. One final question if I may: 'Why did you assign a private investigator to determine whether your mother had met with foul play rather than discuss your concerns with local police? Taking matters into your own hands, perhaps?'

I hear a faint drumbeat and see Stafford performing a celebratory tap dance with his fingers.

'No. Not at all,' Alexander bounces back. 'If you've researched the facts in issue, as I presume you have, you will know my consternation was with the hospital itself. Given that a court-ordered autopsy confirmed my suspicions of malpractice, you would therefore be cognisant that *that* is no matter for the police and therefore vindicates my decision to engage the services of Miss Watts.'

I conceal a smile. *Good one Alex. Maybe Stafford has met his match after all.* I am pleased to hear that they wind up on gentlemanly terms, with Alexander inviting Stafford to contact his office if he requires further information. Stafford would do so regardless of any invitation from a suspect.

Stafford seals the DVD and then grabs my arm – which surprises me – and expresses concern for my safety. It is self-preservation, he claims, that prompted someone to raid my home, and that person might now be one step ahead of us both. 'They'll know you've got incriminating evidence against someone. And this Alex knows everything you've got.'

I do not share Stafford's view, because my intruder could have waited in an advantageous position and injured or killed me, had he or she wished. No, my safety is not at risk – only information I hold. I coolly brush him aside, satisfied that I am more than capable of looking after myself.

I return to my car and for the first time ever check the tyres and lift the bonnet to inspect plug leads, brake lines and hydraulic fluid levels. Paranoia? Dunno. I've never been the victim of car tampering and haven't known anyone who has, but haunted by the scene of racing downhill – without brakes – towards a cliff or intersection is enough for me to heed Stafford's warning.

Happy that Fiona has not been sabotaged, I head home.

28

Saturday 18 March

I cling to the ambitious hope of being able to provide Stafford information sufficient to gain a conviction. I head to Southampton.

I don't bother with an advance phone call. If Rachel is home, I'll speak to her. If she's not, I'll have the opportunity to pillage her apartment and hopefully identify something that will link her, however remote, to at least one death.

I squeeze into a parking bay, embarrassing local garbage contractors as they pluck treasures from the hard rubbish. Their truck is adorned with divorced teddy bears manacled to the grille. Metres of silver tinsel frame the windscreen. Given that it is months before Christmas, I applaud their creation of the flamboyant float.

It is certainly Christmas when I knock on Rachel's door; she opens it with a broad smile. *Must be expecting someone else.*

'Oh, hello,' she welcomes. On recognising me, she descends into somnambulant quietness.

'Hi. Rachel. We have to talk. It can be here or the police station. Which do you prefer?'

I've changed my tack from the innocent, pleasant face

I'd previously presented. Now, I seize control. I'm playing a long-shot, a hunch that has been riding me since Thursday night.

Rachel stands in defiance: 'What if I don't want to talk to you anywhere?'

'Easily fixed. I'll just phone DCI Stafford and have him 'round here within minutes. Then, there'll be no option.'

'All right. I've got no idea what you want, but let's get it over with.'

We enter the lounge room-come-studio-come-storage area and sit apart on the clothing-strewn sofa.

'Rachel. I want to speak about your mother. You made it quite clear on my last visit that you have an intense dislike of her.'

'I don't think anything of her. How would you feel if your mother gave you away, then later wanted nothing to do with you?'

I know how I feel, but I'm not going to enter into a contest over who is the most disadvantaged adoptee. Some of us grow above such things, whereas others harbour a lifetime grudge. Rachel supports a grudge strong enough to make things difficult for her mother. I try to dilute the potentially volatile confrontation: 'I'm not sure how I'd feel, but I think I would be anxious or upset to learn that my mother had no interest in me.'

Rachel remains despondent: 'She's gone on with her life, like we all do. At least when her mother died she must have begun to feel what loss was all about.'

'Yeah, right.' I jump in: 'You contacted your mother on your eighteenth birthday, twelve years ago?'

'Told you all that. She just said, "Life goes on" and stressed that she wanted nothing to do with me.'

'And she didn't? I mean, you just went on with your life?'

'Too right. Like I didn't want nothin' to do with her after that.'

Now it's my turn to emulate Stafford, to reflect her words like an echo, and let her sink herself: 'So how did you know her mother died?'

'Er, you must have mentioned something about it last time you were here.'

I'd mentioned nothing of the sort. My questions had related only to ascertaining paternity. Rachel's answer gives me the impetus to push harder.

'Right. And I suppose that news upset you?'

'Didn't worry me either way since I didn't know her.'

'Let me tell you, Rachel, that last time we spoke, our conversation was directed to locating your father. Remember that?'

'Yes. And you asked about my work and my paintings.'

'Right. There was no conversation at all about your grandmother.' I draw a conclusion and take a massive gamble. If I lose, the interview will be shot, Rachel will have the upper hand and it will take me a while to regain the initiative. However, if I win... 'You knew her, didn't you? You actually knew her and visited her in hospital?'

'What if I did? It's no crime.'

Yes!

Rachel is rattled. She glances around, fidgets and can't sit still. I battle to suppress tears, because in empathising with her situation I feel a maternal bond with the girl who's probably never experienced the mother/daughter connection. I press on: 'How often did you visit? I suppose you planned on being there when no one would see you? Perhaps you don't even know your mother's sister and brother? How did this all come about?' So much for the investigator's creed. *One question at a time.*

'I couldn't care less about them. I felt sorry for my grandmother having a bitch of a daughter like my mother. I think it was also my grandmother's fault that my mum abandoned me. It's all about upbringing, isn't it? I can see how your mind's working. You think that I've been hassling my mother because of what she done. Why would I do that? I told you I'm glad to be rid of her and if I never saw her again it wouldn't worry me. You should have seen them congregating in the hospital car park, like working out who would go in first, who to watch out for, who would buy flowers, cake, and magazines. It was pathetic. You'd reckon they were just waiting for her to cark it so they could get back to their own life.'

'So how many times did you watch those gatherings?'

'Like both days before gran carked it and a few times before that when she was in.'

'Rachel, I want you to listen carefully. How could you possibly have known that your gran was in hospital if you'd had no contact with the family?'

She stares at me with bloodshot eyes. She's either had a very late night, or is on the brink of tears. My throat swells. We share the sisterhood of abandonment and now I, too, am pushing her away. She has been vulnerable for her whole life, more so after learning of her adoption. I'd not broached the subject of her adoptive parents, but I assume that since she'd not denounced them like her own mother, they must have been fine step-parents.

I am overflowing with unanswered questions. I must unlock her heart and extract all she knows about her grandmother.

'Rachel. You know I'm here as a private investigator. I am not the police, so I can offer help and counselling should you need it. But you must help me too. This is important, and I understand you might be protecting someone. Who told you your gran was in hospital?'

'I just knew. I found out myself, sort of a deduction. I'd known about my gran for years, in fact since the time my mum told me about my natural mother. After experiencing the emotional trauma of my mother's rejection, I did a family trace. I'd always wondered if I had brothers and sisters.

'I found nothing about my natural father, but I was able to trace my mother's genealogy back to her mother's birth certificate. I finished with the name Joyce Beecham.'

'Just like that?'

'No. It wasn't "just like that". There were no good genealogy sites on the internet then, or at least no easy means of tracing ancestry, and there were no easily accessible archived records of Births and Deaths. I had to do everything manually, like searching through pages and pages of names, cross-referencing, tiring my eyes poring over microfiche, and then, the source of most disappointment hit me – the unanswered and abusively responded phone calls.

'I think I might have been perceived as one of those annoying telemarketers who persistently phone at dinner time or when you've just sat down to a good dose of evening television. They ended up deflating me: "Can you call another time?" "No. I don't care who you are, and if I had missing family I wouldn't care either". "I'm sorry love. I don't know a Joyce Beecham, but good luck to you".

'I was inspired by the nicer people, or at least those who helped me remain motivated and devoted to my cause. Strange though, I don't really know what my cause was. I wasn't looking to start an intense family relationship – far from it. I think I was keen on learning what sort of family raised a girl – and mum was only a girl when she had me – like only twenty when she callously disposed of her daughter for no reason other, so I assume, than to remain single and career focused. I only presume she was single. By the time I'd examined the Births and Deaths records I had no mind to start on the marriage archives. I thought that as no father was recorded on my Birth certificate, there might have been hidden circumstances like mum didn't even know who the father was or some other dark secret.'

Rachel reveals her past with a fine and even temperament. I share her contempt for her mother, but know I am premature in so doing.

'So at some stage you found Joyce Beecham?'

'Sure did, after going through three phone directories. She lived with her husband, George, I think it was, in the Sheffield area. You know what? She never even knew her own daughter had been pregnant. She explained how she didn't see Meredith very often, something to do with eloping with some old dude, but she was surprised to, like, hear my claims of being her granddaughter. Initially, she treated me warily, and wouldn't discuss anything family related "unless and until" – her words – I could show her satisfactory proof of my claim. That was an inconvenience I didn't want. I turned around and photocopied the records I'd already collected and carted them all the way back to damn Sheffield. I wondered if it would end in disaster, but once I'd been able to confirm that I was family, she expressed shame and embarrassment. I don't think many women would refuse the opportunity of getting to know a granddaughter, no matter what the circumstances.'

'Just to fast-forward, how did you know she was in hospital?'

'I'm getting to that, if you'll give me the chance. A moment ago you're satirising me by intimating I found gran "just like that" so I give you all the details of what happened and how I found her and now you're pushing me. This is hard you know. It's pretty emotional to recount this. Ah, forget it. Like I'm over it now. If you want information, get it from the hospital or her family. What have I got to do with all this anyway?'

I can't very well tell Rachel of my theory that she'd killed her gran to get back at her mother. In view of what she's just told me, I believe it unlikely that she would have done such a thing because of the fondness she'd developed with her gran. 'I'm sorry Rachel. I don't want to upset you. I'm simply trying to eliminate as many people as possible from this enquiry. Every relation and acquaintance of your gran, especially those who visited her in her last days have been questioned by police. I'm just not sure if the police know about you being part of the family.'

'Well, you trot off and tell them then. I've got nothin' to hide and if you look deep into that friggin' family, I'm sure you'll find what you're looking for, for I reckon that any woman capable of sacrificing her daughter could just as easily sacrifice her mother.'

Good point.

'Did you know it was my gran who told me that she was ill a couple of years ago? She deemed it her duty to inform me. She assumed the role her daughter never played; she loved me; invited me to her home; lent me money for my studies – which I repaid – and kept silent to other family members about my presence in her life. Yes, gran got a message to me, through the hospital, and arranged that I be permitted to visit in the mornings, two hours before normal visiting hours. There were days when I was working and couldn't get there until evening. Gran texted when her children would be visiting, including my mother, and that it like, might be best for me if we didn't meet on that particular day. How right she was. But I took that as an opportunity to suss the family, like to see maybe aunties and uncles or whatever, and that's when I put two and two together about the car park scene of avoiding each other.

'I found in gran what I never had with my own mother. My relationship with my stepmother was good, but once I found out that she was not my maternal mother I saw her differently, sort of like a placebo mother. That sounds cruel and disrespectful, I know, but that was my feeling. And you know what? No matter how much I love her, it still is.

'I suppose what I'm trying to say is that if you think I've got anything to do with my gran's death, you're wrong and way off the mark, and only wasting time in finding whoever is responsible.'

After an hour and a half, my best summation is that Rachel is forthright and honest. For all the venom coursing through her veins, none is sufficiently potent to drive her to kill her grandmother.

29

Saturday 18 March

I push Alexander and his problems aside to make way for Rachel. The similarity of both Rachel's and my own problems disturbs me. *Why do so many mothers forego their children?* We share similar childhood memories, we'd both learnt of our adoption as teenagers, and have ever since craved love and acceptance. Rachel's open heart has helped me understand a few things about myself, just as I hope I have been able to help her.

Catharsis accompanies me on my impromptu walk to the beachfront. Whilst home is a refuge where the day's worries and problems evaporate from my being, the beach is a secondary haven where crashing waves stimulate thoughts, and soft sand soothes rash instincts. I can lower my pulse rate and blood pressure just by sitting on a chunky rock, on the soft sand, or in a decrepit toilet cubicle in the beachfront conveniences. And that is where I think over the past two weeks.

Talk about diving in at the deep end. "You may be able to help me with a small family matter." *Shit. What would I have done had it been a major catastrophe?* I feel as if I've spent the past fortnight peering into a kaleidoscope. The smallest twitch changes the focus: Meredith; Roslyn; Alexander; Rachel. All I want is his cheque so I can finally eject the three 'B's': Beecham, Bennington and Bullshit, and return to strolling along the High Street, enjoying coffee and cake at a café whose tables spread onto the footpath where commerce takes precedence over the free-passage of pedestrians; where mothers struggle with prams to negotiate errant table legs and chalkboard menus prominently displayed in the centre of the pavement; where birds dart from nearby rooftops and shop fascias to compete for discarded crumbs, sandwich crusts, flakes of Cornish pastry and remnants of all-day English Breakfasts clinging to plates awaiting clearance by young waitresses sacrificing their leisure and study time to earn a few pounds to purchase the latest CDs or top up their prepaid mobile phones.

I crave walking into shops to sift through racks of jeans and tops, hoping to find a bargain in my size, which I'm ashamed to concede, has marginally increased since my last shopping expedition in Worcester. And I covet looking at babies in prams (not that I want my own – pram or babies) and I need to pat dogs' heads all in a need to regain normality.

Brushing these thoughts aside, I arrive home to find a business card wedged in the door jamb: "*Ring me urgently. Alex*".

Not now. Not today of all days. Just pay the bloody invoice and let me out of this. I've done all I can and more. I'm tired and aggrieved, especially after devoting most of the day to pursuing Rachel – at my expense.

I know twists and turns will confound us during major investigations. I've participated in cases where prime suspects have been exonerated or discounted at the last minute, and

I've seen the exact opposite where the eloquent sweet-faced, victim was, in fact, the perpetrator of a Barclay's Bank robbery.

That was two years ago when Simone Harlock, a Barclay's employee for the previous thirteen years, had bled internal information to a boyfriend, who, in turn, later robbed the very branch where she was employed.

The efforts of a diligent detective, whose name now escapes me, penetrated Simone's veneer of innocence, for it was Simone who had custody of the alarm override code – the same code that her luckless boyfriend had punched into the time-delayed mechanism of the bank's vault.

Whatever the cost, I have to phone Alexander. I trudge upstairs to my apartment, flick on the kettle and notice the answering machine's tiny red attention-grabbing light. Not a good sign, I think, then immediately exchange that with the prospect of having a job enquiry, or better still, an offer for the evening.

You have three messages. Message one, Saturday 9.28 a.m.: 'Hello Olivia, it's Alex. Pick up will you.' SILENCE. 'Please phone me urgently.' *End of message one.*

Message two, Saturday 10.15 a.m.: 'Alex again. Hi.' *End of message two.*

I wonder why he hasn't called my mobile if there is such an urgent pressing matter. I pick up my bag, and even before reaching in, remember I'd switched it to 'SILENT' on entering Rachel's home. I rip out the phone, and sure enough, there are two messages from Alexander and nine missed calls from his home and mobile phone.

Message three. Saturday 11.00 a.m.: 'For God's sake, Olivia. This is most urgent. Please phone me or if I'm out of reach contact Sergeant Glosser at St Austell.' *End of message three.*

I flick through my mobile's memory and press 'Alex Mobile'.

He answers immediately: 'Olivia. There's been a development. Get here right away. I'm at St Austell CID. Roslyn's been found dead.'

'Oh no. All right. I'll leave now. What happened? Where?'

'Can't talk right now. See you soon, okay?'

'Sure. On my way.'

I hesitate, confused as to why he wants me. An instruction rather than request. I've completed the brief; we have no romantic attraction that I know of – well, I certainly have no inclination to hang myself off his arm as a permanent fixture, so I can only surmise he wants me for companionship, or, and I've thrashed this through my mind a thousand times, as a means of bolstering credibility. I know police will ordinarily see through such subterfuge, but a lawyer accompanied by a private investigator can present a formidable barrier to police procedures. I presume that will be my role.

I'd already discounted Alexander as a suspect for his mother's death. I now hope I'm not being dragged in to support an alibi.

Alexander rushes up as soon as he sees me. *Here we go; he's got to get in the first word.* That worries me. Before I've even straightened Fiona in the parking bay, Alexander's peering through my window like a child drooling in his favourite toyshop. He opens my door and before I've extricated myself from the vehicle he laces his arms around me, squeezing air from my lungs: 'She's dead, Olivia. She's been murdered.'

I think it strange that he immediately claims murder, because the police would not pronounce a cause of death until certified by a pathologist. 'What do you mean?' I ask. 'Where? How?' I realise I am as dumbstruck as he, and probably just as irrational.

The police called me an hour ago. They told me a member of the public alerted them to Ros's office where she was found by a passer-by laying on the floor with a massive head wound. From the description of the injury, Roslyn had to have been murdered – or accidentally killed, if we stretch legal boundaries – because her skull was fractured to such an extent that the injuries could not have been sustained by her merely falling over.'

'Does Roslyn work alone?'

'Look. We're all the same. You, me, Roslyn, and any business person. We put in the hard yards. There's always work to do – mornings, evenings, weekends, Christmas. There's orders, accounts, VAT returns, tidying and all the tasks we don't get time for during a *normal* day's work. It's not unusual for Ros to go in early to plan weekend advertising or prepare for an auction. But how anyone else would know that, apart from her staff, is beyond me.

Guilt rises. 'Are you all right? I'm sorry. That should have been my first question.'

'Yes thanks. Good as can be expected. First mum, and now Ros; it's a bit hard to take.'

'So why'd you call me? I don't know what to make of this. I've finished your file. I thought I was out of it.'

'I know. I should have fixed you up already. You're back

on. There's something strange about this whole situation. Just doesn't make sense. I really need your help now, Olivia. The police want to interview me again. I know the routine; if I don't agree, they'll probably arrest me.'

'Jesus. You're joking. They've pinned you as a suspect?'

'Don't fret. They're clutching at straws. Some coppers are like that; just want to stitch it up quick. Sorry, with due respect to your former occupation.'

I need no convincing or apology – that's the reason for my leaving the job.

'Tell you what you can do for me, Olivia. There's a guy called Martin Crowley I once worked with. Brilliant lawyer, works out of a Westminster office. Can you give him a call? Should be under Archbold Chambers – has a couple of rooms there. Give him an overview of my situation. In the meantime, I'll tell these goons I'll not be saying anything until I've got my brief.'

It strikes me as odd that Alexander wants me to contact Crowley when he could just as easily, and more effectively, do it himself.

We walk into the CID foyer where 'Wanted' posters and Missing Persons information overlap each other, forming a giant mural. A row of stained plastic seats wards us off. Alexander strides directly to the reception desk. 'I was speaking to DS Glosser a short time ago. He's waiting for me.'

A man of humungous proportion, dressed in a bedraggled suit, waddles to the counter. His craggy face bounces above a monolithic seven-foot frame. His keg-like stature would look more at home in a cell of over-exuberant drunkards rather than one heading an investigation into the death of a local identity.

He looks at me. 'Glosser.'

Man of few words. Before I speak, Alexander announces: 'My fiancée, Olivia Watts.'

'Good morning, sir,' I offer, pleased with my new status as Mrs Beecham elect.

'If you can come this way, Mr Beecham. I'd like to clear up a few points about your sister's movements.'

I walk with Alexander, following Glosser through the reception doorway and into a maze of corridors.

'You can wait here, Miss Watts. We shan't be long.'

'Olivia's with me. She'll be taking notes.'

'Is she legally representing you?'

'I thought I didn't need legal representation. I'm here of my own accord to assist your enquiries. While I'm assisting you, Miss Watts is assisting me by maintaining a record of our conversation.'

Glosser admits defeat, looks to me: 'Very well. Tag along then.'

So I tag along to the interview room where Glosser is joined by a similarly gigantic WPC.

'Mr Beecham. Perhaps you could tell us how long your sister has worked at Beach Real Estate?

'My sister co-owns the agency. Perhaps you start by telling me what happened and why I'm here?'

I am comforted that Alexander is savvy in legal practice, otherwise DS Glosser might steamroll him into divulging information best kept to himself.

'Very well, Mr Beecham. We received a 999 call that a woman appeared injured, laying on the floor of a real estate office in High Street. One of our cars responded and discovered a Caucasian woman of approximately fifty-years-old on the floor. The officer found no positive vitals. He radioed for an ambulance and advised dispatch who subsequently arranged for the duty inspector and myself to attend. The area was cordoned off and as we speak investigators remain at the scene searching for evidence that might identify your sister's assailant. So you see, Mr Beecham, there's very little I can tell you. Any way you can assist could help arrest whoever is responsible.'

'Of course I'll help, but quite honestly, I know little of my sister's movements. It's not as if we're a close family sharing weekend dinners and the like.'

Glosser drops his elbows to the table. 'Perhaps we could start with this: are you aware of anyone with a grudge against your sister?'

'No I am not, and it is presumptuous that her attack was premeditated by a person or persons known to her.'

Glosser's face matures to a shade of claret. He glances at the silent WPC and motions her to leave the room. She either does not understand his vague direction or is not prepared to breach protocol and leave him alone and open to accusations. She remains fixed to her chair.

I'm amazed by Alexander's summing up of the situation, yet my concern grows that he is prevaricating rather than being objective.

Glosser continues: 'Mr Beecham. Maybe you think I have just walked straight out of the academy. Wrong. I haven't. I've done my homework, you see, and I'm fully versed with recent events in your family, so no one, not even you, is immune to questioning. Now let's start afresh. Who would you suggest had a grudge against Roslyn Beecham?'

Alexander shoots me a furious look, raises his eyebrows

in a manner that says thank goodness you're here to witness this, then turns to Glosser: 'I'm more than happy to assist your enquiry. One suggestion I'll put forward is that it was a random attack – a robbery gone wrong. I know nothing of Roslyn's business practices, her opening times, her client lists. Hell, I don't even do her conveyancing because I don't want to risk a potential conflict of interest suit.'

'So, you have not engaged your fiancée to help immunise you against prosecution for the death of your mother?'

Bloody hell. That's a bold move. Alexander obviously thinks likewise because he's out of his seat addressing the WPC: 'Please ensure you have that statement noted word for word; "You have not engaged your fiancée to help immunise you against prosecution for the death of your mother." Would you please be so kind as to request the attendance of the duty inspector or station commander so I may consult with him in the presence of DS Glosser?'

WPC Collins, I read on her name badge, looks to Glosser. He nods. Beads of perspiration roll from his brow like morning dew drops cascading down the side of a plastic water butty. He's crossed the line and knows that very shortly he'll be paying for it.

Collins returns with Superintendent Ambrose. He presents as an eager salesman ready to overcome all objections. 'Morning Mr Beecham. We have a problem? I'm sure this is resolvable. I have no need to convince you we're only interested in concluding this investigation with urgency. I know DS Glosser here has a slightly different manner about him than you may have previously encountered in your professional role.'

'The problem is, Superintendent, your sergeant

pointedly accused me as responsible for my mother's death by implying Olivia,' – he points to me, – 'is here to "immunise me against prosecution".'

'I don't think that is the case Mr Beecham. DS Glosser has a rather, let me say, robust means of interrogation. I'm sure no charges have arisen from the interview, have they?'

'Not at this stage,' replies Alexander, 'and nor shall there be, because unless you wish to arrest me, I have donated enough of my time to your cause.'

'I don't know if that's entirely practical, Mr Beecham. I'm sure you understand that your cooperation and preparedness to assist in the enquiry relating to your dear sister's tragedy can only be construed as positive?'

'Certainly, Superintendent. Equally, I'm sure you understand that unfounded allegations and accusations against the unblemished character of a professional person can be deemed slanderous and considered as a negative impact on your department?'

I am back in the constabulary. Caught in the crossfire of wit between force command and a suspect. From my experience, the police always come out on top; their protocol, regulations and front-line pleasantries saving them from ridicule and allegations of utilising underhanded investigatory techniques. Fair to say that only few engage in such practices, but when instances like this surface, there is always a senior officer prepared to back his charge to the hilt – no matter the circumstances. Only on rare occasions had I ever heard of an officer being reprimanded or disciplined for 'bringing the constabulary into disrepute' as the scenario is coined in the Police Operational Handbook.

Alexander motions the Superintendent aside and beyond

my range of hearing. I dare not follow, for fear of being labelled an eavesdropper – which is a fitting description of one of my hidden attributes. A moment later they smile and shake hands like reunited Freemasons. Alexander calls me over and together we bid farewell to both Superintendent Ambrose and DS Glosser.

'What happened there? I ask.

'Just set them straight,' Alexander enthuses. 'You see, I was playing squash this morning and signed on at the club at 6.20 a.m. Given that the club has CCTV and that I played three matches with three different opponents, it will be extremely difficult for Glosser to pursue any claim of my involvement. I showered and changed at the club and didn't leave there until 7.50, at which time I headed straight to work. Ambrose is also a member of the club so it took him no time to make a couple of calls to clear this up. Nevertheless, we're no further advanced. I'm waiting for news from the crime scene.'

I'm continually amazed at the way guys fight and brawl, knock each other's heads about, break arms, lose teeth, and then, before even five minutes have lapsed, they share a beer with each other as if nothing had happened: 'Sorry mate. It was all my fault.'

"Nah, I shouldn't 'a' said what I said."

"It's all right. It was my fault. Let's just forget it."

"Nah. Fuck you. It's really my fault an' I can't forget what I said to ya."

Soon enough it's on again – fighting over who was at fault for starting the original fight.

That's pretty much what happened between Alexander and Superintendent Ambrose. Alexander had fired the familiar slur: 'When are you going to focus your attention on catching criminals instead of wasting time arresting mourning family members?' I thought it was uncalled for, but in a sense, Alexander was right, because he expostulated that police had done little since examining Roslyn's office. Sure, they'd door-knocked the immediate area, interviewed staff, and searched the premises. There was no blood, other than Roslyn's, and no tell-tale footprint left in a pool of blood that is the trophy of serial scriptwriters. Collecting hair samples in the hope of identifying DNA was near hopeless in a busy public office, but police did manage to bag fibres and hair retrieved from the immediate vicinity of Roslyn's body. The only positive outcome of their efforts was finding a tiny purple sequin. It would be unrelated of course; probably fallen off a Barbie or young girl's party dress.

I am surprised Glosser had told Alexander that, unless he was aiming for a specific reaction. The police must have had something of substance to justify questioning Alexander. I know from experience that police don't reveal evidential clues unless they have potential for advancing the enquiry. *Why has Glosser given Alexander information of the crime scene status?* And then I wonder why, only hours earlier, Alexander had told me to continue enquiries.

'Alex. I have to speak to you about my engagement. I'm sorry to raise this now, but what are you asking of me? You've told me I'm back on, but surely this is a police matter now; they'll be strategising their procedure as we speak.'

'Olivia. I was thinking of protecting my own interests when I phoned you. I didn't want to go to the police accompanied by a lawyer; it seems so defensive and I didn't want to convey an impression that I had something to hide.'

'You haven't, have you? Be frank with me, Alex.'

'Bloody hell, Olivia. I've just committed myself to paying you for another Christ knows how long and now you're following the lead of that Glosser creep and putting it on me?'

'I hope you don't react like that in the witness box. You'll be rattled by the prosecution in no time.'

'Olivia. You can have faith in me and continue our agreement, or if you feel your investigation is compromised by your belief, however conceived, of my complicity, we may as well settle now.'

'I don't mind either way. The question will be asked by better people than me. Speaking of whom, I got your Mr Crowley. Gave him the gist, but told him to not come down straight away. I left it that if he's needed one of us will call. Now what we should do is put our heads together and decide who would be most advantaged by the loss of your sister. That's my reckoning, anyway. There has to be a reason behind this, and sure as hell it is more than coincidence. These aren't indiscriminate killings – as if I need convince you of that.'

'There's no common link, Liv. Mum didn't have much to leave, and I honestly don't know what Roslyn's got stashed away.'

I overlook him calling me 'Liv'. I've had that conversation before and now isn't an appropriate time for lecturing. 'Okay. I'll tell you what I'll do. I'm going to sniff around Ros's office. The police should be finished by now. Any idea who'll deputise for her?'

'None at all, but as part of a franchise I'm sure someone will step in to ensure the doors remain open.'

My voice breaks to a plea: 'Would you come along with me, just in case I have difficulty gaining access?'

Alexander agrees, and accompanies me to Beach Real Estate, where a woman stands sentry over a cleaning crew. Alexander performs introductions.

The short, stocky woman with the bearing of a museum curator is Susan Davies, Roslyn's second-in-charge. She permits our looking around the office, subject to her observation. I'm uneasy with one eye fixed on Alexander and the other zeroed on me.

'Something wrong?' I cheekily ask, as her eye follows my every move.

'I don't know.'

One of those, I think. The short, simple answer that prevents any prospect of engaging communication. I despise dealing with these trumped up holier-than-thou types who feel it's an imposition or betrayal to assist anyone outside their clique group of friends.

'A woman has just died here. This gentleman's sister. It would be helpful if you would be kind enough to assist us.'

'I told the police everything.'

'Good. Did you tell them if anything was missing from your cash box or rental receipts?'

'They didn't ask.'

Great. Doesn't answer my question directly, but it does illustrate the police did not consider robbery as a motive. 'Did they ask if there was any damage?'

'No. They didn't. But Ros was obviously in here because the front door's okay and the back's still locked.' *Even better. She's opening up.*

'Are you able to tell me what Roslyn was doing this morning? Perhaps her diary's on her desk?'

'I got no idea. The computers weren't on; her office is in there, you can check her diary yourself.'

'So you've got no idea when she opened?'

'No.'

'By the way, what time did you get here?'

'Five to nine as usual. Straight off the bus.'

I walk into Roslyn's office. A handbag sits on her desk. If I were still a police member I would log it and seal it as evidence. I peer inside. No diary. There is a mobile phone which I discretely remove and slip into my pocket. I yell out to no one in particular: 'Mind if I fire up her computer?'

Susan replies: 'Go ahead. It's only got property listings on it.'

Yeah sure. I bet there'll be a swag of emails and maybe even Facebook registrations.

I am right. But no emails offer clues to the morning's tragedy. And then I notice a familiar folder. Mine. Amongst others, my 'Forensics' file has been accessed. I laugh.

'What is it?' Susan calls out.

'Sorry. Clearing my throat.'

Even though I'd seen the long hair spilling out of my flat, I would never have pegged it as Roslyn's. Now, it makes sense. Roslyn has made a career out of inspecting properties of all descriptions from large commercial enterprises to small homes and even smaller flats – like mine. During those inspections, she's obviously acquired a selection of keys to suit most types of locks. She could even have made a hobby of collecting historic keys and lock chambers. In her dealings with locksmiths, if she was possessed of an inquisitive nature like mine, she could have learnt a few easy-entry methods, and maybe accumulated various master keys. No wonder there was no sign of forced entry on my front door.

She'd embarked on the mission purely as a fact-finding exercise. Perhaps she wanted to retrieve incriminating information, or maybe she was trying to help her sister. Whatever her motive, she savoured good fortune by pocketing my memory stick, because sure enough, this is my stuff. She must have thought she'd landed a gold mine of her mother's autopsy information. Too bad. The file was Worcester University material from my suspended Criminal Forensics course. After the risks she'd taken, Roslyn hadn't gained a thing.

I return to the task at hand. 'Susan, I wonder if there's an appointment book at reception or a log of phone calls? Perhaps we can determine from that if Roslyn had arrived early at someone's request.'

'There is no master appointment book. Every sales person, and we have three, maintains their own diary and appointments.'

That confirms my initial belief that Roslyn has a diary. It would be the first thing she'd remove from her bag on arrival, so I am now concerned that it is missing, although what would motivate a person to steal it evades me.

'And the receptionist's log?' I repeat.

'No such thing. All sales enquiries are distributed equally between the agents, unless the caller asks for a consultant by name. If that person is unavailable a message slip is put on his or her desk.'

Roslyn's desk is clear. Her waste basket – one of the best sources of incriminating evidence – is empty. I have no means of ascertaining Roslyn's reason for the early attendance. There is a vague possibility that an enterprising police officer has seized slips, or even the diary. But why then, wouldn't he take her bag? 'Okay then. I'll have a chat with the receptionist later in the morning.'

'Why don't you speak to her sister?'

Alexander swings around. 'Meredith? Meredith was here?'

Susan shrinks behind a partition: 'I'm not certain about this morning, but she's been here a couple of times in the past week. Listed a property with us, but there's been problems. From what I overheard, and I shouldn't be saying this because it's not my listing, someone's lodged an injunction to suspend the sale.'

That'll be Gerald Geddes.

Alexander fumes: 'For Christ's sake why didn't you mention that before?'

'Come on Mr Beecham. Her own sister's hardly going to, you know, do that to her.'

If only you knew. I butt in: She was here when you arrived?'

'No. No one was here except—'

'Except what?'

'Well Ros, laying there in such a state, blood and coffee all over her.'

'So for all we know, Roslyn might have simply tripped and fell, with the most disastrous consequence.' I turn to Alexander: 'Sorry Alex.'

I bid farewell to Alexander. He leaves for his office. I'm sure he'll tender his apologies for the day unless he is required in court.

I arrive home to find no cards stuck in my door and no message light flashing on the phone. My mood changes when I notice a pool of water at the base of my defrosted fridge. I'd left its door open while making my morning coffee.

Loose ends infuriate even the most patient person. From my late teens, I've been unable – or if I tell the truth, *unwilling* – to repair fractured friendships that stem from female bitchiness rolling into a full-scale hate relationship. That's how I am. Forget to return my lipstick or mascara? Too bad, you're no friend of mine.

As I grew older, loose ends dangled at work when I had to decide whether to leave a job on principle because a newer employee gained promotion over me. Later, more loose ends fell into my lap when I engaged in simultaneous relationships with two guys. I had not consciously set out to deceive them, and I had announced that I could not offer monogamy. When I fell in love (as I then thought it was) with two truly eligible bachelors, the loose end syndrome again swung into play to such an extent that I could not decide between the two; I could not muster the fortitude to tell them of my predicament – for I did not want to deceive either – so I simply packed up my flat, left my job and resettled nearly two hundred miles away in Essex.

I reflect on this lifetime of indecision as I struggle to find sleep. I haven't changed, or learnt anything. I want to help Alexander, more for the credibility and accolades my business could earn, but I also want out, because I am out of my depth. This isn't a simple missing person or cheating partner case. From my original charter of having to determine whether a woman's death was natural, a result of malpractice, or, at worst, murder, I'm now trapped in a web of deceit, subjected to the idiosyncrasies of a dysfunctional family, and find myself bang in the middle of what must be considered as four murders. And, I've submitted my final invoice; I'm on a high after finishing my first file, only to be re-hired days later. I start to wonder whether I'm really cut out for this.

From what I can ascertain, the police have made no headway into the Joyce Beecham matter, despite their having unlimited resources at their disposal. Then again, I should remember that I'm not in the loop, as they call it. I would be the last to know the status of their investigation. If not for Stafford, my first tips would come from a news bulletin or morning paper.

30

Sunday 19 March

I wake with a resolution to wrap up the case – or cases as they've become – within forty-eight hours. A firm commitment. I've had enough. My gut feeling screams *target the family*. There are too many coincidences to convince me otherwise, although the death of Nora Geddes remains a red herring. Many a criminal investigation has turned upon the smallest piece of evidence: a strand of hair or nail clipping; a simple word or words spoken within earshot of the wrong person, or the exemplary analytical skills of an investigator.

My skills, so I keep telling myself, are up there with the best. I've no doubt, big call I know, that had I remained in the CID, I would have attained the status of the legendary Sherlock Holmes. I have not discarded that objective – I've merely adjusted it. I can see the multi-storey office now, next to The Gherkin, enormous neon sign blazing 'Watts Happening? Investigations – delivering the science of Sherlock'.

I snap out of my lunacy and scan the pages of notes compiled over the previous fortnight. So many clues interlink, so many relationships are common, yet so many questions remain unanswered. *Time to change tack. If I'm going to resolve this within two days, I'd best adopt a successful formula.*

The reverse chronological investigation is a strategy often applied to serial crimes. The underlying principle is that the more offences or indiscretions a perpetrator makes, the sloppier he or she becomes. It is not so much a matter of his or her being careless; it's their overwhelming confidence in the ineptitude of investigation officers to seize upon the skimpiest fragment of evidence and treat it as an essential element of crime resolution.

Employing this strategy, I revisit Roslyn Beecham's death. The police remain clueless, unless they are withholding pertinent information, which is understandable because of my working relationship with Alexander, who, for all I know, could still be a suspect. However, there seems to be an unexplored avenue of hope. Glosser indicated a lack of evidence, but contradicted himself by mentioning bagged hair strands and a purple sequin.

It should have struck me straight away. With my thoughts wholly trained on Alexander's predicament, I hadn't reacted to a vital clue. Put it down to first-case nerves maybe, but only days earlier I'd seen a sequinned top. The police would have no clue of its existence and relationship to the investigation. Continuing my reverse investigation procedure, I spread across my kitchen table the folder of case notes, photographs, and the printed files I'd misappropriated from Cornwall and District General Hospital. So much for renting a downstairs office, I've hardly used it in the three weeks I've been in Newquay.

I draft my theory, which, once supported with evidence I'm going to gather over the next 47 hours, will be the springboard to charging one person with four murders.

It's not one of my greater cerebral conquests to conclude that Roslyn is Rachel Bennington's aunt. Interestingly, nothing I'd learnt from Roslyn suggests the pair know each other, yet Rachel is aware of Roslyn, presumably through her research uncovering lost family.

I'm not mistaken when I recall seeing a purple sequined top amongst the pile of clothes on Rachel's couch. Does that mean Rachel killed Roslyn? Her face doesn't fit, but who does look like a murderer? The link breaker is that Rachel could not possibly have murdered her paternal grandmother, Victoria Bennington – assuming, of course, that the good Lord Bennington *is* her father. I contrive a new hypothesis: Rachel had embarked on a mission to avenge being discarded, venting her pent-up aggression on those who mattered most to her mother, namely Joyce and Roslyn Beecham. I deplore this innovative thought process because it seems as if I'm indiscriminately painting Rachel as the suspect, even though I'm wholly objective. I won't succumb to emotional attachment, the bane of investigations and working relationships. I've been there before.

In the same manner as I once assembled jigsaw puzzles as a child, I complete the picture. No wonder no one has ever been suspected of Victoria Bennington's death. It makes sense, I now prophesise, that she *must* have died of natural causes. I arrange for Hamilton to obtain a copy of her Death Certificate, with added hope that he might be able to locate the certifying doctor. The remainder of the puzzle assembles itself quicker than Stafford's attempt at the Rubik's cube.

Beneath her facade, Rachel is a conceited child full of venom. She has carried vindictive baggage over many years. On my second visit, she told me that she and her gran had maintained contact over the years. Rachel had every opportunity to visit her grandmother and I remember her recounting watching family members gather and evade each other in the car park. My present focus is to link Rachel to the insulin overdose which has now been established by autopsy. Insulin is freely available. No prescription? Log onto pharmacy dot com. But for all I know, Rachel could be diabetic.

From there, and now I'm winging it, Rachel decides to sink in the boots and implicate her mother in the death of her patient, Nora Geddes. A simple enough exercise I surmise. I'd demonstrated the simplicity of posing as a cleaner, so I have no doubt that Rachel would be able to perform a similar subterfuge. Maybe she'd posed as a voluntary worker, selling flowers, or she'd entered the hospital under the auspice of sketching portraits of patients for their family. Unfortunately, until I hear from Hamilton, I have no knowledge of how Mrs Geddes died.

Finally, I have not discovered why Roslyn has been killed. Had it not been for the purple sequin, I would still be facing a blank sheet when it comes to identifying Roslyn's murderer. Now, I think I'm further advanced than the police. I imagine Glosser in his office, red-faced and scratching his bulbous head trying to draw out clues.

I continue speculating. There is no reason I know of for Rachel to despise Roslyn or level animosity toward her. It might simply have been another irrational ploy to attack Meredith's emotions.

I make coffee. Sit down and revise the theory. I've ventured to the far-fetched, using knowledge of serial murders having evolved from traumatic childhoods and negative family dynamics. In my Worcester forensics class, I'd been studying the cases of Fred and Rosemary West, the Yorkshire Ripper, and other reprehensible subjects, and had learnt that in most cases there was a logical (in the mind of the offender) reason or explanation for their grotesque killings. There were cases of boys being pampered by their mothers, only to grow up despising women. Others killed for jealousy because they couldn't be what they wanted: a woman. Then there were the dozens of women killed and maimed for reasons of sexual deviation, and abhorrent acts of child killing by thrill-seeking bored teenagers – or even younger, as was the case with the pair convicted of Jamie Bolger's murder.

Growing up an only child, I have never experienced, first hand, the jealousies and emotional traumas developed by siblings in early childhood. Certainly, I've witnessed it during visits to friend's homes, where children fight over dolls, games, television channels and attention from their parents. I've also seen the results of retribution: beheaded and amputated dolls, missing draughts and chess pieces and bans prohibiting television favourites. Such vindictive traits are frequently carried through to adulthood, the repertoire expanded and perfected.

It's now up to me to prove just how Rachel has wiped out three women. I grab my bag and car keys, leap out to my car and head, hopefully for the last time, to Southampton. Had I not been so impulsive I would not have spent a fortune in time and money making three such trips. Working for myself has burdened me with new disciplines, disciplines I am yet to refine. Enthusiasm overrides sensibilities, yet I still achieve results, albeit slowly.

As I enter Southampton's metropolis, I have less than 44 hours to meet my target.

Rachel answers the door, cigarette in mouth, paintbrush in hand.

'Hello Rachel. We need to talk.'

'What this time? We talked yesterday.'

'Yesterday, you didn't tell me everything. Things have changed.' I invite myself through her doorway and into the kitchen. 'Tell me, Rachel, when was the last time you visited Plymouth?'

Her face twists. Surprised that I know something I shouldn't.

'Haven't been there for ages. Can't remember when.'

'Rachel. You can't keep messing with me. Right now, you're a suspect in a serious crime. The police have evidence, but they don't know what I know.'

'So what makes you think you're so smart?'

'Because a piece of your sequinned top was found on the floor of Beach Real Estate where Roslyn Beecham was found dead yesterday.'

'I never even touched her. We was just talking. Like the whole family is fuckin' crazy. I only wanted to warn her.'

That stings me. I can't think fast enough: 'Warn her? About what?'

Rachel hangs her head. 'Oh shit. I'm really in this now. It all started when Alex phoned me about gran—'

I see Rachel as a cauldron of shocks and surprises. 'You

know Alexander? You've spoken to him?' She throws me right off-guard because Alexander has never mentioned Rachel. I give no leeway. 'Rachel. When did you first speak to Alexander?'

'Ages ago. Remember the other day I told you about finding my mother and grandmother? It was shortly after my mother pissed me off by still rejecting me that I met gran at her home. It was pretty discreet because she was on edge about one of her girls arriving without notice. I think I told you that I felt she was trying to make up for the mother I never had, and that included telling me about Meredith, Roslyn, and Alexander. I'd worked out Meredith for myself, but gran filled in many blanks. She told me to not contact Alex and Ros because if it got back to Meredith there would be all hell to pay, as she put it. I didn't know like what she meant by that, but I understood that a woman who could give up her birth child could be capable of anything.

'I ignored gran's direction. I sometimes fall into depression and loneliness and wonder if that could have been what drove me to contact Alexander. Maybe I was just looking for a big brother when I had no one else. Not that I needed friendship, I just wanted to feel normal.'

Every syllable of Rachel's pain sears my skin, for I too experience similar feelings of not belonging. Even now, I wish I had a brother or sister to confide in, exchange ideas, brag about work conquests and share birthday and Christmas celebrations.

'It was not until gran was first in hospital that I phoned Alex. I wanted to meet him at the hospital as a surprise, but then because gran had told me not to contact them, I didn't know if gran had actually told them about me. I certainly didn't want to create a scene or cause him distress. I took the chicken's way out and rang him. At least I would have been able to like, handle rejection over the phone.

'It turned out that gran had not told Alexander, so he was wary at first – more than wary, he didn't believe me. I rattled off some family details, courtesy of gran, which made him even more curious. I know that he later spoke to gran about me, but I never found out what was said. I imagine there were no kind words for Meredith.

'I s'pose I'm going on a bit here, but I'll tell you why I had to see Roslyn. I think Alex had learnt a few things about Meredith because of your investigation. He told me how sorry he was about my gran and said that everything would work out. I didn't really get what he meant by that, but then I didn't really, and still don't, know how to take Alex. He's so quiet and reserved and from what I could work out, aside from his work he has nothing. I'm sure he was his mother's favourite. I don't know whether he is, or was, a follower of euthanasia, but some things we discussed about his mother's health surprised me. I mean, he is a lawyer – I just expected, like, a different outlook. He somehow seemed to accept that life is disposable. I suppose in a way, it is.'

Rachel speaks like a woman on a mission, far removed from the Rachel I met a week ago. At first, she was a harsh, dry desert with little to offer but heat and aggression. Today she is the Garden of Eden – full of life, hope and wisdom.

Her acknowledgement of life being disposable strikes a chord. Yes, life is disposable and sometimes we accept that only too late, by which time no restitution for lost times can be made, no goodbyes can be expressed and no final words of love can be offered to those we once hurt and forever cast aside.

Despite my intrigue with Rachel's monologue, I try to coerce her to the point: 'So you saw or spoke to Alexander recently?'

'Yes. We spoke often. He once told me he'd more in common with me than with his sisters, but then we are, like, half the same blood, aren't we? There was something he said one day that made me shiver. Maybe it was the way he said it, but it was just after gran died when he came down to see me to, I suppose, console me.

'He was telling me how he believed his sister, Meredith I mean, had "knocked off" his mother. I first thought he was drunk to say something like that, but he was totally coherent. I said: "That's my mum you're talking about" and he said, "I'm sure you wouldn't miss her". Maybe I wouldn't, but that wasn't the point.

'He rambled on about his sisters being an embarrassment to him and his legal practice. I'd never heard him or seen him like that before so when he said, "I'm going to fix my sisters once and for all," I panicked and became over-concerned. I didn't give a shit about Meredith, but I felt I had to tell Roslyn that her brother had like, lost the plot and might do something to them.

'I was like, fuck me – excuse the language. I've seen grief capture people in different ways. That was two weeks ago. I didn't hear from him until a few days ago when he rang to tell me to keep a low profile and not contact anyone in the family. When I asked why, he just said that the result of an investigation into the death of some Nora woman was about to be released and that it didn't look good for Meredith.'

'So what's that got to do with you and Roslyn?'

'Because he'd told me that Roslyn had something over Meredith – sorry, but I still can't call her mum. I don't know exactly what it is, but I panicked, knowing how nutty Meredith is, so I went to Roslyn's office; I had to find out why she was threatening Meredith. She doesn't care about the wider family, only money.'

Aha. Did Roslyn know more than I thought she knew, or had Meredith confided in Roslyn only to find that she'd turned on her? My stolen USB memory stick again comes to mind.

'Roslyn wouldn't accept that I was her niece. She wouldn't believe that her own sister hadn't told her about me. I don't know what she really thought of me, but she told me to get out, shouted like, in very strong terms. The bitch. I refused to leave. Then she grabs me and shoves me outside. Can you believe that? I nearly bumped into a guy walking along the street. Wish you'd find him. He'd tell ya'.

'What time was this?'

'I dunno. Like about quarter past eight? I bet that's when the sequin came off my top.'

This doesn't get any easier. I have no reason to question Rachel's account but I see another shade of Alexander's character.

'So what happened after Roslyn pushed you out of the office?'

'Happened? Nothing. All right, I yelled out a few choice words, like "stuff you, Roslyn you bitch" and then I walked down the road for a snack before returning home.'

'Look Rachel. I'm not really sure what's going on here. We've got nothing to go to the police with, but I am concerned about your safety. Do you have somewhere else you can stay for a couple of days?'

'I guess so. Why would I be in danger? I haven't done anything.'

'Just a precaution. If your gran's named you in her will, it's very likely that you could be in danger. Remember that three members of *your* family have met suspicious deaths.'

31

Sunday 19 March

I leave Rachel's home with a different perspective than I held when I arrived. The information gleaned from her could either help or hinder the enquiry. I think about Alexander's mannerisms and his resolve to see this matter to its conclusion – no matter what. I grab my phone. It is time to call Stafford for an information exchange.

I look at the phone. What the frig? It isn't my phone. I freak, thinking I've picked up someone else's by mistake, when I remember snaffling Roslyn's phone from her bag. I fumble through its menu to 'Calls Received' and see that Roslyn had received Rachel's call two days' earlier. I scroll to the next ten numbers and freeze. Roslyn's day had been punctuated by calls from both Meredith and Alexander – just three days before her attack. I can't read anything into this, but I sense a great urgency within the family to exchange six calls over one day. And it must have been of much greater significance than arranging a dinner party.

I crank Fiona into life and leave Southampton, hopefully for good.

Minutes after joining the 70-mph traffic flow, a white van races up behind me, lights flashing. Granted, I am sitting in the right-hand lane daydreaming, but there is no need for this imbecile to ride within inches of my butt honking and flashing. I slide across to the middle lane. The van follows, maintaining a gap of only inches.

I've long believed drivers of white vans have a self-appointed right-of-way over our roads and motorways. I've read their (the literate ones at least) Letters to the Editor complaining of old biddies and bingo players clogging London's arterial roads with their 50 to 60 mph Volvos and Peugeots humming along to Beethoven's Moonlight Sonata, while these alleged 'professional drivers' assume priority of the roads with the status of an emergency vehicle.

The driver behind me is not professional. I've given him the right-hand-lane, but he persists in tailing me. I move to the left and again he follows. There is no signwriting on the van's sides or front, and he is travelling too close for me to be able to read the number plate. All I can identify is the three-pointed 'Mercedes' star, and the driver's thin face masked by the customary baseball cap and wrap-around sunglasses. The glasses are superfluous. Either he is a fashion icon or preparing for an eclipse. The morning news had not predicted such an event; today's weather is set to be cloudy and gloomy.

My outlook is also gloomy. I remember that before being waylaid by my interest in Roslyn's phone, I was going to phone Stafford. Like a trick or treater, I plunge my hand back into my bag and retrieve my own phone, only to then grapple with the difficulty of checking the menu, scanning the road ahead, and watching a mirror full of Mercedes grille.

I hold the phone to my ear, hoping the van driver will

think I'm calling the police. I expect him to panic, but he doesn't back off an inch. An approaching services exit could be my saviour. I exhale relief and then inhale despair, realising that two miles is a long way whilst driving under duress. I indicate and move back to the centre lane, only to see the van replicate my move. I slow to 70 mph and increase to 90, poor Fiona screaming, and still the van persists in its magnetic attraction of her rear end. At one stage, he drives so close that I actually feel my car surge forward. *The bastard hit me.*

The services exit approaches. I hold my position in the centre lane hoping that I can make a last-minute swerve to the left, fiercely predicting there will be no traffic in the left lane to obstruct me. My mirrors remain full of Benz as the exit rushes towards me. The left lane is not yet clear, although there is a minute gap – sufficient for me to slingshot through if I time the manoeuvre to perfection. I wait until the last second. As the Armco barrier divides the motorway from the exit ramp, I wrench the steering wheel, jerk my car across the motorway, and into the slip lane. The car fishtails like an aggressive pendulum. I miss the steel railing by inches and skim the gravel shoulder. I fist pump the air like Lewis Hamilton winning his fiftieth grand prix. The van continues, defeated on the motorway. But before I turn my head toward the cafeteria he sidles in to the emergency lane and stops.

From the apron of the service court I watch the van, with hazard lights flashing and reversing lights ablaze, inch back to the exit ramp. I am certain the driver can't continue to watch me while he dodges cars and lorries leaving the motorway. As he finally accesses the ramp, his intention can only be to drive into the service centre. I grab my phone from the passenger seat and dial 999. I feel foolish for not being able to relay my exact location nor the registered number of the van that has tailed me for nearly twelve miles. I am pleased to hear that an area car is nearby and will attend within minutes.

The van appears at the top of the exit road. I drop the phone and pull up next to a petrol bowser where I top up with unleaded. I lock the car and race into the service kiosk, pay for my fuel and tell the attendant that I'm waiting for the police.

'You can't leave your car on the forecourt.'

I tell him to sort it out with the police because I'm not leaving the kiosk.

The van driver parks in a service bay and feigns checking tyres or similar antic. At the same time, a police car enters the refuelling area.

I rush from the kiosk, approach the officers, identify myself as the caller, and point to the van.

'Any witnesses, miss?'

'Maybe. But no one's stopped.'

'Any damage?'

'Well, look at me. I'm shaking, I'm stressed and I'm still panicking about what he was going to do. Look! He's driving off.'

'We need to be satisfied an offence has been committed before we approach him—'

'He hit my bloody car. I could have been pushed off the bloody road.'

'But you weren't. Any damage to your car?'

I survey the rear of my car and see no new scratch or

dent amongst the ripples of car park casualties. This would probably be the only time I'd curse the resilience of plastic bumpers. Bloody hell; I once tapped a car in a Pay and Display and inherited a repair bill of £320 for a thumbnail dent in the front bumper of a BMW.

I know the police routine. No personal injury. No property damage. No witnesses. A minor traffic offence has been disclosed which will most definitely be denied by the van driver – if they catch him.

I quickly explain the case I am working on, my link to DCI Stafford – where I hoped a touch of name dropping would assist me – and plead with them to question the driver. A constable scribbles his name and number on a corner of his running sheet. Rips it off and hands it to me: 'Call me in a few hours. I'm off at eight.' I don't know whether to take that as an invitation for a night out, or whether he wants rid of my complaint before 8.00 p.m. I promise to relay Gilby's attitude to Stafford.

On arriving home at 5.00 pm, I phone Gilby, who happens to be in the station on a break. He advises that he's been unable to locate the white van without a registration number. 'There's dozens on the motorway,' he offers, which I accept as his way of ending the matter. Quite rightfully, I suppose, because from his perspective I'd disclosed nothing more than the possibility of an over-aggressive driver, keen to complete his day's final delivery.

Such is the problem with reporting a minor offence. What do we expect of the constabulary? The van owner would pleasantly admit his indiscretion: "Yes. I tailgated her for five miles, gave the bumper a bit of a tap to move her on, followed her to a petrol station where I intended to give her a piece of my mind, then after deciding against that, I drove off." The police officer would appreciate such honesty and consequently dispatch the driver with a stern warning.

But this is not a case of a frightened female venting frustrations to police. I know I was the driver's target. The lane changes, the tap – supposedly to scare me into pulling over – and then following me into the service centre, were all intimidatory actions. I will not let it rest because it is too coincidental that I would be targeted so far from my home, but only a stone's throw from Rachel's. And more importantly, only minutes after speaking with her.

I should not have placed my trust in PC Gilby. Long ago I'd learnt my father's favourite expression: 'If you want a job done properly – do it yourself.' I remember him teasing my mother after he'd picked a ball of fluff from the floor after mum had hoovered; he echoed it after mum made his cup of tea and he gruffed it when mum ran his bath too warm. I later understood how sarcastic my dad was, for my mum did everything to please him and convey her deep love in the only manner she knew how – by being a good wife. Dad truly loved her, but had an uncanny way of unsettling her. I guess the fun was in the making up.

On reflection, I should not have relied so much on Gilby. I should have applied my natural inquisitive manner at the service station and asked the attendant if I could review his security tape or DVD of the van sitting in the service bay.

I phone the service station and speak with Dominic, who had been the attendant on duty at the relevant time. I learn that he cannot reproduce a CD without authorisation from his manager who will not be on duty until 7.00 a.m. the following morning. I am not prepared to wait 26 hours for information I need now. 'Can I come back and have a look at the tape so I can identify the driver for the police?'

Dominic hesitates: 'I can't see any harm in that.'

I drive the 90 minutes back to the service centre and see Dominic. I show him my identification which he fails to realise gives me no power or authority to enter his premises and view the images. He guides me behind the counter, presses 'search' on the DVD recorder, and programs in 1550, by some means recalling the time of my earlier visit.

'How'd you remember that?

'I made a log of the police attending; just a thing we're supposed to do. It's mostly for drive offs and stuff. The boss just wants to know when the police are here. He prob'ly slips 'em a slab at Christmas.'

The angle of the van affords me a reasonable view of the driver, although the cap and thick jacket prevent me from getting much more than a blurred image of his facial features. I recall from his checking the tyres that he is approximately five-foot-seven and medium to chubby build with a pale complexion. The same as another five million British males. This means little though, for the real reason I want to view the security footage is to obtain the registered number of the van. I'd convinced myself that Dominic would be too cautious to release such a treasure, so I have to once again employ devious means to retrieve it in a roundabout manner.

The number is easy to read. On the inside of my hand I write GH10 176. I thank Dominic for his help, buy a coffee for the road and a chicken burger that had just been placed under malfunctioning halogen heat lamps.

I want a quick report on the van's ownership, but am

reluctant to call Gilby. It is also not the right time to solicit help from either Ambrose or Stafford because that would mean recounting the whole experience all over again. I am sure they'll be too involved in other pressing matters, Roslyn's death for one, than to be distracted by a laughable traffic matter. Perhaps I am fishing in the ocean of non-biting prey.

Right now, I need Hamilton's expertise.

I press his number into my phone. 'You've called the amazing H,' the voice mail squawks, inviting me to leave a message.

I muster my most seductive voice because a woman's power is wrapped in a parcel of expectation – give that parcel to a guy and you've won him over. 'Never burn your bridges' said my father, the man of proverbs and clichés. 'Hi Hamilton it's Oliv—'

'Hello Olivia. My favourite sleuth. Sorry. Screening my calls for a while. A few women want me to entertain them; I'm having to reduce the field for a while.'

'Come on Hamo. Your field's been fallow since last week. Listen, I need help. I'm studying history and need info on Golf-Hotel-ten-one-seven-six. I'm on my way home. Can you call me in an hour?'

'I'll do better than that. I'll drop 'round – nothing like personal service.'

'No Hamilton. I'm flat out at the moment and dependant on what you find, I may be even busier. However, I will reward you once I've completed this case, which, hopefully, should be tomorrow – all being well.'

I'm saddened by putting off Hamilton because I'm forever appreciative of his sedulous devotion to providing information and resources. I drive home at an easy pace, watching traffic, bridges, and overpasses flash by, and shudder as white vans whizz by in either direction. I nibble on the cold burger and aid its digestion with luke-warm coffee. I will not arrive home until nearly nine o'clock; too late to do much of anything except sleep and subconsciously plan the next day's activities. I hope Hamilton will have the information I require, but just as quickly dismiss the optimism, believing that if someone is prepared to mount such brazen intimidation on a public highway, they'd be smart enough to do it in either a stolen vehicle or one fitted with false plates. If that is the case, my day will once again end on a negative note.

32

Sunday 19 March

I've not been home long enough for my kettle to boil when Hamilton phones. 'You're gunna love this,' he announces.

Here we go again. Hamilton concealing his findings in a shroud of suspense. I am tired of having to prise every single detail from him. I liken his antics to a puppy bouncing for rewards after performing tricks. I am beyond caring about training and rewards; I just want to wrap this case and pick up a simple, straightforward file.

'Okay, Hamilton. I know you're good. I know you're efficient. What am I going to love?'

'My new couch. No, not really. Your white Mercedes van is a rental. Registered to Commercial Rentals in Manchester, but could have been hired from any one of their forty-eight national outlets.'

'Shit! Just when I'm on the verge of thinking we're on the way, another hurdle pops up and destroys my whole line of thinking. What the hell am I supposed to do now, start phoning forty-eight rental stations and ask if they've rented a white Merc' registered GH10 176? If I start tomorrow morning I suppose I could be done by lunch.'

'Olivia. You worry so much. Surely the info's not that

important. As you said, it was only a minor traffic offence.'

'He could have run me off the road, stuff you! His sole purpose was to intimidate me. I must have something big enough for someone to want me silenced.'

'You're not *that* important. I think you're jumping to conclusions, Olivia.'

'Jumping to conclusions? Yes, Hamilton, that's what I'd expect from someone in your position. *You* weren't there.'

'Settle down Olivia. I don't mean it that way. I mean you're jumping to conclusions about the driver. How do you know it was a guy?'

He's got me. I cast my mind back to the "guy" in my apartment. Surely, I can't be caught twice? Have I been taken in again and accepted the obvious? How could I know who was driving? I've made the classic error of assuming. Twice. How many times have I heard the formula? If you assume, you make an 'ass' out of 'u' and 'me'.

Once again, Hamilton strings me along, toying with my emotions, delighting in my suffering, controlling me like a yo-yo on a pliable string.

'You bastard. You've got more, haven't you?'

'Da-dah. Yes. And this one you'll really love. I was able to access, with great difficulty – but not beyond *me*, of course – the data base for Commercial Rentals…'

Here we go again. I'm going to get the mega-story of Hamilton's five-minute mouse clicks which led to the information. He'll stretch it out and purport to be the greatest computer hacker of all time. *He probably is.* His words hit the target.

'… and I found the van had been signed out from their depot on The Esplanade, in St Austell, Cornwall.'

'That's a great help, Hamilton. You're wonderful. I'll head down there first thing in the morning.'

'You don't want to hear the rest, then?'

I should have known he would not give up on his suspenseful oratory. 'Of course I do H. It can only get better.'

'It does. Anyway, as I was saying. Where was I? Oh yes, the van was rented to a woman. I think you know that all rentals require licence information for identity and insurance purposes. I managed to trace these details after lifting them from Cornwall's data base. It's quite simple really; but you have to know about MYSQL programming—'

'Hamilton! Shut the fuck up and tell me who it was!'

'Meredith Bennington.'

I reel back in my chair. 'Holy shit. You know who that is, don't you?'

'I think it'll be an unconvicted murderess. A simple thing like road-rage might be her downfall. I think we may be able to nut this out together. I'll bring 'round a pizza.'

I let Hamilton's cryptic invitation slip by, thank him for the info and offer a rain-cheque using the worn excuse of being tired and about to go to bed.

I'm too hyped up. The word 'pizza' has whet my appetite. I punch 'pizza' into my phone. Pancho's is predial number three, ranked in order of importance beneath 'mum and dad' and the reinstated 'Dave mobile'.

Talking to myself to accentuate the validity of my thoughts, I play through the events of the previous three weeks as I interpret them. I discard Rachel and now focus on Meredith who I still believe had accelerated her mother's death, and it seems beyond doubt, now, that she'd similarly aided Nora Geddes to heaven. Both tragedies mirror the death of her ailing mother-in-law, Victoria. I am puzzled over Roslyn's death and wonder how a woman can harbour so much hatred of her own sister. From what I've seen and learnt of Meredith, nothing is beyond her.

I open my front door to the pizza driver, resplendent in orange shirt with green and red chillies screen-printed on the front. I give him £10 and motion to keep the £4 change. I sit down to a large Pancho's Special, accompanied by a flat, half-bottle of chardonnay – the first half used as a Saturday night sedative. *So what's next, Liv? I just want to be rid of it. Now. Nothing's clear-cut, just too many surprises. I don't even know who I am anymore. I've got enough info on this Beecham family to know they're all off the planet.*

I convince myself to leave cleaning until morning. Within minutes I am in bed, the smell of garlic and leftover pizza crusts wafting through my room. I pick up my mobile. 10.02 p.m. No, not too late to phone him.

'Stafford.'

'Hi. Did I wake you?'

'No. I'm on night shift. Just about to head off. What's up?'

'Need to see you. Desperately. About this Beecham case.'

'As I said, I'm on duty tonight. Name a time.'

'Shit. I've had hell of a day and just this minute clambered into bed. This can't wait though. I'll freshen up. Can we meet somewhere?'

'Olivia, what have you got? This had better be worthwhile.'

I explain the day's events, my meetings with Rachel, the white van and how it ties in with Hamilton's information.

'Very well. I've not much on. You get some sleep and I'll see you about midnight.'

I'm pleased to not have to set out into the night and drive along the motorway where I'd probably be hypnotised to sleep. I can do that well enough in my own home. So anxious am I about sleeping through the midnight alarm, I'm drifting in and out of sleep when my front door bangs with such force I think that someone is trying to break in. I groggily pull on track suit pants and a top and race downstairs to silence Stafford before the neighbours do.

'My, Olivia. This is a side of you I haven't seen. Someone steal your hairbrush?'

'Very funny.' I thrust my fingers through Rastafarian tangles in a vain effort to tizzy myself up. 'It's been a difficult couple of days. Come and sit down.'

I pour coffee while Stafford sits at the kitchen table opening his laptop and removing a manila folder from his attaché.'

'You're a victim of road-rage now?' he asks with tilted head.

'I hope you take it more seriously than did one of your colleagues. When I learned who was driving the van, my case of road-rage, as against a minor incident, was avowed.'

'But you don't know who was driving. I've spoken with Gilby. Olivia, I've come prepared.'

'At that time, I didn't know. And, I might point out, Gilby didn't *want* to know. Since then I've got information, evidenced in a printout, that Meredith Bennington hired the van. I bet Gilby didn't prepare you with that.'

'He didn't need to, Olivia. Meredith may have hired the van, but you have no proof of identity that she was driving at the time of the alleged incident.'

'It wasn't an "alleged" incident. It happened. And if it wasn't Meredith driving, who was it? I reckon she knew I was getting to the truth and after somehow finding out that I've spoken with her daughter, she's targeted me.'

I sit two coffee cups on the table, remove a solid bag of sugar from a cupboard beneath the sink (which explains why it's solid) and pour a half carton of milk into a small jug – not for presentation, but to conceal the expired 'use by' date on the carton.

Stafford chastises me about Blackstone's *Evidence and Procedure,* which he claims I've forgotten since my academy training. I concede that I cannot prove beyond reasonable doubt that Meredith had been driving the van. But I am not presenting evidence in a court of law. I am considering facts and scenarios that will help us reach a conclusion or at least steer us toward determining who is responsible for atrocities which have escalated far beyond a simple case of researching a suspicious death.

'Dave. You get a copy of everything from Ambrose?'

'Yes. That and more. He spoke to a witness in a local shop who remembered Roslyn buying a couple of lattés just before eight in the morning. She's clear about it because she opened the shop before her official sign-on time of eight.'

'Two coffees? That's interesting.'

Stafford's eyebrow dances: 'Why?'

'SOCO bagged only one cup.' I offer a wry smile at having done my homework. I continue: 'But she saw no one we could identify as a suspect?'

'Unfortunately not, but we've pinpointed the time.'

I consider Stafford's double-standard: 'That's as open to conjecture as is Meredith driving the van. The time of buying coffee has no relationship to her attack other than *suggesting* she opened her office at eight o'clock or thereabouts.'

'And that's a good start because it gives us only a one hour window to investigate, because, as you'd know, if you'd done *your* homework, Miss Davies arrived at the office at nine.'

'Five to nine – if it makes any difference. Okay. Let's settle down here. The haze disturbs me. This shouldn't be a battle of wits between us. We used to get on so well – I don't know how we got railroaded. Anyway, have you made anything of a sequin thing found on the floor? It was logged by SOCO.'

Stafford laughs the question aside: 'Fell out of some hippy's hair I suspect. Or maybe Roslyn was set upon by the fairy godmother.'

'That's not really funny. You may be surprised to know that I know, and can prove, where the sequin came from. And believe me, it *is* related.'

'My. You have been busy, haven't you?'

'I might go and review my "*Evidence and Procedure*" first.' I deal the Hamilton Holt card of suspenseful revelation and spend fifteen minutes explaining the Meredith and Rachel connection; of how Rachel had found her gran through ancestral information, forged a strong friendship and ultimately had watched Meredith, Roslyn and Alexander attend the hospital. I explain how Rachel had been granted unlimited access to the hospital, a fact that neither Stafford nor Ambrose had unearthed, and I offer ample proof that anyone could have visited Joyce Beecham without their identity being logged. Stafford expresses surprise that a family would hold on to such a secret for over 30 years to which I reply many families have succeeded in similar or worse concealments for twice as many years.

The first cup of coffee restores only half of my usual radiance and alertness. I pour us both a second.

'Your theory doesn't hold water,' Stafford interjects. 'Why would Rachel want to warn Roslyn about anything? How would Rachel know that her mother's a threat to anyone? Just because she'd been abandoned at birth doesn't mean her mother's predisposed to criminality. The kid, sorry, I presume she's not a kid anymore, has a huge chip on her shoulder, but that doesn't make her an authority on the mental capacity of a mother she never knew.'

Stafford, as usual, makes sense. I have already questioned my own conclusions. Heading my thoughts is the knowledge of Meredith renting the van, and for a reason that still evades me, why she had tried to frighten me into running off the motorway. While running that through my mind I postulate how far Meredith would go to protect herself.

Stafford continues: 'Your revelation of the sequin's ownership does shed a different light on the investigation. It crystallises a line Ambrose put to me after he'd delved into the background of your lawyer friend. You see, Ambrose had an uneasy feeling about this Mr Beecham. Word is that this Beecham's been getting it off with a younger woman – that may well turn out to be your elusive Rachel.'

'Don't be ridiculous. She's effectively his niece.'

'Not effectively, Olivia. She *is*; you've established that yourself.'

'So what? Rachel told me her grandmother, Joyce, whose death we are investigating if you haven't forgotten, had tried to bring unity to the family by telling Rachel about her uncle and aunts. Rachel's already told me of visiting the hospital and seeing both her mother and Alexander. There's nothing clandestine about that. And as for "getting it off", that's a trite unfair – you make it sound like a behind-the-scenes dalliance. Rachel has already told me how she saw him as the brother she never had. Alexander helped reconstruct the Beecham side of her family tree.'

'All right then. Let's leave him aside for the moment. You came to me a couple of weeks ago with a file of documents and bank statements of Meredith Bennington's accounts. We've substantiated her earnings and deposits far exceed her regular income. She was beneficiary of funds legally pledged to her through various wills and Powers of Attorney. We have no reason to believe there was any coercion or unlawful measures employed by her. However, there is an ethics issue of how a person charged with the responsibility of caring should be permitted to profit from their patient. Back to Ambrose and his little discovery. Did you know that Alexander had prepared the paperwork and acted for Meredith in formalising those agreements?'

I am floored. 'No way. He would have told me. In fact, he did mention once that he wouldn't even do Roslyn's conveyancing for fear of conflict of interest.' I could not accept that Alexander had double-dealt me. I understood the conflict if Alexander were to accept Roslyn's instructions; remember, her name is also Beecham – it would stand out like the proverbial dogs' bollocks. Meredith, on the other hand, was a 'Bennington'. Not quite so obvious.'

I want to eject him and go back to bed. Right now, there would be nothing better than burying my head under a duvet. If I have been dudded by the very guy who contracted me, I'll turn the corner and seek my own vengeance.

Many times I've been deceived by guys – most women would relate to this – but we only find out when it's too late. We give our heart, our soul, our love, and our whole being to the one who sweeps us off our feet. He brings flowers, chocolates, and intimate gifts, makes us feel special, on top of the world and so happy that we've successfully found that one special love. Then, when we are so hooked and unable to recognise or accept any love in the world other than his, we're taken to the candlelit dinner in the fancy, exclusive restaurant; our heart fluttering in expectation of the big question: *Will you marry me?* Instead, we are introduced to the black zone of emotion.

'There's something I have to tell you,' he says, the tone aggravating butterflies in our stomach.

We're on guard. *Oh, oh. What's this?*

'You know I love you very much and I should have told you this long ago… I shouldn't have waited… I'm married you see… It's been over for a long time and we're working toward a divorce… I just thought I should let you know.'

And of course, us women, seething inside and wondering how any guy can produce so many words from his mouth in just one breath, cop it sweet. Never mind the fact that the guy's got his bread buttered on both sides; we'll sweetly reply: 'Oh really. Yes, you should have told me. How long have you been apart?'

'I'm still looking for a place. We sleep in separate rooms though.'

Of course we all know he's telling the truth – he just slips into her room every second night for a quickie while we're sitting at home thinking he's sleeping in hardship on the floor.

Bastards.

Stafford has been wrong before, but not very often. I do not want to accept that Alexander had double-played me. I can't see how he has, nor can I see what he would gain from it.

'Dave. Please go with me on this. Alexander has nothing to gain. He's got no reason to kill his mother or Geddes and there's not enough disharmony or evidence of any fractured relationship between him and Roslyn. Sure, they're a bunch of misfits, but Alex is not involved. Meredith, on the other hand, is a different kettle of fish.'

'Tell you what I'll do, and we gotta do this quick. I'll haul in Meredith's ass tomorrow afternoon after I've slept. I'll tee it up with Ambrose.'

I know protocol won't permit me access to the interview. I've been fortunate to accompany Alexander during recent questioning, but I am disappointed that I won't see the fruits of my labour mature under Meredith's interrogation. 'Why don't you do an informal first up in the morning? She obviously feels safe at present, but the threat of a formal interview might allow her time to prep a story. I don't wish to feather my own nest, but if we both attended early, say, under the pretence of the old 'routine enquiries' we could legitimately question her in relation to her sister's death. There is a possibility that she may not even know her sister's been killed. Would Ambrose have released her name yet? Would Alexander have told her? I sincerely doubt it.'

'You expect me to do a full night shift then front up at 8.00 am or so for an interview?'

I tuck my hands under my chin and pout: 'You've had no difficulty staying up all night before, if I remember correctly.'

'Very well. Meet me at the northern end of Pin Oak at eight on the dot.'

33

Monday 20 March

I stir from four hours' restless sleep, drained and fearing the remaining twenty-four hours of my self-imposed target. Later in the day I'll probably flake out in a chair in the police interview room. I flash back to fragments of questions I dreamed I'd ask Meredith, seriously doubting that I'll get the chance to pose same to her.

A revitalising shower helps me dress myself without toppling over. I apply a puff of rouge but still look as if I've spent a night on the town and proceeded straight to work. In my younger days, I'd done exactly that, but this time I miss the euphoria and enjoyment of having scored an evening's alcohol and heart-pumping casual romanticism which is my facile definition of a one-night-stand.

I gather my Beecham file, which has expanded to three thick inches, courtesy of Hamilton Holt. Within it there is enough to sink one person, and thereby elevate my line of reasoning over Stafford's, who still maintains Alexander is well and truly in the frame. That's when I phone Alexander. I should have done so the previous night, but I'd stopped short. Things go terribly wrong when one starts interrogating the very person who's paying them. Disregarding the early hour, I forge ahead with my idealistic pursuit of justice. 'Hi Alex.'

'Morning Olivia. You sound troubled.'

'In a way, yes. Stafford's speaking with Meredith today. Last night he mentioned you'd been providing legal services to Meredith. Is that correct?'

'Yes, it is. And I act for my mother and I could have acted for Roslyn but I advised against doing so because of a perceived conflict of interest. Why? Is there a problem?'

'Didn't you query your sister's role as beneficiary to some of her patients, let's say Nora Geddes in particular?'

'Why would I? Those documents aren't initiated by Meredith. Since you want to grill me, though I don't see why, I receive the documents after they've been prepared by the assignor's legal firm. In plain terms, Mrs Geddes instructed, I forget now who it was, but let's say Smith and Smith; Geddes instructed them to commit her wishes to contract. Smith and Smith would have advised her of the risks and benefits, *before* preparation and signing. Only after those steps were agreed and attested to would I receive the documents. My only role is to check the documents and witness Meredith's signature. 'Olivia. I'm not stupid, you know. Stafford or Glosser the Tosser's got to you, haven't they?'

'Not really, but I do think they're covering their butts. I guess I'm covering mine. Believe me, Alex, when I tell you that I did say my piece and claimed wholeheartedly that I believed you weren't involved.'

'Thank you for the favour.'

Sparse morning traffic allows my timely arrival at Pin Oak Avenue. Stafford is slumped over the steering wheel. Shock befalls me. I can't take another catastrophe. No. Not today. I fear for his safety before realising that he's probably driven straight from the office and has taken the chance to snatch forty winks.

I grab my phone and file, walk over to his car, and tap on the window. He jerks to attention as if he's been woken by a teacher in a school classroom.

'Give us a smoke,' he mumbles.

'You don't smoke, remember? You haven't started again, have you?'

'No, of course not. All right. Let's go and see if our host's got the coffee on.'

We push our way through hovering mist. Stafford raps an authoritive knock on the front door. I admire the garden. It weeps for attention.

A female voice breaks the stillness. 'All right, all right, I'm coming. There's twenty-four hours in a day, you know.'

A frosted panel in the front door illuminates before a somnolent Meredith greets us: 'Not interested, thank you very much. I'm not religious, I don't complete surveys and I don't buy door-to-door.'

Meredith's sarcasm flies by us. She obviously hasn't remembered me from her mother's home three weeks earlier. And why should she? A black pant suit makes me look like a weathered scarecrow and smudged makeup accentuates bags beneath my eyes, making me look thirty years' older.

Stafford takes control by inviting us inside. 'This won't take long Mrs Bennington. I take it you're still married?'

Very good, I smirk. He snuck that in.

'Come in, if you must. Yes, I am still married and have been for twenty years. I don't see that changing.'

'Mrs Bennington. We're here for two reasons. First, we offer our sincerest condolences on the loss of your sister and assure you we are working toward a speedy apprehension of whoever is responsible.'

'Good. I should think so. A woman isn't even safe in her own office.'

'Mrs Bennington. You know your sister's working habits and starting times?'

'Not really. We have discussed the unsociable nature of both of our jobs; mine as a nurse – or carer, most recently – and hers with her out-of-hours inspections and contract signings. You don't think it was a disgruntled client, do you?'

'We don't know what to think yet. We're sifting through leads and public information.'

Meredith looks quizzically to me.

'Public information? It was so early, wasn't it? Surely no one saw anything happen?'

I don't answer because I take the comment as an inquisitive statement. A victim's family will always be grateful for public input and will always treat it with the expectation that any information will be beneficial. Quite often, something that seems irrelevant, like a postman cycling across the High Street, can be highly significant because he might be able to pin-point an incident by the timing of his round, or, he might have seen something or someone that might later be considered pertinent. Meredith's attitude suggests that she knows there were no witnesses. I muse: *How could she possibly speculate that no one saw anything happen unless she was there?*

Stafford remains mute on her response and continues regardless: 'Are you aware of your sister suffering a stress complaint?'

'No. We haven't seen each other much since mum passed. Frankly, there is a bit of dissension in the family. Our brother's pointing fingers left, right and centre over mum's passing, and, oh no, now this. I'm just a mess.'

'You weren't in agreement with Alexander seeking an autopsy, were you? I mean, there was a question mark, wasn't there? Your mother's health was reportedly good?'

'Mum's been up and down for a couple of years. It was just her time. Alex is looking for a scapegoat because he won't accept that it was time for his precious mother. The hospital's own doctor had no concerns that mum's death was anything other than natural. Surely, that says something!'

'But he was found to be wrong. The autopsy disclosed, among other things, elevated BSLs and foreign food stuffs in the stomach. Tell me about Rachel.'

'Rachel? What's she got to do with this? She was adopted years ago. I wouldn't even know where she is, and what's more, I wouldn't even care.'

I fight to remain silent.

Stafford fires explosive questions. 'But you've seen her recently, haven't you? She had some questions about her, em, paternity and reasons for her adoption?'

'No. I've never seen her. She phoned me briefly some time ago.'

'You see, Mrs Bennington, we have evidence that might link Rachel to Roslyn's office. So anything you can help us with may speedily resolve this.'

This is one of Stafford's favourite tactics. Throw out a safety net for his suspect and nominate someone else for them to accuse. He invites Meredith to seek refuge in his confidence, knowing full-well that she will implicate Rachel.

Her dead-pan facial expression elongates to a helpful smile as she releases her hands from the tight clench upon her lap.

'I don't think Rachel even knew of Roslyn. Only recently, according to her, did she discover her true parentage.'

'So you didn't know that she's being seeing Alexander?'

Meredith jolts upright in the chair. 'No way. The little bitch. She's got nothing to do with our family. She's got no right sticking her nose in everywhere, then blabbing to others in secret meetings in her flat.'

'So even though, by your own words, you only spoke on the phone "briefly some time ago" you know she lives in a flat?'

'Well I presume she does. She doesn't look to have the means to live in a house of substance.'

'And she doesn't look to have those means because you deduced that from her appearance. Isn't that right?'

'Yes. Of course.'

Stafford creates heightened expectation as he shuffles through the manila folder, removes a page, and then hands it to Meredith. I gather he is about to up the tempo and barrage Meredith with questions that will test her patience.

'Mrs Bennington. I'd like you to look at this,' he says, pointing to the double-sided page.

'So? I rented a van to do some moving.'

'And where did you do the moving from and to?'

'Perhaps it's time I consulted my lawyer. I'm not taking any of this. I can drive a van when and where I like.'

'Yes, you can, and I repeat my earlier advice, you can call a lawyer, even Mr Rosenberg, anytime you like. You can ask us to leave if you want to.'

Meredith calms: 'Look, I've got nothing to hide. I was

going to buy a new bed, but on the way changed my mind, so I didn't need the van after all.'

'Perhaps you could look at the mileage charge. You travelled nearly two hundred miles. That's a lot of travelling for a change of heart. Must have sacrificed a good bed.'

Meredith looks at the floor as if shrinking herself into a speck of dust and trying to conceal herself within the plush-pile carpet.

I can't take it any longer. The mention of the white van combined with Meredith's denials boil my simmering rage. 'You drove to Rachel's home in Southampton. You spied on me and followed me back along the M40 and hit my car. I pulled into a service centre and you reversed and watched me until a police car arrived.'

'You're in a dream world, love. Why would I follow you?'

'Perhaps you'll answer that in a moment,' Stafford interjects.

He removes a series of photos from his folder and hands them to Meredith. 'These show the van at the Exeter Service Centre at 3.30 p.m. yesterday. Can you identify the person kneeling at the rear wheels of the van?'

'No.'

'I put it to you that the person in the photo is you. What do you say to that?'

Meredith remains downcast and starts crying. 'I don't know,' she says. 'My whole life's been a misery. I can't go on. I should have stopped ages ago. It's just gone too far. You've no idea what I've been through as a child, neglected by my parents while mum was gallivanting with every man in town, then I marry a doddering old fool to get out of home, only to find he wanted no more than the ego trip of flaunting me before his stately friends at lodge meetings and the like, and his mother, the old granny, received more attention from him than I did. There I was in the kitchen making meals for the three of us while he's upstairs consoling her and telling her I had no "domestic skills". I heard them talking about me as if I were a hired house-maid. Well, I fixed her, didn't I—'

'I think we should continue this later,' Stafford says. 'You really need to call that lawyer now.'

'Fuck the lot of them. Fuck lawyers, my brother, nurses, mothers, fathers, coppers, private dicks. Fuck everyone. People have got in my way for long enough. I'm finished. Bloody Rachel's fault. Should never have been born or even conceived. Friggin' Lord Bennington. What an arse. "It'll be all right, love", he said. "I'm impotent – I can't go starting a family at my age, can I?" Friggin' arrogant bastard, putting paid to my career and my figure. That's all people ever done to me; destroyed dreams and plans. Just take my mother. Everything was fine 'til she started harping on to me years ago: "When you going to start a family, love?" Of course I never let on about my kid, Rachel whoever she is; mum wouldn't have anything of me giving up her first grandchild, so I never saw her while I was pregnant, but she started years ago, "Merri, we need some little squawks in the night, some giggles in the day". I was dealing with my own squawks in the night with my geriatric patients, but never had the giggles during the day.

'Mum later relied on Ros and me for her care and I was happy to help, but every time I saw her I faced the same inquisition: "Merri, when are you going to find yourself a nice husband?" Poor bitch didn't even know I'd been married for 20 years to his lordship, the crotchety old fool. I couldn't take it anymore; I had to divest myself of my mother. Bloody Alex and his autopsy. It should've never shown up. The insulin should have metabolised in her system, that's why I knew the cause of death would be signed off as natural cause. The hospital had already notified me that her life was in peril. Her death was expected – I just helped it along.'

"Divest myself". I recognised Meredith's words with an irony that I'd once felt when the anger of my adoption boiled within. But never could I bring myself to even shout at my birth mother, let alone divest myself of her.

Meredith continues her harangue, trance-like, ignoring Stafford's requests to keep quiet. He calls for an ambulance. Meredith is in dire need of help and medication. But she continues, single-mindedly: 'Then another old biddy latched onto me, old Nora, who insisted on paying me to attend to her garden twice weekly. What did she think I was – a bloody horticulturist? So I kept up her gardening for a couple of weeks, then I got waylaid because of the shemozzle over mum's death. Some bloody annuals died, didn't they? Dunno how she found out, some bloody Gestapo relative I suppose: "Oh dear granny Nora, your anemones are looking rather poorly; your garden looked so prim before your illness. Now it looks as if it belongs in a vacated council estate". I got a tongue-lashing from bloody Nora. Well, I wasn't going to take that, was I? I couldn't let her get away with it. One has to maintain control of their life, don't they?'

Stafford and I don't get the chance to answer her rhetorical questions. We study each other, open-mouthed, wondering when, or if, Meredith will resume her senses.

But she keeps going: 'Poor Nora passed in her sleep, quite naturally of course, choked on something she shouldn't have been eating, a gobful of éclairs or toffee – she should have known better – but then I knew she'd accept my gift.

'And my stupid sister. I'd had enough of her too, with her Alex this and Alex that and Alex thinking of the family because the hospital's to blame for mum's death and that was okay for a while until he got the bloody court order then it all came out didn't it; it wasn't the hospital's fault – well, perhaps it was Alexander, perhaps he wanted rid of her too; perhaps he wanted rid of Rachel because he felt sorry for her and perhaps he wanted rid of Roslyn too because she was a more successful business person, but I beat him to it, didn't I, and perhaps he wanted rid of you too, Miss Watts-it, who can't keep her nose out of other people's business – oh yes, I know what you've been up to, setting them all against me, spreading rumours to Rachel, hopping along to Alexander's office at his beck and call, collaborating with Mr Sherlock here to gather everything you can on me; well, you got it all, I don't give a shit, I'm sick of this tired, pretentious life I lead, all false, my stupid false marriage – being paid to stay married, what a fool and a joke I've been, oh I need a drink, where's my cup of tea, oh I didn't make one, oh how I wish I had someone to serve me as I'd served them all those years; they can serve themselves now, let them find someone who cares like I did, changing dressings, sheets and nightbowls, listening to all their stories of hardship, but did they ever listen to mine? No, of course not, get it over with Mr Sherlock, just charge me or whatever you're going to do. Just get me out of here.'

I take hold of Meredith as she collapses to the floor. She

salivates profusely, a liquid, bubbly rage erupting from her soul. She has vented her anger on everyone she knows – not a kind word for anyone. On the few occasions I've seen her, she's always been so composed, save for discarding her clothes at Nora Geddes funeral. I should have read the sign. What rational person would do such a thing? Anywhere. Who knows what lies beneath the facade of normality?

Sirens wail outside and cease before I open the front door. Paramedics examine Meredith, who now shivers on the floor, Stafford holding her hand in quiet consolation. I sense it is the first time ever that someone has shown compassion to Meredith Bennington.

Stafford phones Ambrose and updates him, apologising for not alerting him to the morning's interview, excusing his omission in the name of night-shift fatigue.

I accept that my Beecham file can now be permanently closed. I phone Alexander and detail the morning's events, at the same time advising him of Meredith's debilitating condition and that she is enroute to the Cornwall and District General Hospital. I arrange to see him later in his office where we'll finalise our working arrangement.

He asks about his sister's admissions. I tell him that they weren't really admissions – just the ramblings of a traumatised woman. I continue that there is sufficient evidence to support Meredith's rant. Insulin detected in Joyce Beecham's tissue samples was identified as having the same chemical structure as 100 ml insulin syringes I retrieved from Meredith's First Aid kit.

Although Nora Geddes' death had been proclaimed a death by misadventure, a statement made by a fellow Happy

Valley resident tells of Meredith swamping Nora with bags of toffee and chocolate éclairs. A copy of the statement has been sent to the Medical Board along with a request from Happy Valley's director to de-register Meredith Bennington.

A coffee cup found in Meredith's car is identified by a cafe assistant as one that she sold. Forensic analysis proves that coffee saturating Roslyn's clothes is of the same chemical composition as dregs sourced from the cup.

Finally, I advise that the increasing burden of evidence against Meredith Bennington might never proceed to court because Meredith stands a good chance of being assessed as unfit to plead.

I refer Alexander to DCI Stafford and Superintendent Ambrose for information about forthcoming proceedings. I have no doubt that Meredith has painted herself into a hopeless position. She admitted detail that will be extremely difficult to retract.

I am so glad to be out of it now. All I want is to return home to catch up on the sleep I've been deprived over the past three weeks. I promise myself a week off. I'll visit my mum and dad. Perhaps spend a whole day with them. Funny thing about parents. You don't miss them until you're re-introduced to the fact that they won't always be there. I am determined to not leave my love for them unstated.

I'll call Rachel and offer my apologies about the fate of her mother. I'll encourage her to visit her mum in hospital, but I hold little hope of her doing so. Perhaps I could introduce her to my own step family and try to belatedly give her just a glimpse of what it's like to grow up with real love and real support and a real identity of who we are.

I'll commission her to sketch Alexander and me together in commemoration of my first job performed under Watts Happening? Investigations. And what a job it was.

The journey home is uneventful. Fiona sings sweetly, there are no vans to distract me and no phone calls to answer. On arriving home I open my front door to the stale odour of pizza and coffee, reminding me of Hamilton's visit. I'll phone him to update the events of the day. I walk into my office and open the blinds. Scattered notes and files lie across the desk. Anyone looking in from outside would think that I'm running one heck of a busy agency. I amble over to collect my phone's awaiting message. I turn up the volume and press PLAY: *Hello. My name's Thornton. You don't know me, but you come highly recommended. Interested in a big job? If so, call me. You need to be ready to start.*

I don't recognise the number.

Here we go again. Business is going to be good here. I toss a coin: Heads, I phone; Tails, I sleep.

Heads.

Epilogue

I am grateful to have achieved a result within my self-imposed forty-eight-hour deadline. I'm further gratified to find Alexander's cheque, in the sum of £2,000, on the floor. I've earned every penny of it.

A spot remains in my heart for Rachel, or more particularly, her circumstances. After two phone calls and a visit, I finally convinced her to undergo DNA profiling to ascertain her parentage. I think my own experiences as an adoptee helped her realise that maybe she's not stuck on her own. On that, I had no argument from Lord Bennington. To the contrary, I think he honestly looks forward to the prospect of having an adult child, although I detect a deep down, traditional wish, for a boy to 'carry on the family name'. High fives to egotistical males.

DCI Stafford did me a favour by giving me the coffee cup found in the back of Meredith's car. Yes, it had been purchased by Roslyn on her fateful morning, and yes, it was the cup from which Meredith had sipped. And that was the very reason I wanted it – to aid DNA profiling.

The results proved with 99% certainty (they'll never put their neck on the line by stating 100%) that the good lord is Rachel's father. I guess there'd been occasion for post-separation dalliances, or 'sex with your ex' as is commonly phrased. To each their own.

Rachel has moved to Wiltshire Manor where she operates a successful studio. She attributes her artistic streak to her father's peculiar ways, which now include prototype canvas stretchers and picture frames made of papier-mâché.

Meredith Bennington pleaded guilty to three counts of murder. She is due for release on her ninety-second birthday – ironically the very same age of her first victim, although she did manage to evade prosecution due to the passage of time having eroded all prospects of procuring sufficient evidence.

Lord Bennington mounted a legal challenge against his mother's will. Setting a legal precedent to ensure Lord Bennington himself did not profit from the challenge, the judge determined that all proceeds of the will previously granted (insomuch as they applied to Meredith Bennington) shall forthwith be retrieved and distributed to Rachel Bennington as next of kin. The will's invalidity saw Lord Bennington instruct his lawyer to issue an immediate divorce petition. It succeeded unopposed.

One puzzle continues to confound me. The locket. I churn two scenarios. The first: Rachel might have unwittingly dropped it at the hospital while visiting her grandmother. By chance, Meredith later picked it up. The second: Meredith *did* know where Rachel lived so she performed her own burglary to remove from Rachel the one link to her parentage.

After visiting Meredith in Holloway, I found I had been wrong on both counts. After Meredith calmed from the surprise of seeing me (even though she hadn't had to knock back visitors with sticks or insulin jabs) she spoke quite freely. A mother will always talk about her daughter – no matter the state of the relationship. Her revelation astounded me. At no time had Meredith given the locket to Rachel. She had intended to drape it around Rachel's neck on leaving her with the Department of Social Services. However, in the ruckus of embarrassment and screaming baby she simply forgot. The locket became a 'I must get around to doing that' project of taking it to the DSS for on-forwarding. It never happened, so Meredith wore it as a memento of her inhumanity. Only because of a broken clasp was it in her pocket on the day she visited me. Another sense of irony. A broken clasp on a locket helped deliver her into Her Majesty's pleasure, just as she had delivered the young baby inside the locket into Her Majesty's care.

PAIGE OFFERS A PREVIEW OF OLIVIA WATTS' NEXT CASE IN THE 'WATTS HAPPENING? INVESTIGATIONS' SERIES.

CLOCK FACE OF ILLS
AVAILABLE NOVEMBER 2017.

Prologue

Phillip McMaster slams the bill on the table. Two tumblers of Dewar's Scotch whiskey jump in protest. Heads turn from adjacent tables. Silence fills the lounge.

'You fix this and make sure you fix that Angelo pratt,' wheezes McMaster.

'Pay your own friggin' bill,' recoils Jeff Main. 'I'm here to do you a favour. I never wanted in on this in the first place. I'm the paperwork man, not an action hero you pull out of a Mattel box to perform at your beck and call.'

McMaster reinforces his demand with the gesture of a politician placating the public. Opens his palms in retreat. 'Okay Jeff. Settle down. I've got the tab, okay?'

Phillip, known to colleagues as Phil, a seasoned detective inspector who found his niche placement in a small regional office, has bedded down in career hibernation. He'd long ago settled into a comfort zone; happy to drift along from one file to the next, to do only as required, and no more. Promotion and career progress – long-gone aspirations of the once eager officer – have disappeared into the nicotine-infused ceilings of Worcester CID.

Five years earlier, his sonorous instructions boomed across rooms and offices with the mellifluous harmony of Placido Domingo. Today, McMaster huffs like a punctured blacksmith's bellow, legacy of his daily 60 cigarette dependency. His physique also resembles the bellow: puffed up and full of hot air. At 42 years-of-age, and after 22 hard years in the constabulary, Phillip McMaster personifies the role of desk sergeant. His medical records should note 'obese', but the constabulary chooses to play down the condition as 'slightly overweight'. Spider-veins criss-cross his sun-deprived complexion. Glowing cheeks and nose pay homage to Dewar's redeeming powers. Thin, peppered hair sprouts like bleached wheat stalks ravaged by a plague of locusts, and the skin beneath his eyes sags like a pair of old saddle bags flung over the bony back of a prairie horse.

For McMaster, life parallels the game of Snakes and Ladders. He slides beneath promotional opportunities; he falls into pits of depression propagated by marital disharmony; and his alcoholic dependency drops him into a fantasy criminal underworld.

He'll climb out of holes in allegations of impropriety and he'll step up the pace of an investigation until he nails his suspect. His mental capacity is reputably top of the game. Locked away in his cerebral safe are the names, faces and crimes of every person he's arrested and prosecuted during his generally non-eventful career. He also remembers the few he's freed, his eyes closed to the activities of those he believes capable of furthering his agenda; and he zealously guards mental profiles of those recruited into his clandestine empire of chicanery and scams.

McMaster lives by his self-conceived doctrine: 'financial security is the ability to seize opportunity and shield it from authority's eyes'. He applies the creed to all manner of deceptive conduct, from swapping bar codes on B&Q's power tools to returning items of clothing for refunds after wearing them to one-off functions. *Why rent a dinner suit when I can buy one from a retailer with a lax return policy and claim a full refund the following day?* If the sales assistant objects, he coolly removes his wallet and lays it on the sales counter – making sure it falls face up to clearly display his police warrant card. The hapless assistant buckles to the innocent intimidation and cheerfully completes the refund.

For the past five years, he's held permanent ownership – under the auspice of 'reservation' – over a rear table at the Knight's Arms. It is now a renowned rendezvous point for informants of dubious background who provide information for both his judicial and personal interests.

The small room is still, as if a mute button has silenced the pair of wide screen televisions hanging above the bar. A six-square-metre ceiling of straw, mud and cowpat render, crudely brushed with the mandatory magnolia, and illuminated by six 25-watt power saving globes, reflect glistening beads of perspiration from Main's brow.

McMaster glares: 'I know you're the paper man. But I'm the head man, aren't I? For the past year, I've papered your pocket with real bills – tens, twenties and fifties. Now, I'm thinking that if you want our little arrangement to continue, we have to come to an understanding. Right? There has to be some sort of hierarchal order. Right? You see where I'm coming from?'

Main knows exactly where. He'd once skimmed profit from McMaster's share portfolio after being authorised to sell 12,500 shares in a small trading company. Main had no way of knowing that Phillip McMaster was the major shareholder of that registered company, and that McMaster knew *exactly* what the sale should have returned.

McMaster had turned the tables to his advantage. Rather than report Main for criminal deception, he recognised the ingenuity as an exploitable trait. To date, his scams and schemes have lined Main's pockets with more than £40,000.

McMaster continues: 'You remember how you tried to, shall we say, rip me off?'

'I've apologised a thousand times for that. You never let me forget it – it was a poor business decision.'

'And I make the good decisions, right?'

'Yes, Phil. Always.' Main shrinks into a small-time thug, afraid of his menacing Mafia-styled boss.

'Angelo's not pulling his weight. We've got to get that property deal sewn up. Quick.'

'Yes. Of course. I thought we'd sealed it.'

'Well we haven't. You were too soft on that fuckin' wog bastard.'

Main turns to the beeping shrills of the cash register. 'Better keep your voice down. There's not enough distractions.'

McMaster sets a ferocious glare. 'Fuck distractions. You're a distraction.'

* * *

The brass mail flap snaps shut. Letters topple to the floor. I grab the bundle and shuffle the envelopes like a deck of cards; throw aside a BT bill, Office Plus stationery account, a window envelope addressed to my business name – Watts Happening? Investigations – and a large, brown Readers' Digest envelope promising to excite me because I've made the final cut in their 'Last Chance Draw £1,000,000 prize pool'. I hadn't even entered the damn thing, but now choose to enter it in the bin.

Since establishing my agency some six months ago, I have undertaken enquiries from missing persons to untimely deaths. I proudly take credit for helping a lawyer solve a suspicious family death – an enquiry which resulted in my contribution to solving two related mysterious casualties.

I'd originally set up in Worcester, but moved to Newquay in Cornwall as part of a career, slash, sea change. I later succumbed to the magnetism of my geographic roots after a chance Worcester file pulled me past my old flat and office. The 'To Let' sign dangling from the window hung as an omen – a divine invitation beckoning my return. Flushed with funds from recent well-paying files, I flashed six months' advance rent before the landlord, and, well, he couldn't resist the sight. Then again, it might have been another sight; my loose, flouncy top sliding down my shoulder, teasing him with an ample hint of silken, mauve bra strap. Turns grown men to water. Too bad for them. Whilst there's not much in the bra, it's the hope of getting their hands on the merchandise that hypnotises them to my commands.

I am about to head out to deposit Alexander Beecham's £2,000 cheque when the phone startles me.

'Hello. Olivia? Superintendent Jack Thornton.'

Shit! I recognise the surname. I was supposed to have returned his call last night. I freeze. Even the innocent freeze when a police officer calls. But this is business; I learn that I am invited to conduct 'a spot of observing'. Excitement rises. *Nothing better than the chance to get my teeth into a big one.* I relish assignments of a covert nature; the darkness of tailing and observing; slithering around, chameleon-like, tracing a target's every move. I explain my reluctance to enter into another working relationship with police, especially after having been castigated over my harmless association with DCI Stafford.

Thornton confides that it was Stafford who recommended me. He goes on to describe how he often relies on external sources to drive further into investigations that challenge the propriety of police members. He boasts that I've been singled out because of my belligerence, devotion to duty, and the fact that I utilise every available resource to achieve resolution.

Documented in my Personal History File is the cruel analogy: 'like a dog with a bone'. The term could be taken as a compliment, but in the world of officialdom, it can also be seen as derogatory.

I anticipate his use of the term 'observing' as a full-on, closely monitored watch over a senior police officer whose identity would be code-named throughout the investigation. His real name might never be revealed. To me. What Thornton does not know is that I am one who shifts the earth to uncover little snippets invariably concealed from all but those immediately beneath command.

I feel uneasy about spying on former colleagues. It is not a role to be proud of, or one to gloat about at Christmas parties, but at the same time I recognise the need for underhanded surveillance to help keep the constabulary scrupulously clean. I arrange to meet Thornton at the Worcester CID office, an inconvenience I would defray by blending those hours into later invoices – assuming I agree to the collaboration.

* * *

On completion of an enquiry into the ownership of recovered stolen goods, McMaster drives home along the A44, the BBC broadcast of the third Test between England and Australia playing in the background, and smoke curling from a cigarette in the foreground – typically flouting the constabulary's no smoking in police vehicles policy.

A red Renault flashes by. Blonde hair wavers from the driver's window, attracting McMaster's attention. Had the driver been anyone other than a young female, he would have continued rolling along, counting six-ball overs, and sweating as the required runs-per-over became more and more unattainable.

The visual draws him to the speedster. He maintains a steady pace of eighty-five miles per hour behind the Renault before uncharacteristically intercepting it. He flashes his headlights and then, in a move creating more danger than the offending driver's actions, pulls alongside the car, holds up his badge, and motions her to the verge.

Both cars turn in to a convenient lay-by where McMaster withdraws from his Vauxhall, lights another cigarette, and walks up to the Renault's window. Colour drains from the young woman's face. 'Sorry, I've had a hard day at work.'

McMaster studies her: about twenty-years-old, bottle-blonde hair, deep brown eyes of Mediterranean or Middle Eastern background, and skin glowing like rich Crème Caramel. A trace of fine black eyeliner rolls down her left cheek. She wears the attire of a waitress: white blouse, a black lace tie pinched at the neck and a black linen skirt riding high on her thighs. Conscious of McMaster's gaze, she drops her hands to her lap.

'So, what's the rush?'

'Just late. I'll be honest. I just wanted to get home. I know I was going a bit fast, but I was careful.'

'What's your job? You work in a restaurant?'

'Not quite. Heavenly Spirits. I'm a manager.'

'So, what's that, a fortune telling shop?'

'No. Wines and spirits. We specialise in spirits – the wine's just a sideline.'

'Girl after my heart.'

She cringes.

'I'll have to make a note of this. What's your name and address?'

'No please. I can't afford to be fined. I'm going through a bad trot at the moment.'

'I'm not saying you'll be fined, but I must record your details as a person I've spoken to whilst on duty.'

'Rose Maree Hernandez.'

McMaster scratches Rose's details into his notebook, and for added verification obtains her work address. He huffs out a lecture about the dangers of speeding and finishes with a menacing glare: 'You may hear something within the week.'

* * *

McMaster pulls into the driveway of Ashton Hill. He'd discovered the property eight years' earlier during an afternoon's cruising about the countryside in an unmarked police car. He jumped at the opportunity to acquire the property and instructed solicitor, Steven Weston, to acquire the estate 'at all costs'. McMaster warily educated Weston about his interpretation of 'at all costs', not the least of which was encouraging other parties to reach a favourable agreement either by legal threat or cash under the table.

Seven months' later, after succumbing to McMaster's persistent phone calls disguised as requests for 'progress reports', Steven Weston secured the Title of Ashton Hill.

Bordering the McMaster property lies Blackshaw's Mill. Surrounded by 25 fertile Gloucestershire acres fronting the River Avon, the former textile factory was long ago converted to a family home. Today, the only survivors of the eighteenth-century mill are two huge water wheels that once drove a score of antiquated bevelled cogs which creaked and groaned crude mechanical agitation to the wash and dye rooms.

For the past fourteen years Giuseppe and Maria Caruso have lovingly tended the property. Its heyday returned a regular income from sheep sales, baled hay, and grazing the local pony club's horses. Now, only wild grass is loosely rolled as cheap chaff for livestock and mulch.

Giuseppe is one of Britain's early invasions of European migrants, having arrived with his parents in 1962 and settling in Manchester – then home to a strong Italian community. At sixteen-years-old he was apprenticed to his father, Giuseppe senior, who was a master craftsman in laying terrazzo. With the advent of fibreglass and resin shower bases, and vinyl and ceramic tiles, terrazzo lost favour with builders. Young Giuseppe could have followed fellow tradesman into kerbing and paving, but laying daily expanses of dull grey concrete failed to offer the same job satisfaction as the sparkling, glittery medium he had enjoyed for twenty-odd years. He disappointed his father by joining Royal Mail as a sorter. He earned no reprieve after progressing to mail deliveries in the Manchester area.

Giuseppe Caruso is the quintessential master of the home, and of his wife. Tall, and prematurely silver-haired, his dominant bearing often obligates elder siblings to rescue their mother from his wayward fists. He creates arguments from the most trivial circumstances: late meals; clothes not ironed properly; overspending at the supermarket; and his wife's frequent molly-coddling of their youngest child.

* * *

'Miss Watts?' A young constable approaches and escorts me to Thornton's temporary office. I supress my knowledge of the building and its occupants, preferring to leave that history clinging to dusty architraves and faded blue curtains.

The introduction springs surprise. Thornton stands in contrast to my perception of senior officers, typically typecast as five years' pre-retirement, anaemic complexion – save for the liquor-reddened nose, the uniform-issue fifty-inch belt buckled into the third extra hand-punched hole, and a wealth of travel brochures piled on their desk beneath unsolved-crime files. Thornton, however, is elf-like: short in stature, ectomorphic frame, and a flushed look as if he'd minutes earlier completed the London Marathon – or just finished 'interviewing' a young female constable eager for promotion.

'Hello, Miss Watts. Pleased to finally meet you.'

Why? Small talk, or has my reputation preceded me?
'Thank you, sir.'

I don't know why I address him as 'sir'. Force of habit – the indoctrination of hierarchical respect instilled in me by my police officer step-father and later forcefully repeated through school and college.

Thornton sedates the atmosphere: 'Call me Jack please. You're not in uniform now, although I must say it was a loss to the constabulary to hear of your resignation.'

'One of those situations, sir. I hope you accept the awkwardness of the predicament I faced. I felt extremely uneasy about overriding DI Marchant, but if we pledge to represent justice, I believe that justice has to be given the best opportunity of being served. Idealistic, I know. But as my presence here attests, I'm a person who stands by her word.'

'And that's precisely why you're here, Miss Watts, because of your ethics.'

'Better forget the "Miss Watts" bit then. It's Olivia.'

Needless to say, I wondered what was coming. Why recruit a recently resigned member who'd lagged on a superior officer? And why is this driven by the upper echelon – a superintendent for goodness sake?

Thornton presses on: 'The target is a private investigator. Gillian Trotter. Know her?'

A queasy uneasiness chills me. *Reporting the activities of one of my own. That's* worse *than investigating a copper.* It revives the fallout of the Worcester CID incident, the very reason I'd left the constabulary. I'm still recovering to this day, not through emotional stress but through the regret of having sacrificed a magnificent career and all of its financial benefits. But there's a rider: I'm far happier for having commenced my own agency. Now, a potential conflict smacks me in the face in the form of Thornton's requesting me to inform on a colleague.

'No. I don't know her.' And that is for the better, because if I did know Trotter, I would instantly decline the job.

Thornton proffers a long-winded analytical speech in which he convinces me – not that I need convincing – of the need for accountability: 'it benefits taxpayers; it's their money,' and 'not all police officers are squeaky clean; think of the bad apple syndrome.' He smiles and opens a manila folder. 'No vipers and no problems. We have a situation, and I think – no, I know – that you're the person to look into it.

'The situation is, Olivia, we have an officer, an inspector at that, who we believe is compromising the ethics of the constabulary. That will not concern you because we already have Internal Affairs and a PI seconded to that cause.'

I immediately feel second-rate, being called in to assist as a back-up to their preferred outside help. My dismay is short-lived.

'We have strong reasons to suspect that the investigator tasked to inform us of matters pertaining to that detective inspector is not acting in our full interests. We have suspicions of Trotter short-delivering investigatory material, and that she may be *too close* to the target. Your task is to shadow Trotter and update me, and only me. There's a loose cannon somewhere – it's either her, or we have an internal problem. I can't afford to have information flowing to anyone but me. I will be your only – and I stress *only* – contact, and you'll submit invoices only to me.' Thornton pens his mobile number on the back of a card and passes it to me. 'For all intents and purposes you don't exist.'

I don't mind not existing; it's been on my wish-list for some time. But what haunts me is whether Thornton is going to pay me £45 per hour from his own pocket? If so, that suggests the enquiry is most definitely not *official*. On the other hand, hundreds of scenarios deserve varying levels of confidentiality. Mine is not to reason why. Just do the job and deliver results. And bank the money.

Thornton spills the folder's content across the table and points to three photos. Trotter. He details how she has been 'installed' in the Knight's Arms as a part-time bar attendant working hours that coincide with McMaster's lunch breaks and shift completion. Gillian Trotter looks every bit the expensive escort, overdressed and over made-up. And over ugly. The snaps fail to disclose whether she is in disguise, but her proximity and demeanour with McMaster oozes with the passion of a family reunion.

On Thornton's winding up the meeting, I accept his recommendation to 'trial run' the Knight's Arms for a spot of lunch. I walk into the pub with the confidence and deportment of a female CEO and take a seat in a dusty alcove beneath a flickering fluorescent light. Difficult to see, difficult to *be* seen – but I do recognise the face behind the bar. No need to double-check Gillian's profile.

With good fortune, a separate meals counter provides a safe haven for me to order a Chicken Parma and cappuccino. My concern is that a woman on her own in a pub *always* stands out. Most guys believe that a single woman in a pub is on the make. I know different. Excuse my crassness, but they're thinking with their dicks. Why can't they accept that a girl has to eat, and might just want to drop in to a good value pub for a meal and a glass of cider? The greasy £2.99 café should not be the only venue where we can sit undisturbed.

I swipe away time on my mobile, checking emails and a couple of blogs and message boards to which I regularly contribute. Three little characters, A44, pricks my attention. The road is one of my most travelled out of Worcester. I read a rant about sleazy coppers who patrol the A44. I type out my alter ego cyber chick message to stir the pot:

> *Yeah. Agree wid ya. I had an old fogy try it on. Reckoned my car would fail a roadworthy check but sed hed let me off if we could cum to an agreement. I havent done nothing yet coz Im scared of what might happen. Cant afford to fix my car. I spose the best thing in these situations is to stay strong. They cant do nothing if we dont give em the chance ☺ .*

By the time I arrive home there'll probably be another twenty replies.

Bugger me. Talk about a trial run. I've barely put down the guy's photo when he walks in, strides up to the bar, orders a drink and strokes Gillian's hand as he hands over a £5 note.

From beneath the table I aim my phone and snap off a couple of quick shots. Their intimacy might be totally innocent. Perhaps Gillian is over-playing the role. My interest, however is tuned not to their dizzy gazes, but to their conversation.

While Gillian ogles McMaster, I flick through Thornton's notes. Thumb to Gillian's address which I assume will be a budget rental somewhat like my own: lounge room converted to a home office, main bedroom demoted to a lounge room and the second bedroom barely accommodating a king-size bed and small dressing table – a dual purpose establishment set up to claim tax deductions on home purchases that can be written off as office expenses.

I take the scenic route home – a circuitous thirty-mile detour – solely to check out Gillian's address. I locate the average, two-bedroom terrace in one of Cheltenham's quieter back streets. It reeks of rental: weeds sprout across the frontage, cobwebs span windows' corners, and flakes of white paint fall from windowsills like coconut from a lamington. Local real estate professionals would declare it a 'renovator's delight awaiting tender loving care'. I dump my car in a side street and trek back to the building. Knock on the door. No reply. I disadvantage myself by standing in view of the half-dozen neighbours who have little other to do than gawk out of their windows. That rules out lock picking and window forcing. I reschedule the search and find mission.

Although only three hours have passed since downing the Chicken Parmigiana at the Knight's Arms, I fancy a cake-hunting stroll along Cheltenham's High Street mall and swanky arcades. I've covered only fifty metres when a flashing sign catches my eye: Heavenly Spirits. It is heaven-sent because if not for a faulty electrical component known as a fluorescent starter, I would have continued blindly by the bottle shop. I take advantage of the find to top up my two-bottle alcohol cupboard. I walk into the store, acknowledge a young woman stacking shelves and browse the liqueur section. I snub the droned 'Can I help you?' with the retail customers' stock response: 'Just looking, thanks.' To negate any perception of ignorance, I look up, and after making facial contact, read the sales staff's name badge: Rose Hernandez.

I spend an inordinate amount of time scanning the kaleidoscope of coloured liqueurs in their pleasant and peculiar bottles. I settle on my standby of Bailey's Irish Cream, approach Miss Hernandez and ask if a new taste sensation has recently captured the market. She looks at me as if I am crazy.

'Sorry,' I stutter. 'I thought you might be able to suggest something nice. I don't want to waste twenty quid on something I'll later tip down the sink.'

Hernandez switches from the couldn't-give-a-damn attitude to sales mode and suggests I try Orange Shock which is bottled in two sizes: 375 and 750ml. I grab the smaller sampling and hand her a debit card along with one of my business cards – a recently instituted self-promotion practice.

* * *

With Saturday's shift commencing at 6.00 p.m., McMaster settles in his conservatory to enjoy a home-cooked lunch. His estrangement from wife, Gloria, means that the meal of eggs, sausages, bacon, beans and tomatoes, smothered with chilli sauce, is 'home-cooked' by himself.

Don McLean's 'American Pie' wails from a pair of Bose speakers. With a full mouth, McMaster utters a ridiculous proposition: Why has no one composed a song about Spotted Dick? An opportunity awaits an aspiring artist prepared to deliver a unique rendition through one of the new-talent productions: *I get my kicks from Spotted Dicks*.

A frantic banging on his back door competes with a shrieking voice: 'Mr Mac, Mr Mac. Come quick. My husband. He's a fallen down. Not good. Not good.'

McMaster slams the remaining inch of whisky down his throat like a toilet cistern dropping its ten-litre flush.

He races to the door. 'Maria, what is it? Joe's hurt?'

'You musta come quick. Please.'

McMaster realises that Maria has hobbled 300 metres across the uneven pasture to his back door. He grabs a set of keys, helps her to his car, and moments later pulls to a halt at the Caruso's back door.

Leaving Maria in the vehicle, he bounds to the rear door, eases it open and steps inside. The room holds the tang of a commercial galley whose residual aromas of garlic, tomato paste and boiling pasta cling to walls and ceilings. On the floor, Giuseppe lays motionless, face down, arms outstretched above his head as if he'd tried to soften the impact of a fall. McMaster lifts Giuseppe's splayed wrist and checks for a pulse. Nothing. He rolls his neighbour over and commences CPR – preservation of human life taking priority over yet-to-attend paramedics and crime-scene investigators. He pushes down on his patient's chest – 100 to the minute. Nothing. Repeats the series: press and press and press and press. No twitch. No sudden jerks. No eye movement. No sign of recovery. He bends over and heaves air into the man he has for the past few weeks treated with disdain.

Maria props in the doorway, hands clasped to her face.

'Phone 999,' McMaster yells, while silently berating her for having not already done so. His resuscitative efforts fail, as do those of paramedics who arrive twelve minutes later.

'Maria. Your husband on any medication?'

'No Mr Mac. He's take nothing. He's healthy. He'll be all right?'

McMaster accepts the grim task. He pulls himself from the floor and takes Maria's hand. 'I'm sorry, Maria. He's gone. Could be a heart attack. We'll know more after the medics have finished. Is there someone I can call?'

Maria clasps her hand to her chest and lets out a piercing 'Noooo.'

McMaster tries again. 'Let me get someone to sit with you. Who can I call?'

'I have my Angelo, but I'm prefer be alone.'

The Coroner, who attends in double-quick time, reports a fracture at the rear of Giuseppe's skull. He cannot determine, on location, whether the break was caused by the deceased falling to the floor or whether it was occasioned pre- or post-mortem. He leaves the cause of death open, subject to autopsy.

Maria Caruso now has the added strain of wondering whether someone has murdered her husband.

* * *

Further information and book news available at www.paigeelizabethturner.co.uk